ADAM AXIS

Path of Tyranny

Sin of Gluttony

Contents

Introduction

Right and Wrong
Black and White
Sin and Virtue
Good and Evil

There are countless stories where these forces clash against each other. A hero fighting for the poor and meek while the villain proclaims their utter superiority and power. You know who to cheer and jeer for in these stories. You know for whom the story wants to win in the end. It's almost sickeningly horrible how often this plays out isn't it?

Then, there are stories where things are not so clear. Where those that seek to upend the status quo commit horrible acts. Or maybe the bad guy has a point, just enough of one where it would make anyone question if maybe their the ones in the right. These stories and their overly grayed and tragic tones. Where's the fun? Where's the levity?

This... is not a story like those. But we are getting ahead of ourselves. After all, every story starts with a beginning.

It Starts with a Beginning

Far to the north, where breath freezes mid-air and the snow bites skin like sharpened teeth, lies a land so arrogantly pristine it seems to exist only to mock softness. Towering peaks jut like stone fangs into slate-colored skies, their jagged edges draped in endless snow, not for beauty but as banners of nature's cruelty. Between them crawl dense tundra forests silent, black-limbed things that rustle like whispers in a crypt. Here, the cold doesn't simply chill. It tests. It peels. It punishes.

Thus, we begin our little tale and find ourselves in the quaint, unassuming town of Glimisvellir, a speck of civilization that boasts an age older than most dusty tomes could recount. Once, it fed a grand temple far to the north of even these frozen wastes, but those days are long gone. For the ancient site of worship and devotion is now only attended to by the dead, buried under centuries of frost and forgetfulness. Glimisvellir's true origins? Lost to the ages, much like the gods who once frolicked and fought over these peaks. Steeped in a history they barely remember, the people of Glimisvellir cling to one simple truth: they are ancient and owe nothing to the world beyond their walls.

Outsiders? Pah! Parasites. They come with smiles and

schemes and leave with scars if they leave at all. The Glimingar have been burned before. And fire leaves a long memory.

Ah, but let's not romanticize this frozen relic, shall we? Glimisvellir is no peaceful backwater sipping tea with ghosts of the past. No, it snarls at the world with chapped lips and frostbitten fists. Not so long ago, the town's mantra of mistrust was put to the test when a woman, whose name if you were to utter now would be met with scowls sharp enough to slice the frostbitten air, dared to tread their hallowed grounds. She wasn't a priest, nor a trader looking to profit from Glimingaric savage hospitality. No, she was something far more dangerous, a woman with a miserably sad sob story. Poor her, alone and heavy with child, seeking refuge in the last place that would ever care. But now, she was gone and whose remaining tie to the world would soon be dealt with in the coming days.

Glimisvellir, a steadfast devotee of survival, lay cradled at the confluence of two towering mountain ranges, beneath the cascading grace of a river birthed from their lofty peaks. Growth here is a myth whispered by city folk and laughed at by stones. Streets don't bustle; they crunch. Buildings don't rise; they lean. The stone? Older than memory, older than sin, laid when this place had meaning beyond simply being.

The Glimingar do not till. They scrape. They trap. They forage. If it isn't clawed from rock, plucked from thornbush, or dragged bleeding through snow, it doesn't go in a pot. Here, patience is a predator's virtue. Warmth is a currency. And trust? That's the rarest meat of all.

But let us narrow our gaze, hmm? Past the town's broad strokes to pinpoint, shall we say, the 'hero' of our narrative.

Perched atop the village, like a vulture surveying its wasteland, rests the hill that Glimisvellir was built around and straddles with a certain stoic pride. Atop it was the Great Hall of Glimisvellir, a building that maintained myth and legend from across the great north. A structure as imposing as it is central to the town's pulse, flanked by ancient dwellings and the ever-watchful local church. It is here, amidst these venerable stones steeped in history and whispered secrets, that we shall encounter our protagonist, the so-called 'leading man' of this tale.

And within the church, they gather. Not to pray, oh no, the gods have long since packed up and abandoned this sorry realm. What's left is ritual. Mourning in performance. The scent of damp furs clings to the pews, and every breath fogs in the stale chill, as if the very building holds its breath in perpetual grief.

Among them, fervor varies; some are mere onlookers to the ritual of mourning, while others are devoutly entwined with the tears of holy abandonment. For all mortals of this world feel it, a missing piece deep within them. A glimpse into this church might find what we are looking for.

Let's pan across this solemn gallery. Look there, our first contestant.

Our gaze momentarily settles on a man exuding strength and a certain regal bearing uncommon in this most isolated and tribal of towns. There he sits, in the front pew, embodying the paradox of attentive piety and restless anticipation, one leg bouncing with the pent-up energy of someone itching to be out on the hunt rather than caged by solemnity. He's the type to think of himself as a drengr as the locals would call it, a warrior in every sense of the word. The kind who'd sooner die than let Glimisvellir change. Pity that everyone seemed to buy his act. Is this our leading man? Ha! No, no. He is just a little too polished, a bit too keen on his own reflection in the town's collective admiration. He's the kind who walks like his boots alone keep the earth turning, a protector of old ways and traditions if only anyone else took his posturing as seriously as he does.

And beside him, a spark. A girl. Sharp-eyed, wild-browed. She shifts like she's ready to bolt, fidgeting, clawing at invisible chains. She's not meant for stone pews nor quiet contemplation. There's a wolf's breath in her chest. She'll run, one day. Or burn the place down trying.

But not today. Not our heroine. Not our interest. She will have her tale… but not this one.

Our view slides over another, broad-shouldered, apple-cheeked, and as dumb as packed snow. The kind who gets called "full of potential" by old widows with bad memories. A brute born to bark and swagger, nothing more. Not a glimmer of wit behind those eyes, just the dull flicker of inherited malice. Which is always a nice touch. But being born to bully and being born for greatness are two different things. Moving on.

Behind him, skirting the stone wall like smoke, the black-smith's son. Soot-smudged, eyes darting. He avoids the altar like it might swing a hammer back at him. He comes not to pray, but to not be seen not praying. His rebellion? So small. A whisper against a roaring furnace. He resents his fate, yes, but lacks the fire to reforge it. He'll rust away before he ever makes sparks.

No, no, no. Still wrong. Too grey. Too obvious. Too boring.

No, none of these fine specimens will do. Our tale doesn't crave a champion of the people or a force for all that is just and right. How utterly dull that would be! We're in pursuit of something, or someone, with a bit more… shall we say, entanglement? We're in search of someone with a bit more rot in the core, a character who doesn't fit neatly into anyone's mold, least of all his own. Someone with the complexity of a rusted blade, still sharp enough to cut, and just twisted enough to be interesting. No hero or saint, for what's the fun in predictable righteousness?

Someone with rot in the marrow.

Someone who makes the story interesting.

And then a noise.

Subtle. Barely a sound at all. A scrape of wood. A flutter of dust from the rafters. But those who know what to listen for, like her, sharp-eyed and wild as ever… hear it. And they smile.

Curious, aren't we?

Let's peel back the veil. Let's lift the snow from the stone. Let's see who had the gall to slip away during mourning, and why his absence tastes so deliciously like disobedience.

Outside, a young lad had just executed a daring feat, escaping from the Church's towering belfry. A long plank of wood wobbled and slipped along the icy surface of the open tower window, to the ruined remains of the home that stood next to it. A splash of water on the structure's side of the bridge, then frozen solid to secure the plank. A clever trick, but who is this little interloper so brazenly sneaking out of the house of the abandoned faithful?

Ah, behold our protagonist, draped not in hero's garb but in the rags of tragedy. An orphan by birth and by nature double cursed in a town where the gods themselves have long since turned their backs. Once, the heavens graced mortals with miracles, their faithful receiving blessings and a warm fuzzy feeling in their souls. But something happened; one day these gods just up and left. Never to be seen again. Now the world wears their abandonment like a scar. And our boy, forsaken by both the divine and the mortal, finds no solace in the cold hearts of Glimisvellir. Communal love? Ha! Not here, where pity is as scarce as sunlight in the dead of winter.

"Finally, at least now I'll have some answers." A grin twisted across his unusual face, one not made for joy. His skin, as pale and mottled as old parchment, was etched with dark veins. His nose, barely there, and those eyes, vivid green and pupilless, made him look more like some horrible thing of fish and beast that crawled out of the sea than a young boy. Malnourished and marked by scars of neglect, he was a portrait of survival against the odds.

Once he was safe in the ruins of the old house that no one seemed willing to claim and repair. Space was limited in Glimisvellir so it was unusual that no one was in a hurry to collect such a prized spot that the building stood on. He kicked the soggy end of the board loose, letting it clatter to the ground below. A temporary triumph in a town that's never had room for him. He pulled out an old bundle of pages, his prize stolen from the priest of the church.

Flipping open the book, he skimmed through parchments with eager fingers, but his excitement soured into frustration. The scribbles were foreign, indecipherable. His mother's diary, her name boldly written on the first page, but the rest? In a tongue he couldn't read. A year of painstaking, secret lessons in literacy, all useless against these strange symbols.

"Hah, as if my luck was ever bound to change," he muttered. The sting of disappointment was softened by the small victory of having stolen it at all. Slumping to the floor, our boy let the weight of his failures press down on him, simmering in frustration and the bitter aftertaste of his hollow triumph. He lay still, listening as the distant murmurs of the church crowd began to fade, replaced by the droning clatter of boots on cobblestones. He dared a glance through the blackened frame of the crumbling wall, catching sight of Glimisvellir's faithful filing out, their faces as grim and weathered as the stones beneath them. His lip curled at the sight of Thrain, the so-called town hero, strutting like a peacock fresh from battle despite the hunt happening later in the day. Why fuss over a single hunt when the whole town's teetering on the brink? But that was not our little man's problem, it was everyone else's.

He lingered until the streets emptied, pondering his next move. What options did he have, really? Retreat to the embrace of a warm, loving family? Seek out the wisdom of a sagely mentor who saw potential in his odd little black heart? Perhaps find solace in the arms of some girl who could see past his grotesque appearance to the soul beneath? None of that. Ah, but life isn't so kind to our leading voice on the stage. Bereft of warmth, guidance, or love, he slipped away into the shadows of back alleys, skirting the edges of Glimisvellir like an unwanted stray.

He slunk toward the town's rear gate, a place he knew better than any warm hearth, a gateway to the dense, unwelcoming forest that loomed at the valley's edge. The trees offered solitude, necessity, and an escape from eyes that never ceased judging. With his mother's diary tucked into his ragged coat, there were chores to be done out in those trees, so he ventured forward. Only a single step. One step before he found himself surrounded on all sides by the playful youth of Glimisvellir.

"Why hello there all, can we not do this today? I've got chores." The boy's grin was as forced as it was crooked, a thin veneer over the simmering irritation beneath. The only thing he tasted was bitter anger that must be masked by false sweetness lest the game be lost. He would not give his tormentors the satisfaction of seeing him despair or even rage at his lot in life.

But children are cruel and rarely understand the complexities and dedication that the Cursed Born boy put into his craft. Their play was simpler, more direct, and so his face was shoved to the ground, followed by the familiar barrage of fists and feet. A sadistic game they never tired of playing, and one he was forced to endure time and time again. Ah, the art of brutality. Such a shame no one appreciates the classics anymore.

"Freak!"

"Just go and die Cursed Born!"

"How many more days is it now until you're finished?"

"The whole town is getting ready to celebrate!"

The huddle of snarling children encircled his prone form, their kicks and jeers coming with the unrestrained glee only youth can muster. In any other time or place, these brats might be held up as paragons of politeness, obedient little angels. But here, looming over a much despised pariah, they were free to unleash every bit of malice they could muster on someone who was, by silent decree, undeserving of mercy.

Here in this one instance, where cruelty wasn't just condoned but actively cultivated as far as one could see, they could torment without consequence, indulging in violence that would shock even the most lenient of saints.

Ah, Glimisvellir, the stage for the world's most predictable tragedies. And here we have the children of the chorus, reciting their lines with all the enthusiasm of a bloodthirsty mob. It's almost poetic, if you're the cultured and refined sort to find poetry in mindless cruelty. Our beleaguered lead was one such sort, if the roles were reversed. But alas, he suffers under a hail of tiny, cruel feet, one can't help but wonder: where's the hero when you really need one?

Our poor Cursed Born knew better than to fight back. He learned early on that resistance only brought harsher retribution later from these delightful little creatures. But what of the adults? Surely someone of aged wisdom and compassion would step in. Oh no-no-no, they were different beasts altogether. They wouldn't give him the time of day long enough to strike at him, but they were more than happy to turn a blind eye when their offspring did it for them. In the past, the tattered boy had tested that willful ignorance of his existence and paid dearly for it.

Here, among Glimisvellir's icy streets and colder hearts, no one cared about the nuances of blame or the ethics of punishing a boy for his birthright. Pain was his constant companion, and what did it matter now? He would be dead in a week, and then the town would need to contend with the misfortune that waited outside their gates.

Ah, and for those wondering why our unfortunate lad has marked his own calendar with such grim finality, let me enlighten you. The dogma of the Church of the Orphaned

World is as unforgiving as the stones it preaches from: at thirteen, an orphaned child is no longer an orphaned child, no longer shielded by ancient, shared grief and clerical doctrine. And for our leading man? His upcoming birthday isn't just a passage of time; it's the countdown to a ceremonial blaze that will mark his end. A fire lit by irrational hate, misplaced spite, and a twisted sense of communal justice.

Of course, it's not just his infernal lineage that fuels their hatred though that's a fine garnish on this wretched dessert. But let's not forget the delectable cakey core: their loathing for his mother, a woman they slandered with venomous zeal, branding her with terms as vile as 'rotten foreign whore' a phrase they didn't hesitate to hurl at her son loudly and often.

Finally, the delightful tykes had their fill of cruel sport. The chorus of giggles and mocking jeers drifted away, fading into the distance as a lone malnourished form remained curled on the ground. But not all had dispersed; a cluster of the older bullies, those who were on the cusp of adulthood themselves, lingered. They stood around him, each wearing that smug, self-satisfied grin of someone who believes they'd just won a grand wager. Chief among them, as always, was Borstig, the ringleader of this charming little troupe. Pig-headed and barrel-chested, he crouched beside his prey and flicked at his deformed ear with the lazy cruelty of a boy who knew he would never be punished.

"Patch yourself up with your infernal Seidr. Bet you love being your own little healer, huh?" Borstig taunted, his voice thick with mockery. Each flick of his fingers was a small, deliberate act of petty violence, like plucking the wings off a fly. "Come on, bastard, you think this is a holmgang? Fix yourself up and try again, if you've got the stones for it."

One of the other boys, clearly more interested in their next mischief, nudged Borstig.

"Borstig, leave him. Hrodgeir's brother promised us a horn of mead tonight. Don't want to be late and have him change his mind." Ah, more important tomfoolery was in store for these young rascals. The promise of boozy sips enticed the fresh teenagers, and so the tubby brute ceased his bullying of the chosen subject of our tale. But with a parting gift, a hefty boot to the gut and some parting words that cut deep to the core of the Cursed Born.

"Count yourself lucky, bastard. A filthy half-breed like you would've died alone anyway. At least now, you'll burn surrounded by people who know you best." I'm sure that Borstig had spent far too many weeks coming up with that. It was delivered in that fashion, like he had rehearsed it in his head to sound smart and witty in front of his friends.

They scampered off, their hearts aglow with the warmth only youthful wickedness can kindle. Not a single one paused to ponder if their deeds might cast long shadows, heralding ghosts of retribution. Alone now, our fated Cursed Born lingered on the cold ground until the echoes of their mirth faded into silence. Only then did he muster the strength to rise once more, a solitary figure amid the remnants of his latest ordeal. The cold cobblestones, slick with a fresh dusting of snowflakes as sharp as iron filings, bit into his knees as he pushed himself up, even the very stones of the town itself seemed to try and teach the all-important lesson its people did.

"Ugh… about time. I've got things to do." He muttered, brushing off the dirt from his tattered rags. While the rest of Glimisvellir's privileged wrapped themselves in warm furs, stitched with care, sealskin and reindeer hide to fight off the biting cold, his clothes barely shielded him from the wind. But who in their right mind would spare a thought for a Cursed Born? Never mind the fact a 'right mind' is out of style anyway. Wrong mind is so in this season.

Battered and bruised, but not broken, our young almost-man was far from ordinary. And why, dear Listener, would we waste our time on the mundane? No, our story clings to this boy because he is something far more though that spark of destiny remains a well-kept secret, even from him. Just another lost soul? Ha! Not quite. He's the linchpin of our grand tale, a hinge on which fate itself may yet turn.

"Li-Li-Li-Li Li-Fir-Me-Wa." With a chant that seemed more like a secret whispered to the wind, our Cursed Born wielded a bit of the arcane, two fingers aglow with a soft, healing luminescence. Touch by touch, his bruises vanished, as did the pain, a neat little parlor trick for our not-so-ordinary lad. Ah yes, a protagonist with the gift of magic, a mainstay of any great story.

"You know, I'd almost feel useless now that you can patch yourself up like that," came the teasing voice, followed by the sudden arc of a cooked trout wrapped in boiled cabbage leaves, flung expertly through the air and landing neatly in his hand. "Almost."

Sarcasm, sweetened with a playful grin ah, now here's a face worth noting. Brune, a girl maybe a year shy of his age, stood there with a defiant light in her eyes, free of the scorn or pity that laced the looks of others. In Glimisvellir, where girls were expected to stay close to the hearth, stitching and stirring, Brune bucked tradition with a gusto. She was just as comfortable with a knife in her hand as she was a needle, equally at home hunting in the forest or gutting a fish. Having the town's golden boy Thrain as her brother certainly gave her some room to be different, but it didn't make her any more liked in a place where tomboys were as welcome as a snowstorm in spring.

"You're a braver man than I if you eat that. Last time she tried cooking, she burnt it so badly I could use it in my dad's furnace," quipped another voice, rougher, with the rasp of smoke and steel. Jorund, the blacksmith's son, bore the marks of his trade soot-smudged, calloused hands, and hair singed at the tips from too many close calls with the forge. Despite the grime and the weight of his work, there was a sturdiness to him that seemed unbreakable, a resilience hammered into every bone.

"Should I dare? What's the harm in dying early?" The Cursed Born eyed the fish, turning it over as if it might bite. He examined the food like a jeweler assessing a counterfeit gem, suspicious of even the most basic meal fish and cabbage, the simplest of Glimingar staples. And yet, somehow, Brune had managed to botch it in the past. A remarkable talent, really.

"You're lucky I'm feeding you at all, Frost-Bite. You need all you can get with how stunted you've turned out." Her words along with the mocking giggle at the end did get a reaction out of the normally corpse deadpan look he wore most of the time. She knew just how to poke at him, and Jorund, sensing the impending sparring match, took a step back, smirking at the familiar dance.

"Oh yeah? And how are you going to find a husband, you giantess?" There was… a bare minimum foot and a half between them. Was it because he was short or she was tall?

It didn't matter. She, along with the boy, were the only ones willing to be friendly with him so they were the only people he would compare himself to.

"Well, I don't need one, I can do everything that a husband would do and better." Brune retorted, flipping her bright blonde braid over her shoulder with exaggerated flair. His own hair, if it could be called that, was a stark contrast, more akin to spiky quills than any human locks.

"No, stop, cease this madness," Jorund interjected half-heartedly, retreating to a nearby stump, content to watch from the sidelines. He knew this little performance all too well, the playful barbs, the mock indignation. He'd seen it a hundred times and never tired of it.

"And nothing a wife would do, but probably worse." The budding of a true vile laugh existed in that proud chuckle that came after the comeback. Stunting it, however, was a snowball that hit him in the back of the head. Brune's aim was true, and in an instant, the simmering tension broke into a flurry of snow and laughter.

There it was a rare, fleeting moment of genuine happiness. A snowball fight among friends, a brief respite from the cruel reality that lurked just outside their little circle. Ugh, this nauseating display of youthful exuberance, this sickeningly heartwarming scene of camaraderie… let's draw the curtain on it, shall we? There are far grimmer things waiting, after all, and this saccharine nonsense won't last long.

The impending execution of a teenage boy wasn't just a morbid pastime for Glimisvellir; it was a distraction from a far more grave threat. You see, Glimisvellir now found itself staring down the barrels of a formidable menace quite literally. An entire artillery regiment, bristling with cannons and soldiers in absurdly tall hats, had taken interest in the ancient walls that had protected this stubborn town for centuries. Conform or be crushed, the ultimatum from the south was clear. Ah, the classic guise of conquest masked as unification, propaganda draped in patriotism.

Once, Glimisvellir's response to such threats was simple: lock the gates and let their warriors do the talking. Sneaking through hidden tunnels, they would strike like ghosts, turning the tables on any would-be invaders. Glimisvellir's land was unforgiving, known only to those born in its icy embrace, and their shrewd tactics, towering walls, and a bone-chilling moat fed by glacial waters kept even the mightiest armies at bay. But the winds of war had shifted.

Cannons, those relentless harbingers of modern warfare, now threatened to shatter walls that had once scoffed at battering rams and catapults. Glimisvellir, once an unassailable fortress of stone and ice, now faced a cage of its own making. The Glimingars, fierce defenders of their frozen realm, found themselves ill-prepared for this new era of thunderous artillery.

So, you wonder, with the shadow of war looming, can't the arcane arts tip the scales? This is a world of magic is it not? Regrettably, magic isn't the panacea it's often fancied to be. In the world we find ourselves in, true Mages number as cockroaches living in a grand cathedral; they exist, oh sure. but relative to the size of their home it is not many. Only a select few in any given hamlet are touched by their mercurial hand, and Glimisvellir? Well, it's got just a pair of these mystical misfits in this generation.

Don't get started on the spells themselves… a maddening cacophony of eight words used in sets of four, up to ten sets for each spell. Math, there is a mathematical element in the combination of words in sequence. Throughout the ages, some level of common understanding of how these equations work out has spread but beyond a certain vital number of fundamentals, it's all random. Knowledge is hoarded, every secret and scrap of divine understanding kept for each Mage for themselves.

As the cannons loomed large, Glimisvellir's warriors clung to their old guerrilla tactics, ambushing the invaders in the narrow passes and shadowy forests. But these were no ill-prepared foes. They were well-armed, disciplined, and, crucially, well-fed. For two weeks, a grim stalemate ensued, with the usual allies of starvation and frostbite mysteriously absent. A direct assault on the gunlines ended in disaster, a harsh lesson quickly learned. The town's invincibility, so long taken for granted, had become a quaint myth, crumbling under the weight of modern warfare.

The tension simmered, curdling into a bitter brew that the townsfolk were unaccustomed to sipping. So, they latched onto a more familiar spectacle, the approaching execution of a Cursed Born, a diversion to keep their minds from the cannon fire echoing just beyond their walls. It was a grim pageant, a twisted festival to momentarily forget the impending doom, with the Cursed Born as the centerpiece. His moment in the spotlight was soon, and the town was all too eager to play its part in the macabre performance.

"Enough, Orphan, let me go!" Ah yes, the boy's name is indeed Orphan. Out of all the labels thrown at him over the years, it was the most consistent, and the least crude, so it just stuck.

"Well, that's ninety-nine to ninety-five. Shame I probably

won't clinch the bet before my birthday rolls around." With a casual flick of his fingers, the ice shackling Brune dissolved into water, trickling harmlessly away. No dramatic flares or searing heat, just the simple manipulation of water from one state to another. Each Mage in this world has their own peculiar gift, and Orphan's? The power to tweak water's state at will ice, liquid, or vapor, as long as it's pure enough and within sight. So no, he can't turn anyone's blood to ice, don't get your hopes up.

"Four of those fights you cheated, so it's actually the other way around. You think you're some kind of skald, making up stories? Just don't end up like one of those drunk idiots spinning lies at the Sumbel." Their spectator chimed in. He hopped off his little seat and walked back over, happy to be dry and not soaked like the girl. That was why he never engaged in these silly fights. After all, why jump into the fray when watching was so much more amusing?

Orphan smirked slightly. "Maybe I am a bit of a skald. Wouldn't mind telling tales instead of dodging snowballs all day."

Brune rolled her eyes, wringing out her damp sleeves. "You? A skald? Please. You'd need more than a few clever lines to impress anyone."

"Who says I don't have them?" Orphan shot back, a glint of mischief in his eyes. In truth, he'd always been fascinated by the skalds' songs and flyting duels the way words could be wielded like weapons. If things were different, perhaps he might have pursued that path.

"Well, it's like racing against the thaw, and then you pull that ice Seidr," she grumbled, tugging off her coat and shaking the drips off. Orphan's magic didn't make the air colder, but there was still a chill that lingered when he was done.

"A win is a win, Brune, and this one has been getting even better recently," Orphan retorted, a rare hint of smugness seeping into his usual monotone as his gaze lingered a tad too long on his friend, who was maturing faster than the seasons changed. Ah, the impetuousness of youth. Under normal circumstances, such behavior might be chided as foolish, but with Orphan's grim countdown, who could blame him for seizing the moment?

"Shut up. They won't stop growing, and I'd much rather look like my father's sister, lean and quick. Instead, I take after my ox of a mother," Brune shot back, irritation flaring as she adjusted her coat. Orphan met her glare with his typical calm; he feared nothing, certainly not her anger. He'd learned long ago to bear the taunts of children rather than the ire of their parents.

"Or worse, you might grow up to look like Thrain. He's already blurred the line enough," Jorund added, earning a disgusted look from Brune.

"Shut up, Jorund! Don't you dare compare me to that self-absorbed idiot," she snapped, but the smith's son only grinned, clearly pleased with her reaction.

"Lucky then I won't win the bet, and you'll have to start acting like a proper girl then." Anyone else who spoke to her like this probably would have gotten a split lip and a black eye for their trouble. Brune was a violent little monster, even more so than the other brats in the village. The benefit of being the beloved little sister to the town's best tracker and hunter meant no one could touch her or else suffer his wrath. Perhaps that was why, in such a patriarchal and traditional society as Glimisvellir's, she could be the way she was. Or maybe so much attention was given to the Cursed Born that no one paid attention to the normal troublemaker in their midst.

"Out of everything you could have actually listened about from all these idiots it had to be ' how to be a man'. Your uncle is a pathetic drunk, how could he possibly be the kind of man you'd like to be?," Brune grumbled as they made their way toward the forest's edge, where Glimisvellir gave way to untamed wilderness. This forest, with its dense underbrush and thorny paths, was a natural barrier, as effective as any wall.

"And apparently, my devil-loving mother is your amazing role model.. So, who's really in the wrong?" Orphan replied, not with venom for Brune but for the woman who'd brought him into this mess of a life. He resented her not for dying but for doing so poorly at her scheme to stay on the town's better side. If she'd just toed the line, perhaps he wouldn't be the walking target he was today. And yes, the cruel irony is, he's right, though not in the way he believes.

"How can you even say that? She was gone before we could even walk," Jorund interjected, puzzled as they leapt down to the creek that marked the town's unofficial boundary.

"Doesn't matter. I just like the idea of a woman bucking the old rules," Brune shrugged, letting logic slip away in favor of the romantic notion of rebellion. Orphan glanced at her, a hint of admiration flickering in his eyes. Perhaps that's why he enjoyed the tales of defiant heroes and sharp-tongued skalds who challenged the world with words and wit.

"Besides, if I win the next snowball fight, that's game over," Brune said, nudging Orphan with a teasing shoulder bump. Jorund watched them, rolling his eyes at the unspoken tension simmering between the two. It was obvious to everyone except, perhaps, to them that their friendship carried more weight than either was willing to admit. Not even Orphan's impending death could change that.

The trio ventured deeper into the forest, leaving the faint glow of Glimisvellir far behind. Both Orphan and Brune knew the terrain well; their shared history of exploring these hidden places was what had brought them together in the first place, though each had sought solitude for different reasons. As they walked, Orphan found himself quietly composing lines in his head, snippets of verses that he might one day dare to speak aloud.

They clambered down into a small cave, where gnarled roots of ancient trees clawed at the earth and the steady drip of melting snow provided a constant, rhythmic echo. This was a secret spot, a place usually reserved for quiet reflection or solitude, but today they weren't alone.

Blissfully unaware of the many kinds of dangers, they navigated the descent, moving from the steep entryway to the flat expanse below. Faintly glowing vines clung to the stone walls, casting an otherworldly hue. A trickling stream, coaxed into existence by Orphan's magic, wound its way through the cavern, and clusters of mushrooms grew in abundance enough to sustain someone if they didn't mind a monotonous diet. But today, food wasn't the reason for their visit. Instead, they gathered around a small, weathered box filled with vivid flowers nestled at the back of the cave.

"Is there a reason your uncle have you growing these things out here? His whole place is already stuffed with weird plants from the south. Your uncle's no better than a Völva and just as crazy," Jorund muttered, leaning in to sniff the flowers. He immediately recoiled, his face twisting in disgust. Orphan's amused smirk told him that he'd expected the reaction.

"That's why. They stink. But he says they're an important ingredient for the Jarl's medicine. He asked me to fetch them now that he's done with the rest." It might seem strange a boy awaiting execution helping to prepare medicine for the very man who had decreed his death. But Orphan bore no particular grudge against the Jarl; in fact, he was one of the few who only ignored Orphan's existence rather than occasionally tormented him. That made him more tolerable than most, and besides, what else did Orphan have to do?

"The Jarl is sick? Looked fine at the Sumbel last night," Brune remarked, eyebrow raised. It struck her as odd, but the pieces didn't quite fit together in their minds.

"It's not that kind of sick," Orphan explained, carefully plucking the petals as he'd been taught. He separated them into one bag, roots and stems into another. "Uncle says it's a mind sickness. Makes him see things that aren't there. The Jarl who sees shadows in daylight,' mmm... I should write that down later."

Brune chuckled. "You're hopeless Frostbite. Maybe stick to Seidr before you embarrass yourself with bad poetry."

"My poor devil-spawn heart, how will I recover?" he retorted, feigning offense. "Even the greatest skalds started as the town embarrassment. No one is born great... except for the great and mighty Thrain! Should we try again one last time before I'm sent to the pyre to cut his ego down to size?"

"Tempting, but last time we pulled a prank on Thrain, he nearly killed you. And his whole speech about you 'corrupting' me? Ugh, it was humiliating," Brune said, changing the subject as she covered her face, the memory still fresh and embarrassing. Thrain and Orphan had been at odds since the beginning, their rivalry fueled by Thrain's self-righteousness and Orphan's mere existence.

"It was nice having him gone the past few weeks. Shitty now he's back." The conversation meandered as Orphan continued his task, the smell growing worse with each plucked petal. By the time he'd finished, the stench was nearly unbearable, forcing all three to gag.

"Finally. Let's get out of here and into the open air," Orphan said, stuffing the bags into his tattered coat. They scrambled back up to the forest, grateful for the sharp, fresh air that greeted them. But that was the only bit of pleasantness that came to them.

Instead of the lip of the cavern that Orphan had intended to grab ahold of, his entire arm was instead hoisted up by a gloved hand twice the size of a full grown man. Yanked up out of the cave, the poor and weak boy soon came face to face with a folktale, a myth among hunters, truly more a monster of the wilds. Nearly nine feet tall, the man was cloaked in a fur coat stiff with ice, its face obscured save for small, clouded glasses that revealed nothing to those who dared to look. Those hidden eyes stared directly into Orphan's vivid green ones.

"Two? What pretty little emeralds you have in that skull of yours. Count yourself lucky."

Hunters whispered of the Winterman, an apparition in the woods. When beasts cornered men, this towering figure would emerge from the shadows, its breath turning the air to ice, its movements slow and deliberate, as if time itself bent to its will. A hungry mountain lion or an angry cave bear, these would prove a challenge to skilled hunters. But to this creature, killing these beasts looked effortless as it would pierce the neck with an arm size bolt from its crossbow.

Brune's gasp shattered the silence. She and Jorund stared, frozen not just by the cold but by the sheer impossibility of seeing this legend in flesh and bone. Demons, Fiends, and Devils are real, dear girl; why wouldn't this monster be, too? Her voice, shaky and edged with dread, broke the spell, igniting fears that their fates were now tangled with Orphan's. The moment stretched, the air heavy with the chill of something ancient and unkind, as the Winterman lifted Orphan with one powerful hand, holding him aloft like a rag doll.

"What an interesting find on my morning walk. A different kind of interesting too. Lately, it's been odd men with tall hats, bright clothes, and strange weapons." Its voice was unexpectedly warm, a stark contrast to its frozen appearance. It dropped Orphan unceremoniously onto the snow, its towering shadow swallowing the children whole.

It had been a long time since these kids had felt fear. No, that's not right. It's more like they've never known fear. Until this very moment, the three of them had never felt that most vital of emotion as what they called fear as before was so tepid compared to what they felt now. It could no longer be called such in their minds. That primal feeling all animals have when they just know they are about to die meaninglessly, about to perish just to feed a stronger being its daily meal.

"Jorund, what do we do? I can't move." An unfamiliar sensation to Brune. She hadn't cried in many years, partly out of principle and proudly because nothing had done something to her worth crying over. But now? Oh yes.

Tears streaked down her face as every ghastly horror story she begged her brother and his friends to tell her about the Winterman repeated in her mind at blazing speeds. The fun, she enjoyed being brave in the face of such outlandish stories that must have only been made to scare little kids. They couldn't have been real, right? Dear girl… they were real, even worse they were made soft and easy to swallow.

"I… I don't know," Jorund admitted, all defiance drained. His rebellions seemed absurd now, childish acts of resistance against the ordinary. This was something altogether different, an authority beyond mortal understanding. But there was one among them that was mad enough to defy all logic and sense to babble and cry in a corner for mercy.

Despite the terror, something stirred in Orphan. The stunted, malnourished boy no match for even the smallest predator pushed himself up and stood between his friends and the towering figure. His arms spread wide in a futile, instinctive gesture of protection. Even with all that fear, there were things that a man had to do.

"What are you doing, boy? Trying to be a hero?" The Winterman's voice rumbled, a mix of mockery and disdain. The word 'hero' spat out like a curse, stripped of its grandeur. There was a vanishing understanding in Orphan there, such words brought comfort to others but were meaningless or worse to him. What was a hero but a fool that risked himself for others, what nonsense.

"I don't have much, but I'll fight to keep what's mine." His voice held a different kind of fear, not the primal terror that seized his friends, but a cold, logical dread. He couldn't win, but he had nothing left to lose.

"Greedy little thing, aren't you? Wanting so much." The

Winterman's laugh was muffled, its amusement more chilling than any threat. Without another word, it turned and disappeared into the forest, leaving a hollow silence in its wake.

"That... that didn't happen, right?" Brune stammered, clinging to the hope that this was some hallucinatory trick, maybe a side effect of Orphan's strange plants. "Just... something from your uncle's flowers?"

"I think we're better off remembering it that way," Orphan murmured, his voice flat, but something within him had changed. Fear, true fear, had touched him, shaken him in a way nothing else ever had. Without another word, they bolted from the cave, scrambling through the forest toward the false safety of Glimisvellir.

For the first time, Glimisvellir felt like a refuge, its walls less menacing than the cold, vast unknown of the forest. For Orphan, the pyre awaiting him now seemed almost a mercy compared to the raw, untamed dread of the Winterman. The stories he'd once dismissed as wild exaggerations now felt all too real, their weight pressing against him with a new, terrible clarity.

They returned to Glimisvellir, a town caught between the old world and the new, its skies filled with the banners of an advancing army and the whispers of things far worse. This is the precipice upon which our tale truly begins: a town stubbornly clinging to its past, its people lost in the comforting cruelty of tradition, and a future that will not be denied. The tides of change are coming, relentless and unyielding, promising a reckoning that will reshape Glimisvellir and its people in ways they cannot yet fathom.

Words of the First

Orphans, widows, and cripples' pain
Thieves in moonlight, shadows gain
Gods forsake the crowns falling like rain

The Curtains Open

"He was real! I saw him!" Ah screaming, though not the bellows of the tortured but rather the petulant outburst of a child struggling to be taken seriously by the grown-ups around him.

"Yes-yes, the Winterman. Did he kill you? Because that would save everyone a bit of trouble." The voice came from amidst the clatter of pots and the shrill hiss of boiling kettles, nestled within the Great Hall of Glimisvellir, or more precisely, within a small, cluttered annex traditionally reserved for crazed witch women called Völva. This space, once a sanctuary for seers and mystics of great renown, Yet now, it hosted a tenant of… decidedly lesser renown.

Gone were the venerated druids and wise sages of old. In their place was Gerfinn, Glimisvellir's resident herbalist and dabbler in the arcane, whose devotion to his craft was rivaled only by his devotion to the bottle. Gerfinn possessed a certain knack for brewing salves and elixirs that soothed aches of body and spirit, but it was clear that his residence in this hallowed space was more due to the absence of better candidates than any love for this wayward son of Glimisvellir. Had there been another with the faintest spark of magic, this sanctuary would have been theirs.

Once a place of order and reverence, the annex was now an ode to chaos. Clay basins lined the walls, cradling flames beneath an assortment of pots and kettles that bubbled with dubious concoctions. The heart of the room was dominated by oversized boilers, their contents known only to Gerfinn, if even he could keep track. Potted plants spilled across every available surface, their leaves tangled with clutches of drying herbs. It's a tangible representation of the herbalist's mind: cluttered, unfocused, but undeniably that of a craftsman with a deep, if not somewhat blurred, passion for his work.

Orphan rarely strayed far from this corner of the Great Hall. As the town's only other magic user and healer, Gerfinn received the Jarl's support, a lifeline that inadvertently extended to his unwanted nephew. For Orphan, the arrangement was a mixed blessing. Gerfinn's drunken neglect meant the boy often went hungry, but it also granted him the freedom to scavenge the hall's leftovers in the early hours, a small act of defiance that kept him barely fed. The toll of this scavenger's life was evident in Orphan's slender, underfed form, his skin stretched taut over bones that bore the marks of his scant and irregular meals.

"No, he didn't kill me. I'm still here, obviously." It was a simple observation to make and a stupid question to ask if taken seriously. The exchange, though seemingly trivial, was laden with the unspoken nuances of their relationship, one that hung by the thread of the man's whims. A bond, if it could be called that, anchored not in familial warmth but in a begrudging promise to a brother, now serving as the flimsy lifeline for Orphan's basic needs. Most of the time. Usually.

"For now. You get my fucking plants, boy?" Gerfinn barked, his voice rough, like gravel scraping over iron. His face, a map of old burns and scars, told the tale of countless failed experiments and a younger life raiding coastal villages. Once bright blond hair had long since dulled to a pale, lifeless yellow, a casualty of his reckless pursuits. Only his craft and magic explained his non-corpse status. Misusing talents better left for someone else to keep his hands limber and wrapped around the ale horn instead stiff and cold. Yet behind the weathered exterior, his eyes remained sharp, gleaming with a cunning that had outlasted his youth. He thrived on chance and deception, a gambler whose skill lay not in cards but in exploiting whatever fortune lay within his grasp.

Orphan, uninterested in further banter, silently placed the two bags he had retrieved onto Gerfinn's makeshift alchemical altar, a cluttered workbench that doubled as a dumping ground for failed potions and questionable ingredients. A short mocking sequel escaped the drunk gambler as he scooped them up and excitedly skipped over to a separate cauldron of bubbling soup. Without ceremony, he tossed in the stems and roots of the bright yellow-orange plants Orphan had painstakingly grown in the hidden cave. The brew bubbled on, unchanged in color or scent, though the mingling aromas of the room made it impossible to tell.

With his task complete and his presence seemingly superfluous, Orphan announced his departure towards the meager sanctuary of his bunk. There, he planned to immerse himself in the enigma of his mother's diary, hoping against hope that the script might reveal its secrets to him through sheer willpower or magical whim. It was a better use of his time then planning out some doomed scheme to escape the coming pyre. Biting, clawing, and fighting his way out was senseless even if it would have been satisfying. No, he was smarter than that. At least he knew he was smarter than the stupid fools that hated him for all the wrong reasons. Why hate something on the fault of someone else, waste of hate and spite at the end of the day. Let a person disappoint and or enrage you themselves instead.

Orphan was acutely aware of the grim arithmetic of his situation. A scrawny, untrained boy pitted against a town of hardened fighters and hunters, all bound to the land they knew like their own breath. The very notion was absurd, a fool's errand destined for failure. Moronic of the highest order! Even if he could somehow sway the townsfolk, their hunger for the spectacle of a Blót was too deeply rooted, a convenient distraction from the encroaching doom beyond their walls.

"Get back here boy, I don't need you skinning your snake back there or muttering Words of Invocation all night. Gods lost know I don't want either of the results to be staining my floors. Or even worse you think up rhymes shoddier than your last attempting at flyting me boy. I've heard better insults from tavern drunks when they're passed out." The drunk's slurred command cut through Orphan's thoughts. He gestured impatiently to the stool by his cluttered workspace, leaving no room for argument. Orphan rolled his eyes but complied, his insolence simmering just below the surface. He knew when resistance was pointless.

The cauldron's simmering sound marked the slow passage of time. Gerfinn, focused on his work, added a final flourish to his concoction: a handful of inky beans and a dash of ochre dust. A brisk stir, the clatter of a lid, and the herbalist leaned back with a satisfied grunt. But the satisfaction faded quickly, his grin replaced by a pensive scowl as he paced back to the chaos of his laboratory, casting a critical eye on his collection of flasks and herbs.

There, amidst the vials and the verdancy, sat Orphan, the child thrust upon him by a brother whose ineptitude was only matched by his timidity. Not tied by blood but bound by a begrudging sense of duty, the herbalist found himself incapable of outright despising the boy or his sibling. But he could smack him around a bit from time to time.

"Ow! What did I do now?" It was rare for his uncle to just hit him for no reason, even if it was just a quick smack to the backside of his head.

"I told you not to keep muttering the Words of Invocation. You ain't going to find the fucking Words to turn yourself immortal. Blessed with the Majorus of Life you may be, the number of sets for something like that would be too fucking high." Gerfinn's voice dripped with scorn. Magic, after all, wasn't a gift neatly packaged or uniformly understood. The so-called "blessing" of magic was more like a cruel puzzle, different for every soul cursed enough to wield it.

It wasn't the same for each person. What one sequence of the Words of Invocation did for one magic user did not mean it would do the same or anything at all for another. Even if they had the same attunement to the Cardinal Points of Magic. There was a small consistency, there in fact existed the same spells for everyone and there tended to be an average number of sets for each one. Orphan knew the Heal spell, anyone with a Life Majorus could cast Heal. But… could they do it with only two sets? Unlikely. And even if they could, every word past the first set would be entirely different. This individualism bred a culture of secrecy among mages. Knowledge was guarded jealously; spells were not shared but hoarded, each word a currency in a world where magic could mean power, survival, or destruction. Revealing the secrets of one's magic was akin to stripping naked before a crowd exposing vulnerabilities best kept hidden.

The fabric of magic was a tapestry of intuition and intellect, where practitioners could sense the push and pull of their power with each uttered Word of Invocation. This intuitive guidance, this subtle nudge towards the right combination, was the line dividing the adept from the inept, the brilliant from the mundane. In this dance of chance and skill, how one responded to magic's silent whispers could elevate them to the heights of arcane mastery or condemn them to the obscurity of the ineffectual.

"Yes, Uncle Gerfinn, I'm just a talentless, ugly half-breed with nothing to offer… oh, wait, except for that shortened version of the Heal spell I discovered." Orphan's sarcasm was sharp, cutting through the stale air between them. He knew the value of his accomplishment, even if no one else acknowledged it. In any other context, he might have been lauded as a prodigy. Here, he was just a cursed boy with a rare stroke of luck.

"Don't let it go to your head, brat. Every mage gets lucky once," Gerfinn growled, refusing to acknowledge the talent hidden in his nephew. The Heal spell was basic, but reducing it to two sets was no small feat. If it had been any other child in Glimisvellir he would have jumped for joy at the prospect of a real apprentice, even better that they had Life as their Majorus instead Minorus like him.

"You didn't even realize you had Seidr until you were twenty. That's not exactly early," That comment earned him another smack to the back of his head, but Orphan took it with a grin. The idea that someone could miss the pull of magic for so long was laughable to him; it had been part of him from his earliest memories.

"That's normal for a pure human, you damn half-breed. Now shut up before I start aiming for your cheek." The room fell into a heavy, uneasy silence, more a battle of wills than a truce. Orphan briefly considered asking about his mother's diary but quickly dismissed the idea. Gerfinn's hatred for her burned as hot as Orphan's own, and the risk of him destroying the last piece of her was too great.

In the dimming light of the coming days, the shadow of Orphan's fate grew ever longer, a grim reminder that the sands in his hourglass were swiftly falling. With only three days left before his flame was to be extinguished, the sense of inevitability hung dense in the air, a silent testament to the finality of his destiny.

The space they shared was marked by years of uneasy cohabitation, filled with fraying edges and unspoken resentments. In thirteen years, no bridge of understanding had ever been built between them, only a precarious truce that barely held. To Gerfinn, Orphan was nothing more than a cursed mistake, a vile remnant of a hated woman who should never have set foot in the North. And to Orphan, Gerfinn was a failed man clinging to the last shred of his worth, defined solely by his fading talents and bitter survival.

But while respect was lost entirely between them… an alliance of convenience was there. As both knew they were not normal people, they were a bit abnormal, different… twisted. That being said, the elder did feel one duty towards his junior, if for no other reason than the haunting memory of his own flesh and blood compelled him.

"Orphan, let's hear them once more," Gerfinn ordered, his attention still fixed on his bubbling potions. The command was more habit than anything else, an old ritual meant to instill some kind of discipline, however misplaced. Disobedience was not an option unless Orphan fancied a fresh set of bruises.

"Fine. Not that it matters when I'm dead in three days," Every single day this happened. A list of things that the drunken gambler wanted drilled into the boy's mind. And truth be told it had formed much of Orphans ideals, what he had strived to be. "Every man must be Strong, so that he can protect what is his. Every man must be Diligent, so that he may have something to call his own. And every man must be Cunning, to prevent someone from stealing what he has."

"That's right. My brother was none of those. And he paid the price for it when your whore of mother came through the gates. Wrapped him around her finger and killed our parents just so she didn't have to do a moment of work to get what she wanted." He should have come home sooner, leaving behind his days going out as a worthless víkingr on a crew that hated him and a captain that delighted in tormenting him. Maybe he could have stopped it all. But Gerfinn knew that wasn't what fate had in store for his brother.

He hated how weak and pathetic his brother was in his final moments. Trampled by a mob dragging out his wife to a pyre not too dissimilar to the one being prepared now. But try as he might, he couldn't hate his brother… only the weakness.

"What was she really like?" Sarcasm. Not some last moment's plea of an innocent boy wanting to connect with the ghost of his own mommy. No-no. Orphan had never once felt a longing to know any more about his mother than what he had already been told. A story well known to him, but perhaps

A woman, clearly not a native was found at the gate of Glimisvellir. The settlement by which this realm got its name opened its gate only by mercy, helping a poor pregnant woman nearly frozen by the cold. The Glimingar, perhaps against their better judgment, let their compassion override the warnings of the old crones who spoke against the perils of welcoming strangers. Oh, the delicious irony! A simple act of kindness, a momentary lapse in their guarded existence, sowing the seeds of their potential undoing. But, patience, every tragic downfall has its own delightful pace.

While the newcomer expressed her gratitude for the Glimingarn begrudging hospitality, it was glaringly apparent that her presence was more of a burden than a blessing to them. Their concept of mercy did not extend beyond the gate's threshold, offering her no more than a corner in the great hall. Instead of proper lodging, attendance, and supply of coin. The space was shared with the town's assorted castoffs and forgotten souls. She tried many-many-many times to explain just how important proper environment for mothers are for the health of a baby, but for some unknown reason they, The Glimingar, it seemed, were as adept at misunderstanding as they were at extending the most minimal of courtesies. Oh, the relentless efforts she made, to no avail!

Ah, but there was one shining beacon of understanding amidst the sea of indifference, a young man. Not burdened by the trivial pursuits of hunting, building, or dabbling in the arcane arts. No, his talents lie elsewhere, in the noble art of being aimlessly led around by a flock of goats. Yet, in this tapestry of mediocrity, he emerged as the unsung hero, the solitary figure of empathy in a world bereft of such. For he alone grasped the true essence of the woman's plight, recognizing the dire necessity of lavish gifts during trying times. Yes, while the others busied themselves with their mundane tasks, this young visionary perceived the woman's profound distress... for expensive things.

Quick as a wink, they were wed, immune to the desperate pleas of his family, for he was smitten, hopelessly in love. And just in the nick of time, tragedy struck with theatrical flair his parents succumbed to a ghastly fever. How utterly convenient! But fear not, for his new bride was there, a beacon of solace in his sea of grief. And, oh, what a stroke of serendipity that in the wake of death, they found a new abode, inheriting the family home for the eldest son was somewhere far away and unaware. Fortune does have a peculiar sense of humor, doesn't it? A tragedy here, a windfall there, all tied up with a neat little bow of marital bliss.

There before him unfolded the tableau of an idyllic family life, or so it seemed. A doting wife, ever so encouraging, urging him to chase after every coin, for the sake of their budding family. A tragic necessity, really, leaving her to bask in the solitude of their inherited home. His returns were infrequent, and their encounters fleeting, yet her joy was palpable or so he convinced himself. The sumptuous gifts he lavished upon her? Mere tokens, of course, not the keys to her effervescent happiness. No, she was simply overjoyed at the sight of him, not the trinkets he bore. All her time really had to be taken up by the child.

The child, not of his blood but destined to be his, was a different story. He knew that he would come to love it as his own… eventually… hopefully. A curious chill crept over him every time he looked at it, an unsettling whisper to his very core. Yet, he clung to the belief that love, that great conqueror, would prevail. Surely, when his own flesh and blood entered the world, those paternal instincts, currently absent, would awaken. Yes, all would be right. Meanwhile, he'd muster through the unease, awaiting the day when genuine bonds would form, dispelling the sinister shadows cast by this unnerving infant.

Nothing would get in the way of their happiness… well that angry mob might. All sorts of accusations and false stories of his wife being some witch with nothing but Malice in her heart were being thrown about. They said that she seduced him, singled him out for his simple mind. All slander. He begged. He pleaded. Any and all effort was given to assuage everyone of their fears. It was all for naught. The mob, fueled by fear and ignorance and perchance the whispers of the self-righteous, breached their sanctuary. They swept him aside with the ease of a child discarding a ragdoll. As shadows encroached upon his dimming sight, her terrified screams pierced the chaos, the crowd's cries for a pyre a grim symphony to his failing senses. But fear not. For in his final fading moments, he was not alone.

A brother only recently returned from his wayward adventures south now saw the results of his folly. There he was, the eldest sibling, perched silently beside his deathbed, offering no words, no solace, no healing spells from his repertoire. His inaction spoke volumes; it screamed that the end was nigh, too nigh for magic or miracles. Surely, that's why he merely sat there, idle, as his brother's life ebbed away, right? There couldn't possibly be any other reason for his passivity in the face of familial demise. How… comforting it was, to have him there, a silent sentinel to his final moments. One last request, the only thing that he could do now.

Ah, the mob's thirst for vengeance didn't stop with the witch; they clamored to cast the Cursed Born into the flames alongside the mother who bore him. But they were denied their blood. Salvation came with a clerical nod, as the local priest begrudgingly declared that even the offspring of the damned had the right to draw breath, only if orphaned. Though he chastised the mob for not killing the child first and then the mother. Such were the Church of the Orphaned World's ways. So, the child was allowed to live. Another act of mercy. Who knows if this one will be rewarded just as the last.

"She was beautiful, I'll give her that much." he admitted reluctantly. "And… I know she loved you. Or at least I knew that she was most vicious to those that threatened her pregnancy with you. Take that what you will."

The admission hung in the air, an uncomfortable truth neither of them wanted to confront. Orphan clenched his fists, his knuckles white against his knees. He didn't know what to hate more: the possibility that his mother had loved him in her own twisted way, or the idea that Gerfinn was feeding him a lie out of some misguided attempt at kindness. Both options were infuriating in their own right.

Orphan had always assumed the town's hatred was rooted in something deeper than just his lineage. Glimisvellir's disdain for him had always felt personal, more visceral than simple bigotry against a Cursed Born. If his mother's actions had poisoned the town's opinion of him, then her legacy was a heavier burden than he'd ever realized.

Glimisvellir was about as far from the Devil kingdom of Hell as one could get. At most they had to deal with Fiends every now and then but never Devils. The spawn of Tyrants, the dynasties of Malice, the inheritors of the World. The Glimingars had only ever glimpsed a handful of Devils in all their long history, each sighting remembered more like a ghost story than a real, present danger. Unlike the southern cultures, Glimisvellir did not bear the scars of a people constantly tormented by the agents of Malice. Their disdain for Cursed Born, those born of devilish unions, was less visceral, driven more by ancient prejudice than by the tangible fury of those who had suffered under Malice's yoke.

But Orphan's misery wasn't born solely of his cursed lineage. His mother had soured Glimisvellir's tolerance, her defiance and manipulative charm leaving a lasting stain. In truth, the town's animosity was fueled as much by her actions as by Orphan's blood. If not for her, perhaps he might have merely been a strange child on the fringes, not a marked boy awaiting his execution. Or… nothing would have changed and he was doomed from the start, what fun.

Regardless of the reason for this revelation or the truth of it, we are saved from this soppy conversation by the blaring of trumpets, a sound alien to Glimisvellir's warhorns, yet one that's become all too familiar of late. While the mismatched duo of uncle and nephew scramble to witness the source of this cacophony, let's not dally and head straight to the action. How convenient.

Behold the gates of Glimisvellir, marvels of old-world craftsmanship forged with Runes enchanting them with the powers of Ice. Freezing anything not of native blood with a touch. These gates had withstood the onslaught of raiders, rebels, and beasts, mocking every battering ram and scaling ladder. Today, however, they did not stand against a threat but opened wide for a procession of horses and riders whose pomp and regalia were as out of place in Glimisvellir as roses in the snow.

The gates groaned open, ancient iron straining like a beast roused from sleep, its breath mingling with the crisp, bitter scent of snow and pine, a smell that would cling to the Teutons' clothes, unwelcome and unfamiliar.

A Teuton party of three men and a single Neustrian woman entered the town with all the misplaced bravado of conquerors who had never tasted this land's unforgiving bite. You could always tell who was in charge by the most elaborate hat, the biggest weapon, or simply the one who towered above the rest. They held their heads high and why shouldn't they? They were important people. Very important… somewhere else. But here they were just strange men with funny hats and really big moustaches.

"Herr General, is this parade-ground spectacle truly warranted? The Soarlings at least pour you a drink before they try to cut your throat. Here we earn only glares and an affront to proper table manners. What concrete gain do we secure from this venture, beyond entangling ourselves in avoidable complications?" asked one rider, his voice heavy with the weight of bureaucratic skepticism. He sat third in line, his eyes narrowing as if trying to calculate the exact degree of nonsense unfolding before him.

At the forefront was the General, a man whose very existence was a testament to the virtues of his homeland:

precision, discipline, and an almost comical reverence for tradition. His square jaw, bristling mustache, and a face creased with old battles gave him an air of stoic authority. Though, perched atop his head, a bicorne hat, the ultimate symbol of his military prowess. Remember, in the realm of pomp and circumstance, the one with the most ludicrous hat is king... or general, in this case. His uniform was a striking clash of red and orange, punctuated by a somber greatcoat to ward off the northern chill. Medals glittered on his chest, each one telling a story of valor at least in theory. His companions wore similar attire, though their lack of such decoration marked them as lesser, their gaudy uniforms mere echoes of his.

"From a military standpoint? Glimisvellir is of negligible value. A patch of ice and rock on the map's last line. They breed skilled fighters, perhaps, but what is a handful of hunters against our battalions? At best, it is a skirmish won, not a war decided." the General responded, his words slipping from his mouth like cold steel. He spoke in the sharp, clipped dialect of Teutonreach, a language as stiff and unyielding as the men who spoke it. It was a deliberate choice, a way to remind the Glimingars of their outsider status.

The party pressed on, indifferent to the wary eyes that tracked their movements from every shadowed corner of Glimisvellir's streets. The riders held their heads high, secure in their misplaced confidence. Important men and women in their own realms, but here? Just foreign intruders, wrapped in strange colors and boasting titles that meant little in the unforgiving north.

"Economically, they are a liability. Any ore in these mountains lies entombed beneath layers of logistical absurdity.

The cost of extraction would bleed a state budget white before a single ingot reached the foundries. From a fiscal standpoint, Glimisvellir offers nothing to the Confederacy but red ink." the bespectacled Teuton noble said, his voice clipped and efficient, much like the calculations running behind his sharp gaze. His sharp gaze, peering through spectacles, seemed to appraise the world solely in terms of profit and loss. With a dismissive nod, he turned to Lady Delacroix, the Neustrian in their midst, as if passing the burden of cultural judgment onto her. "But perhaps you, Lady Delacroix, see some merit in this place that we do not?"

"The Soarlings are savage but welcoming, the Glimingar are traditional but isolated. The lowlanders are seafaring raiders with might makes right as their moral code, these mountain dwellers live off hunting, gathering, fishing, and herds and so have an extremely rigid way of life and morality. The only things they share are cultural heritage, norms, a few traditions, and a language. But. The Glimisvellir are viewed with a certain romanticism by the rest of the untamed north and have managed to carve out a reputation even within our courts. Both the Chancellor and the Heads of States agree that Glimisvellir would make an excellent jewel in the crown of humanity. As one of the oldest settlements still standing, it has a direct link to the Age of Gods. That kind of prestige, mon cher, cannot be bought, only claimed. Beyond that, though, they're just another Soarling village that pretends they are better than their lowland cousins," Lady Rinelt Delacroix replied with a polished but disinterested air. She was dressed in Neustrian finery, her elegant attire at odds with the rough, wind-beaten backdrop of Glimisvellir. The burn scar creeping up her neck to her jaw was a stark reminder that she, too, had faced her share of harsh realities, a blemish that, paradoxically, augmented her intriguing allure.

"Prestige and Legitimacy, one is being grabbed up like coins tossed to starving masses and the other is quite short supply as of late for the Confederacy." the Teuton officer continued, unable to resist another dig. "Oh, am I speaking out of turn General Hermenigild?" The bespeckled cocksure man covered his mouth in a fake show of shame. I wonder if it's his daddy or mommy that paid for his nice suit and over inflated ego? Seems to be the type, as opposed to the simple but elegant livery on the General's sword, his was covered in intricate flowers of silver and gold. One an officer that affords himself small luxuries vs… nobility and their antics.

"The Emperor is a child, the Republic's congress is rotten with patronage, and as for the Víteli…" Hermenigild exhaled through his nose. "It is best we do not begin that list." His voice a cool reprimand wrapped in weary pragmatism. Unlike the others, his uniform was functional, designed more for endurance than show. His chest bore medals not for vanity but as quiet acknowledgments of duty and loss. He looked every bit the hardened soldier, his presence commanding without the need for theatrics. "Prestige alone won't bring order. We need practicality, and that's something the Chancellor understands well."

As they rode deeper into Glimisvellir, the party of southerners cut a stark, unwelcome figure against the austere landscape. The Teutons, wrapped in their uniforms of authority, exuded a kind of disciplined arrogance, their every movement underscored by the weight of their homeland's militaristic tradition. In contrast, Lady Delacroix's Neustrian elegance set her apart as an outsider even among the outsiders, her presence tinged with a subtle defiance that mirrored Glimisvellir's own stubborn spirit.

Glimisvellir's citizens, watching from the safety of doorways and shadowed corners, sizing up their uninvited guests with a mix of suspicion and silent contempt. These visitors, with their foreign airs and self-important posturing, were a jarring intrusion into a world that had long thrived on its own terms. The Teutons' sense of superiority, the Neustrian's barely hidden boredom, it was all out of place here, in a town that had weathered more than its share of storms without any help from the outside.

But what is all this? Who are these uptight... I mean fancy people that look down on the stupid... no wait... simple honest folk of the land. Yes. Those words. Ah, to understand this little spectacle, we must broaden our view. Glimisvellir's rugged landscape is merely a speck on the northern edge of a broader world. Beyond these mountains lies the Soarlands, a land of fjords, jagged coasts, and hidden settlements. To the west stretch the Skjar Isles, and beyond that, the cold expanse of the Mørkstraumar Sea. Southward lies the continent of Ereth, a realm of conflict, ambition, and enough bloodshed to paint a thousand sagas.

It is where these pompous puffed-up peons come from. For centuries upon centuries the people of Ereth warred, slaughtered, and lots of bashing-over-the-many-heads. Overall, a great time. Power arose and fell, so-called saviors and dreadful tyrants carved out their own places in history. But now things have changed and for the worse. The three largest hegemonies of Ereth have united to form one Confederacy of Ereth, determined to unite humanity for the betterment of all. The altruism would be vomit inducing if it wasn't so painfully obvious it was all a big fat lie. No mortal man is immune from his own vices and sins.

This Confederacy is still in its early stages, nothing really works as intended and much of the founding nations still operate on their own. These specific representatives that concern our story come from the newly established State of Teutonreach, formerly the Empire of Teutonreach. A hardy industrial powerhouse of staunch fortitude. Emphasis on the fort in fortitude, as you can't throw a stone in Teutonreach without hitting the stone wall of a great bastion or castle. They are the unwavering shield of the Confederacy... that everyone hates because they have completely given up on the gods returning.

The Teutons halted their procession outside the Great Hall of Glimisvellir, where Jarl Hlodvir, the chieftain of the Glimingar, awaited them alone. His warriors were scattered throughout the surrounding snow, watchful sentinels ready to pounce at the first hint of betrayal. But Hlodvir needed no entourage to make his presence known. A giant of a man covered in scars earned from his favorite pastime, fighting bears. And those beasties grow quite big this far north. Jarl of the Glimisvellir only ever went to the strongest. No heavy coat to shake off the cold, only a leather vest and a couple dozen necklaces of bear teeth, one each a victory. One or two of those bones could be of less ursine origin too.

The Teutons dismounted with careful precision, their eyes flicking over the crude stone structures of Glimisvellir. Disdain simmered beneath their practiced facades as their polished boots sank into the slushy snow, a minor indignity that stung their pride more than the biting cold. This was not the manicured parade grounds of Teutonreach; it was a far cry from the civilized courts they were accustomed to.

"I greet you, Jarl Hlodvir of the Glimisvellir, as agreed," The general had brought his best diplomatic voice to bear as he stepped off his horse. Meant nothing, his opposite did not look amused or impressed in the slightest.

"The only reason you're not feeding the crows right now is because your boy earned this meeting by nearly matching me in our last skirmish," Hlodvir responded, his voice a deep, gravelly rumble that carried more boredom than hostility. His words were less a greeting and more a blunt statement of fact. He had no interest in pleasantries; this was an obligation, not an opportunity. At his remark, the Teuton delegation glanced toward the smallest of their number, a nervous, mousy man with four fingerbone earrings dangling from his ears. He quickly averted his gaze, shrinking from the sudden attention.

"Though he doesn't look it, that one's got more guts than most of your lot. It's the only reason I've agreed to let you all inside." Hlodvir's lips curled into a faint, mocking smile before his expression turned cold again. "Now, let's get this over with. Freezing my balls off here."

The Teutons stiffened at Hlodvir's crude finish, momentarily thrown off by the Jarl's unfiltered language. In their world, such talk was unbecoming of any man with a title, especially one meeting with foreign dignitaries. But this was not Teutonreach or Neustrian high society, where words were sheathed in etiquette and veiled threats. Here, words were as sharp as axes and just as unrefined a reflection of the brutal honesty that defined life in the north. And what is crudeness if not the simplest, most unvarnished form of truth?

Following Hlodvir into the Great Hall of Glimisvellir, the door groaning shut behind them as they stepped into the heart of the ancient settlement. It was a world unto itself, a place shaped by centuries of fierce independence and unyielding winters. Built from the first timber felled by Glimisvellir's founders, the hall had grown from a simple waystation into a sprawling longhouse that stood as the town's beating heart. It was all that was needed. Its thick beams were darkened with age, carved with intricate designs of serpents, wolves, and knotwork that whispered of forgotten hands and lost tales.

A great hearth ran the length of the hall, its flames casting restless shadows on the walls lined with shields, banners, and trophies from hunts and battles. The chief's seat, a rough-hewn throne adorned with antlers and ancient runes, stood on a raised dais at the far end, a crude yet commanding symbol of authority. The Great Hall was the soul of Glimisvellir, every beam and carving a testament to a people who bent but never broke, who endured every hardship the world hurled at them. A place to sleep, eat, and trade beds would be made and food would always be ready. It was all their home as much as it was the Jarl's.

The Teutons, more accustomed to glittering parlors and marble courts, found the Great Hall's rough timber and unpolished stone unsettling, a place where grandeur felt like defiance rather than design. The grandeur they were accustomed to the scale and mightiness of Teuton castles or the gilded elegance of Neustrian opera houses was nowhere to be found here. Instead, they found themselves sitting on furs laid out before the dais, the chief's throne looming above them as Hlodvir took his seat on the ground. There were no chairs; traditions demanded that none rise above the Jarl, a practice whose origins had long been forgotten. The true meaning was because they were too poor to afford chairs so they just sat on the floor. Hehehe.

"Speak. I'll hear you out before I cast you back into the snow," Hlodvir growled, his eyes scanning the visitors with a mix of disdain and dark amusement. Figures moved between the wooden pillars lining the hall, shadows of the curious Glimingar watching the southerners with wary, calculating eyes. The Teutons felt the weight of those stares; one officer shrank into his collar, unnerved by the silent scrutiny, while another sat straighter, his pride armoring him against the unspoken judgment.

Lady Delacroix was the first to rise, her Neustrian grace in stark contrast to the rough surroundings. She offered a crisp curtsy, the gesture as precise as it was insincere, before launching into her speech a mix of carefully rehearsed lines and improvisation that betrayed her lack of genuine regard for the Glimingars. Already she knew how all this would end, it was only her job to play her role in it all upon this stage.

"Jarl Hlodvir, I come to you with a final offer of peace. By the will of the Chancellor of the Confederacy of Ereth, and sanctioned by the Heads of State, Glimisvellir is invited to join the Confederacy as the capital of the Soarlands province." Her voice was even and inviting, in that diplomat way that was supposed to sound humble but came off as patronizing. There was some snickering from the sides, but the Jarl said nothing as he waited for the invaders to finish up their words that he so graciously allowed. The silence went on for an uncomfortable amount of time, enough to make this high and noble lady wither a bit under his stare. "As a tribute to your history and the respect you command, we…"

"I have seen your vinegar and found it lacking, so now you thought to bring honey. Well it would seem I am not a fly because you forgot to bring anything sweet to my ears." Hlodvir interrupted, his voice sharp and derisive. His smirk sent a shiver through all but the most composed of the Teutons, their expressions stiffening under the Jarl's mocking challenge. "You speak of making us a capital, but of what? The Soarlands do not stand with your Confederacy, else our lowland kin would be here at your back."

"The Havi of Níðavellir has pledged her support," Lady Delacroix countered, though her confidence wavered under the several unamused snorts to this very untrue statement. "Her city stands with us, and others will follow if you lead them."

"Mmm, the chance to lord over weak and soft thieves who can barely keep a tavern together and standing for more than one season. No. I do not think so. Try again." His mockery cut deeper this time, and the barely restrained laughter of the Glimingars echoed his disdain. The Teutons' façade of diplomatic composure began to crack, their indignation slowly seeping through as Hlodvir's blunt rejection met their lofty propositions.

"What is it we cannot offer you, Jarl? Trade, wealth, advancement in every useful discipline. The Confederacy unites the three great Savior nations; no other human realms can claim such a lignée. Only those with statehood in the Confederacy trace their origin back to a Savior. Our aim is merely to give humanity the unity the other civilized peoples already enjoy. Ma foi, it is not such an outrageous dream." Lady Delacroix's voice rang with practiced conviction, but beneath it lay a veiled arrogance. Elves, Dwarves, Naga all had forged unified societies while humanity remained fractured, forever clawing at its own borders. Because while they are the most numinous of all and occupy the most land of the planet... they are also the most stupid and shortsighted most of the time. Greedy and arrogant little things that must have control over all. Capable of both wondrous and terrible things.

Hlodvir scoffed, the noise harsh and dismissive. "Last I heard from the priests, there have been six Saviors since the Age of Gods. Of those, one fucked off across the unending ocean, never to be seen again. Two founded kingdoms in the east that, if the priests can be believed, still stand to this day." All of the Teutons looked very uncomfortable as the Glimingar brought up two very politically charged topics and one that was easily shooed away. The largest and most successful of the human nations claim to have divine origins. And in a world in which the Gods have been proven to have abandoned their flock, Divine Right... is oh so valuable.

"Ahem, well the status of the Empire of the Great Winds as a Savior kingdom is up for debate since the Sixth Tyrant ended the Divine Line of Emperors. So, they don't count. And the entire subcontinent of Suvannabhumi is composed of hundreds of small city states and no one single leader stands among them." The Lady tried and failed to say that two of the founding nations of the Confederacy are more like successor states than is polite to say in the correct company.

"Enough. You offer riches and glory when we Glimingars have no need of the former and have plenty of the latter.

This is merely like every other time you outsiders come to Glimisvellir bearing your claws and teeth. You want a trophy, and nothing more." He rose from his seat, and the clattering of bear teeth strung around his neck echoed through the hall. The Teutons hesitated; for all their military training and bravado, they were unaccustomed to facing such raw, unbridled defiance. Hlodvir loomed large, the embodiment of a strength that was primal, almost otherworldly. More than one Teuton found themselves wondering if they were truly in the presence of a mere mortal.

The general was the first to stand, regaining his composure almost immediately. He had faced demons, devils, and monstrositics born of Malice, but it was the unpredictability of his fellow humans that always gave him pause. "So, you're refusing our offer?"

"I never considered it in the first place." Hlodvir replied, a dangerous gleam in his eyes. "Go, and when you return, know that we will turn the snow red once more." His gaze lingered on the youngest Teuton, the only one who hadn't yet spoken. The youth held firm under the Jarl's piercing stare, refusing to flinch or look away. A small but defiant victory in the face of such overwhelming presence.

The delegation rose and departed, their exit marked by tense, controlled movements. None dared glance back as they made their way through the hall and into the biting cold. The gates of Glimisvellir closed behind them, sealing them out once more.

But in their wake, something had been left behind. Hidden beneath the furs where the delegation had sat was a folded slip of paper, seemingly unremarkable at first glance. As the hall emptied and the doors shut, the paper began to move, its edges twisting and bending until it sprouted tiny legs. The now spider-like creature scuttled free, slipping through the shadows as it crept toward its unknown target, silent and unseen.

"Get to sleep, boy. I'll need you running errands early tomorrow, and you talk back more when you're groggy," Gerfinn barked as he and Orphan made their way to their corner of the Great Hall. The boy offered no retort, slipping away to his cramped bunk with the practiced silence of someone long accustomed to being dismissed.

Gerfinn watched him go, a crooked smile creeping across his scarred face. The evening's spectacle had been amusing watching the southern dignitaries bluster and flounder against the impenetrable wall that was Hlodvir. The Jarl's refusal had been as predictable as it was gratifying, a reminder that Glimisvellir would never bend to outsiders, no matter how many medals they stuck to their chest or how much oil they rub into their mustache. Chuckling to himself, Gerfinn returned to his cluttered workspace, the simmering cauldron at its center burping quietly in the flickering firelight.

His smile widened as a small paper spider skittered across the floorboards, coming to rest at his feet. The little construct unraveled, revealing a single leaf within its delicate folds. It was unremarkable at first glance green, slightly dry, and utterly innocuous. But Gerfinn handled it with the care of a man who knew its true value, carefully tipping it into the bubbling pot without letting it touch his skin. The leaf sank, releasing its essence into the clear, roiling liquid, transforming it in ways that only Gerfinn understood.

Everything was falling into place, every piece set on the board. The Jarl was strong and diligent, fierce enough to claw his way to power and tenacious enough to keep it. But cunning? That's very funny. No-no-no. Hlodvir had a warrior's mind, sharp but direct, built for battle but not for the tricksy games or old fashion backstabbing and shadows kind of play. To him, a threat was to be met head-on, not scurried around like some rat hiding from torch light. After all, he allowed those frilly southerners to come into his home for the chance to gloat in their faces about how much he didn't care about their offers. Lesson number one, never let your enemy into your home unless you plan on never letting them leave it.

But Gerfinn, he was not a man of brute strength anymore. Once he had been a strapping young man capable of much troublesome violence. Fond memories of better times with his crew pillaging and stealing from fat rich southerners as a víkingr. But those days were gone. A small tremble of the hand and aches on an old wound on his back saw to that.

His hands were marked by burns and scars from years of toiling over cauldrons. His power now lay in the subtle art of manipulation, in potions and poisons brewed in secret. While others fought with steel and muscle, Gerfinn fought with whispers, with slips of paper that scuttled in the dark, and with leaves that hid their lethality behind a facade of helpful healing. He stared into the boil, watching as the liquid shifted, its color deepening into something more sinister. The concoction was nearly ready, and with it, Gerfinn's plans would begin to unfurl.

It was like he'd told Orphan: a man must be strong and diligent, but above all, he must be cunning. Hlodvir had power, but Gerfinn had patience and a mind bent toward the long game. He was content to wait in the shadows, biding his time until the perfect moment to strike. When that moment came, the Jarl and everyone else would realize that battles weren't always won by the strongest fighter, but by the cleverest player.

For now, he'd wait. He had gotten very skilled at that.

Words of the Second

Compass of faith guides
Unwilling souls in raging tides
Hope blooms where darkness dies

A Orchestra of Cannons

"Hey, come on, I've been here for five minutes already," Orphan called out, his voice barely rising above the rhythmic thud of hammers against wood a macabre symphony as they built his pyre. The fishmonger, busy at his stall of mottled, half-rotten catches, finally deigned to glance down at him. The man's face twisted into a familiar scowl, a blend of disdain and a begrudging recognition that Orphan was still, unfortunately, alive. Added to that was the same mocking smile the poor unfortunate soul wore to grate on the townsfolk's nerves. What did he have to be happy about? Nothing but their annoyance.

"What do you want, brat? I was almost pretending this morning wasn't going to shit until you showed up," the fishmonger grumbled, his hands stained with the slick filth of fish guts. His gaze shifted, as if he might dismiss Orphan as easily as yesterday's catch, already starting to stink. If there had been 'a yesterday's catch'. The siege had made it impossible for the few fishermen of Glimisvellir to make the arduous trip down the mountains to the coast to perform their craft.

"Really? Not one of you can just act like I'm a normal kid today, huh? Just once. Y'know, before…" Orphan's voice trailed off, eyes flicking toward the towering stake rising in the center of town, where flames would soon lick at his heels. Back to the man with a deadpan stare. Ah, the cherished rituals of the Glimingaric traditions, upheld with the fervor of fools who've mistaken cruelty for justice. Burn the boy, purge the blight. It was all so predictable, so dreadfully quaint in its barbarism. Glimisvellir, your dull dedication never disappoints. If only it weren't so dreadfully banal.

The fishmonger leaned over his stall, lips curling in a mockery of a smile, voice sweet as soured mead. "I don't know what you're on about, you damned wretch. Not like I've ever thought of tossing you up here with the rest of this muck. Could pass for one of these slimy things, don't you think? Flayed and filleted, right proper."

"Now that's no way to treat a poor child, orphaned in world and spirit." Pah. Whatever fun might have been had, a fish smacked in a man's face comes to mind, was stopped by the kindly voice of a very honest and very trustworthy old man. Both Orphan and the fishmonger looked up from their glaring eyes to see the town's sole priest and representative of the Church looking at both of them with a mix of disappointment and disapproval. "Orphan, you've made such progress since coming from the Sorrows of Denial, can you please find it in your soul to move past the Trials of Anger before your timely end?"

Ah, the Church of the Orphaned World. So very sure that each and every person in the world is actually a crying baby wailing away for a divine daddy and mommy to make every bad thing go away. No. Perhaps, just perhaps… people can change… grow out of old needs and habits.

The current actor upon the stage to signal and showcase

this particular brand of stupid, was dressed in the traditional garb of the priesthood. If a bit modified for the cold. White and black robes that hung heavy on the old man frame, disguising any sense of what sort of build was under them. Though, the right arm sleeve was quite loose, possibly due to the lack of an arm. Then a veil of strung beads covered his face, each supposedly earned when the man successfully helped a poor soul reach the next step in their proclaimed Journey of Grief. But Orphan could see, between the strings of beads was a face of judgement hidden behind professed concern.

"Don't waste your time on this devil spawn, Eberulf. You should be getting out of town. I'm sure your countrymen wouldn't mind letting you through." There was only a half-hearted attempt at being civil. There was a decided split in the town on the matter of faith, many felt nothing for the loss of the gods while others desperately wanted someone to give them answers and a way to feel better about themselves. Weak and pathetic, quite so.

"Now-now, all on this world deserves to find solace, even the infernal." But does the Infernal need your pretty words priest? Nevertheless, the older man paid for the fish Orphan had come to collect and with a gentle nudge began escorting the Cursed Born child away from the market.

"Come again, Orphan, always a pleasure," the fishmonger called with false cheer, watching him go with eyes full of malice barely disguised as mirth.

"Fuck off," Orphan muttered under his breath, barely sparing him another glance. Why waste energy on their little games when there was work to be done, even in the shadow of death? He had no time for their half-hearted jabs and pitiful cruelties. Even on the last day of a condemned man, one still had his duties. That's what set him apart. The boy with nothing left still had his principles, a steely conviction none of these hollow souls could muster.

Orphan's fear was tempered by the one thing they could never take from him: his principles. A conviction forged in spite of the world's cruelty, unyielding like the frozen peaks that loomed over Glimisvellir. These people? They had no principles. If they did, they might have found a shred of decency to spare for an orphan. Not that the Lamenting Record, that wretched holy text they clung to, ever mentioned what to do with a Cursed Born like him. Orphan had learned to read by tracing the priest's sermons against those pages, matching hollow words to their twisted doctrines. Burning a poor, malnourished, parentless boy at the stake? That was all them, an extreme exaggeration of a traditional Blót, stirred by the hands of small minds.

And yet, for all their fervor, not one of them lived by any creed worth dying for. Orphan would die; he'd known it for as long as he could remember but he'd go down more principled than the lot of them. He was certain of that, more than he'd ever been of anything. Even now, the whispers around him only proved his point.

"Did you hear? The utlanders promised to make us rulers over the entire Soarlands." The voices carried like gusts of bitter wind, ignoring him as they always did unless he caught their eye. But Orphan had long since mastered the art of slipping between their notice, a ghost in ragged clothes, hovering at the edge of their vision.

"Really? What a ridiculous thing. We don't need them." Ah, there it was the correct response. The kind of staunch, chest-puffing defiance expected of any true Glimingar. Pride, the unbending backbone of their people. But pride is a fickle thing, prone to cracking when temptation finds a way in.

"Yeah… but…" And there it was. The first fissure, the tempting promise of power creeping in like a serpent's hiss.

"We really are the only real choice." Vanity.

"Someone should put some order to the lowlands." Ambition.

"Maybe winter could be a bit easier if we had some help." Laziness.

"Would it be so bad to accept?" And there it was: doubt, the first nibble at the rotten apple of surrender. They'd been too long without a proper fight, these Glimingar. Too long since the last serious attempt to conquer them, too many years spent believing their walls and traditions made them untouchable. A fortress against time itself. Against the very concept of Change itself.

But not this time. Not with cannons and steel facing their stone. The last invaders had been easier to dispatch of. Barbarians, witches, things from children's tales that could be hacked apart with axes and swords. This was different. This was the Change. And the Glimingar, stubborn fools that they were, never handled change well.

The warriors and proud men, the Jarl among them, were too wrapped up in their own strength and past glories to see it. Blinded by old victories and the lure of new songs sung in their honor. Violent men of peace dream of war, and often find the taste far more bitter than they were expecting by the end. Orphan saw the truth plain as day, a truth they all chose to ignore: this was a battle they couldn't win, not with valor, not with pride, and certainly not by pretending the world hadn't outgrown them. They did that a lot, pretended not to see the obvious truth in front of them.

"You hear them too, don't you Orphan?" Eberulf's voice was a bit more stern, a little more honest in his feelings. They stopped at the midpoint of a stone stairway that separated the upper markets from the lower ones. Orphan rested his head on his arms as he leaned on the edge of the railing, uncaring for the priest's games. There was always something… easing about the old man to Orphan. Perhaps it was because Eberulf was one of the few that actually sought Orphan out for something other than torment.

"Yeah, of course I do. They never hide what they say around me. I'm just surprised it's happening this quickly." A shrug, uncaring about the troubles of next week. Why do so when he won't be living to see it.

"People will always seek out the comfort of certainty, of knowing that their next day will be the same or better than the last. This is a first for them, a siege is a horrible thing, young Orphan. Though it's far from a true siege." A hint of disgust and bitter resentment eh? They both looked down to the Lower Markets of the town and sitting in the middle of it a large and finely crafted stone archway that led down into the ground. Glimisvellir, the town of layers of stone and timber stacked upon itself like the bones of old gods, had a market that mirrored this stratified mess. The upper part, cozied up to the Great Hall. Down below, the lower market sprawled toward the mouth of the valley's tunnels, the hidden veins of Glimisvellir where people scurried about like ants beneath the earth. "These people are not trapped like others would be, hmm… as we can see."

Ah, and here comes the greatest hypocrite of them all,

making his grand entrance as if he were a bloody hero returning from the front lines. Out of those tunnels strutted none other than He-Must-Always-Be-Right, basking in his moment of glory.

"I've done it, they said it couldn't be done but I did it!" The words rolled out with a smugness so thick it could choke a bear. There he was: Thrain, the golden boy of Glimisvellir, the best hunter, the pride of the town, and, oh yes, Brune's overprotective and self-righteous brother. Tall, broad-shouldered, with that annoyingly perfect jawline and hair that somehow managed to stay clean despite the grime of battle he was the kind of man ballads are written about. In any other tale he might be the focus and his origin story given what is to come with all those angry guns outside the wall.

"Two whole winters these little pests have been killing our elk and ruining everything they touch. No more!" He crowed, like a victorious warlord who'd slain a dragon. Behind him, more Glimingars emerged from the tunnels, carrying the spoils of their hunt. Strung up like trophies were short, twisted figures no taller than a large child, but with a mischief and malice that far outweighed their size.

"Is it true? The Fiendpit is gone?" Aren't they under a siege right now? I think they have more to worry about than just some inconsequential little troublemakers. What did they ever do to you all? Besides kill, steal, and destroy everything they could. Poor innocent little Imps that do nothing but cause a little mayhem to brighten up the days.

"Burned it myself. Was a bit sad that now our friends on the outside won't have to deal with them either but only a little." He joked but that might actually be a big reason why they haven't attacked yet. The little things that they were now unceremoniously pilling up like kindling, which was likely their intended fate, were a crafty sort that wouldn't hesitate to interfere in any big battle between humans.

Fiends. The living scourge of Malice made manifest, crawling out of their pits like vermin birthed from the world's darkest nightmares. They roam the lands in packs, hordes, or sometimes alone, leaving chaos in their wake. They are the world's most enduring curse, the stain left by the Masters of Malice. Glimisvellir's own personal brand of hell had always been these Imps, and now their little Fiendpit had finally been dealt with... or so they hoped.

The bodies of these particular Imps were a hodgepodge of mismatched parts, arms too long, legs too short, heads perched awkwardly atop grotesque, insect-like torsos. Blackened stones stitched together with sinewy, yellow tissue gave them an unsettling, piecemeal look. Some had wings like dragonflies, others mantis-like blades for hands, each bearing some dreadful mark of their progenitor. Born as tiny miseries, they scuttle about until, by some miracle of Malice, they live long enough to cocoon themselves, growing more meat and muscle, until finally they transform into Demons larger, nastier, and infinitely more troublesome.

"He's probably asking about Brune now, haven't seen her since we came back from..." Careful now, he caught himself before saying anything important but not before giving away that there's something to be hidden.

"It is only natural for a brother to be protective of his little sister. But yes, Thrain has been unable to find his way to the Garden of Acceptance. Fear of losing more than he already has, terrible burden he carries." Orphan scoffed at the priest's words as they both watched the hunting party be received by the townspeople. But the brief happiness that came with thinking that Eberulf had missed his slip up, melted away as he felt the priest's hand on his shoulder. "Orphan, I know the potential in you. I want to…"

"You reckless demon! How dare you put my precious little sister in danger like that!" Thrain seemed to have learned what happened with the Winter man. As the hunter was now running up the stairs toward the pair. And why not be angry. He knew better. He'd seen the Winterman himself once, and the memory clung to him like a stubborn shadow.

It had been on his third hunting trip, his first alone, a bid to prove himself a man worthy of song and saga. But what he found in the woods was no easy trophy. An entire mammoth, far from its herd, lay sprawled in the snow, its skull pierced and its belly torn open in a way that no human could replicate. Thrain hadn't dared approach, and just as he was about to turn back, he caught sight of the massive figure, looming, standing over the carcass with a predator's indifference. The Winterman. For a long, breathless moment, they stared at each other across the distance, hunter and beast locked in a silent standoff. Then, with a casual shrug, the Winterman dragged the mammoth away, leaving Thrain with a terror that still curled his stomach when he slept.

The weight of a sibling's overbearing guardianship pressed down on him a burden he wore like a badge of honor. Their father had been swallowed by a sabertoothed seal not long after Brune's birth, leaving Thrain to fill the void. While their mother had shriveled into a husk of a person by grief, a shadow of her former self. For Thrain, Brune was a wildling without a leash, and it infuriated him that she spent her time with the town's least desirable.

"Stop it Thrain! This is not the time to be reckless!" Eberulf shouted as Orphan ran back up to avoid the vengeance of the town's golden boy.

Now, this wasn't a new dance for them. Thrain had made a habit of chasing the little Cursed Born around town, usually after spotting him within so much as breathing distance of his precious sister. Sometimes it ended in an escape, sometimes in a thorough beating. But today, oh, today was special. Today, that fear simmering beneath Thrain's bravado, the primal terror of the "demon" so close to his sister combined with Orphan's looming execution made the air crackle with violence. Restraint? That had long since melted away like snow in spring.

A crashed stall there, an overturned cart of cabbage there, oh dear oh my they're quite destructive now aren't they? Even gathering a small mob of chasers behind them, I'm sure the townsfolk trying to stop Thrain are very confused. They must save a boy slated to die the next day from the local superstar. But fate has many plans in place, and often they upturn the schemes of men.

Boom.

Boom.

An extra big boom for sound measure.

The Teutons had finally grown tired of waiting. First, they took down a watchtower. Then came the windmill poor thing, never stood a chance. Lastly, the gatehouse, once so proudly defending Glimisvellir's walls, crumbled. They had graciously given their terms... no... not terms. Benefits, offers, just tribute to the Glimisvellir. Beyond a shadow of a doubt, the Confederacy bowed and pleaded to the Jarl of the

Glimingar to join them peacefully but woe is to the faithful of diplomacy they were rejected. I'm sure that's how certain parties consider that to be the truth of the matter. Instead of accepting the fortune befalling them, the Glimingar would be forced into submission as a stolen jewel of conquest. And now? Well, now the Teutons were done playing nice.

The city descended into chaos. Screams echoed through the streets as people scurried about like headless chickens no, worse. Like headless chickens set on fire and chased by ravenous dogs. Oh, it was glorious. The panicked masses knew instinctively what was coming, and their traditions told them to flee to the tunnels, to trust in the strength of their walls and the unforgiving river that surrounded them.

But tradition was a rusted shield against the weapons of today. Their walls, those prideful stones that had repelled so many in years past, were now crumbling under the weight of the Teutons' might. Reinforced ladders like great wooden spears rose to meet them, sturdy enough to climb walls twice as tall. Glimingar were fearsome killers, yes, but only when the land itself fought alongside them. They were ambush predators, not sentinels. Their skills were honed in the wild, not on battlements. The frozen north, once a loyal ally that crippled any would-be conqueror, had lost its bite. And the enemy had new tools, new tactics, unlike anything the Glimingar had faced. The foe had grown stronger, and Glimisvellir had refused to change.

And change, dear Listener, waits for no one.

Now, what of our little Cursed Born, hmm? Amid the chaos, with the skies shaking from the Teutonic cannons and the townsfolk shrieking like startled gulls, what would a boy do? Why, he ran home, of course. The simplest instinct, bred into the bone: find shelter, find safety, find the familiar. Thrain was long lost in the melee behind him, and Orphan hardly cared. Whether the golden boy was trampled in the panic or crushed under the rubble of his own hubris, it made no difference. Orphan's eyes were fixed on survival, darting through the mess of overturned carts, fallen market stalls, and the crumbling buildings that threatened to bury Glimisvellir's stubborn pride.

The Great Hall loomed ahead, but the main gate was a seething knot of people, all clawing at the doors, fists pounding against the thick wood, demanding entry. Oh, look at them, like rats scratching at the walls of a sinking ship. And here was Orphan, wading through it, invisible, slipping past the mob that would've happily turned on him had they the presence of mind to remember he existed.

He tried the small side entrance to his uncle's quarters first. Locked. Of course it was. Gerfinn, the consummate coward, was no doubt drowning himself in cheap spirits, ignoring the world as it burned around him. The other private doors were just as stubbornly shut. No one was letting the likes of Orphan in not today, not ever.

That left only one option: Orphan's own secret way. Hidden at the very back, the cellar entrance was covered in a thick sheet of ice that had been for as long as anyone could remember. None had ever bothered to fix it, nor suspected Orphan had his own little way in. With a wave of his hand the ice shimmered, turned to water, and slipped away, revealing the entrance. It was a trick that he had used several times when he had been purposely locked out of the building.

Sliding in, he pulled the cellar doors shut behind him, sealing himself in the pitch-black underbelly of the Great

Hall. But darkness? Ha, that was hardly an obstacle. Orphan's green eyes glowed faintly, cutting through the shadows, a devil's gaze that saw more than the mere mortal could ever hope to. He stepped carefully, navigating around empty wine bottles and frozen puddles, an echo of his uncle's perpetual indulgence. For a fleeting moment, the thought crossed his mind: just stay down here, wait it out. What was one siege compared to a lifetime of being hunted by your own? At least the Teutons had terms. He knew, in his gut, they would see him no kinder than the Glimingar, but at least magic had value, a bargaining chip he could play.

But the gnawing truth was there, wasn't it? A spark of ambition that kept him moving forward his fate wouldn't change by hiding in a cellar.

Orphan crept through the narrow passageways, quiet as a whisper, until he heard the wet, rasping sound of someone choking. He knew that voice; anyone in Glimisvellir would. Strangled gasps filled the hall beyond, pained and gurgling, each breath a futile struggle. Orphan moved closer, years of practice at staying unseen guiding his every step as he peeked into the feasting hall.

The grand chamber was all but deserted, save for six figures. Two of them were already dead Hlodvir's concubines, sprawled lifeless on the floor, their pretty faces twisted in their final moments. Orphan didn't spare them much thought; they were vain little dolls, empty-headed and pampered. Even their deaths seemed fitting, robbed of all dignity. But the chief still struggled, his breaths ragged and failing, clinging to life even as it slipped away.

Well, well, it seems today was full of surprises.

"Come on, give up already!" Thrain's voice was as sharp

as the boot he drove into the Jarl's head, sending Hlodvir sprawling back to the ground. The once-proud leader of Glimisvellir, now just another stubborn old man bleeding in the dust. Behind Thrain, dear old Gerfinn stood with his usual look of dispassionate detachment, his eyes half-lidded, uncaring. And there was Priest Eberulf, the smug architect of this sordid affair, watching with a self-satisfied smile, as if he'd just laid a perfect trap. The first two were the last that Orphan thought would be working together on a coup. The fact they were doing something like this was perfectly in character though, Thrain didn't like taking orders and wanted to be the center of attention and Gerfinn... well... It is obvious that the man had few scruples about loyalty. But together? No.

But there is that Priest there, and in his hand was the necklace of bear teeth. Though those bones weren't what made it special. It was five finger bones of an ancient Hero, a relic of the past that had been passed down from Jarl to Jarl. But now it had been stolen away in the confusion of the attack... the concubines had been given one job during all of this and the fact Hlodvir was stripped down to just his trousers meant they completed their task. Traitors deserve their just rewards huh? I'm sure these three traitors would agree readily yes-yes.

"You little... I... I trained you. Did a shit job though... always complaining and dragging down hunting parties." Blood dripped from between Hlodvir's teeth, his vision blurred and he could feel all sensation in his fingers and toes begin to vanish. Small pieces of glass were still embedded into his face from where Thrain had thrown the glass bottle at him. He thought it had just been booze, it was just one of the many on the tables from last night's pre-battle feast. Who could have blamed him though, how could he suspect that such a common-looking thing actually held in it a potent poison able to bring him to his knees.

"Tell yourself whatever helps you die easier," Thrain sneered, his eyes alight with something far more dangerous than anger. "I'm destined for glory, real glory not this frozen little pit you call a town." With every word, Thrain's voice grew louder, tinged with something more than just self-belief, a resonance that felt almost... unnatural, like the echoes of a drumbeat no one else could hear. But before his grandiose proclamations could go any further, Eberulf, ever the puppeteer, placed a calming hand on Thrain's shoulder, the picture of serene manipulation.

"You should've accepted the Confederacy's offer, Hlodvir," Eberulf murmured, voice smooth as oiled steel. "A Hero has been found among your people, one chosen by Fate itself, and it's high time he be used against the forces of Malice, not left to waste away in this gods-forsaken tundra." A Hero, is it? Oh, the capital 'H' gives it away, doesn't it? A touch of divinity, a sprinkle of destiny it's all very grand until you realize it's just another tool for the likes of Eberulf. But let's not get ahead of ourselves; there's more to being a Hero than just a title. In this world, names are sharp things, and some cut deeper than any blade.

"And you, Gerfinn?" Hlodvir rasped, turning his bloodshot gaze to the last of his would-be executioners. "I suppose you think-"

And just like that, he was gone. No final retort, no desperate struggle. Hlodvir collapsed, the fight drained from him as poison and betrayal stole his last breath. One moment he was accusing, the next he was a heap of wasted flesh, his body crumpled on the stone floor. Not a battle, not even a scuffle, just a swift end delivered by those who lacked the courage to face him head-on. No song would be sung for Hlodvir, no grand saga of valor or vengeance. It was a pitiful, mundane death, fitting in its own sad way.

Ah, but isn't that the beauty of it? Heroes and villains alike dream of glorious battles, only to find their fates in dark corners and poisoned cups. There's no poetry in it, no honor, just the cold, hard truth that this world doesn't care for your story. It moves on, indifferent, leaving the corpses to rot.

"Alright, so this is the part where you two kill me because I'm a drunk embarrassment, is that it?" Gerfinn's voice dripped with weary sarcasm, like a man unimpressed with the whole business of betrayal. His own little scheme had played out better than expected, but the finer points of duplicity still needed hashing out, and his partners in crime weren't quite on the same page. They needed guidance, the fools.

"Indeed," the priest snarled, barely able to maintain his veneer of piety. "Orphan has his uses elsewhere, your request to keep him alive and by your side borders on the Sin of Greed. Intolerable." Eberulf's anger simmered beneath the thin mask of his clerical calm, his fury held in check by the frail illusion of righteousness. Oh, just drop it, Eberulf. You're not fooling anyone, not even yourself. Orphan, hidden in the shadows, found himself stunned. Someone had actually tried to keep him alive? That was new. Unsettling, even.

Thrain meanwhile didn't need any further reason to pull

out his hunting knife and strike right for Gerfinn's eye. Orphan watched… and was surprised with himself at how much his chest hurt at seeing his uncle go down. The force of Thrain's body and thrust pushing down on him into the floor, it would easily crack a skull and kill the man. The young boy's hand reached for his own throat in a mix of nervous unconscious action and conscious effort to keep himself quiet. But one last cunning trick from the former víkingr saved him.

Gerfinn's form began to disintegrate, crumbling like the cap of an overripe mushroom squeezed to pulp. Thrain leaped back, eyes wide with shock, while Eberulf stumbled away, staring in horror as the floorboards around Gerfinn's remains began to rot and swell. Fungi of all shapes and sizes erupted from the mess, thick stalks and sickly caps forming a thick blanket over the spot the body had once been. Finally, from this grotesque garden, a hand clawed its way free, and then another, pulling forth a body from the fungal bed.

"Everyone forgets I'm more than just an old drunk with a knack for brewing," Gerfinn's voice rasped, emerging from the shroomy figure that slowly, unnervingly, reassembled itself into his human shape. Each breath that passed through his reconstituted throat sounded less like a man and more like something scraped from the darkest depths of Malice.

"Yes, yes… Majorus Cardinal Wind, Minorus Life, which grants you the Compound Magic of Spores. But to find a Blessing as powerful as this!" Eberulf stammered, caught between outrage and fear. The priest had fancied himself the puppet master, a righteous hand guiding a Divine Right Bearer, and yet here he stood, blindsided by a trick he hadn't foreseen. Foolish, really. Men of faith are quick to forget that their gods don't play favorites anymore if they even still play at all.

"That's what you all think, and that's why I like it. Keeps things… interesting. Afterall it paid off this time quite well no?" Gerfinn chuckled, twisting his neck until it popped, his body settling back into something almost human. The room fell into a tense silence, the din of the ongoing battle outside and the banging of the doors to cover the awkward quiet up. "I'll keep to the plan, but my terms still stand."

"No! Not after what that Devilspawn did to my sister!" Thrain spat, his voice seething with the misplaced fury of a man convinced of his own righteousness. "Turning her against me, filling her head with lies, he's a menace, and so are you! I say we put you to the flame as well" Orphan winced. None of it was true, of course. Brune had disliked her brother long before she and Orphan ever met, and if anyone was a bad influence, it was Brune herself. But Thrain never could see past his own delusions, blinded as he was by the image of his perfect little world where he was the hero.

"This is a great Hero chosen by the gods?" Gerfinn sneered, turning back to Eberulf with a grin that spoke of deep, seething satisfaction. "Then we're all doomed, aren't we? Sure, you could burn me, but first you've got to drag me there. And you've no idea what I might do on the way."

"Mages are always so difficult," Eberulf muttered, his frustration boiling over. Magic users were a gamble in the best of times; one might hold only the simplest of spells, while another could, through sheer luck or malice, unleash a cataclysm that no one could control. Gerfinn was the latter, a walking, talking disaster waiting to happen. "We could perhaps…" Eberulf began, but Thrain cut him off with a furious roar.

"No! No more games! I am the Hero! I command, and you will obey! The Cursed Born dies, here and now!" It's a funny thing what is right and wrong. Just whom gets to decide which is which? In times past it was the gods who decided that. They would argue amongst themselves over the correct way for the world to operate and their followers would faithfully submit to their decrees. The gods were Infallible after all, and to deny their word would be punished with Annihilation. But the gods were gone. So who decided what was right and wrong now?

Reality bent over backward to accommodate this new Right that Thrain had set forth. Cracks in the very space itself began to form, like spiderwebbing through glass before it shattered. What was right and wrong clashed with the authority of rulership. The dominion of Sovereignty roared against the decrees of Infallible. And like a window that had been assaulted by an angry child with a rock, it did shatter. The various pieces of reality burst apart and in the end rather than a compromise, a break in powers occurred in which neither party got what it deemed to be its due. Reality forced its hand, and young Orphan tripped forward and into the view of the three adults.

"Fuck. He's seen us, Wi-Wi-Wi-Wi Wa-Li-Fir-Fir Wi-Da-Fir-Da Da-Wi-Wi-Wi." Gerfinn muttered, the proceeding Rights Clash taking the other two men aback. Before anyone could react he recited the spell. His incantation ripped through the air like a whip, a burst of wind that sent all three men sprawling. Thrain crashed against the far wall, Eberulf was flung into a corridor, and Gerfinn's own body hit the floor with a sickening snap, crumbling into a familiar mess of mush and rot. This time, he didn't get back up.

But the wind hadn't just scattered the conspirators, it had also blown open the barred doors, giving the frantic mob outside an unfiltered view of the carnage within. And oh, what a sight they beheld: their Jarl dead, their Hero and priest battered, and the Devil-Spawn himself standing amidst the wreckage. It didn't take long for the howls of rage to begin, the half-whispered fears of the town whipped into a frenzy. They'd come here to kill Orphan anyway; this was just the excuse they needed.

The hall erupted into chaos, but Orphan was already moving, ducking back into the cellar. He turned the spilled wine and booze into slick ice, buying himself precious moments as the mob struggled to gain footing. Then he was running again, bolting through the secret exit at the back. The only place left for him now was the forest, a tangled mess of roots and snow that the townsfolk feared more than the boy they hunted. There, at least, he could lose himself. There, he might have a chance.

Because out there in the dark woods, anything was kinder than the people of Glimisvellir.

Words of the Third

Minds kept sharp and bright
Duty's song, soft and light
Legacy's rewards, never in sight

First Act's Lullaby

The last thing he remembered was cold though not the kind of cold he had known all his life, not the bite of northern winds or the numb fingers of frozen nights. No, this was deeper, colder than the grave, the kind that creeps into your bones and makes a home of your soul. He'd stumbled, fallen face-first into the snow, and felt it burn his skin like a whip. A fleeting sting, really. It was the cold that followed that mattered. It had crept up on him, slowly, with patient glee that wanted to devour him whole. And it would have, too, if not for that one little ember that refused to go out: pure, unrelenting spite.

Ah, spite. What a thing to keep a man alive when he's already halfway dead.

Orphan had always thought his death would be quick, a burning agony on a pyre of their making. But this cold? This slow, creeping end? It didn't fit the script. His body refused to believe it, refused to accept the way his life was slipping away into the snowdrifts. His spirit dug its heels in, just long enough for someone or something to take pity on him. Heh, pity. Let's call it what it is: impulse.

When his eyes finally fluttered open, Orphan wasn't met with the familiar sting of freezing wind or the gritty embrace of snow. No, what he found was something so alien to him that his mind stumbled over it like a drunk man trying to stand. A blanket. A real blanket. Not some patched-together scrap of fur, but a thing of genuine luxury. Silk, embroidered lace, and soft wool, all conspiring to make his skin itch with discomfort. It was too… nice. Too soft. He wasn't used to anything this fine, and it almost made him want to crawl out from under it and sleep on the floor instead.

The room around him was no less unsettling. Hand-carved furniture, polished wood and marble, and décor that screamed of wealth far beyond anything Glimisvellir could offer. Exotic trinkets lined the shelves, each one from a place Orphan couldn't name, let alone imagine. Everything was grand, oversized cabinets and tables towering over him as if built for a race of giants. And maybe they had been. The walls were stone, smooth and gleaming, but not the kind found in any castle or hall he'd ever seen. It was like he was inside a cave, but no cave that nature had shaped.

"I'm dreaming," he muttered to himself, though even that felt wrong. Dreams were chaotic, disjointed. This place, for all its strangeness, had a sense of order to it. Coherence. "But how could I dream of this? I don't even know what half this stuff is."

He rubbed at his eyes, half-expecting them to clear away the illusion, but the room remained stubbornly real. A chill crept down his spine, reminding him that he didn't belong here. No poor orphan cursed by gods-long-gone had any business waking up in a palace.

His hand instinctively moved to his chest, checking for the weight of his mother's diary. It was still there, tucked between his skin and the worn leather of his vest. His fingers curled around it, reassured by the familiar weight. At least that hadn't been taken from him. From what he could tell, he was whole, unspoiled. But that only confirmed one uncomfortable truth, whoever had saved him didn't know him. And that was a problem. A big one. Because if they didn't hate him on sight, they soon would. They always did.

Orphan pulled himself out of the massive bed big enough to hold five, maybe six people, if they were friendly and immediately felt his legs buckle beneath him. He hit the floor with a thud, face pressed into the plush rug. He wasn't sure whether to be grateful or irritated. Maybe both. The truth of it was, he was weak. His body felt drained, hollowed out by hunger, thirst, and whatever days-long sleep he'd just crawled out of.

How long had it been since he'd blacked out in the snow? His stomach churned with emptiness, reminding him that it didn't matter how long it had been, it was long enough to hurt. Every inch of him ached, but not in a way that could be fixed with magic. No, this kind of weakness couldn't be healed with a spell.

Magic ate the same fuel the body did. You didn't use magic with willpower or the mercy of gods. Magic used the same chalonic energy that the rest of your body did. And Orphan didn't have enough to spare. If he tried to cast even the simplest healing spell right now, it'd be the last thing he ever did.

He needed food. He needed it soon.

But food didn't come free. Not ever. And kindness? That was even rarer. No one did anything for free in this world. Orphan knew that much. Whatever had saved him from death had its reasons, and those reasons wouldn't be kind.

He grimaced as he forced himself to his feet, legs trembling under the weight of his own body. It would not take long to find out what those reasons were. And when he did, he'd be ready.

Fate, for once, showed a glimmer of sympathy to our dear Orphan. The sound of footsteps echoed from beyond the nearby door. The thought of who saved him overpowered even the gnawing hunger twisting his stomach. Could it be the invaders? Perhaps they'd found him and taken pity? The foreign decor certainly fits that theory. But no, it wasn't the Teutons.

The figure that darkened the doorway had to lean to fit under the arch, despite its considerable height. The moment he stepped into view, Orphan knew the Winterman.

"Well, well, already up. Been two days. Must be starving," the Winterman said, its voice a low rumble beneath the layers of heavy wraps and coats that hid every inch of it. Not a hint of skin was visible. In its gloved hands, it carried a tray with two sets of perfectly prepared dishes, one large, one smaller, clearly meant for Orphan.

Without so much as a word, the Winterman set the food down in front of him with a grace that belied its massive frame. Meat, vegetables, two kinds of soup, a plate of cheeses and crackers. To drink, a glass of red liquid and a horn of something darker. Then, as if this were the most normal scene in the world, the Winterman carried its own plates to a small table and sat with a deliberate, almost formal air. It had even been thoughtful enough to give Orphan just one spoon and fork. How considerate.

Orphan stared at the food, eyes wide, stomach tight. He hadn't said a word, but the Winterman didn't need his words.

The air itself seemed to hum with the being's amusement, as if it could feel the boy's shock and fear like a tangible thing.

Finally, after minutes of silence, Orphan managed to ask, "Why are you doing this?" He didn't dare look up. Not that it would matter, the Winterman had perfected the art of hiding behind his scarves.

The Winterman's voice came, thick with smug superiority but somehow not mocking. "Even I have a soft spot for the pitiful of this world. And you, boy, are pitiful."

Orphan's gaze flicked back to the food, doubt creeping in. Poison? A trap? But no. If the Winterman wanted him dead, there were simpler, quicker ways to dispose of him than this elaborate charade. His stomach growled, reminding him that fear was a luxury hunger didn't allow.

The first bite shattered the dam. Tears welled in his eyes, rolling silently down his cheeks. He'd never tasted anything like this luxury wasn't even the word. He barely understood the flavors, their richness, their warmth. All he'd ever known were scraps: bits of meat too small for the butcher, moldy bread no one else wanted, whatever he could scavenge from the feasting hall after dark. This? This was beyond imagination. Every bite was a revelation, a reminder of everything he had been denied.

And maybe, just maybe, a seed was planted. A seed of hunger, not just for food, but for more. A taste for this comfort, this power. Why should this be out of reach for him? Why had it been, all these years? Some awful gnarled its way into existence in Orphan. Something voracious. Something desperate. Something… evil.

Then, of course, the other realization settled in the one almost too impossible to accept. He was thirteen. He was alive. The fire meant for his pyre hadn't been lit. For years, he'd lived with the knowledge that he wouldn't see this day, that his end was marked. That to dream of anything was a foolish notion. To travel beyond the lands he hated so. To maybe confess silly disgusting feelings of affection to a certain someone. To sing and slight in poetic rhymes to halls and jarls. These things were wanted or desperately desired but cast aside in the face of reality. And yet here he was. Alive. Breathing. That was never supposed to happen.

There'd been no hope of escape, nowhere to run but the frozen wilderness. And even if by some miracle he reached the lowlands, they would kill him just the same. He'd always known that. Or thought he had. But today was the day after his birthday, and against all the odds, he was still here.

"I don't know what to do." Orphan's voice was quiet, his focus entirely on the soup in his lap, its yellow tint catching what little light there was. Such an insignificant thing, yet it held his attention like nothing else.

"Stupid boy. That means you have options." The Winterman had finished before Orphan had even started, its plates and bowls neatly set aside.

"Options?" Orphan asked, his voice carrying the weight of disbelief. "What options do I have? There's no place in the world that would let me live. What choices besides death do I have left?" He wasn't sure if it was despair speaking or something worse an old, suicidal comfort in the familiar. Better the fate he knew than the unknown.

"You have more than you realize." The Winterman's words were accompanied by another low, rumbling laugh. It stood, looming above Orphan, before lifting him effortlessly by the back of his neck, like one might carry a misbehaving cat. But

Orphan wasn't some passive animal, and though his attempts to squirm free were futile, he fought back instinctively. His anger was a spark, dim and flickering, but there all the same.

They passed through more rooms of impossible wealth and luxury. Every step further revealed more of the Winterman's hidden domain: tapestries, plush carpets, exotic trinkets that glinted in the soft glow of oil lamps. But there were no windows. Heavy drapes hung as though concealing glass that wasn't there, the only light coming from softly glowing sconces. Light music played in the background, the scratchy sound of a record player weaving through the warmth of the space, making it feel almost like a dream. It wasn't until they reached a heavy, steel door thick with bars and bolts that the illusion of comfort was broken. This, finally, looked real. Utilitarian. Cold.

The Winterman swung the door open with a groaning whine of metal against stone. A gust of icy wind hit Orphan's face, biting through his skin as the outside world intruded once more. The cold lingered, wrapping around him like a shroud as they exited the hidden home. He shivered, already longing for the warmth of the cave behind them.

They reached the edge of a great cliff overlooking the entire Glimisvellir Valley. From this vantage point, Orphan could see it all, the conquered town laid out like a ruinous map beneath him. Smoke still rose from the blackened buildings. Foreign flags fluttered in the bitter wind. The camp of the invaders was alive with movement, their forces already spreading into the town like ants claiming new territory. Glimisvellir had always prided itself on being unconquerable, the oldest settlement of humankind, its people steeped in pride and tradition. Now, its legacy lay in ashes.

"After the first strike, they pulled back. Let the chaos stew for a while," the Winterman's voice rumbled, calm and almost conversational. "Guess it got worse after the chief was killed. Didn't make him a martyr, so the people didn't stand and fight to the last man like they would have. Then the Teutons really let loose and took out about a third of the town by the looks of it. When the gates opened, they just marched in."

Orphan listened, his eyes fixed on the smoldering remains of his home. The townspeople had blamed him for the chief's death, hadn't they? Every ounce of their rage had been focused on him. But even as he looked upon the smoldering town he could only feel deeply satisfied. Knowing that the people who had wanted him dead were suffering and he wasn't, in his heart it felt great. After all, why shouldn't it? Why deny yourself the joy at seeing such delicious irony.

The Winterman dropped Orphan into the snow with an unceremonious thud, his feet sinking into the crackling snow. Orphan took a step forward, closer to the cliff's edge, drawn to it as if it might offer some kind of answer. All it would take is a little push, for him to start tumbling down. Though he had never been at the top before, only at the bottom. So maybe, just maybe the nudge wouldn't push him over the edge to fall... but to fly.

Survival had always been a strange thing to him. On one hand, he had known the day he would die, felt a kind of grim comfort in the certainty of it. Dying early, though? That was unacceptable. Letting the Glimingars see his body broken and cold before they had the chance to burn him? It would mean they won. And Orphan? He hated losing. Hated it with a fire that had never gone out.

But the thought of not just surviving but thriving? Three

days ago, he would have spat at the idea. Yet here he stood. Alive. Two days beyond his thirteenth birthday. Two days he should never have seen. Luxury and riches had been laid at his feet, if only for a fleeting moment. And now he wanted more. He wanted life. He wanted power. And he wanted to make those who had tried to crush him pay for it. He wanted to spite them all, and perhaps… perhaps he wanted something beyond even that.

"You think I have other options. What if I said I was interested?" Orphan's voice was low, almost lost in the wind, but there was sharpness there, something that hadn't been there before.

"Tell me, kid. Have you ever wanted to rule the world?" The Winterman's voice was thick with anticipation, a smile felt even through the layers of cloth as it placed a hand on the boy's back. Gently, it steered him away from the edge. Away from that fall and toward something else.

Further down the cliffside, beyond treetops and frozen hills, the town of Glimisvellir was unraveling in slow motion. Not just poorly no, it was a masterclass in incompetence. The fools couldn't even fix their own homes. It was almost comical. The few builders who hadn't perished in the assault were utterly lost without their foremen. They had tools and materials aplenty, but without plans or guidance, they were like children with knives dangerous and useless all at once. Ah, but humans do love to brute-force their way through problems, don't they? It seldom ends well.

But the lack of repair was merely the tip of the iceberg. A mob of angry Glimingars had gathered outside the Great Hall, their frustrations barely held in check by the bayonets of Teuton soldiers. They weren't foolish enough to challenge their new overlords directly, self-preservation still trumped outrage but they demanded answers about the most mundane of things: food, water, shelter. Basic needs turned into luxuries overnight.

Normally, hunters, gatherers, and fishermen would provide for the town. But with many of them dead and the rest in disarray, the food stores dwindled quickly. The Great Hall's cellars held reserves for emergencies, but none had anticipated an occupation. And now, under new management, the leaders were preoccupied with far more important debates.

"By every forgotten name of the gods, I implore you General do not do this. Gerfinn is not the man you have been led to believe he is, there is no honesty in him. No genuine attempt to travel down his Journey of Grief." Priest Eberulf's voice strained against the indifference of his audience. It was an affront to the priest Eberulf's very real and very uncompressed moral fiber. His objections fell on deaf ears, particularly those of General Hermenigild, who seemed more amused than concerned.

"Meister Gerfinn was instrumental in the transition of power in Glimisvellir," the general replied smoothly, "and he has the endorsement of the new Governess of the Soarlands."

Ah yes, Lady Delacroix the Teutons' carefully placed political authority, and a woman no less. Not like they explicitly knew about Glimisvellir's patriarchal culture vs the Soarlands' more utilitarian equality. Bitter about how this all happened perhaps but not vindictive enough to pull a stunt like that. No-no-no.

"Oh please," Gerfinn interjected with feigned humility, "I had such a small part to play in all of this. I cannot accept such a duty. The position of Jarl should go to someone more deserving."

What a performance. Both he and Lady Delacroix danced their little dance, words flowing like honeyed poison between them. They were enjoying this, reveling in the charade while everyone else in the room watched, powerless to stop them.

"But you must, mon cher Gerfinn," Lady Delacroix purred, her eyes alight with both mischief and genuine affection. "Only you can be trusted with such an important task. The integration of the Soarlands into the Confederacy hinges on Glimisvellir's development into something truly civilized and modern, n'est-ce pas ?"

They shared a glance a brief, intimate connection that spoke volumes more than their public words ever could. In a room full of people, they might as well have been alone. Two minds, sharper than any blade, united by a mutual disdain for the mediocrity surrounding them.

"Ugh, we all know they're bedding each other, ja?" The four-eyed bureaucrat pompous and perpetually unimpressed muttered to General Hermenigild and Eberulf. Meanwhile, Gerfinn and Lady Delacroix continued their verbal waltz, utterly unbothered.

"Officially, I must protest such accusations against Madame Delacroix," the general replied, his tone as flat as the plains of Teutonreach. "As third cousin to the Head of State of the Third Republic of Neustria, and currently engaged to the brother of the Head of State of Imperial Teutonreach, any rumor of impropriety is unwelcome in the Imperial Court."

It was as much a threat as it was a stress-filled admiration that yes indeed something quite lewd and scandalous was happening here. But the truth hung in the air like a thick fog everyone knew, and no one could do a thing about it. Lady Delacroix's 'soft exile' from court was as much a political maneuver as it was a scandal. Intrigue and backstabbing are such delightful pastimes.

"All the more reason to keep Gerfinn from power," Eberulf pressed on, his desperation seeping through his practiced facade. "That is a man that sailed with a known crewmate of the Twelfth. The Sin of Ambition is clear and obvious here, you cannot allow it to take root. Poisoned soil is no place to start a garden."

The very trustworthy and very honest priest was not a native to the area, but he knew what was at stake. The possible turning of a land toward the Light of Righteousness rather than the Shadow of Malice. Oh the Soarlands never openly consort the Fiendish nor did they seek out the Infernal, but they were most certainly not the allies of those that fought against the forces of Tyranny. Eberulf knew the goal of the Confederacy, or at least the general outcome, was to find a strong new member to count among the States.

While not a Savior Nation, the Lands of Soar were large and rich in natural resources. The people were strong and fierce, potential laying dormant. At the moment the only other candidates that could possibly join the current three States of the Confederacy were... let's see here... ah... a recently established communist regime and a monarchy on the brink of all out civil war. Yes. Perfectly acceptable I'm sure. Regardless, the Soarlands were less problematic even if they required some work. All the more reason for the Church to make sure that the beginnings of this new nation weren't sullied with a possible legacy of Malice.

Eberulf words fell flat. Gerfinn and Lady Delacroix paid him no mind, their attention solely on each other. In a world of pawns and petty players, they saw themselves as the only true intellects, a king and queen moving pieces across a board only they understood.

"Oh, but I heard something interesting before leaving Aemstelredamme," The haughty officer spoke, his tone dripping with smug teasing. "Upon news of our success, an entire monastery of clerics is set to descend upon Glimisvellir mein lieber Pater. They're eager to investigate rumors of a Seat of Power of the northern gods hidden in these mountains. Imagine Glimisvellir becoming as famous as Köllen and Zawra." That shut the ever-so-pious Eberulf right up. The legends of cities like Köllen and Zawra were known even in these forsaken parts glittering spires of wealth and devotion, throngs of faithful singing hymns in hopes that the absent gods might cast a fleeting glance their way while priests work to shepherd them through their grief. Perhaps a lesser man of faith and virtue would see himself at the helm of such grandeur, basking in reflected glory. But unfortunately, we find ourselves with not of a lesser man but one of that most awful and disgusting of traits, genuine belief in the betterment of the soul.

"It's not about fame or glory, or even the politics of humanity… this is a fight between Malice and Righteousness." No, it wasn't. Not anymore. For thousands of years the world was divided between those that suffered and wept for the old world, that which had been ruled and ordained by the Gods. When men did not think for themselves but danced to the tune of beings who by no obligation would care if those same men fell dead during the performance. And those on the other side were… well… of a more selfish proclivity. Seeing their own needs as more important than the whims of Gods who were so ready to abandon the flock.

"Genug. Enough." General Hermenigild's voice cut through the air like a blade. "We have achieved what we had come to do, a garrison will remain to keep order. The Confederacy will recognize Glimisvellir as the de jure power in the Soarlands. Once Glimisvellir is brought up to proper standing they can petition for Statehood and the collective force of the Confederacy will be brought to help it gain control over its recognized borders."

With that definitive dismissal, the general put an end to Eberulf's scheming. The pompous bureaucrat beside him snickered openly, delighting in the priest's humiliation, and trailed after the general as he moved toward the true leaders in the room.

"If the two of you are finished," Hermenigild addressed Gerfinn and Lady Delacroix, "I'll be departing at dawn. I've grown quite a distaste for this northern cold."

"Oh, but by all means, stay a few days, mon général," Lady Delacroix purred, her eyes never leaving Gerfinn's. "You've been such a delight, and it will be some time before my social circle here matches my… standards."

Even I can't tell where her genuine offer ends and the empty flattery begins. But then, that's the art of it, isn't it? While one might expect a highborn noblewoman to excel at such games, it's a rarity among Teutonic ladies. The Soarlands and Teutonreach share many views on women and power, but Teutonreach has recently been forced to engage with such pesky notions as liberalism and equality.

"No," the general replied flatly, turning on his heel and leaving no room for argument.

Soon enough, the Great Hall emptied, leaving only the three architects of Glimisvellir's downfall. Their plan hadn't been grand Glimisvellir, despite its historical fame, was little more than a large town of seven thousand souls. A single traitor and a bit of fortunate timing were all it took. Now, they could finally enjoy the spoils.

Gerfinn offered his hand to Lady Delacroix, a mocking parody of the courtly manners she was accustomed to. She accepted with a sly smile, allowing him to lead her through the disarray of the feasting hall toward the chief's dais. A large chair had been dragged from another room to serve as a makeshift throne; traditions mattered little to them now. They had but one spectator, whom they could not give a tiny bit of care what he may think of them. Judgement, after all, was a right not held by all men.

"You two, how long are you going to pretend that you have any loyalty to your oaths? A year, maybe two if we're all so lucky. Or maybe you will keep your promises, just to different masters." They stopped their accent just before their throne, to look back to the accusations being hurled their way. For his part, Eberulf's own resentment and bile were bubbling to the surface. One mistake, that's all it took for this world to be shaped into being. And at their laughter at the priest's bemoaning, the anger boiled and roiled ever hotter.

"Tell me Eberulf, you seem so insistent on dear Gerfinn here to not be the Jarl. Is there another candidate more fitting or is it just that you question my intelligence to be incapable of choosing a suitable leader for the town?" she began, her tone teasing yet edged with genuine curiosity, "Because I find myself quite satisfied with my choice."

"Lets see here, I'm an accomplished Mage and proven my ability as a víkingr for years, oh and I have this," Gerfinn chuckled as he spun the bear call necklace of the precious Jarl in his hand. It rang of power, softly echoing from the few pieces of not-bear on the piece. The new Jarl and Governess ascended the dais, there he settled onto the throne, and she gracefully perched herself sideways on his lap, legs draped over the armrest. "Oh look, I'm sitting here too. I think that makes me the Jarl doesn't it?"

They looked quite the picture, an unkempt herbalist and a highborn lady entwined in a pose that blurred the lines between power and intimacy. Anyone stumbling upon them might suspect treachery brewing. But no, their bond was forged in mutual disdain for the world around them and a shared belief in their intellectual superiority.

For years, ever since discovering his magic, Gerfinn had been treated differently. Revered, even. It was intoxicating for a time, being hailed as the future of Glimisvellir. But when his progress stalled whether from lack of luck or motivation the adoration faded. The Glimingars had no use for those who didn't contribute to their narrow definitions of strength and honor. Stripped of their praise, Gerfinn threw a tantrum like any child would. Running down to the lowlands to join a Soarling crew and become a víkingr. Something not unheard of among the youth of the Glimingar. But time and misfortune have their ways with mortals, eventually he returns. And resigned himself to being the town's healer and herbalist, seeking solace in other intoxicants.

Meanwhile, in the courts of Teutonreach, Lady Delacroix

navigated a world rapidly changing yet stubbornly clinging to old ways. Teutonreach, one of the mighty Savior Nations of Ereth, was advancing swiftly but doubling down on selective traditions. Freedom, equality, the rights of women and non-humans ideas celebrated in theory but often strangled in practice. Power was shifting from the crown to those who wielded pens instead of swords. For a woman like her, smart, witty, and undeniably beautiful only the last trait truly mattered to her male counterparts.

Their unlikely union began with a single misdelivered letter, intended for the very intelligent and certainly very discreet priest of Glimisvellir. Upon seeing the botanical diagrams and alchemical notations, Eberulf had promptly handed it off to Gerfinn, assuming it was meant for him. And so began a correspondence that would end a millennium of Glimisvellir's isolation.

"None of those things gives you the right to rule." A slip of the tongue, from the most ironic of places. Eberulf cursed his luck and stormed out of the hall not wanting to witness the continued folly in front of him.

The crowd outside were still quite irate as one would be when possibly facing starvation. But Eberulf was currently in no mood to even keep up to the vague appearance he held on this stage, kindly old man. Instead with a scowl on his face and without a word to the panicking people he moved through the mob with a force that none knew he could have had to him. He was of course just an old one armed man right? Right? Those robes are quite heavy and could potentially hide some bulk under there... huh.

A few tried to follow him to the church just down the road. A modest, round building with a solitary room and a tower sprouting from its center, offering humble quarters to the priest and a perch for a lonely bell. Today, like most days, it was empty of worshippers. Eberulf slammed the door behind him, leaving him all alone… for the most part. There was one person in the building. The very kindly and not at all callous priest moved through the pews before opening the door to the tower that was his home, finding Thrain exactly where he left him.

A garbled shout of protest attempted to exit from the hunter's mouth only to be muffled by the gagging cloth tied tightly around his head. Nothing else bound him, yet he knelt in place, arms locked behind his back by what looked like some invisible force. Eberulf looked down at the golden boy of the village in unfiltered fury, in a petty act of needed stress relief back handed the trapped young man leaving behind a harsh red mark on Thrain's otherwise pretty features.

"Gods away, look back to your humble servant for the briefest of moments and grant me the temperance to deal with fools and heretics." With a withering look down to Thrain, the priest gave a silent warning before undoing the gag. After a few coughs and adjustments, Thrain opened to speak again only to be immediately cowed into silence by another look. "Only questions, no statements or definitive outbursts. The Right of Infallibility is becoming stronger, I can no longer keep it suppressed in your mind."

"We made a deal didn't we? Uh… damn it… you would keep this power in check and I could stay with my sister if I-" Another backhanded slap came to interrupt his words.

"Silence. I can do far more than just cripple you, Thrain." Eberulf, the ever beleaguered priest, pinched the bridge of his nose, struggling to maintain his composure. He reminded himself of his sacred duties: to guide the people through their eternal grief over the lost divine, to comfort those who've lost all they hold dear, to warn the world of Malice and its servants, and most perilously, to aid the Heroes, the Oracles, and the Saviors.

"Then I should be the Jarl, not that scum, Gerfinn!" Thrain's voice reverberated off the stone walls, each word laced with indignant fury. And with that declaration, an imperceptible ripple spread through reality subtle, unseen, yet altering the very fabric of truth behind the eyes of all mortals.

"Y-yes. Yes, you should be the Jarl," Carefully choosing his words, he knew he had to correct that Statement before too much damage was done. As much as he wished for Gerfinn to not be the Jarl, Thrain was an even worse option. "But you aren't and you shouldn't want to be, you can be greater than just a chief of a backwater mountain village. So say it, you shouldn't be Jarl"

He had to force these words out as something fundamental in his soul believed that Thrain should be Jarl of the town. It was a truth but not the one that needed to be true now. He was desperately trying to dance around the new reality Thrain was unconsciously weaving. Thrain should be chief; it was now an undeniable fact etched into existence. No one else deserved the role more than he. Eberulf knew this was the dangerous power of a Hero with a Divine Right, warping reality with mere assertions. Knowing it was one thing; countering it was another beast entirely.

"I would need to leave my sister, that can't-" Screams followed an unintelligible string of words that came from Eberulf's lips. A spell had been cast and then Thrain felt only pain. It was like every other sensation in his body was gone except for pain. Then as quickly as it came it was gone. "Please… not again."

"Say it."

"I… I shouldn't be chief." And like that reality recorrected itself back to account for this new Truth.

"It's bad enough I lost Orphan, the boy would have been perfect for the Repentant. But, I'll need to settle with just sending a Hero to Atlas instead. By the Gods Lost, this is more excitement than my old bones can take." This was not how he'd envisioned his tenure in Glimisvellir. When assigned to this remote northern outpost, he'd welcomed the prospect of a quiet life. Nothing ever happened here until everything did. The town had been dull, its greatest scandal a foreign woman and her devil-spawned bastard. After her pyre cooled and the townsfolk redirected their scorn to the orphan, life had settled back into monotony.

Then came the Confederacy's arrival. Letters from his colleagues in Atlas spoke of a unified humanity, and Eberulf saw opportunity. A chance to climb the ecclesiastical ladder, perhaps even apprentice under a Cardinal. It all seemed so perfect.

Until he mistakenly handed that pivotal letter to Gerfinn, the one meant to connect him with Teutonic nobility. The oversight had cost him dearly. And now, a Hero had emerged, complicating matters further. But he'd managed to steer Thrain away, at least for the moment.

Now, all he could do was wait and hope that his efforts would bear fruit. An easier, more prestigious life awaited him, surely deserved after all his hard work and… adaptability.

But fate, as always, had a twisted sense of humor.

Words of the Fourth

Hearts racing with Greed
Swift desires intercede
Speed fades, avarice recedes

Paths Better Not Taken

It was a rare spectacle when anything from beyond the borders of Glimisvellir dared to disturb the serene yet unforgiving forests nestled among the mountains. Yet, change, like a relentless invader, cares little for the status quo. Roughly a century ago, one such anomaly arrived, and its mere presence did cause much disturbing. Not intentionally, at least for now that is. A bizarre, cloaked figure emerged from the south, its origins shrouded in mystery. This figure, with a peculiar audacity, waltzed into the snow, trudging forward without apparent aim or reason.

Its cloak, a dark wraith trailing in the pristine snow, etched a line in the earth that stretched back to realms untouched by frost. Mysteriously, no footprints marred the path of packed snow it left in its wake. This long, long line in the snow extended on as the being made no stops for its entire time in this land. Days turned to weeks and anyone privy to this creature's journey would have lost count of how long it had drifted. Aimless it wandered through the snow as this poor soul was quite lost. Headless. Directionless. Utterly Adrift.

Both predators and prey, in their dim-witted simplicity, had become acutely aware of the anomaly: the crunching cadence of what they thought was a two-legged being disturbing their mundane existence. It wasn't like they were trying to hide. Why would they? After all, even the feeble-minded fauna of this land, with their limited wits, could sense when a superior predator was in their midst. Only the bravest or maybe furry creatures of the most stupid variety mustered the courage, or foolishness, to draw near enough to glimpse the enigmatic wanderer.

At first glance, the creatures would behold nothing more than a jumble of crudely stitched hides cloaking the being from head to toe. The keener eyed would spot beneath the hood two sets of lightly yellow glowing eyes. Every so often, the cloak would contort in peculiar fashion, as if something was twitching underneath. It could be a man... of a sort? Maybe a wretched being, grotesquely twisted by some arcane mishap or a vile, dark enchantment. Regardless of its origins, the forest's natives, guided by their primal instincts, steered clear of this ominous figure.

And so, a legend grew, of a strange wandering cloaked man whom if the survivors are to be believed, should never be approached unless one has a death wish. These shell-shocked hunters, more kissed by fortune's whimsy than embraced by any divine favor, whispered fragmented tales of companions swallowed whole by the very earth. Brash lads, puffed up with the need to flaunt their valor, boldly declared their quests to vanquish this phantom and seize its head. Alas, their boasts were their last, their disappearances a silent testament to their folly. And frankly, the world's better off without such buffoons. And now two new figures found their way into those same desolate lands.

"Could you have given me some shoes?" Barefoot in the snow, for what could be miles. Orphan followed the

Winterman through the Glimisvellir mountains away from the town of the same name. There hadn't been any more explanation, but what was he going to do?

"Could have, didn't feel like it. Besides, you have that nifty little trick." Tis true, Orphan had been making a great use of the Heal spell to fix the frost bite that had been nipping at his exposed feet. But his suffering wouldn't continue on for too much longer as the two neared their destination, a ruined tower jutting out the peak of a hilltop. Old and ancient it was, only kept stable by the sheer amount of ice that had frozen the stones solidly together.

The Winterman opened the gate that led inside, Orphan hurried on in as cold stone was better than frozen dirt and feet of snow. Inside was a little cleaner than one would expect from a ruin such as this. Several crates covered with tanned leather littered around with several bundles of camping supplies leaning against them. Several oil lamps that were being lit by the giant of an occupant illuminated the rest of the room. Orphan meanwhile sat down in the middle of the space and began his best to get warm by huddling close in on himself, there was little else he could do.

"Okay. We're here. What now."

"Now, I leave you to your fate, kid." The Winterman laughed before sitting down on one of the many creates, no sound coming from the weight pressing on the wooden box. The little Cursed Born didn't so much as gasp or try to feign shock at this statement. The idea that he was just going to get dumped off and left to die? Perfectly within expectation at this point. "Damnit, you're no fun."

"No really, you said I had another option so what is it?" For the first time since waking up, Orphan felt the air around the Winterman change. Despite his face being covered there was always this lighthearted sense of uncaring jovialness. Like there wasn't anything that could make this monster take things seriously. But now that changed as the beast of a man leaned forward and his entire demeanor seemed to drop.

"You were a pious little boy and went to church right? Did they tell you about why the gods left this world?" Orphan nodded, church had been one of the few places that he could go without expecting to be run out of. The gods had left the world after a single mortal proved to be so heinous and cruel that they demonstrated the unworthiness of all mortal kind. That person would go on to create the Devil race and ever since then the gods refused to return so long as Devils and Cursed Born existed. The young man repeated this to the Winterman who nodded at this approved version of events. "Close… but the truth?"

"The truth? Then what actually happened?" Perhaps it was his personal distaste for the opinions and facts of others, but Orphan had always assumed that the story given by the Church of the Orphaned World wasn't the full truth. Plus, the priest in Glimisvellir always looked so nervous when giving his sermons when Orphan was in view.

"It was caused by one person, that is true. But it wasn't that the gods abandoned the world because of them, it was because they had stolen the very thing that gave the gods ownership of the world. The Divine Right of Sovereign." The air stiffened but for a moment, reacting to a series of events outside the view of the mortal and out of control of the divine. Stolen? Who could steal from a god? A thief, that's who.

What is a god? A king is a god to a peasant, the difference in fundamental Rights and abilities make it so. Then a god must have Rights to powers beyond that a mortal could possibly hope to attain themselves. Divine Rights. What rights could a god have? To be at the highest of positions in existence must come with some powerful perks, yes? Well… off the top of my head. To never be wrong. To destroy whatever they want. To know everything. To be praised and believed in by all. To judge a person's soul. And to rule the world.

"They could have stayed, remained gods with all their other powers. But then they would have to ask permission for anything as they were no longer the rulers of the world. And that was unacceptable. So instead of staying by the people that loved and worshiped them, they left. Without even a word to their prophets because they couldn't do so without being allowed to." A crack back to the Winterman's previous mood came and went as he finished speaking. Like talking about an old friend he once knew and lost, the times they had and the fleeting moment before they never saw each other again.

"But what does any of this have to do with me?" It was nice and all to be told an earth-shattering truth of the beginnings of history but Orphan was too cold and hungry for anything except himself. Typical teenager already.

"It has to do with you because you have that Divine Right in your blood. Every Devil and Cursed Born do, just a small little piece of it. But you can claim it all, and become a Tyrant." To this half dead boy whom being at the bottom was the natural state of things… this sounded all so ridiculous. Like telling a drowning man that he has just inherited a massive palace in the middle of expansive farmland. Sure, that sounds fantastic but given the current circumstances it doesn't help much does it?

"I'm… having a hard time believing that." A disappointed sigh and a hung head later and the Winterman continued on, likely questioning just what he was doing.

"I'm not saying you can just suddenly become ruler of the world, also based on your reaction I'm guessing you don't know the meaning behind the title of Tyrant right?" A shake of the head is the answer that the Winterman was given. In all likelihood the people of Glimisvellir avoided telling Orphan about this topic to prevent him from getting any ideas as a child. Can't have a dream if you didn't know the dream existed.

The history of the world is shaped by the exceptional. The talented and the ambitious. Nations rise and fall on the efforts and sacrifices of those Marked by Fate itself. And in this world those given the Divine Rights once held by gods even more so. Because after the gods had left the world, these Rights that held such power and authority did not just disappear. They needed to find new worthy candidates to hold them. This is where the Divine Titles and their bearers come from.

Six Divine Rights exist in this world, each with their requirements and privileges. Five of these manifest in those that are suitable to have them. While the last remains tied the bloodline of the First Tyrant, the one who stole the Right and began this new Godless age. To this day in history, twelve individuals have held the Title of Tyrant and the Right of Sovereign. Their lasting influence on the world can never be erased even by the combined might of the righteous and pure of the other Title Holders. The Winterman tried to explain all of this as best he could to the weakened Orphan, and the young man did try to retain it all. But one can only do so much on an empty stomach.

"So you want me to become a Tyrant, me?" Orphan's disbelief was palpable. The idea was absurd, like asking a fish to climb a mountain. Sure, he'd fantasized about power who wouldn't, after a life scraping the bottom of humanity's barrel? But this? This was a step beyond wild dreams into the realm of madness.

The Winterman shrugged, unconcerned. "I don't care what you do. With the Confederacy marching in, this valley's about to get crowded, and I prefer my solitude. Thinking of heading East. Haven't been there in ages." He began uncovering the crates scattered around the tower, peeling back layers of worn leather. Inside were cured meats, jars of preserved fruits, and bottles of spirits that caught the dim light. He plucked a bottle with a practiced hand. "There's about a month's worth of supplies here if you're careful. And with that little trick of yours, water shouldn't be an issue."

Orphan watched him, frustration gnawing at his insides. "But you haven't explained how I'm supposed to become this… Tyrant." The door to the tower stood ajar, a gaping maw letting in the cold. The Winterman seemed ready to leave, but he paused, perhaps indulging in one last bit of mischief.

"First, you'll need an Archfiend. There's been one roaming these lands, has for about a century. Be cautious; it's more likely to devour you than listen to you. Second, you'll need a Seat of Power, a place still touched by the Divine Spark of the gods." He took a swig from his bottle, the liquid vanishing behind his scarves. "That's all you need. I'm curious to see if you can pull it off. You're not the first I've set down this path, but you might be the first in a long while to succeed." With that, he stepped out into the swirling snow, pulling the door closed behind him.

Silence enveloped the tower, pressing in like a weight. Orphan stood there, the enormity of his solitude settling over him. Slowly, he moved to the pile of discarded leather tarps, crawling beneath them in search of warmth. Survival first; grand destinies could wait a moment.

What options did he have? With the supplies left behind, he might make it beyond Glimingaric territory, perhaps reaching the lowlands. Maybe he could hide his cursed lineage, blend into some Soarling village. But then what? Live in the shadows, always one misstep away from discovery and execution? The stories he'd heard were grim: Devils and Cursed Born hunted mercilessly, or worse, corralled into squalid ghettos. His only distant hope was the fabled lands far to the south, where snow was a myth and Hell the Devil's kingdom might offer sanctuary. A fool's hope.

Staying here was equally laughable. The idea of surviving alone in this frozen wasteland was almost comical. He was all skin and bones, lacking the strength or knowledge to hunt or fend for himself. The wilds would swallow him whole. Yet another grievance to lay at the feet of Glimisvellir's townsfolk; they hadn't just shunned him; they'd left him utterly unprepared for life.

As he huddled beneath the tarps, a grim resolve began to take shape. This insane notion of becoming a Tyrant, it was madness, sure, but what did he have to lose? Every other path led to a slow death or a miserable existence. If he was going to risk dying, better to die reaching for something monumental. The allure of it tugged at him: the Right to Rule the world. It was preposterous and yet, it made a twisted kind of sense.

Decision made, Orphan set about preparing. Over the next week, he consumed more food than perhaps he should have, trying to build up some semblance of strength. He fashioned crude winter garments from spare cloth and leather, layering himself against the biting cold. The Archfiend was his first objective. He knew nothing about it, save that it wandered these lands and was dangerous beyond measure. But the Seat of Power that he had a vague idea about. Ancient ruins that whispered of forgotten gods didn't move, after all.

At dawn, he stood at the tower's threshold, swathed in his makeshift attire. Behind him, a sled laden with supplies was roped together with a meager arsenal against the unforgiving wilderness. In his hand, a sharpened wooden pole served as his sole weapon. It was a pitiful sight, really. A boy, barely more than a ghost, setting out to challenge fate itself.

But stories worth telling seldom begin with wisdom.

The journey was brutal. The sled emptied quicker than he'd anticipated, his supplies dwindling as the cold gnawed at him. Twice, he was set upon by wolves, surviving only by the skin of his teeth and the edge of his magic turning snow to water, then freezing it to trap the snarling beasts. Each encounter left him more ragged, his clothes torn, his body exhausted.

Days bled together. The wilderness stretched infinite and indifferent around him. No signs of life, no wolves, no birds, not even the whisper of wind through the trees. An oppressive silence that felt like the world's breath held in suspense. He knew enough to recognize the omen: death was near.

But dying out here, alone, carried a certain grim satisfaction. Better this than giving Glimisvellir the pleasure of his demise. As he stumbled forward, the snow stinging his raw skin, he felt a perverse pride. If this was the end, at least it was on his own terms.

He collapsed, the cold embracing him like an old friend. His vision blurred, the world fading to a blank canvas of white. Somewhere deep inside, that stubborn ember of spite flickered. This wasn't over yet.

"So little meat left… so much bone… but not to gnaw on?" The voice was a discordant melody of chittering clicks and guttural hums, each word a jagged edge slicing through the silence. Orphan mustered the last of his strength to lift his head. Where there had been nothing moments before, now loomed a towering figure draped in crudely stitched leather. Unlike the Winterman, this creature's face was exposed, a grotesque visage that defied any natural order.

Its head was an unsettling fusion of insect and nightmare: a bright yellow carapace streaked with orange, sharp and angular like that of an immense ant, but stretching back into an elongated skull. Two pairs of luminescent eyes, devoid of pupils much like Orphan's own, stared down at him one set larger and perched above the smaller. The mouth was a horrifying assembly, akin to a crab's mandibles flanked by razor-edged pincers, with tiny feeders incessantly writhing, eager to draw anything into its abyssal maw.

"Archfiend," Orphan whispered, recognition laced with dread. Of course it was. No other being could possess such perfect hideousness.

"Only for stew. Too skinny. Too bony. Not enough meat.

No bait anymore… prey now knows it is hunted. But hunger still… so hungry." The creature glided toward him, its cloak trailing in the snow without disturbing a single flake. Its eyes gleamed with a ravenous desperation, a bottomless pit seeking to consume.

"W-wait… please…" Orphan's voice was a frail thread in the icy air. This was it, the first step toward the fantastical future dangled before him. But fate's threads tightened like a noose; to the Archfiend, he was nothing more than a morsel.

"Crunching bone, among the snow, it is all that I know." The Archfiend's words were a macabre rhyme, a song of hunger and inevitability. Orphan might as well have been a carcass already.

"No… Tyrant… I need you." The declaration cost him dearly, each word pulled from the depths of his waning strength.

The Archfiend halted. Its hunched form straightened, rising to twice the height of a man. It turned fully toward him, newfound interest igniting in those alien eyes.

"For what cause dost thou seek to ascend as sovereign o'er the realm entire? Love? Power? Revenge?" Its voice was different now. Still the same in pitch, but now it was clear, smooth and expecting. Almost as if an entirely different person of the same species was now talking. But its question stoked a fire to Orphan's heart, the very last of his strength burning inside of him. An indignation, an all-consuming anger that forced his weakened form to give one last spiteful declaration.

"All of it," Orphan rasped, a fire igniting within his chest. "I've been stepped on and spat upon my whole life. Thrown into the cold more times than I've had warm meals. Is it wrong for me to want better? Is it wrong for me to want to live more than a wretched pariah? I want everything this world has to offer! Everything that's been denied to me and more! And I don't care what I have to do to have it. For no other reason than I want it."

Despite the closeness that death now had over his heart, Orphan's resolute conviction in his answer bled through into his words. He was done having nothing to his name. Done being at the bottom. He wanted everything this world had to offer him. A life of luxury. Love and adoration. To stand at the very top and look down on everyone else.

"Yes… yes," the Archfiend hissed, an unsettling satisfaction in its tone. "Ne'er have I encountered avarice akin to that since the master, and hunger akin to the mistress." It turned away, gliding back toward the remnants of Orphan's sled. Darkness encroached on the edges of his vision, but he fought to stay conscious, to see what would come next.

"A commendable beginning," the Archfiend continued. "Thy first utterance upon this frozen expanse that merits an answer. Come forth, my progeny, let us assay the mettle of this spawnling."

A slender, clawed appendage extended from beneath the creature's cloak, deftly hooking the rope of the sled. The ground trembled ever so slightly as the earth itself seemed to assist, lifting Orphan onto the makeshift board. Then, from the depths of the Archfiend's being, a piercing cry erupted a sound that to human ears would be the shriek of a thousand cicadas, but to other entities of the tundra, it was a summons.

The Archfiend moved forward, dragging the sled with effortless grace, the cacophonous call echoing into the desolate expanse. Whether Orphan lived or perished was part of the trial, a test for the would-be Tyrant.

Things stirred in the shadows of the Glimisvellir tundra, weaving through the twisted trees and echoing caverns of the mountains. A call had been sent a resonant, unearthly summons that rippled through the very marrow of the land. Imps, young and ancient, scurried and scrambled, drawn inexorably toward their broodsire. Demons, more cunning and cautious, cast wary gazes skyward, pondering what could have awakened the great Archfiend of the Seventh Tyrant: The Locust Lord, the Maggot King, the Ever-Gaping-Maw… Archfiend Beelzebub.

They converged upon a single, yawning cave deep within the heart of the Glimisvellir mountain range, a place so remote that no Glimingar had set foot there in over three millennia. The air thrummed with the cacophony of chittering voices, a symphony of anticipation that echoed through labyrinthine tunnels plunging deep into the earth. The path led to a cavernous chamber dominated by a bubbling lake of obsidian tar, its surface breaking and reforming with each languid burst. The walls dripped with viscous black slime, forming grotesque honeycomb structures that pulsed like living things.

At the very center, upon a small island of jagged stone, stood the Archfiend, towering and terrible, with Orphan limp at its feet. Around them gathered Imps of all shapes and sizes, their beady eyes gleaming with a mix of fear and reverence. In the shadows, more formidable figures lurked Demons, their gazes sharp and calculating, awaiting what was to come.

"We, a ceaseless swarm, hath been astray," the Archfiend's voice resonated, each word a guttural echo that seemed to originate from the depths of the earth itself. "I, shrouded in the mists of loss, have roamed aimless. But now, shall we find a master? A fresh purpose? A newfound Tyrant? Shall the earth once again reclaim the riches and sustenance of the surface world?!"

A thunderous roar erupted as Imps screeched and stamped, their fervor shaking the very walls of the cavern. The Demons remained silent but inclined their heads in acknowledgment. The Archfiend hunched back down to the unconscious and barely breathing Orphan. Without further ceremony it pushed the dying child into the lake of pitch and watched as he was claimed by the darkness. They all waited… and waited… and waited some more.

Orphan for his part barely noticed that he switched from dying by starvation to dying by drowning. Well… it did feel a little different. He had almost drowned once before when one little kid pushed him into the river. Too bad for the town that someone had dove in to recuse him not knowing just who it was that had fallen. But this did not feel like that time. He was warm now but not burning. Just warm.

Strength seeped back into his limbs, tentative at first but growing steadily. The medium surrounding him was thick, almost gelatinous, resisting his movements yet supporting him. He sensed other presences shapes nudging and brushing past, stirring echoes in the murky depths. A sudden surge from below propelled him upward, the warmth intensifying, coursing through him like liquid fire.

He could not see that he bled, all across his body finger sized needles were poking into his flesh as he was forced up. Not a single piece of him, however, gave into the pain. Nothing the bullies he had could compare to this, but all the same pain was pain. It ripped at him, trying to flay him alive. Picking his body apart piece by piece. Trying to change him. But none of it mattered, what could he possibly care about when death was so much more frightening. And he had accepted death a long time ago.

He broke the surface with a gasp, expelling a torrent of blackened ooze from his lungs. The pain subsided, replaced by a ravenous hunger that clawed at his insides. Weakly, he dragged himself onto the island's edge, the tar clinging to his skin like a second hide. No sooner had he caught his breath than he felt a cold, sharp point pressed against his cheek.

"Well, damn… I was hoping for a fight," a rough voice grated, laced with disappointment. "Been ages since I've tussled with a Returned Revenant."

Orphan looked up to see a figure unlike any he'd encountered, a Demon. It shared some traits with the Imps he'd seen lifeless on the outskirts of Glimisvellir, but this was a being of an entirely different order. Its body was a seamless fusion of glossy black rock and sinewy yellow flesh, with insect-like features that were both alien and unsettling. A single fly-like wing twitched restlessly at its back, and its head, more helm than face, regarded him with undisguised scrutiny.

Four more Demons encircled him, each unique in their grotesquery. Their carapaces gleamed like polished armor, and their eyes shone with a predatory intelligence. Orphan's heart pounded, but he refused to show fear.

"Hold thy hand, Abezethibou," another Demon intoned, its voice smooth yet commanding. "He hath endured and thereby earned the privilege to continue upon his journey. Henceforth, our role be only to lend aid in his onward path."

Abezethibou withdrew his spear with a disgruntled huff.

"Always spoiling my fun, Arcon," he muttered, stepping back. Orphan pushed himself to his feet, muscles trembling but functional.

He finally beheld the Archfiend Beelzebub in its full, horrifying glory. The creature's serpentine neck was as thick as a man's torso, stretching upward to support the monstrous head he'd seen before. Rows of small appendages lined its spine, twitching rhythmically. Its main body was a mass of obsidian and pulsating veins of yellow and orange crystal, supported by six double-jointed legs ending in razor-sharp talons.

"Yes, our lord Beelzebub," the Demons intoned in unison, each bowing their head.

"Canst thou ne'er cease to be the faultless little soldier, Abezethibou? Some of us, indeed, do our duties as intended rather than implied." Arcon chided, its tone edged with judgmental scorn. Unlike the others, Arcon was clad in attire reminiscent of a Teutonic officer, complete with a tailored coat and polished boots an anachronism that only added to the surrealism.

"Some of us prefer duty over dalliance," Abezethibou retorted, its single wing flicking dismissively.

"Ever so eager for that final release, aren't you?" sighed Sorosma, the smallest among them, its form resembling a mantis with delicate, scythe-like arms.

"We did win the wager on how long it'd take the young master to return," Carelena chimed in, its coiled chitinous tendrils swaying like hair.

"Speaking of which, should not someone procure sustenance for the poor boy?" suggested Lirochi, the sole Demon with overtly feminine features, a lithe figure with a face that, while plate-like, bore an uncanny human beauty. "Thou there! Go forthwith and fetch nourishment for the young master."

As one of the Imps scurried off, the Archfiend addressed its progeny. " Mine eldest offspring of this realm, thou hast arrived and beheld the resurgence of our novel lord. Perchance, it may be one among thee to ascend unto the heights that I, too, possess." The five demons of the Archfiend bowed and moved back as their broodsire slipped between them and Orphan who was still trying to process everything. He had never seen a demon let alone be witness to their… quirky nature.

Imps are nearly mindless little troublemakers, going about making mischief and mayhem wherever they go. Only when in the presence of their betters do they shape up; even then, they maintain a very simple mind. Not demons oh no. They have lived long enough to evolve into clever and intelligent beings, capable of leading their younger siblings to battle. The oldest among the demons can be even a match for a seasoned Hero. Killing machines and beasts with a cunning most sharp.

"Then that's that? I'm one step closer to becoming a Tyrant?" Orphan murmured, more to himself than to the Fiends assembled before him. Yet, they heard him, and a chorus of eerie laughter echoed through the cavern. Even the colossal Archfiend emitted a sound reminiscent of amusement.

"A single stride, indeed," Beelzebub intoned, its voice reverberating like the rumble of distant thunder. "Yet numerous more await thee. 'Tis truer to declare thou hast been granted leave to embark upon the inaugural journey." The Archfiend slithered its immense neck around Orphan, encircling him in a living barrier. The myriad tiny appendages lining its neck writhed subtly, each movement sending a ripple of unease through the young Cursed Born. He could not shake the sensation that any one of those limbs might dart forth and pierce his flesh without warning.

"The Magic of Malice hath not denied thee," Beelzebub continued. "That is all."

"Then what is next? To seek a Seat of Power?" Orphan's question hung in the air, met with a collective stare from the Fiends that suggested he had spoken out of turn or revealed more than he should.

"How dost thou possess such knowledge?" queried Carelena, the most outspoken among them. The Demons exchanged glances, their expressions inscrutable, save for the subtle tilts of their insect-like heads.

"Uh… I don't know his name, but the Glimingars call him the Winterman. He's the one who told me about becoming a Tyrant." Orphan shifted uncomfortably under their gaze. The Fiends murmured among themselves, their voices a susurrus of chitinous clicks and archaic whispers.

"We know naught of such a being," Beelzebub spoke, its tone contemplative. "Yet, it matters not. Before we concede thee the candidacy of heir, thou must surmount two more ordeals. Five Demons, five questions. Begin, our progeny."

The Demons formed a line before him, their monstrous sire looming behind like a grotesque backdrop. Hundreds of Imps clustered around the periphery, their excitement palpable. At a signal from Beelzebub a single, resonant stamp of a taloned foot the cavern fell into an expectant silence. A knot tightened in Orphan's stomach. This was more than a simple interrogation.

In unison, the Fiends intoned, "Blessed by the Curse, baptized in the unholy, to be judged by thy servants and thus given thy first step along the Path of Tyranny."

Suddenly, a searing pain gripped Orphan. His skin felt aflame, as if boiling from within. He gritted his teeth, refusing to cry out. This was never going to be easy. Orphan was never under any illusion that it was. Why would life suddenly start being easy?

"To what principles wilt thou hold thyself?" Arcon stepped forward, its voice echoing with resonant authority. "By what standard are we to measure thine own expectations? That is our query as Arcon, Demon of Gluttony." Bones snapped and a little boy fell onto his knees. None of the Fiends did anything to help him as every single bone in his body broke a hundred times over. But he did not die, the pain was excruciating. His entire body was rejecting the concepts of structure and health.

It was never said that this would be easy, to gain something one must either give up something in return or suffer for their desires. To become ruler of the world meant to travel along a road of skulls and broken dreams. As far more than just Orphan here, are attempting this very trial. Dozens every year seek out the Archfiends and hope, dearly so they hope, to achieve that first step upon this hallowed path.

There are in fact eight Archfiends that exist in this world, two that live in Hell and seven that roam the lands. Devils and Cursed Born alike seek them out; it is the promise of Tyranny in their blood that draws them in. First, one must find an Archfiend, survive the initial encounter, invoke the desire to become a Tyrant, and then that desire must speak to that particular Archfiend. Then the second stage comes, where we are right now with young Orphan. The hopeful candidate must be baptized in a Spawning Pit and not be subsumed by the Magic of Malice. All in all, far more survive to this point than one might expect. Devils of Hell often study and train themselves for this very process all their lives and Cursed Born so very often naturally develop the qualities that make themselves survive until this stage. But now is when a great deal of the chaff gets tossed aside.

Answer it, he had to answer the question even after all the damage had been done. That was never more evident as Orphan heard every Fiend take a single step forward. The threat was clear. He needed to answer quickly. Thankfully the words came out as easily as they had the uncountable number of times he said them before.

Summoning every ounce of will, Orphan forced the words out between ragged breaths. "Every man must be strong, so he can protect what is his. Every man must be diligent, so he may have something to call his own. And every man must be cunning, to prevent others from stealing what he has."

Despite everything that had happened, Orphan still knew those words his uncle made him recite. He didn't even hold a grudge against Gerfinn like he did with the rest of the Glimingars. For if nothing else his uncle gave him a direction to live by. And one that seemed to satisfy, as his body regressed back to the point before the question was asked. He still felt unbearably warm and his skin too tight, but the rest of his body felt… better than before. Stronger even.

"Then shall we have a ruler who is neither weak, indolent, nor a fool," Arcon declared, nodding approvingly. It stepped back, allowing Sorosma to advance for the next question.

"Does thou fear death?" Sorosma's voice was a haunting whisper, echoing through the cavern like the rustle of dry leaves. Suddenly, a vile rot began to consume Orphan's body, flesh clawing and peeling away as patches of corruption spread across his skin. The warmth that had bolstered him moments before was snatched away, replaced by a chilling emptiness that gnawed at his very core. Yet, amidst the encroaching decay, Orphan's response came swift and unwavering.

"No."

An almost palpable silence followed. Sorosma blinked its multifaceted eyes, taken aback by the immediacy and sincerity of his answer. "Oh… well then, that is settled," it murmured, retreating with a slight bow. The rot receded as quickly as it had come, leaving Orphan's body not only restored but purified. Any lingering impurities were purged; his blood flowed richer, his vitality enhanced. Disease would find no foothold in him now.

"Ha! Thou canst not even frame a question rightly, canst thou, Sorosma?" Carelena teased, a chittering laugh escaping its mandible-like mouth. Stepping forward with a flourish, it addressed Orphan. "Now 'tis our turn. What manner of Tyrant shalt thou be? Wilt thou skulk within shadows, weaving plots unseen, or stride boldly at the helm of grand legions?"

There was no mirror, but Orphan felt his features contorting, twisting into grotesque shapes. His skin stretched and bulged unnaturally, as though his very essence rebelled against him. It was an agony of identity, a corruption of self that struck deeper than physical pain. The urgency of the question pressed upon him. Unlike before, the answer did not spring readily to his lips.

He envisioned the archetypes of tyranny: the ruthless warlord drenched in the blood of foes, the cunning puppet master pulling strings from the shadows, the imperious king commanding obedience through sheer presence. One step. Each path held its allure and its perils. But Orphan had never confined himself to a single vision; his goal had always been singular to rise above, no matter the means. Two steps. Time was slipping, and he sensed the Fiends' patience waning.

"I'll be whatever gets me what I want," he declared, his voice steady despite the chaos within. It was the truth of his heart. Principles were tools, methods were means to an end. If deception served him, he would deceive; if brutality was required, he would be brutal. He had lived at the mercy of others' whims for too long. Now, he would claim his fate by any means necessary. A flicker of doubt sparked: was his answer too vague, too self-serving?

"Mmm… a candid reply," Carelena mused, its many eyes narrowing thoughtfully. "Thy resolve is admirable, yet remember: versatility is a weapon, but so is conviction. Do not shackle thy potential by clinging to a single guise."

As Carelena stepped back, the twisted sensation gripping Orphan's body began to ease. Orphan's body and face cracked back into place… or more accurately better into place. Before he knew that he was ugly, that had always been one of things the Glimingar liked to mock him with. But now… everything was far different than before. His skin took on the smooth pallor of polished ivory, the sickly paleness replaced with an otherworldly allure. The black veins that once marred his complexion became delicate tracings, like ebony filigree beneath the surface.

The quills that sprouted from his head arranged themselves into a dark, lustrous mane, sharp yet striking a crown befitting his emerging stature. Gone was the hideous fishy visage that he once had, now it was now perfectly human, not only that but perfectly symmetrical with nice little high cheekbones too. If one were to look upon this Cursed Born they might actually forgive him for that sin on his looks alone.

Only two more demons to answer. Lirochi was next and while usually her humanish face was that of concern and almost caring visage, now it was serious and judgmental.

"Thou aspirest to be a ruler; what wilt thou do unto those whom thou dost rule?" Everything felt so still and lifeless to Cursed Born. As if all the color in the world was bleeding any. But it wouldn't stop slowly even the outline of things started to blur into nothing. The question you idiot, answer it and it will stop!

"I… I…" He could barely hear his own voice as it vanished into the everything. Those under him. What would he do with them? He did not care overly about most people but that didn't feel like an acceptable answer. But this was the worst trial yet. It didn't hurt but it attacked the feeling of existing itself. All of reality was melting into this meaningless gray blob for Orphan. Quite a boring story for us to witness if it stayed like this. He had to say something. "Uh… um… no I got it. Like any craftsman with his tools, work them hard and well, but keep them in fine condition."

"Ugh… we suppose that is the best we can hope for at this moment." In a snap it all returned brighter and more vibrant. Even just touching the ground again Orphan could feel every edge and crease of the stone floor. The world itself felt more than it ever had been. He looked up to the last demon, the one that had been holding a spear tip to his face when he had woken up. What would this warrior ask of him?

"Have you killed yet?" Nothing happened. No traumatizing pain or earth-shattering ordeal. Just this question that Orphan knew he had the wrong answer for. These were demons, fiends of malice. Killing wasn't a question of morality to them. But he had come this far with the truth, can't start lying now.

"Not yet." Moments passed by and none of the Fiends took a step closer. Abezethibou just cocked its head to the side and sighed.

"Bare minimum he's not unwilling or making a fuss about killing. Enough for now." Like before nothing changed as far as the boy could tell. At least logically, but something in his soul did tell he was different now. Deep and primal, that he had changed after answering that question.

"It is done. With the blessings of Fortitude, Resilience, Guile, Sensation, and Instinct given! Our Lord hath been discovered! May he proceed to ascend as the Thirteenth Tyrant of this world. The Right of Sovereign shall be stirred, and now we shall discern if it shall be bestowed in entirety."

Words of the Fifth

Mother of failure, hush
Slothful echoes softly brush
Sleep soundly, in graves of dust

Audience of Monsters

"And he's out. By honest thought, we did not believe he could manage it," Carelena murmured, slithering over to the collapsed form of the new Heir Apparent of Gluttony. The Demon's head tilted, peering down at the boy's still-breathing body, where the residual effects of the metamorphosis rippled under his skin, a silent testament to the havoc that had been wrought.

"He survived by the skin of his teeth. You all felt that his answers to the last three questions were nigh unto lacking." Tis true, Arcon's complaints were not unwarranted. Its charge was valid, for there was no denying the boy's precarious footing. Each of the Fiends present had sensed the frailty in his responses, the uncertainty. He was standing on the edge of a precipice, saved by little more than sheer dumb luck. Ah, but what story doesn't grant its protagonist a few well-placed strokes of fortune? After all, aren't the most gripping tales filled with just such coincidences?

"A year and two months in the Pit," Sorosma remarked, its insect-like limbs twitching at the edge of the black tar lake. "A long time, by any measure. Speaks of conflict, of ambition clashing with fear." It fiddled absently with the edge of the pit, a finger tracing the blackened, inky depths from which they all had once emerged. Born of the raw Magic of Malice, Fiends were forever tethered to its depths. And every Tyrant… yes, every one of them had to survive their baptism in those same wicked waters. Afterall, can't have some sneaky virtuous-type trying to fake their way into power. No-no-no, only those with a selfish, callous, hateful heart can survive such a bath.

"He's young, and given what Lord Beelzebub said about his state when first approached the broodsire, he must not have had an easy life. At the very least must have suffered a traumatic event prior to finding us." The only one that seemed, 'Seemed', to be a caring and tender person, Lirochi. It had gathered several of the imps to begin prepping a suitable home further in the cave. The little darlings were so excited to be hosting so many of their elder kin and a possible new lord to serve.

"Enough!" Arcon's voice boomed, silencing the murmurs. It strode forward with heavy steps, the air shifting as it approached Orphan's prone form. Without a second thought, it hoisted the boy up, slinging him in its arms with graceful care. "Lord Beelzebub has departed. We cannot sustain it in a stable state with our current food supply. The boy is the Heir Apparent to Gluttony, and as such, we shall treat him as though he already holds dominion over us. Lirochi! Sorosma!"

"You can't-" Both began their complaining, but.

"Just do it." With three simple words, no more argument was brokered. The Demons all looked to Abezethibou as it lazed about at the shore of the Spawning Pit.

"Yes!" Both Demons snapped to attention, their deference immediate and unquestioning. To disobey Abezethibou would be to invite swift and merciless destruction. But Arcon took no time to waste to use this gifted authority.

"Make haste to the southern lands and spread word to our kin. Any fiend skilled in the arts of order, carpentry, or the craft of sustenance bring them hither at once. The swifter we establish our stores and provisions, the swifter shall Lord Beelzebub make his return. And seek also a demon steep'd in the vices of Greed or Lust, for their presence too shall be needed in this dark endeavor." The last request caught both Demons off guard, but they did not challenge the command. With no more words, they departed, slipping out of the cavern into the frozen wilderness beyond.

As for the ones who remained…

"Greed or Lust? What exactly are you planning, Arcon?" Carelena's curiosity laced its voice as it followed their kin deeper into the tunnels. Around them, Imps scurried in a chaotic dance, carrying scavenged materials, wood, metal, whatever they had plucked from the remains of dead Teuton caravans.

"The boy shall not endure till his Crowning, not with a Will so feeble as it doth now appear. We must immerse him deeper in the cravings that do already grip his soul. Indulgence, it seemeth, doth lie at the heart of his hunger; thus we must seek out the other Sins of Indulgence, that his desire may grow and his strength be forged." Arcon's tone was grim, a low rumble of consideration. All Fiends were intimately bound to the ebb and flow of the Magic of Malice. Born from it, they could feel its rhythms, its unspoken desires. Each of the eight Cardinal Points of Magic steered the world along a specific course, and Malice… well, Malice had its own direction. Fiends were its truest manifestation, creatures molded by the darkest aspects of power and desire.

"He arrived in a season of dire need, his responses lacking though they were, and with the favor of Lord Beelzebub," Arcon continued, its voice cool and contemplative. "There is promise, if properly nurtured." A twisted smile, not of warmth but of expectation. *And what wonderful teachers he has now. Beings of cruel hunger, inhumane to the extreme, and devoid of all sense of selflessness. After the scheming old drunk that was his uncle, this is sure to be quite a step up isn't it?*

"He is young, well young enough to be yet unfirm in his habits. And already he doth incline towards the ways of Malice." The excited giggle that came out of Carelena unnerved the other Demon more than one might believe.

Arcon debated if it should send out Carelena as well even as they finally reached their destination. The deepest part of the tunnels lay a cave, roughly hewn and beaten into shape over the past year. Crude by any mortal standard, yet it bore the vague semblance of a proper chamber wooden planks and beams, half-rotten and splintered, lined the stone walls and ceiling. Scattered throughout were pieces of furniture, damaged and worn, scavenged by the Imps from the remnants of Confederate caravans. It wasn't luxurious, not by any stretch, but it was far better than the miserable bunk Orphan had called his own for most of his life. And that, of course, was the point.

The furniture had been in better condition when it was first stolen. The Imps had easily plundered finer materials: wood from wagons, metal fixtures from looted camps, even rich fabrics from the dead. They could have crafted something far more suitable, especially with the skilled carpenters that traveled north under the new Governess's orders. It would have been simple to capture one of them, to force them to build a proper dwelling for the Heir of Gluttony. But that was not what the Demons wanted.

No, Orphan needed to crave more. He needed to be made to hunger for what had always been denied to him, to feel the sting of insufficiency, the yearning for power that could never be sated. It was a hunger that must be nurtured, fed, until it consumed him completely. What better way to instill that desire than to starve him of comfort, even in victory? What nasty-nasty little minds we have here, ey?

"When he doth awaken, then shall we begin to discern with what manner of will we are dealing," Arcon said, laying Orphan's limp form upon the shoddily made bed. The creaking wood barely supported his weight. "-We shall school him in the arts of administration and in matters of general learning. Carelena, thou shalt instruct him in the ways to comport himself as nobility steeped in Tyranny. And Abezethibou shalt train him in the art of war and combat."

They stepped back, a moment of silence passing between the two Fiends as they contemplated the odd reality of their situation. This young, fragile Cursed Born, this half-formed creature of potential, was now their liege an Heir to Gluttony and, possibly, the next Tyrant. Few ever claimed the title of Master of Sin, fewer still found a Seat of Power. Yet here lay a boy on the cusp of achieving both, the mountain looming above as his next conquest.

Not long ago, these Fiends had operated in isolation, each selfish in their desires. By their very nature, they craved more for themselves, as was the dictate of Gluttony. Food, wealth, power they wanted it all, and they wanted it without sharing.

But they were also a Swarm, bound to their broodsire, Lord Beelzebub. They would never disobey it. For now, their personal grudges and hungers would be set aside. Once Orphan took the mantle of Master of Gluttony, their selfish desires would transform into a brutal competition for glory, each Fiend seeking to bring honor to their lord's name whether on the battlefield or in the shadows. But until then, the Swarm of Ravenous Hunger had to focus on building its Hive.

And what of the boy around whom this Hive was being built? Did he dream, as he lay in unconscious repose?

Not quite. The images that flickered behind Orphan's eyes were more like memories than dreams, though they felt foreign, unfamiliar. In them, he was starving, his body caked in filth, and the world around him barely acknowledged his existence. He had nothing. No family. No friends. Nothing to call his own. The people in the temples, they had everything: wealth, food, power. And they kept it all for themselves, hidden behind grand walls, never sharing with the likes of them. But… this poor dirty little thing… it could steal… it did that all the time. And they were oh so desperate.

Orphan awoke drenched in sweat, gasping as though he'd just surfaced from drowning. The images from his dream or whatever it had faded quickly, leaving behind only the visceral feeling of desperation. A gnawing, hollow sensation. The kind of need that clung to your bones. That much, at least, was familiar. And so, he did what he always did when a nightmare came.

Not even registering where he was, as so ingrained was this ritual he had, he sought out the tools to write. A practice he had forced himself into to better teach himself how to be literate, and to make use of the terror of nightmares. Ever so practical Orphan had become. Thankfully, an ink quill and empty book lay on a less than pristine desk nearby. Quickly he jotted down a small poem, trying to make sense of what he saw. The words flowing out despite his mind barely understanding them.

> Orphans, widows, and cripples' pain
> Thieves in moonlight, shadows gain
> Gods forsake the crowns falling like rain

"Just a dream. Just a dream," he muttered to himself as he finished, though the words felt thin and unconvincing. Desperation wasn't something you could simply dream away. It clung to you, and deep down, he knew that.

Still catching his breath, Orphan finally took in his surroundings. The stark contrast to his last awakening was jarring. No opulent furs, no warmth of the Winterman's cave, this place was rough, bare, like a rundown cabin carved from the belly of the earth. A bed, simple and uncomfortable; a table and chair, all mismatched and worn; a small dresser topped by a cracked mirror, and a large cabinet that looked ominously big enough to hide a body. It was modest, bleak even, but compared to the life he'd known in Glimisvellir, it was a significant improvement. And that was the cruel irony of it better, but not enough.

Stare. His gaze locked on the cracked mirror, and he felt a jolt of recollection. The changes. Slowly, cautiously, Orphan pulled himself away from the desk and shuffled toward the mirror, unsure of what he'd see.

The reflection that greeted him was striking. Gone were

the fish-like features, the grotesque shapes that had always marked him as something other. His face was human now pleasant, even handsome though his eyes, hair, and skin still clung to an eerie inhuman beauty. The alien green of his eyes and the sharp quills that passed for hair now added an ethereal, almost regal quality. He no longer looked like the outcast, the thing people recoiled from. No, now his appearance could inspire awe or fear, something powerful enough to unsettle or captivate.

Yet beneath that beauty, his body remained the same slight and willowy, too thin and small for his age. He still looked frail, and by all rights, he shouldn't feel any different. But he did. Despite the reflection, he felt stronger, more solid, as if something deep within him had changed beyond mere appearances.

Still, he needed answers, and they wouldn't come from the mirror. Which is definitely why he didn't spend a half hour making poses in front of it, admiring this new version of himself. No, that didn't happen.

Pushing the door open, Orphan stepped outside and nearly jumped back at the sight of the five Imps waiting for him. It hadn't been that long ago that these creatures were the embodiment of nightmares, each one a potential death sentence for someone as weak as he had been. Yet here they were, not enemies, but… cheering? Hooping, hollering, clicking, and buzzing in their strange insectoid way. They chirped out praises, a cacophony of alien sounds mixed with familiar expressions.

He didn't have time to process it. Before he could say anything, the excitable little monsters were already ushering him along, pulling him toward the chamber of the Spawning

Pit. It had changed since he'd last been dragged there. The structures that filled the space were chaotic, like a fevered dream of ants, bees, and termites mashed together into a single twisted vision of architecture. Ramshackle scaffolding made of scrap and debris bolted onto the walls, with strange towers and shapes that only an inhuman mind could comprehend.

At the center of the madness stood a massive table, rough and crude, set before the shore of the Pit. The Imps corralled him there, depositing him at the table's edge with an odd sense of ceremony. Everything about this place, from the frantic movements of the Imps to the buzzing activity above, was alive with energy and industrial chaos, all centered around him.

For the first time, Orphan truly felt like he was at the heart of something much bigger than himself.

"You're awake," Abezethibou grumbled without lifting its gaze from the mess of crude maps strewn across the massive table. The Demon's mood was sour, its distaste for effort palpable. It was a creature built for hunger, not work, and anything resembling labor was met with disdain unless directly demanded by Beelzebub.

Orphan, still disoriented, glanced around. To his right, Arcon barked orders at groups of Imps, directing them as they built onto the chaotic hive-like structures. High above, Carelena hung lazily in a net, observing the frenetic activity below with the detached amusement of someone who had no intention of helping. The scene was a whirl of movement, every Imp scrambling with purpose, hauling logs, hammering nails, buzzing and clicking in their strange language.

"What is all this?" Orphan asked, his voice tinged with the assumption that their next step would be something grander, more immediate perhaps even a climb to claim his throne atop the mountain range. Yet, this felt like preparation for a siege, not an ascension.

"This is the only Spawning Pool of our brood for leagues," Abezethibou said, still not bothering to look up. "We must fortify it. It will serve as our base of operations, at least for now."

Orphan watched as more Imps dragged in a sled, its surface laden with tree logs and a fresh elk carcass. The air was thick with the sound of saws, hammers, and buzzing wings. It felt like a living organism, each part working in unison to survive. But to Orphan, it seemed far removed from what he had imagined. Where was the grandeur, the power he had been promised?

"But what about the Seat of Power?" he pressed, impatience creeping into his tone.

Abezethibou snorted, dismissing the question as if it were the ramblings of a naive child. "You have yet to fully claim power over even a single Sin, and you think you can claim a Seat of Power? No. You are still a spawnling, mewling and thrashing about in the dark."

The Demon finally looked up, fixing Orphan with a piercing stare. The moment stretched, tension pulling between them as Abezethibou sized him up. It noted the flicker of frustration on Orphan's face, the glimmer of ambition stirring beneath the surface. The boy was growing impatient, wonderful, but also dangerous if not controlled. The demon weighed its next words carefully. Should it stoke the fire of his ambition or encourage him toward a more measured path? Either could shape the boy's trajectory, but Abezethibou had no interest in holding his hand.

"Before you can claim a Seat of Power," the Demon continued, voice cold, "you must first be Crowned as Master of Gluttony. As of now, you are merely the Heir of Gluttony."

Orphan bristled. "What is with all these tests and steps? Seems a bit much for Fiends." His tone carried the faint edge of someone still adjusting to the idea that this was his new life, and not just some twisted game. He still saw Fiends through the lens of Imps simple, crude, and straightforward. And in that view, all these rituals and trials felt excessive.

Abezethibou's eyes narrowed, though it did not rise to the bait of offense. The boy's ignorance was expected. He was not like the Devil-bred nobility of Hell, who spent their lives preparing for the Path of Tyranny. No, this one was a half-starved, beaten wretch from the surface. He had no idea what he was stepping into.

"It is the great work of the Third Tyrant, he was born during the time after the gods had left and the world was still grasping in the chaos of their absence. He desired nothing more than to establish Order, and he did. The Magic of Malice operates on systems, rules, and authority." After all, that's what being a Tyrant is about, using absolute power to enforce your will upon the world. Doesn't it sound so nice, at the top of the ladder kicking everyone else down so you can maintain your stop. Ah... exhilarating.

"So what was that business with the questions about?" The pain and trauma still reverberated in his mind. Suffering had been an old friend to Orphan by this point but that time was different. Not only had he felt the worst physical pain in his life but he had felt himself at the edge of oblivion, the grotesque, and rot. His mind was quite rattled to say the least.

Abezethibou's gaze flicked toward him with a hint of irritation. "I see you actually have questions this time. That's… progress." It wasn't often that a potential Tyrant showed such humility. Most Devil-born aspirants were arrogant wretches, fully expecting the world to hand them a crown. But this one, this one had been battered by life, and while refreshing, it was also grating. Explaining things that should have been common knowledge to anyone with real ambition that was tiresome.

Orphan felt a pang of anxiety. This wasn't over yet.

"The Path of Tyranny," the Demon began, rolling its eyes like it was recounting the basics to a child, "begins when a Devil or Cursed Born displays traits an Archfiend finds favorable. That's the First Step. From the moment the candidate is chosen, they walk the Path, which only ends when they sit upon a Throne and claim their Title. The process, the systems, all of it stems from the Third Tyrant. The whole thing is a bloody ordeal, designed to weed out the weak and indecisive."

Orphan listened, trying to process the scale of what he was being told. He had only just survived the Trial, barely holding onto his life, and now he was learning it was just the beginning.

Abezethibou's tone remained flat as it continued. "The First Steps of the Path are what you've already gone through: becoming the Heir of a Sin. To do that, you had to find an Archfiend which you did, somehow and then survive the magic of Malice. That's what the Spawning Pool was your introduction to the raw power of Dark Magic. After that comes the Trials, which we administered. The purpose is simple: you're still soft clay, freshly warped by Malice. You're malleable, easy to shape. And each question we asked was designed to mold you if you survived."

"And the 'Gifts?" Orphan asked, remembering the pain that accompanied each question.

"The Gifts of Tyranny," Abezethibou explained, its voice filled with mild disdain. "Each question you survive gives you a change, usually useful, but not always. You got lucky with five. The last Tyrant endured twelve."

Orphan shivered at the memory. Five had nearly killed him.

"After the Trials comes the Crowning. That's when you officially become the Master of Gluttony. Right now, you're just the Heir. Beelzebub will crown you, and only then will you have full power over the Sin."

Orphan nodded, trying to take it all in. He had assumed surviving the Trials meant he was almost there but it was only the beginning.

"The Crowning… does it need a grand ceremony?"

Abezethibou chuckled. "Depends on the Archfiend. Some love the spectacle. Others… don't bother. But the crown's what matters. It marks you as their liege."

Orphan's mind raced. "How many Masters of Sin can exist at once?"

"As many Archfiends as there are in the world, that's how many Masters of Sin can exist. No more, no less. But by the time a Tyrant claims their Throne, they'll often have control over more than one Sin. Gluttony, Greed, Lust all of them, if they're ambitious enough. But don't get ahead of yourself. You're lucky you've moved through the process this fast. Most take years to even find an Archfiend. And finding a Seat of Power? There are few left in the world, and they're dwindling."

Orphan's brow furrowed as Abezethibou's words sank in. This world of power and dominion was far more structured than he had imagined, and far more perilous.

"And if a Tyrant falls?" Orphan asked, almost dreading the answer.

"If a Tyrant falls, their Seat of Power is usually destroyed, declared corrupted. It's why there are so few left. Tyrants don't just die, they leave scars on the world."

"And why can't I be Crowned right now?" Orphan's voice carried frustration after enduring the lengthy lecture. The sheer complexity of the rules and rituals from the Third Tyrant left him reeling, but before he could catch up, the Demons burst into mocking laughter. Heat rose in his chest.

"One, because Lord Beelzebub has left us. Its presence would exhaust our resources. Two, you're far from ready. You've much to learn, and even I know you aren't prepared yet." The frustration flared higher. Orphan's anger was a tangled mess aimed at the demon for belittling him, at Glimisvellir for keeping him weak, and at himself for his own inadequacy. "What can you even do?"

"I, uh… I know some herbalism and botany. I'm skilled at hiding… Oh, and I know Seidr with Majorus in Life and Minorus in Water," he stammered, listing his meager skills. He'd never learned to fight or read extensively just enough to scrape by. Oh wait, tell them about your wordcraft, I'm sure that they would love to hear all about that.

"Magic's a start. Life, Water, Malice, Blood… Fleshcraft. At least you've got potential," Abezethibou muttered, unimpressed. "But it's barely a foundation."

"I don't have three Magic Points. No one does." Orphan was aware that Life and Water combined into Blood, but he'd never dared to try learning more.

"Those Marked by Fate do. It's called Optimus. Scourges, Warlocks, Tyrants… They wield Dark Magic, while Heroes and Saviors use Virtue Magic." The titles flew over Orphan's head; his sheltered life hadn't prepared him for the complexity of the world beyond Glimisvellir. "But that's not relevant now. You won't be learning magic yet. We'll start with combat, leadership, and social skills. You'll need them for the next few years."

"Years?!" Orphan's pulse quickened. After accepting death, the sudden expanse of time stretching before him felt overwhelming, precious, yet stifling. The anger bubbled beneath the surface.

"I'd say ten to twelve years until your Throne-Day. That's time enough for training, acquiring Artifacts, mastering another Sin or two, and building your Court." More alien terms. The wider world's scale was beginning to crash down on Orphan, filling him with a growing sense of inadequacy and confusion.

"I don't really understand what you're saying, but I want to learn. I want to get stronger. There's no way I'm getting everything I want in this world staying the way I am." Orphan's voice was firm, determination edging out confusion. Abezethibou had returned to scrutinizing the crude maps sprawled across the table but glanced up at Orphan's words. The words themselves sounded quite humble didn't they. Humble. Whoever said a Tyrant needed to be humble?

"Ha! At least he admits his own foolishness. Who is the wee savage bumpkin? Thou art, indeed," Carelena cackled, descending slowly from the cavern ceiling, lowered by interlocking web strings. Inch by inch, it hovered above Orphan, lazily twirling a clawed finger through his hair. "By the Fourth's rusted hooves, thou hast such vast potential. Young and impressionable art thou, yet thou shalt ne'er advance unless thou dost accomplish thy tasks!"

"Though coarse, we do assent to thy reasoning. He must be fashioned in the proper ways of his own kin." Arcon walked down the shaky bit of stairs to finally join the rest of those in the cave capable of speaking in coherent sentences. "As matters lie presently, he can accomplish naught to further the cause."

"Hey." Just because he was willing to learn and admit he was pretty far behind didn't mean his feelings couldn't be hurt. Hahaha.

"Further the cause? We suspect all he might do is serve as our pet cleric, tending to our scrapes and cuts. How pitiable! What can anyone expect from such a weak and frail frame? Even after the Trials, thou still appear'st half dead." Carelena's laughter rang out, and even Arcon chuckled quietly. The cavern amplified their mirth, and soon a chorus of chittering laughter from thousands of Imps filled the air.

This was different from the mocking he'd endured in Glimisvellir. The townsfolk's jeers and his uncle's cruel laughter had always been background noise. But this collective ridicule struck a nerve deep within him. Mocking him on one of his greatest prides and his greatest shames all at once. His magic was his, nothing could take that away. Heal had saved him and he could do it faster and better than nearly anyone else. To reduce him to only that made his magic feel all the more shallow. Then in the next breath remind him of his body. Oh his body that had been crushed, starved, and stunted. Of course it was a sore spot for him. Beyond sore really, more like a festering wound that cut very deep indeed.

These monsters that did nothing but steal and feast on the land that didn't belong to them. They were the locust swarm that ate everything in sight. Bottom feeders and scavenger, but somehow they thought they were above him? These insects, like ants he would crush under his foot. They were laughing at him. Wasn't he supposed to be their master now in all but official name? Did their broodsire not tell them all that their purpose now was to Help him. This did not feel like help at all no sir.

"Enough!" Orphan's shout sliced through the cacophony. For the first time in his life, he let his anger boil over. "I'm supposed to be in charge here! I'm not going to let you two bugs make fun of me. I know there's a lot I need to learn, but I'm still the one calling the shots! Your Archfiend told you I'm in charge, so what I say goes! The rest of you are no better! And you..."

He turned his glare toward Abezethibou, but his fury began to wane under the Demon's piercing gaze. Oh, you did the bad thing brat, you invoked a name that others are far more loyal to than your own. The primal fear he felt upon first seeing the Winterman resurfaced, chilling him to the core. Abezethibou's eyes bore into him, and the air grew heavy.

The demon's voice, once modulated for human ears, now resounded like a million echoing reverberations layered upon one another, forming words that felt more like vibrations than sound. "I am over seven centuries old, boy, and have seen Tyrants rise and fall. I was among the first clutch of Imps spawned by Lord Beelzebub when it ascended to Archfiend. I alone here hold its authority!"

With a swift motion, Abezethibou slammed its clawed fist onto the table, cracking it in half. The splintered wood shattered as the Demon stepped through the debris toward Orphan, who stood frozen. Without hesitation, Abezethibou grasped Orphan's neck, lifting him effortlessly off the ground. "You are but an Heir, not a Master! But if you wish to become a Tyrant swiftly, I shall give you one and only one requirement to become Master of Gluttony. Fulfill this task, and I will seek out Lord Beelzebub to crown you the very next day."

Orphan struggled to breathe, his hands gripping the demon's wrist. Fear coursed through him, but he managed to choke out, "Fine then… I've been getting by well enough. What is it?"

Abezethibou's gaze remained unyielding. "Conquer your place of birth. Subjugate Glimisvellir."

"What?"

Words of the Sixth

Lustful flames ignite
Passions' dance in the night
Fire's embrace, all is right

A Brief Intermission

Conquering Glimisvellir was not an impossible task. In fact, Orphan's Path to Tyranny would inevitably lead him back to his birthplace sooner rather than later. Beyond the personal symbolism that subjugating the town held for the Cursed Born, Glimisvellir was also the closest settlement to his future Seat of Power. Its domination was essentially a stepping stone he couldn't afford to ignore. But therein lies the problem.

Glimisvellir, in the year since Orphan's departure, had not been idle. It had become both an investment and a passion project for one of the Confederacy's three Heads of State. The town's walls and many buildings were not only repaired but enhanced using superior techniques. Colonists from the south brought with them advancements of the new era: steel rebar, mass-produced concrete, and other innovations that transformed the once-isolated village into a burgeoning hub of activity. The more that came, the Glimingars both cautiously accepted the newcomers and chafed at the new. A bunch of staunch traditionalists that prided themselves on not changing suddenly had an influx of people that were oh so very excited with the progress of the modern day. But the money helped.

How did they pay for all this? Glimisvellir had no real worth to the continent spanning empire in terms of economics… or did it? Hmm… lots of mountains. What could be in them one could wonder. Iron. The answer is a lot of iron. Yes! Prospectors from the south came in droves as the fabled untouched Glimisvellir mountain range was vast and untapped. Ripe for exploiting or in the nicer way of putting it, development. That had been the most recent of news to come to the Glimingaric markets.

"They say there might even be silver and other precious metals I've never heard of,"

"I don't care what they find, so long as these utlanders keep buying my stock,"

"They pay well enough, even if they do complain a lot."

"Most of them seem decent folk,"

"Just wish there weren't so many of them."

As one of the Them, Lady Rinelt Delacroix walked through the market accompanied by two of her guards. Ignoring the dirty stares of the natives and the curious glances of the early colonists from the south. A larger garrison had been established with forces from the Confederacy and along came with them trailblazers and camp followers. Those that smelled profitable ventures and those that sought a new life perhaps. The Glimingar had no say in whom could stay and who would be shut out. That was up to the new Jarl and Governess.

"Heard another hunting party just vanished into the woods." One of her guards muttered to the other from behind. It was indeed becoming a problem, at first it was thought that they were escaping to form a rebel outfit to continue the fight. But… it never came. A year and there had been no attempt to mount a counter-attack on the occupation. Rinelt knew it wasn't because they had done such an amazing job at convincing the locals. No, based on the amount of caravan attacks they have suffered she suspected that the local Fiend population was starting to get to critical levels.

"Can't lose anymore, we barely have enough stores of food as it is. And none of the lads know how to hunt in this godsforsaken wasteland." Glimisvellir was the size it was for a reason, larger than perhaps one might expect from an isolated mountain village, but it got by. Food was always a carefully maintained matter for the Glimingar, hunting just enough, foraging their vast wilderness carefully, and monthly trips down to the sea to fish a mighty haul. But now the population was excessively in excess.

"Both of you hush, once news of the iron veins reach the South every prospector and magnate in the Confederacy will be pouring in capital and supplies." It was logical thinking on her part. With the rapid industrialization of the major powers, their factories and furnaces were ever hungry for more ore. A new source of iron and hopefully coal would bring in another wave of steelworks and thus... ugh... economy. All so very overcomplicated in my ever-so humble opinion dear Listener. The more money one has, the more grubby hands want to dip into your pocket and the more lies you hear every which way.

Nevertheless, matters of economy were not on the Governess' mind this day. It was a matter of culture. The Soarlands had it, but it was wrong. Very wrong. In the minds of the respectable and powerful men and women of the halls of power in the Confederacy you could not get more wrong than a Soarling barbarian. They were everything that the rest of the civilized world was trying to leave behind. Even the Devils of Hell had nobility and class to them. Rinelt was given a task by her Head of State and cousin to find a peer in the Soarlands and she would accomplish this. Turning this backwater and savage land into something akin to a modern nation worthy of Statehood. Maybe.

"I had better be given back my place at court for his cousin, this is far more than just a passing caprice." The Lady muttered under her breath as she ascended the steps to the elevated platform where the Church stood. The early morning light cast long shadows, and the area was deserted, no surprise, since it wasn't a day of sermon. Only the most devout, those inclined to spend their days praying to gods who had abandoned them long ago, would be around; they were few indeed. Still, the church had changed significantly since the shift in leadership.

No longer just a small temple, it had been transformed into a grand house of worship capable of comfortably accommodating a couple hundred people. The main building was a large dome adorned with four stained glass windows at the cardinal points north, south, east, and west each depicting one of the four elements of nature. At the center of the dome rose the spire tower, its windows artistically illustrating the Divine Cardinal Points of Life, Light, Death, and Dark. Flanking the structure were four smaller towers placed, of course, at the compass points. The Church of the Orphaned World was nothing if not thematically consistent. And out in front was a young girl coming into womanhood, sweeping the front and doing everything to not be inside.

"What do you want, it's not the best of times. The old

man is in another one of his moods." Brune sighed as she watched the three foreigners approach. The girl had been living here since its construction, and she wasn't alone. If one were to push open the heavy doors, and walk through the empty pews, you would need to deftly avoid the busy clerics scurrying between the five tower entrances. They had arrived weeks after the town had been absorbed into the Confederacy, pressuring Gerfinn and the governess to build this new church. Why allocate so many resources to a place of worship that most of the town's residents, both old and new, didn't take seriously? Because, until the recent discovery of iron deposits, the Church of the Orphaned World had been Glimisvellir's biggest source of new money. Their quest to explore the mountains in search of the mythical World Tree had funneled great wealth into the town's coffers.

"I'm not here for Eberulf, I'm here for you ma chère. Might we talk inside?" Genuinely trying to connect with a teenager rarely ends well for anyone at the best of times. But maybe it was the fact Brune hadn't been spoken to so kindly in quite a while that softened the girl's attitude.

Life had grown unbearably dull for Brune since Orphan had left town and in such a spectacular fashion, too, killing the chief like that. The only thing she held against him was that he hadn't taken her with him. Admittedly, it would have been impossible under the circumstances, but a girl could dream. No one else understood her the way he did. Even if he disapproved of much of who she was, there had been a kinship between them, a shared sense of otherness as the black sheep among the Glimingar.

Even Jorund had abandoned her, choosing to conform rather than stand apart. Their harrowing encounter with the Winterman had scared him straight, it seemed. After Orphan's escape and the Confederacy's arrival, Jorund became a dutiful son, helping his parents and staying out of trouble. He refused to associate with her anymore. The last time they spoke, he'd shouted that she was going to get him killed one day with her antics. It… hurt her more than she ever would admit.

Things only got worse after her mother had died, made even worse by the awful rumors that she had killed the poor woman. Now, her mother was at the bottom of the stairs and Brune happened to be at the top of them. And yes, there had been shouting between them moments before. But no-no-no, it was all just a big misunderstanding. Certainly, that's what Brune told everyone when they found the body. Thankfully for some reason people did nothing about it despite the fact she knew that she should have been jailed and tried by the Jarl. That had been the law since forever. That did not happen, however. Instead everyone just up and agreed that she now should live with the town's priest, a safe and pious life.

"Sure, I have to get dinner ready anyway." She led the three back behind the main structure and to a hidden away door that led into the private quarters of the church's bishop. Without even a care to Eberulf's privacy, Brune let the Governess in while her two guards waited outside. Though with a quick pass of her hand, one of them passed over a coil of rope to the noble lady.

"What a dedicated man," Lady Delacroix remarked softly, her voice melodic, yet laced with quiet judgment as she took a seat at the simple table in the middle of the room. "Taking in the sister of the town's sole Hero. Quite the charitable type, n'est-ce pas?" She hummed to herself, her contentment undisturbed as Brune handled a basket of food on the table. Brune, for her part, said nothing as she unpacked the groceries.

The two women had never spoken before, though they were aware of each other. Brune knew of Lady Delacroix as the woman who supposedly ruled over the Soarlands. In truth, the governess's control was limited to Glimisvellir and a few of the southern Soarling villages. Brune had overheard Teuton soldiers mention how the Confederacy was dragging its feet on fully declaring war on the Soarlands, but none of it affected her personally. Outsiders, to Brune, were simply strangers with their own ways, eager to impose their changes on the Glimingar.

Lady Delacroix, however, had her own thoughts about Brune. Thoughts she kept to herself, waiting for the right moment. The silence stretched on as Brune began preparing some bread and salted fish, her movements sharp and deliberate.

"Not going to offer anything to your guest, mademoiselle? No manners, I see," Lady Delacroix commented lightly, though her tone held a teasing edge.

In response, Brune brought the knife down with a loud thunk, severing the fish's head. Her expression remained stony as she continued preparing her meal. Living with Eberulf had its perks, decent cutlery being one of them. But still, she harbored a deep resentment for this man not least because living with him had forced her to learn all the domestic skills expected of girls: cooking, cleaning, sewing, and more. Eberulf refused to do any of these tasks. Initially, he claimed such chores were beneath him, but lately, she believed he just found some sort of joy in making her work.

"Come now, I've done nothing to warrant this silent treatment, non?" Lady Delacroix said, undeterred.

"Just don't have anything to say to you, is all," Brune replied coolly. These days, she had little to say to anyone. Most of the town saw her as a murderer, a reputation built on baseless rumors. Yes-yes, quite baseless indeed. The rest were outsiders, and like the Glimingar, they didn't care for outspoken women like her.

"Really? Everyone seems to have something to say to me these days. Quite novel that you don't, ma fille" the governess mused, silence followed again, broken only by the sounds of Brune's knife against the fish and the occasional clink of porcelain. Not tea offered, the Lady was right… no manners at all.

People talk, people gossip, and if you were to listen in you would hear quite a few naughty things. That day by day, more and more individuals whom held no loyalty to the Governess found themselves in town. Money and schemes were creeping in like thorny vines with bright red roses dotting them. Pretty petals bloomed on sharp spikes like pretty words were spoken by lying mouths. Rinelt knew that her power was eroding by the day unless she showed results and built her own powerbase. But it could only come from the locals, any support she had back home would only make the situation worse and none of the other foreigners were options either.

Minutes passed in this uneasy equilibrium. Brune plated her meal and, to Rinelt's mild surprise, placed it in front of the governess before seating herself with her own portion. She dug in without ceremony, entirely indifferent to the noblewoman across from her.

"You truly don't care what others think of you, do you?" Lady Delacroix asked, the question more of an observation.

"Not these people. Not you. Certainly not the asshole who thinks the gods look back only for him," Brune answered, tearing off a piece of bread without looking up. Her mind was already wandering to the tasks she had to complete later and the possibility of sneaking out of town. "But why are you here? What do you want with me?"

"Is it not obvious?" Lady Delacroix replied, her gaze never leaving the diamond the rough before her. If she could turn this pariah into the very model of what women of this nation could aspire to be then everything could start falling into place. That was what nobility was for at the end of the day, to be the goal of the peasants. To be the top of the ladder, after all the top of said ladder needs to be worth the climb, ey? "I'm taking you under my wing, so to speak. A winter rose like you will wilt under such poor care."

Brune blinked, incredulous. The absurdity of it. This rough and uncouth rebel becoming the student of a highly refined woman such as this? The audacity of it. The scandal it would cause in the courts of the southern nations. But that was partly the point now isn't it? Too bad Brune isn't able to see just how deliciously devious this move is.

"You're going to try to make me into some fancy lady like you? Piss off," Brune snapped, her voice brimming with defiance. She had her own plans. Gather enough money, stock up on preserved food, and make her way south, find a víkingr crew willing to take on someone so young and become a skjaldmær. She'd heard rumors of women fighting along-side men down in the lowlands, and anything was better than staying in Glimisvellir, where sooner or later someone would force her hand. She'd be blamed for whatever followed, just like always.

"Not like me," Lady Delacroix corrected, her voice gentle but firm. "Nothing like me. I want you to become more like the real you. Beneath all the dirt and that youthful bravado is a woman who could lead the charge for the changes coming to the Soarlands."

Brune scoffed, but Lady Delacroix's words lingered in the air. The absurdity of the situation was undeniable, but so too was the governess's conviction.

The First Citizen of Neustria, one of the Three Heads of State, was the mastermind behind the Confederacy's expansion into the Soarlands. Lady Delacroix had been sent by him, along with the Inner Council of Prime Citizens, with a singular mission: to elevate the Soarlands into a near-equal of the other States within the Confederacy. The reason? Ideology.

In a world where the gods had long abandoned their thrones, mortals no longer waged wars over faith, but over ideals. For centuries, the battlefield had been split between those who followed the path of the Tyrants, fueled by Malice, and those who knelt before Saviors, exalting Righteousness. Unfortunately for the villainous despots who thrived on Malice, their influence had waned in recent years. Yet mortals, being what they were, continued to fight like rabid dogs over meat and bones.

Democracy. Autocracy. Communism. Republicanism. Monarchy. Blah-blah-blah... so much yelling over how best to abuse and use the poor hungry man in the field and factory. But! It was the world we have now. The Third Republic of Neustria was of course... a republic. As was the League of Vítelíú Cities. Meanwhile the Imperial Empire of Teutonreach was thoroughly an Autocracy led by an Emperor. Each of these Savior Nations were powerful in their own right but for right now the balance of power between these forces was depressingly even. Men that like to rub their hands while cackling madly worked their own magics. And it would not stay that way forever. That was where Glimisvellir and the Soarlands came into the picture, a new counterweight and piece on the board.

The Soarlands had the history, the martial traditions, sheer size, and now a possible economic boom. It appeared as a possible peer if handled correctly. All that stood in their way was the savage nature of the Soarlands. It was still very underdeveloped and a cultural backwater in the eyes of so many other nations. This had to be rectified. But the trick was, the Soarlands' culture couldn't be replaced or else it would just be seen as an extension of whomever replaced them. No-no-no, the Soarlands needed to evolve and become something new but ultimately itself.

"Then you want me to become this new kind of Soarlands noblewoman?" Brune asked, her skepticism laced with a hint of intrigue. After Lady Delacroix's detailed explanation, she found herself more interested than she had anticipated.

"Yes," Lady Delacroix replied smoothly. "Gerfinn and I have discussed this at length, voyez-vous. The changes that are coming to Glimisvellir need to be carefully guided, so that the Glimingar can be elevated as a model for all the Soarlings. As Glimisvellir advances, as it industrializes, the men will need their own example to follow. Gerfinn has already begun preparing himself for that role. I must say," she added with a sly smile, "I've enjoyed the results of his exercises."

Brune frowned slightly, her attention wandering back to the view of the meager food in front of her. Her priestly caretaker lived simply, and had enforced this lifestyle on her. It was a lucky day if she got anything but bread and small bits of meat. But the Lady Delacroix continued, "But a paragon for the women is needed. It cannot be me, I'm another utlander as your people are so ready to call us southerners. But you?" She let the question hang in the air.

The very earliest memory that she had was her mother just standing there, staring blankly forward… doing nothing. A haunting thing to remember for a little girl and one that made her want to just keep moving. She could never sit still during her lessons with the other girls and constantly ran off to just do anything but stay still. It evolved to playing with the older kids who humored her for a time, letting her play in their games as a novelty. But eventually they told her to stop coming around and go back to her lessons on how to be a pleasant little girl, then the games turned to fights. More and more she fell into the need to rebel and reject the stagnation of the Glimingar.

Could she change them? The idea was almost amusing. After a lifetime of others trying to mold her, the thought of turning the tables was appealing. But she was wise enough to understand that Lady Delacroix wasn't suggesting she remain exactly as she was now. Refinement was part of the equation.

"I'm not wearing a dress," Brune stated firmly.

Lady Delacroix smiled. "Oh, don't worry. We'll work on that ma chère."

"And I want that fancy food you rich people eat too."

"Certainly, once you have perfected your table manners." Rinelt smiled feeling confident for the first time in several weeks. This was one piece of a larger puzzle she and Gerfinn needed to solve if they were to achieve anything here. And what was that poor excuse for a herbalist and Jarl doing?

The other half of the town's leadership carried on with his own duties or rather, he was supposed to be. Gerfinn, Jarl by title if not entirely by merit, was in the training yard instead of handling his responsibilities. Surrounding him were three of the town's best warriors, two locals and one Neustrian, all towering, broad-shouldered men. They were only the best because the true warriors of Glimisvellir had long since departed, leaving behind the remnants to carry on the town's honor.

A warhammer crashed into Gerfinn's side, his body splintering like rotted wood. His form scattered into soft, crumbly chunks across the ground, decaying almost instantly into a bed of mushrooms. From the largest of these fungi, an arm sprouted, followed by the rest of Gerfinn as he reformed, pulling himself out of the earth. His little trick had been revealed early on, ever since a disgruntled Glimingar had hurled a spear at him during a feast. The same spear had skewered him to no effect. There was a reason Eberulf had given up trying to kill him.

"You rely too much on your Seidr," Grumbled the man with the warhammer, resting the weapon's shaft on his shoulder as he loomed over the still-reforming Gerfinn. "If you ever want real respect from the people, you'll need to learn how to fight without it."

This warrior, broad and imposing, was Hanef. Beside him stood his nearly identical twin brother, Hring, both of them giants even among the Glimingar. Hring hefted his own warhammer and brought it down with a crash, once again shattering Gerfinn into pieces. The remains quickly dissolved into the ground, as before.

"To be fair, brother," Hring said in a lighter tone, watching as more mushrooms sprouted. "He has been trying to bulk up. You could be a little more encouraging."

"Hring."

"Yes Hanef?"

"Shut the fuck up."" Hanef retorted, his voice as cold as his demeanor. The two of them, though fearsome in appearance, posed no true threat to Gerfinn's leadership. Hring was too much of a follower, content to echo his brother's commands, while Hanef lacked any patience for the people of Glimisvellir. Neither of them had the temperament nor the ambition to lead, leaving Gerfinn secure in his position, despite his... obvious shortcomings.

"He's making progress with his body," said the third man, stepping forward with a smirk, "but his spirit? That still needs work."

The last of the men was the oddest one out. Also a hulking behemoth, but this one was far from the Glimingars' normal sense of style. Instead of heavy furs and leather straps this one was clad in a pastel blue dress uniform that only allowed limited movement... if it were not ripped at the joints as it was. Not only that but there was also a definite contrast in the faces. The twins had a classical rugged scared look to them meanwhile this outsider had regal noble features with caked on white powder and soft blue eye shadow and lipstick. Odd fashion contrasts here certainly.

"I haven't spent my life eating piles of meat and wrestling

bears like you bastards!" Gerfinn snapped, his body reform- ing once more from the earth. While his regenerative ability spared him from the permanence of death or even pain, the sensation of being torn apart and scattered was deeply unpleasant, something more akin to an instinctive revulsion than physical agony.

"A bear of a different kind, perhaps," the Neustrian quipped with a sly grin, earning groans from both Hanef and Hring.

"Fuck! Why couldn't I have gotten the Life Majorus like that little shit? There's a gods-damned spell in that set that just gives you abs. Turns your body into an Adonis no need to eat, sleep, shit, or even breathe. You still can, but you don't have to! Damnit, that would be useful right about now." Gerfinn's voice rang out in frustration as his body finished reforming, the scattered chunks of his being pulling together once again. Despite his repeated efforts, the results were underwhelming. He was healthier now, at least no longer the frail, skinny drunk he had once been but far from the idealized Glimingish warrior-chief he needed to become. Years of indulging in vice had destroyed the body he once had, the one he used to crack skulls and loot villages.

"There are no shortcuts to a great physique," the powdered Neustrian added, striking another exaggerated pose to show off his own grotesquely perfected muscles. "But we'll keep at it, until your body's almost as perfect as mine." His words dripped with arrogance, his display over-the-top and theatrical. Hanef, rolling his eyes, turned his back on the peacocking foreigner when his brother joined in the clownery. He had no patience for such antics.

"Ignore the fools for a minute," Hanef said as he sat down on a nearby bench, his tone gruff. "We got news just before we started training that another caravan from the south was hit by Fiends. It's becoming routine now." He cracked his neck and scratched his beard, looking grim. The supply line from the south had become critical to the expanded population of Glimisvellir. The influx of people, the new demands on the town none of it could be sustained without the steady flow of resources from southern farms. Before all this, the Glimingars had managed their resources carefully, ensuring they never outgrew what their harsh land could support. Now, the town's rapid growth was pushing them to their limits.

Gerfinn sighed, his expression hardening. "Packs of Greed wolves and the occasional Cursed Tree of Envy that's all we had to worry about before. Sure, there was the occasional surge, but nothing like this. Until the Curse of Wrath and along with it small swarms of bugs started popping up it's never been this bad." The Soarlands had always been a harsh, inhospitable place. Only the heartiest or those suited for the cold could thrive. Unfortunately humans are too stubborn and pig headed to get the hint and settled here anyways.

"The southerners' guns have made dealing with cave bears and mountain lions easy enough," Hanef grumbled. "But these Fiends? They're tougher. Smarter."

"We haven't even found the Spawning Pit yet. What really worries me is how coordinated these little bastards are. I'm starting to think one of them might've evolved into a Demon." The tension in Gerfinn's voice was unmistakable. A Demon in the wilds? That was a nightmare waiting to happen. One Fiend becoming a Demon could spell disaster for the entire region. The difference between dealing with scattered Imps and facing an organized force under a Demon's command was staggering.

"If that's true, we're in deep shit," Hanef replied, his expression dark. "I just hope it's a new Demon and not an older one that followed the southerners here. Either way, you're probably the only one left who can survive a fight with it."

"Yeah… guess it's all on me then," Gerfinn muttered, more to himself than to the others. Better not to push back against their view of Hlodvir; it worked in his favor, after all. "We'll set a trap. Even if it's a Demon, it's still a bug. Pile up enough food in one place, and it'll come sniffing around."

"That's the problem," Hanef shot back. "We don't have enough food. You and the Governess have done a lot, but it's not enough. More people are coming in every day, and we can't feed them all." He looked over at the other two, his annoyance growing. "Are you two still posing?!"

Hanef stormed toward the Neustrian and his brother, their ridiculous muscle-flexing continuing without shame. Meanwhile, Gerfinn remained by the bench, thinking over the situation. The threat of Fiends had become more than just an inconvenience; it was a danger that could unravel everything they were working toward. And now, with the possibility of a Demon in the wilds, it seemed the stakes were higher than ever.

The problems were mounting, and Fiends were only one part of the growing disaster. Gerfinn sighed as he trudged back toward the Great Hall, contemplating the many layers of chaos they faced. His lady friend often said that society was just three meals away from collapse, and it was a sentiment he was beginning to agree with. Together, they had used all their magic to cultivate edible mushrooms and fast-growing crops but they didn't have the land or soil for large-scale farming. Feeding the population was becoming more difficult by the day.

But food scarcity wasn't the only issue.

This grand experiment the Confederacy wanted to conduct in the Soarlands was flawed from the start. They thought they could turn the north into a reflection of their own culture by playing nice, sending troops when needed, sure, but mostly relying on money, infrastructure, and the southern way of life to bring the Soarlings into the fold. Cities, factories, governance, peace… It all sounded nice, but they were ignoring the fundamental truth of the Soarlands: it was being forced on them by people incapable of taking the necessary cruel steps to truly force an entire culture to change.

Gerfinn had traveled as a youth, and he'd seen firsthand what the rest of the Soarlands was like. There were two kinds of people in the north: the reasonable ones, who understood the importance of hard work and family bonds but kept that decency reserved for their own; and the unreasonable ones, who only tolerated each other because survival required strength in numbers. The core of Soarling culture was simple: might makes right, and whatever you can take is yours.

The Glimingar knew that back in the Age of the Gods, the Soarlings had a semblance of order, tightly bound to the gods' decrees. But for the past three thousand years, they had lived as they wished, free from divine rule. In the eyes of the Glimingar and Gerfinn himself the Soarlings were little more than selfish children who refused to share their toys.

"Gods long gone, I need a drink." The monumental task before them felt impossible, even if it wasn't theirs to achieve alone. He ignored the sounds of the twins sparring in the training yard and made his way into the Great Hall. A few people were scattered about, eating or chatting idly, but most didn't acknowledge him. Why respect the town drunk just because he now sat in the big chair?

He slammed the door to his bedchamber behind him, making his disdain for their indifference known. Gerfinn hadn't bothered moving into the Jarl's quarters; those were now claimed by his lover, the lady of the Soarlands. He had spent years cultivating this space to his liking and wasn't about to abandon it. Without thinking, he began gathering ingredients, making tonics for rashes and hives. His hands moved automatically, the motions familiar, reflexive. At one point, he reached out to swat at a phantom head that once would have been peering over the cauldron Orphan's head.

He missed the boy. It was a strange truth, but undeniable. Orphan had been an excellent outlet for Gerfinn's frustrations, a convenient whipping boy. And more disgustingly, there were some nagging icky feelings of familiarity and bond that only proved itself stronger than he thought once Orphan was gone. The search parties had found nothing, no body, no trace. Just rumors of wolves, Imps, or even a cave bear from further north dragging him away. He had tried to find the boy, but eventually, they had to give up.

"Now don't you look lost in your work," came a soft, familiar voice from behind, wrapping around him like silk. "Thinking about me?"

A smile tugged at his lips as he felt his lover's arms snake around his waist. "No. Something a bit paler and uglier than you. How'd it go with Brune? The little lynx didn't turn you down, did she?" The idea of turning that wild tomboy into some strange hybrid of noble lady and shieldmaiden was ridiculous to him, but as long as it didn't interfere with his own plans, he wouldn't oppose it.

"She agreed," Lady Delacroix replied with a sly smile. "So you owe me a foot rub later mon cher."

Gerfinn rolled his eyes but couldn't help the warmth that spread through him at her teasing. His attention shifted when he noticed the letter in her hand. "But we've had news. It's not just the Fiends making trouble."

He frowned, taking the letter. "News from court or from the church?"

"It's worse the Havi."

The ladle slipped from his hand, clattering onto the floor. "Which one?"

Her lips curved into a tight line. "The Havi of Horga."

Gerfinn cursed under his breath. It was the worst possible one. The current ruler of Horga, the largest port and strongest castle in the Soarlands wasn't just brutal. He was smart. But worst of all, he had a history with Gerfinn.

Ripping open the letter, Gerfinn read the details with mounting dread. "He wants tribute. Thirty carts of processed iron, ten barrels of pickled fish, five carts of Gluttony Fiend Coal, and three women every month. In exchange, he won't attack us. Grieving souls, Värmod, that'd make a wolf blush from the greed." His hand tightened on the letter, and then, with a growl of frustration, he tore it to pieces. They barely had the iron mines ready, let alone the forges. The Glutton Fiends were a problem too, but nowhere near the scale needed to meet this demand. The pickled fish and women? Insults. Värmod knew Glimisvellir's fish was garbage, and Gerfinn suspected the man was taunting him with the demand for women.

"You know this man?" Lady Delacroix asked, her eyebrow raised as she sauntered toward him. She could tell he had been startled, his hands were shaking with emotion. A rising mix of fear and rage boiled in the man.

Gerfinn sighed. "He was my captain, he sought out those with Seider for his crew. He was… a worthy man to follow. But I had enough of the Soarlings as a whole, so I left. And I didn't do so on the best of terms." Old ties, it seemed, were as fragile as ever in the Soarlands.

Her expression softened, but the tension between them was palpable. "We can't pay this. Even if we could, it would humiliate us. Everything we're working toward gone."

"We won't pay," Gerfinn agreed, his mind racing. "Glimisvellir is still Glimisvellir. Värmod knows he can't enforce this. Raiding the caravans would just bring the southerners down on him. No, this is his way of telling us he won't submit. And if Horga won't fall in line then Mydalsa won't for sure. And it's only a matter of time before the old hag finally drops dead and the next Havi of Níðavellir won't be so on board with all this Confederacy nonsense."

"My cousin won't accept that, the Soarlands needs to become a thriving Republic if… there are things in motion that could severely upset the balance of power in the Confederacy. Soarlings have an intrinsic value in the individual as well as a unified sense of identity. If we could just steer them away from nationalism and toward republicanism then-" Her words were cut off by a sudden throwing of a bottle toward the wall and a forceful grab, shoving her down to the floor. The smart intelligent man that she found love in was now looming over her with a look in his eyes that harkened back to a wildness and a time of savagery. He had never done this before, at least not when she did not ask him to do so. In this brief moment he was a different man, one from his younger days and it terrified and excited her all the same.

"None of that matters. You're thinking too much." The tension grew exponentially, a gasp from the audience if there were one, as Gerfinn's forearm pinned her by her neck, choking her ever so slightly. His other hand snaked its way under her dress, ripping it slightly until it found her breast. "This is what matters. Life and Death, pleasure and fear. Those are what drive the lowlanders. You southerners can't offer either that they can't get themselves."

And just like that Gerfinn moved away, standing up and leaving Rinelt breathless for various reasons I'm sure. If it had been anyone else that had pulled that, something along those lines was what she was thinking but no poor woman. Gerfinn had successfully closed off every means of retaliation you had, no spell casting from the closed throat, and swell luck overpowering him. Still, she liked to believe that they were on equal footing.

"If just… there must be a way. They have to change or they will be destroyed." That was true. The times were passing on from the ages that Soarlings could freely descend from the icy seas and raid the countryside. Cannons, ironclads, and many more wonderful creations of bright minds were coming. But Gerfinn, had a horribly honest response to that pitiful hope.

"People don't change, not without something horrible happening to them."

Words of the Seventh

Locusts whisper dread
Feasting shadows spread
Gluttonous swarm, where nightmares are bred.

Break Many Legs

The sharp smack of a training spear against Orphan's face echoed through the rough-hewn cave. He tumbled to the ground, rolling to the side just in time to avoid being skewered by the blunt weapon's next thrust. Abezethibou's relentless attacks were pushing him harder than he'd ever been pushed before. Every move, every failure, grated on the Fiend's nerves, the boy's hesitation in combat growing more tiresome by the second.

"Attack me!" Abezethibou commanded, its voice a low growl vibrating through the cave. It stood, a perfect defensive posture, wide and unyielding, its spear angled with the precision of a creature that had been using its tool of violence for centuries. Orphan scrambled to his feet, repositioning himself, trying to make his next attempt look like anything more than the blundering movements of a novice.

The fool hesitated once again, his grip on the spear sweaty and unsure. With a determined frown, he lunged forward, thrusting the spear towards the midsection of the Fiend. The movement was clumsy, spoken in so many words to a seasoned warrior.

The Demon didn't even flinch. Orphan's movements were telegraphed clumsy, slow, the kind of attacks that could be read from a mile away.

"Faster! Again!" Abezethibou's voice reverberated off the stone walls, buzzing with impatience. In one smooth motion, it parried the thrust, sending Orphan's spear off course with a flick of its wrist.

Frustration welled up in Orphan as he tried to adjust his stance, his mind scrambling to recall the footwork that had worked, even if only briefly, before. He stepped forward again, this time feinting left before thrusting the spear toward Abezethibou's chest. The movement felt slightly more fluid, a marginal improvement, but still pitifully slow.

Abezethibou knocked his weapon aside with ease, spinning its own spear before slamming Orphan back to the ground with the pommel. Winded, Orphan glared up from the dirt.

"You could teach me by actually teaching me!" Orphan snapped, his voice cracking from the strain.

A week had passed since his training began, and still, he felt as helpless as the malnourished child he had always been. The Gifts from his Trials had elevated him slightly, but they were being squandered on a body too weak and a mind too timid.

But he would not allow himself to stay as he was. Before him was a great task, to conquer his hometown of Glim-isvellir. Doing this would require a great many things but above all else he needed to become strong. His uncle's words continued to ring true for Orphan, like a screeching banshee in his ear. The boy would spend all his time now dedicated to living by the principles that he knew set him above the weak and stupid. So he buckled under and grit his teeth. The indigent sting remained as Orphan continued to suffer under the Demons' torment disguised as teaching only because he knew it would work in the end.

The pain, the humiliation he'd endure it. He had to.

Seven days under the demons' harsh tutelage had taught him many things. Chief among them was that, despite their claims to serve him, these beings didn't care for him, not in the way one would expect. Even the Imps seemed to show more genuine concern than the demons. The lesser fiends would be the ones to pick him up when Abezethibou had beaten him nearly to death or when exhaustion almost claimed him during one of Arcon's thirteen-hour lectures on Tyrant history. But the Demons? No, they were like his uncle: harsh, unyielding, unforgiving.

Still, they were the first to push him toward something greater, and for that, Orphan kept his complaints to himself. He was smart enough to understand that strength only came through suffering. And so he'd endure.

But what the boy hadn't realized was that his silence, his passive acceptance, was yet another weakness. Silly, foolish boy. He should have been demanding their respect loudly, defiantly. He wasn't supposed to endure; he was supposed to rule.

"You learn by surviving," Abezethibou declared, its voice a harsh, resonant growl. "That's how a child like yourself learns. Arcon can try all it likes to shove knowledge and wisdom into that skull of yours, and Carelena can work on painting your tongue silver. But I will brand you with battle scars as your true testament."

As if to emphasize its point, the Demon hooked its clawed foot under Orphan's body and launched him into the ceiling with brutal force. The impact drove the air from Orphan's lungs, a spray of blood escaping his mouth as he felt bones crack first when he hit the jagged stone above, and then again as he plummeted to the ground below. Pain shot through him, sharp and unforgiving, as his body met the cold, rocky floor.

Abezethibou, the eldest of the Fiends of Gluttony, a name cursed by knights, priests, bandits, and bankers alike. For as long as the Sin of Gluttony has existed there has existed a Demon that has destroyed men and women brutally and cruelly, with all the hunger for their suffering that Malice could muster. Such dedication to the finer arts, an inspiration to all. And one who has had the great honor of killing a Hero, a rare feat among the Fiends. Now if only it wasn't such a lazy slacker.

This was the treatment that Orphan had been subjected to, nothing but absolute dispassionate efficiency. Again-again-again, the two ran through this series of beatings, ahem, trainings. Orphan was slowly learning the stances, the movements, the footwork, by sheer trial and error. Every step forward was paid for in blood and bruises.

The day ended, as it always did, with a final, jarring blow. Abezethibou hurled its spear at Orphan, its shaft connecting with his face and leaving his bent nose dripping. Without a word, the Demon turned and left the cave, not offering even a glance back.

The hopeful heir of Gluttony rubbed his face before buckling and falling onto his knees once the demon was gone. This was how they often ended things, without a single word Abezethibou would leave. No words on how his supposed liege was doing, criticism nor encouragement came. Orphan purposefully fell to his side and breathed a sigh of exhaustion. Poor thing could possibly be debating in his twisted little mind just which was worse, these Demons' training or the Glimingars' ire.

He lay there, staring at the barren rock ceiling. The same view greeted him wherever he went in these tunnels of endless stone, illuminated only by flickering torchlight. The smoke from the torches gathered at the cave's ceiling, finding its way out through small holes dug by the imps. Elsewhere in the hive were ramshackle structures made using stolen debris and other ill-gotten gains from the Fiends' raids on the increasing traffic to and from the south. It's not like those Teutons were using any of it being dead and all.

Orphan groaned as he pulled himself upright, his body already beginning to knit itself back together. He didn't even need to use Heal; his Gifts were doing the work for him. Fortitude and Resilience were his saving graces here. Fortitude granted him a level of stamina and physical endurance no human could match, while Resilience ensured his body repaired itself quickly, always recovering from the punishment it endured.

Perhaps that's why the demons pushed him so hard. They knew he could take it. Or maybe they didn't care. No, who was he kidding? They'd beat him just as brutally regardless of his Gifts.

"Fucking bastard." Orphan cursed under his breath as he pushed his arm back into its socket. Even if Orphan could take the punishment better than most humans, he was not immune to pain. But that had long since been an old… not friend but that person you saw everyday on your way home that continued to just make your day all the more worse by seeing them.

Moving out of the solitary cave where his combat training

took place, Orphan entered one of the larger main caverns, a vast chamber in the process of being hollowed out. The path he walked was narrow, just wide enough for two people to walk side by side. On either side of the path, deep ditches fell away into trenches filled with glowing mushrooms. The air reeked of decay, the mushrooms thriving on the corpses gathered from Imps' raids. But Orphan didn't mind the stench; it was no worse than his uncle's lab. Imps scurried and flew around him, baskets of fungus clutched in their claws. While they lived off stone, carving their tunnels as they ate, the mushrooms were their preferred delicacy.

Leaving the fungal garden behind, Orphan slid through tunnel after tunnel. Some of them were already carved with intricate hexagonal patterns, symbols that must have been some form of language. It was becoming painfully obvious to Orphan that the Fiends had an entire culture of their own, one that surrounded him now in its strange, grotesque glory. It was a stark contrast to the way he'd thought of them before as nothing more than semi-useful monsters that annoyed hunters. He chuckled to himself, realizing that maybe he had always harbored a soft spot for the little darlings.

"Thou art three minutes and twenty seconds early; 'tis unacceptable."

A sharp crack pierced the still air as the rod struck Orphan's skull, a sound that echoed throughout the chamber like a director's cue. Arcon, ever the exacting perfectionist, retreated to its precious chalkboard, the pristine emblem of its obsession with order. Oh, how lovely. The only part of this entire festering hive that wasn't a jumbled mess. Perfectly arranged wooden boards, finely woven rugs, and a classroom that stank of ancient books and chalk dust. The smell of… education. How utterly revolting.

Orphan rubbed the top of his head, grimacing. "I've already gotten enough of that today. Can we do away with the beatings?" Oh, poor child. How endearing it was that he thought such a request would be granted.

The Demon ignored him, as it always did, its insectoid limbs clacking against the stone as it positioned itself in front of the board. Arcon, as ever, was a master at wielding the chalk with the same precision as a blade. "Three questions," it began, in that grating, pedantic tone. "One for each minute. If forty-five is equal to the third multiple of A plus five, what is A?"

Orphan's face twisted in confusion as he took a seat, one of many, all empty, of course. A whole classroom, and he was the sole unfortunate student. Was it necessary? No. But that's where the delight lies, doesn't it? A room for an audience of one. The Demon's hunger for significance. The grand maestro of Gluttony, with no one to impress but a begrudging boy.

"Uh…" The boy's blank expression spoke volumes. His mind, I imagine, was trying to crawl away from the scene in abject horror.

"Failure! Children of five winters can solve this!" Arcon snapped, the Demon's voice buzzing with disdain. Ah, but of course, those were noble children. Precious little cherubs whose families offered their pantries and wealth to the Demon in exchange for a perfect prodigy. A crime, a heresy, and yet one whispered about in every dark corner of Neustria and beyond.

"I don't know! Why are we using letters in math?!" Orphan snapped, frustration bubbling up. Oh, the poor thing.

Arcon's eyes burned with disdain as it moved to the next question.

"Name the homelands of the Fourth, Fifth, Sixth, and Seventh Tyrants! We have reviewed this many times, lad thou canst do it!" The Demon practically hissed, tossing a piece of chalk at Orphan's head, which the boy barely dodged.

"Víteliú, Hell... uh..." Orphan's brow furrowed, clearly struggling to recall the information. Arcon stalked toward him like a predator, its claws tapping rhythmically on the floor. "Some island chain... I don't remember the name."

"Akitsushima! Dullard! Thou art a repugnant slacker! Doth thou mean to disgrace Lord Beelzebub with such incompetence?" Ah, yes, the insults. A symphony of belittlement, each note intended to grind away at the boy's fragile ego. Arcon reveled in it, and yet Orphan merely sat there, his eyes glazing over, the Demon's tirade little more than a dull drone to his ears. Not fear. No, just boredom. How quaint.

"Are you finished?" Orphan asked flatly, his tone dripping with irritation.

"The Seventh Tyrant whence did they hail?" Arcon's tone was mocking, but oh, there was something else there too an eagerness. The demon couldn't help it. Despite its cruelty, it saw something in the boy. Perhaps, like a craftsman who delights in chiseling away at stubborn stone, Arcon found joy in molding this particular piece of work.

"Hell," Orphan answered, a smug smirk pulling at his lips. "Queen Sevra was born to the Devil House of Glut. It's from that House's name that we get the word Gluttony. She was of the First Tyrant's lineage and only held the Archfiend Greed's power. Went on to create the Kingdom of Mandé

Glut, still standing to this day as one of the Great Powers of Malice." Ah, the little brat had done his homework, at least when it came to that most girthy and wonderfully plump woman that would go to create the Ravenous Swarm. Such a delightful dream, to consume all that this world had.

"Correct," Arcon begrudgingly admitted. "Last question for thine lack of punctuality. What is the number of noble ranks in both the Empire of Teutonreach and the Republic of Neustria?" Tis a trick, Teutonreach had no official noble titles and the Republic of Neustria had done away with their feudal system in their republican uprising. But at the same time, Teutonreach does have a labyrinthian system of offices, decrees, orders of imperial mandate, and obligations each Noble House had to carry out. This effectively created an unofficial pecking order that only the studious and desk loving bore could fully grasp. Meanwhile while there are legally no more ranks among the Charlen, they still exist in practice. What was once a Duke or Marquis, still presented themselves as such and ruled much of the lands their families had for centuries. The only thing that changed was now nobles had to pay taxes like everyone else.

"Zero," Orphan replied, a glimmer of satisfaction in his voice as he caught on to the trick.

"Correct again, boy." Arcon's lips curled into what passed for a smile, if a Demon could smile. "Since thou didst only err in thine arithmetic, that shall be our focus this day. Thou mayst dream of wading through the battlefield or commanding legions, but I shall ensure thou art not ignorant of the numbers involved. More goes into combat than the swing of a sword or a push on a map."

Orphan groaned in exasperation, already resigned to

the monotony that awaited him. Arcon, ever the cruel taskmaster, launched into the lesson without mercy, filling the room with mind-numbing equations and numbers that danced across the chalkboard.

By the end, the boy's head was firmly planted on his desk, a drool-stained page beneath him. Oh, how Arcon must have loved it, knowing full well the next test would cover everything Orphan had just slept through. A perfectly spiteful plan.

But alas, a delightful little Imp, cheerful as ever, tapped Orphan awake. Arcon was gone, content with its sadistic lecture, leaving the boy to suffer the consequences of his negligence later. And oh, suffer he would. The smiling Imp, however, had a far more pleasant task bringing Orphan to his final lesson of the day.

Ascending to the very top of the tunnel network, Orphan entered the only section of the hive illuminated by natural light. Thin beams of sunlight and moonlight trickled through the cracks in the ceiling, casting dim rays across the most intricately built part of the hive. This was the heart of the Fiends' domain, where the spawning pool lay, along with the food stores, feasting halls, and the personal quarters of the Demons. Orphan often wondered if the decision to place his quarters so far below was truly a security measure, as they claimed, or just another way to break him down bit by bit.

The number of Imps increased the closer he got to the surface, and most of them were older and more experienced. Only the most intelligent and skilled Fiends were permitted to work so near the Spawning Chamber. Here, they carved the stone with precision and reverence, shaping it into smooth, intricate patterns. Earth was sacred to them, the

Cardinal Point of magic they were most attuned to, aside from Malice. Their architecture reflected their insect-like nature, with its minimalist design and flowing lines that even a dwarf might begrudgingly admire.

Orphan for his part had to give it to the Fiends, they knew what they were doing. And that also came with the Demon's lessons. It had only been a week but he had to swallow his pride and admit to himself that they were teaching him things he would need. Beyond that they were damn effective in breaking through his stubborn nature. The little brat was a spiteful monster, he was willing to walk into the pyre in order to deny the Glimingars their preferred outcome of him attempting to futilely escape. Or that's what he told himself, what nonsense. The truth of the matter is simple, he had no other option and had to justify it to himself.

"Welcome, dearest Orphan, our liege, our lord, our ever-greatest master-to-be!" Carelena's gleeful voice rang out, echoing through the amphitheater as the Cursed Born entered. Grand and sprawling, it could likely seat hundreds in its stands. Why would anyone want to spend such precious time and manpower to create such a useless edifice in such a time as this? A hunger for gratification no doubt. The Demon standing at the center of the stage bowed deeply as Orphan walked up the steps.

"Enough," Orphan muttered, rubbing his temples. "My head's still aching from Arcon's lecture." He complained, these lessons were always his least favorite. Learning to fight, that would surely bring him closer to conquering his homeland. Learning to lead and the fundamentals of intelligence and wisdom, that also was very much needed to command an army effectively. But learning to talk in flowery and pretty words? Bah. The boy lacked any respect for the craft of word weaving.

"Oh, most respectable and favored master, we have such grand designs planned for thee this day," Carelena sang, its voice an awful mimicry of a cicada's call. Orphan grimaced, and of course, that only encouraged the Demon. "We have found thee some dancing partners. How exciting!"

"Dancing partners?" Orphan raised an eyebrow, suspicion coloring his voice as several Imps scuttled into the room, dragging two figures wrapped in chains and covered with sacks over their heads. Orphan's eyes widened; these were the first non-Fiends he had seen since leaving Glimisvellir. Both figures were men, clothed in tattered rags, their hands bound by heavy iron chains.

"Indeed! Dancing partners!" Carelena crooned, skipping over to one of the captives. "The dance shall, of course, be long and most educational."

With a taloned finger, the Demon traced a line along the chin of the first man. The last word growled out like a sadistic purr… or as close to as a purr a bug can make. "This one, a Teutons colonist. He hails from a small fishing village to the far south. He dreams of escaping his dull, tedious life to perhaps find a spirited savage wife and civilize her into a proper woman. Ah, such deluded fancy."

With that the Demon lifted the bag off the man's head, he blinked in confusion and looked up with horror in his eyes. Why wouldn't he? He had spent days under the tender mercies of Fiends intent on breaking him into a nice, compliant, harmless little slave. Truly a wonderful bonding experience among Imps and their bigger Demon siblings.

The wretched squirming of the first prisoner was delicious,

in its own way. He groveled as though Orphan were some lofty Devil from the pits of Hell, a mighty noble of Dis itself. Ah, the ignorance of mortals so willing to bend the knee when they believe their souls hang in the balance. This fool, this trembling wretch, thought he stood before some infernal dignitary. How utterly… delightful.

"Please, my lord, your infernal grace, grant mercy to this unworthy man!" the Teutons wept. A laughable display.

Carelena's chitinous foot pressed down on the man's skull, forcing his face into the rough stone floor with a satisfying thud. "Quit your false pleas," it hissed, talons digging into his scalp just enough to remind the worm of his place. Oh, it was all so familiar. Mortal desperation is such an art form, don't you think? The way they cling to life like rats on a sinking ship.

The Demon turned to Orphan, voice thick with mockery. " My dear Heir of Gluttony, this dancing partner shall teach thee all thou need'st to know about those who fervently wish to kill thee whilst simultaneously kissing thy boot." Ah, yes, a valuable lesson indeed. These squabbling sacks of flesh will smile, flatter, and grovel one moment, only to slip a knife between your ribs the next. Better to crush them beneath your heel while you still have the chance.

Orphan, ever the naive little thing, hesitated. "Is… is this really necessary?" he asked, as though mercy was something one could afford in the arena of Malice. The poor boy, still clinging to the vestiges of his mortal mind. A mind that would have to be broken down and rebuilt if he had any hope of surviving this grand stage.

Carelena's eyes flared with amusement, its voice a sickeningly sweet whisper. "Only if thou think'st it, my lord.

Shall I go easy on this worm? Or perhaps let it live to slither away?" Oh, the anticipation Carelena relished watching the boy squirm in his decision-making. The hive watched too, Imps skittering just out of sight, their tiny, insectoid eyes glued to every twitch, every slight motion Orphan made. They always waited for the telltale sign of weakness, ready to swarm if given the opportunity.

But Orphan, bless his cold little heart, didn't flinch. He met Carelena's eyes, his voice firm, even if his heart still fluttered with uncertainty. "Yes, don't damage him while on the stage. Or else he might not be able to play his part." Oh, how the Demon savored those words, its yellow eyes darting back and forth as if measuring the weight of Orphan's will. There was a flicker of something in Carelena's gaze approval, perhaps? No, too soon. But a step in the right direction.

With a theatrical flourish, Carelena moved to the next bagged figure, its voice oozing with venomous glee. "Very well. To our next dancing partner! Perchance something a little more… familiar?" It snatched the hood from the second prisoner's head, revealing a face bruised, bloodied, but still burning with defiance. Oh, how lovely this one had fight left in him.

"Fuck you monsters!" spat the man, his voice hoarse, his body trembling with rage. "No son of Glimisvellir is going to give you anything but their spit!" And spit he did, a pathetic gob of defiance landing at Orphan's feet. How utterly… charming.

Orphan stepped forward, lowering himself to one knee to meet the Glimingar's hateful gaze head-on. Oh, this was going to be wonderful. The man's bright blue eyes widened as he took in Orphan's face so beautiful, so monstrous, those glowing green eyes set against skin that was no longer quite human. The Glimingar's posture faltered, if only for a moment.

"Hello, Veleif," Orphan sneered, his voice dripping with years of pent-up venom. "Got any rotted fish to overcharge me for today?"

Ah, Veleif what a delightful memory. A fishmonger who had taken great pleasure in tormenting the young Cursed Born, slinging rotten fish and insults with equal vigor. And now? Now the tables had turned, and Veleif was at Orphan's mercy. A satisfying reversal, wouldn't you say?

"Orphan?" Veleif's voice cracked, his bravado crumbling. "How? It's only been a year… you couldn't have changed that much!" Oh, the terror in his voice so rich, so full of disbelief. He hadn't expected the little gutter rat to rise from the ashes.

And yet, here he was.

"It's amazing how much can change in a year. So what's happening in Glimisvellir, you all still upset that you didn't get to see me burn?" It was a reasonable thought given all that he had experienced. A lifetime of being the center of everyone's ire. The town pariah that no one could get enough of making him suffer.

"Actually I haven't given you much thought since you abandoned Glimisvellir." Or not.

"What?" Oh no, has someone's ego been shattered? A bit of reveal that one was not so vastly important in the lives of their tormenters. The boy stood back up, taking a step back in shock.

"Haha! Oh that's pitiful! Did you think all of us back in town were pining after our favorite whipping boy?!" Veleif laughed in the face of his captors, unafraid or perhaps he had already given up on living through this. His body was already covered in bruises and cuts barely treated. Why not laugh in the face of death?

"I mean... a little?" Orphan muttered more to himself than to the laughing Glimingar.

"Understand this, freak. The only time I thought about you was when you came to my shop. And even then, it was only because you reminded me of your whore-witch mother. Or when you slunk around the feasting hall, trying to steal scraps like the little rat you were."

Veleif's laughter turned to coughing, but Orphan... Orphan was shaking. Not with fear, no, but with rage. Oh, this was the moment we'd been waiting for. The Demons, the Imps they could feel it too. They circled around Orphan like vultures, watching, waiting, ready to pounce at the first sign of weakness. But instead of retreating, Orphan clenched his fists, his nails biting into his skin.

Yellow eyes hundreds, thousands, each a flickering flame of malice fixed upon their young, lordly heir as he approached the jeering fool. Veleif, the fishmonger, had his smug satisfaction slapped away as Orphan's grip tightened around his scalp, lifting the wretch to his feet like a ragdoll. Oh, how quickly the tables turned. How swift the fall from mockery to... well, something far worse.

With deliberate precision, Orphan touched two fingers to Veleif's bruised and battered face, muttering under his breath. Heal. A spell that, in another's hands, might be wielded with kindness, with compassion. But not here. No, this was no act of mercy. It was restoration for the sake of cruelty. The black eyes and swollen cuts faded, the bruises stitched themselves back together, only for the process to be repeated again and again until the Glimingar stood whole once more.

A touching moment? A spark of redemption? Ha! Mercy? In this place? Foolishness. The thought alone is an insult.

"Escort him out of the hive. I want him gone." Orphan's voice rang cold, detached, as Veleif's body hit the ground with a thud, his confusion palpable as the Imps scrambled to obey. The dear little beasts dragged him away, their crooked limbs scuttling along the stone floor, never questioning their master's whims. They didn't need to. Obedience is their nature, after all.

Orphan's eyes flicked to the other prisoner. "And that one, take him back to wherever you had him stashed. I've more questions for him later."

A soft hiss emanated from Carelena as it watched, its gaze sharp with curiosity and dark amusement. "Interesting. Wilt thou share with thy devoted teacher what thou hast planned?" A dangerous question, laced with mockery, of course. The Demon's amusement was thick in the air, yet beneath it, there was an ever-present threat. This mercy or whatever Orphan dared to call it was not viewed as weakness. Not today.

Orphan waited, his gaze lingering on Veleif's shadow as it vanished from sight. Only then did he speak, his voice as cold and unfeeling as the stone beneath their feet. "Hunt him down again. He's fresh now. Whatever you did to him before… do it again."

Ah, yes. Now that is the voice of true hatred. A hatred that isn't satisfied with mere death or even suffering. No, this hatred requires layers of torment, the breaking of a soul before it even dares to fully comprehend its despair. The demon, well, it seemed almost proud of him in that moment. A subtle nod of approval from a creature that lived and breathed cruelty.

"Thy will be done, Heir of Gluttony. A true embodiment of Glutton for Punishment. Shall we grant him a day's head start? Let him believe, just for a time, that freedom's sweet taste is within his grasp?"

Orphan barely heard Carelena. His eyes had dropped to his hands, clenching and unclenching, as if trying to hold onto the slippery emotions that now churned within him. Disappointment. Anger. Bitterness. How beautifully they all entwined. What could be worse than being hated? Ah, yes. Being forgotten. Being insignificant. To find out that all the pain, all the hatred, wasn't even real malice. Just neglect. Just nothing.

"Sure, but don't let him escape. We can't have him running back to Glimisvellir and telling anyone what he saw." As if there was any risk of that. The hive was well outside the range of Glimisvellir's hunters. But the command was given, and the die was cast.

Carelena giggled a sound that should never, ever be associated with a creature like her. "Very well, my lord. Then let us end today's lesson early. By Lord Beelzebub's empty stomach, we find ourselves quite famished. We are sure Arcon shan't mind if we… filch a few of its victuals, eh?"

The demon sauntered off, ever gleeful, but Orphan's voice stopped her in her tracks.

"Carelena… could it be possible… to gather everyone for a shared meal?" His question was almost absurd, almost pathetic. The boy spoke as if requesting a family dinner, as if that was still in the realm of possibility. Foolish child. Even I cringe at his naivety.

The insectoid Demon froze for a moment, then erupted

into a cacophony of screeching laughter. An alien sound, grating and unnatural, filled the amphitheater. An insect cannot laugh, but if it could, if its chittering mandibles could ever make such a sound this is what it would be.

"Does my request amuse you?" Orphan's voice was dangerously low, but how pitiful. The boy had no real power here. Not yet.

"Nay, 'tis not the request, my lord," Carelena replied, wiping the remnants of its cruel mirth from its gleaming fangs. "'Tis the sentiment behind it. Doth the lonely little monster miss… family time? Perchance not a loving family, yet a family nonetheless? Does thou long for the days of grand feasts, filled with laughter and joy, though never thine own? Those days where thou didst sit in silence, wishing thou wert included?"

"Carelena." Orphan's voice, a feeble warning. Oh, how adorable. He still thought his words carried weight.

"We savored that," Carelena hissed, her eyes glowing with malicious delight. "But nay, my lord. We Demons of Beelzebub share neither food nor feasting table with others. Besides, thou wouldst be wise not to seek companionship with us. For thy mortal mind is more akin to a dog, a bird, or even an insect than it is to ours."

And with that final dagger to the heart, the Demon was gone, leaving Orphan alone or as alone as one could be with a swarm of Imps still scuttling about. Alone, yes, but those words lingered. Twisting, gnawing. Carelena had spoken true, after all. For all mortals share something, some thread, some long-forgotten origin. But the Demons? They are something else. Something unknowable. And Orphan, poor boy, may have begun to understand that in his heart, that he was reaching for something that would never, could never, reach back.

To seek friendship, to seek kinship… even the wicked crave connection, and oh, how many delicious, horrible deeds have been done in that pursuit. So, so many.

Words of the Eighth

Deer forgotten, daughter's tear
Jealousy's grip, whispers near
Forgotten words, linger, sear

Act Two

The clock ticks forward, and we step into a new chapter of our story, one where time itself has wrought its changes on our would-be Tyrant. Six years have passed since Orphan, that fragile boy, crawled out of the Spawning Pit, marked for a destiny drenched in Malice. Six years of relentless training, bitter lessons, and a life forged by the hands of Demons who shaped his every moment. He has grown, matured, but most importantly, his power oh, how his power has swelled.

The Hive of Gluttony beneath the mountains of Glimisvellir has expanded, stretching its tendrils deeper and wider into the earth like an unstoppable infestation. Imps burrow through the rock like ants, carving out great caverns and mining veins of iron, building a crude industry that serves a singular purpose: the growth of their master and the expansion of their domain. Yes, they lacked food, but food was never something that needed to be cultivated, not when there were countless places to raid.

In these years, the initial group of Fiends was joined by others, drawn by the growing strength of this potential Tyrant. More Demons came, bringing with them beasts and men who had thrown their lot in with Malice, hoping to secure favor with Orphan before he ascended fully to his throne. Allies, opportunists call them what you will. But one thing was certain: the Hive buzzed with activity.

But what of Orphan himself? Twenty years old now, seven more than he ever thought he'd see. Surely, he must have changed since we last saw him as that gangly, half-starved wretch. Well, let's take a look.

"Again," came the sharp command, the wooden training spear cracking through the air as Abezethibou chastised his lord. Orphan, now fully grown, found himself once again in the sand of the training pit, staring up at the moonlight filtering through the carved skylight above. The pale light cast long shadows over the ring, a pit dug deep into the earth, the floor a sandy circle for their endless combat practice.

"I know. This is the twentieth time you've beaten me today," Orphan muttered, pushing himself up from the ground, wiping the sand from his loose-fitting furs. His voice, though deeper, still carried that familiar thread of frustration, though it was tempered now with a sense of grim acceptance. He was taller, his frame no longer the spindly form it had been, though he still didn't cut the figure of a traditional warrior. His clothes, made to fit his size, hung loose in places, and yet, despite the unimpressive bulk of his body, his face had changed. The baby fat had melted away, leaving behind sharp, angular features likely thanks to his Gift of Guile he had developed a very handsome face if one were to look past his more corrupted facets. Even has the cute little beginnings of a beard starting to show.

"Then this will be the last round of the day," Abezethibou replied, its voice carrying that same stern authority, the same unyielding coldness that had been Orphan's companion throughout the years. "We'll need you refreshed for tomorrow."

Oh, look at them how far they've come. A painting of words would describe this moment best.

Within the confines of a dimly lit cave turned training room, a seasoned and disciplined warrior executed precise spear techniques. Their movements were a symphony of mastery, the spear an extension of their skill and experience. Opposite them, a less adept but determined student struggled to emulate the finesse displayed by his counterpart. Despite his lack of proficiency, the student demonstrated a willingness to learn, drawing upon whatever experience he possessed to meet the challenges presented by the harsh instructor. In the hive's shadowy depths, the clash of wooden shafts reverberated, echoing the journey of skill development and the mentorship between the two.

And scene. Oh, it also ends with Orphan once again on his butt.

"Thou dost persist in training him with a spear, yet 'tis clear that he hath the makings of a great sorcerer rather than a warrior," came a voice from above the pit, cold and sharp like a blade slicing through tension. Ah, fresh players grace our stage three ominous figures perched at the edge of the pit, casting elongated shadows over Orphan and his relentless mentor, Abezethibou. Newcomers to our budding tyrant's growing menagerie of monsters and beasts.

The speaker was a terrifying creature even among the Demons of Beelzebub. Its body was encased in a shell of sharp, flared spines that jutted outward in every direction, creating a nightmarish silhouette. Its arms, grotesquely long, ended in wicked claws that scraped the stone floor with every idle twitch. Eight glowing amber eyes, burning with the cold, calculating intensity of a true predator, all focused on one thing: Orphan. This was Igurim, second only to Abezethibou in deadliness among Beelzebub's brood. Oh, how it reveled in reminding others of that fact.

To Igurim's right hovered Arogor, another Demon of Gluttony who had arrived but two moons prior. Quickly becoming Abezethibou's favored subordinate, Arogor bore a spider-like maw, two sets of tattered wings, and utterly lacked any sense of self-determination. A perfect underling obedient, efficient, and devoid of pesky ambition.

And then there was the third figure, lazily draped across the edge of the pit with an air of indifference. Ormenu, a Demon of Greed and a far cry from the insect-like fiends that populated most of the Hive. His form was something between a wolf, a horse, and a man lower half shaped like a horse's, covered in thick, shaggy fur, though instead of hooves, his feet were clawed like a wolf's. His upper half was that of a muscular man, also furred, with the head of a wolf but an unsettling hint of human expression in his eyes. A beastly grin split his lupine features as he eyed the pit with predatory excitement. This was Ormenu, a Demon of the line of Mammon. Though the Voracious Pack serves the current Archfiend of Greed Pamersiel, those of previous lines still hold great respect and are many.

"A Tyrant does not linger in the back lines," Ormenu growled, his voice a deep rumble that seemed to vibrate the very air. "He charges forward, hungry for blood, ready to take whatever he desires." His wolfish grin grew wider, lips curling in anticipation as he watched the training below. Neither Orphan nor Abezethibou flinched at his words. They were used to the beast's hunger.

"He shall not enjoy his desires if he be dead," Igurim shot back, its many eyes narrowing, and a tense silence followed. A staring contest of sorts, between two beings of vastly different tastes, one reveling in the raw, animalistic thrill of the hunt, the other savoring the slow, calculated consumption of power.

Abezethibou, in a fit of annoyance, stepped in before the exchange could devolve further. "Ormenu, Igurim, neither of you are here to instruct the young lord in combat. You are here to guide him in matters of mentality and terror, respectively," it said, its voice a calm yet commanding rumble. With a casual motion, it handed the training spear to Arogor, who caught it effortlessly, his wings buzzing as he hovered in place above the pit, ever the obedient helper.

"Now, is there a reason you two have decided to spectate our training match?" Abezethibou asked, its gaze shifting between the two demons.

"Yeah," Ormenu replied casually, rising to his full imposing height and stretching in a manner reminiscent of a wolf shaking off the morning dew. "Lirochi is back. Says she finally found a Whore to join us. They'll be arriving in a village called Krisuvik down south in three days. No luck in finding a Failure, though." With every movement, the strings of trophied teeth adorning his custom leather armor clattered a haunting melody of past conquests. Demons of the Voracious Pack, while crude at their core, had a penchant for the finer things. Their fashion, a blend of savage totems and high-class adornments, spoke volumes of their twisted tastes.

"Very well," Abezethibou acknowledged, its gaze steady. "I'll begin preparing for the journey."

No surprise there. The elder Demon had always managed the critical missions beyond the confines of the Hive, never once considering bringing along the Heir of Gluttony. After all, the boy hadn't set foot outside these caves since he first descended into their depths.

Orphan stood silently, absorbing the exchange. A hint of something flickered in his eyes. Curiosity? Resentment? Hard to say. But one might wonder, dear Listener, when or if the time would come for our young would-be Tyrant to step out of the shadows and into the world that awaited his rule.

All of Orphan's time had been devoted to either his education or his training both demanding, given the woeful neglect of his childhood. He had started out knowing only how to add and subtract, and not very high numbers at that. Just a glimpse into the depth of his ignorance back then.

Orphan climbed out of the pit, dusting himself off with a frustrated grunt. The others followed, shadows in tow as they left the training room behind, the cacophony of the Hive surrounding them. Imps scurried about, claws scraping against stone, pickaxes swinging in rhythmic monotony. The whole Hive seemed to hum with the constant toil of digging, burrowing, and expanding.

"And I'll ask again like I did when Ormenu arrived," Orphan said, his voice edged with impatience, "does this mean we're ready to attack Glimisvellir?"

Ah, the boy's focus never wavered. Glimisvellir, the place of his birth, the source of his deepest scars. Always lingering on his mind. His desire to conquer it was palpable, a festering wound that had yet to be soothed. But, of course, the question was dodged. Ignored. As it always was.

The path they walked was a narrow stone bridge, arching over a colossal cavern. The sounds of construction and industry echoed below. Enormous pillars of rock held the cavern from collapse, their surfaces adorned with honeycomb-like structures made of a grotesque blend of stone, metal, and Imp-secreting fluids. Organic and unholy, like everything the Ravenous Swarm touched. Above them, wooden scaffolding stretched up to where the Fiends lived, their makeshift villages clinging to the stone like parasitic growths. And below, at the base of the pillars, sat the Spawning Pods, grotesque mounds of writhing mass where new Fiends were born.

All Fiend broods possessed two methods of increasing their number, the Spawning pools and their own personal method. The Spawning Pods here were far slower than the shared method of the Pits, but an untold number of them could be made and any Imp could create them given enough time.

"In Arcon's last report," Abezethibou began, its voice unbothered by Orphan's impatience, "the number of Imps fluctuates between nine thousand and eleven thousand. Most of that number would be worker drones rather than soldiers. Though I am pleased that the Swarm has fully transitioned to Hive state. Once you have taken your Crown, the rest of Drone-Forms will begin to spawn."

Oh, yes, of course. That oh-so-important Crown, the ultimate goal for their dear little lord. Once the Heir of Gluttony truly ascended, the Hive would evolve further, its numbers swelling into something far more terrifying. Each Sin had its own evolution cycle, changing and growing to better fulfill their eternal duty to their Masters.

"That doesn't answer my question." Orphan pointed out. He was categorically ignored.

"Still a big horde," Ormenu cut in, his wolfish grin flashing in the dim light. "Why the wait, Abezethibou? The boy should've had his hands bloody on some Soarling marauder and his dick wet in a village girl by now." The Demon chuckled at his own vulgarity, a low growl rumbling through his chest. The brashness of Greed never failed to amuse. Or offend. Depending on one's taste.

The elder Demon's only response was a subtle shift in stance, not missing the slight slump of their liege's shoulders at the comment. "For the first point, he would get himself killed, given his showings in the pit mere minutes ago," Abezethibou retorted, unperturbed by Ormenu's crassness. "As for the second point, Carelena insisted any... social calls would happen on its timeline, not anyone else's. I believe the number of 'dance partners,' as it calls them, has been in the hundreds over the past two years."

A humorless grin tugged at Ormenu's lips. "You bugs really do take Order too seriously. No time for fun and games. Don't even leave scraps behind for me to play with. Those cages you keep are always empty."

The implications of that statement hung heavy in the air, but no one batted an eye. Orphan himself had never asked what happened to the prisoners Carelena brought in for his training, and he had, on more than one occasion, refused to partake in the darker lessons the Demon had prepared. The sight of a sobbing, terrified woman never put him in the mood for Carelena's twisted games. A disappointment to the Demon, no doubt. Orphan wasn't a sadist, just a chauvinist, at worst.

But the fact that hundreds of people had come into the caves and never left was simply accepted as a given among this crowd. Because, in truth, none of them valued mortal life. To them, humans were little more than cattle fodder for entertainment, currency, or sustenance.

"We also can't risk the Church finding out about an Heir Apparent in the Soarlands," Abezethibou continued, ever practical. "We've had enough trouble with the fact I've been spotted. The young master needs to learn how to operate among mortals in a controlled environment."

It would indeed be suspicious if a sudden surge in Fiend activity went unnoticed. The world was well aware of the various ways in which the forces of Malice operated. The Third Tyrant had established his systems and rules over two thousand years ago, plenty of time for organizations like the Church of the Orphaned World to understand and counteract their methods. Better, then, to keep their true strength concealed, presenting a lesser threat to the world while they prepared in the shadows.

"Still think Carelena is wasting time filling your head with all this seduction nonsense. Just take a bitch when the mood strikes you." Ormenu, ever the crude embodiment of Greed's most primal urges, growled his unsolicited advice as they walked. Greed was, after all, savage, cruel, and relentless in its desires.

Orphan, however, was no stranger to such provocations. His retort came swift and sharp. "A real man doesn't need to force himself on a woman. If you have to do that or pay for it then you didn't earn it. And I earn what's mine." Ah, the twisted chivalry of the young Heir of Gluttony, shaped by the bitter lessons of his uncle, the disdain he held for women like his mother, and, yes, even a bit of Carelena's wicked influence. I'm sure that if a certain person in a certain town ever met a particular person in a particular cave that would be a reunion most fiery indeed.

Ormenu, predictably, waved it off. "Eh, too much work. But maybe it's just that I enjoy the scrappy ones when they scream and cry." They passed the halfway point of the bridge, the deafening whirl of Imps flying overhead drowning out conversation for a brief moment.

But Orphan, focused and unyielding, wasn't about to be sidetracked by the vile musings of his demonic companion. "None of this is the point I was trying to get to." He turned toward Abezethibou, setting his foot down as though physically anchoring himself to the moment. His patience had finally run out. "Abezethibou, is my army ready to take Glimisvellir or not?"

This had been building to a boiling point for some time. Again and again, Orphan had been told that to prove himself worthy of Beelzebub's crown, he must take Glimisvellir. The other Demons deferred to Abezethibou's decree without question, but now Orphan demanded an answer. The Imps were numerous, the warriors capable, wasn't the army ready?

Abezethibou's response came like a dagger to the gut, without even the courtesy of facing Orphan as it delivered the blow. "My army? When did I ever suggest that the Swarm was your army?" The words struck like jagged stone, rough and cruel. Orphan froze mid-stride, his mind spinning. Only Ormenu stopped with him; the other Demons of Gluttony continued walking as though the declaration had not just shattered the young man's world.

"What… what are you saying?" Orphan's voice wavered.

He was desperate for clarity, searching his memory for any conversation that had implied otherwise. But the truth was dawning on him that he had assumed, taken for granted, that the forces gathering beneath the mountains were for him, for Glimisvellir. How foolish.

"They will be, if I deem it so," Abezethibou stated coldly, still not bothering to turn. "But I do not. And there is no Master of Gluttony to tell anyone otherwise."

Disappointment: a cruel, relentless companion in the life of the weak. And in this moment, Orphan was weak, too weak to do anything about it. He stood there, utterly directionless, the weight of the Demon's words pressing down on him.

Was Abezethibou expecting him to take Glimisvellir all by himself? Trapped beneath the mountain as he was? Yes and no. Ah, Fiends have their own twisted logic. If Orphan could not struggle, claw, and find his own path to victory, then he was not worthy of it to begin with. He could not be handed Glimisvellir, but he could also not be left to die in a foolhardy attempt. The investment the Demons had in him made him too valuable to lose by mere chance. Thus, the paradox.

"The bugs keep forgetting you lived most of your life without your kind," Ormenu rumbled, hitting the proverbial nail on the head. "I bet you're itching to be out of here." And indeed, the young Cursed Born did want to leave the tunnels, to see the sun, to be among beings who didn't have carapace plating or incessant buzzing. He wanted conversation, real conversation, that wasn't scripted or drowned in weeping. What he'd wanted only moments ago had now become something far sharper he wanted to spite them. If this wasn't his army, he'd find another. If Glimisvellir wasn't their goal, then it would be his.

"What do I do?" The question was whispered to himself, his hands clenching into fists as he stared down at them. They were calloused, rough, but they felt empty.

"I've got ideas," Ormenu growled, grabbing Orphan by the back of his collar as one might grab a misbehaving pup, dragging him toward the tunnels. The young man didn't resist, lost in thought as the beast hauled him through the caverns. What was Abezethibou playing at? Did the Demon expect him to murder his way to power? Or train for another decade until Glimisvellir was so powerful it could never be taken?

They reached the heart of the cavern, the largest of the rough-hewn pillars rising like a monolith. A grand staircase spiraled upward, leading to the nerve center of the Hive, the domain of Demons, Imps, and the chosen few mortals who served Orphan. Along the way were more bridges, some sturdy stone, others dubious-looking rope bridges that swung precariously with the weight of each step. At the top lay the Spawning Pit, the higher quarters, and, of course, Orphan's living quarters.

With a grunt, Ormenu unceremoniously tossed Orphan into his quarters, leaving him to stew in the thoughts that weighed on him. The Hive buzzed with activity all around, but Orphan, for the first time in a long while, felt isolated once again.

For a time Orphan just laid there before getting up and approaching the door. The wood was fine and carefully crafted like he was a prince of some great kingdom, inlaid with silver. They spent all this time lavishing him with luxury all the while laughing behind his back. He knew they did… but not to this extent. A punch. And another. Two fists pressed on the wood, cracking it just a little, before he slumped forward and turned his back onto the closed door. Slowly did the young man slide down, his back against the wooden door in exhaustion.

"Fuck. This would be easier if they all weren't such bootlickers while being such assholes." The young Cursed Born groaned and slogged his way into his quarters. These living spaces had also changed quite a bit in the past few years. No longer were they scraping together boards and damaged stolen furniture. Now it was expertly carved stone in tasteful shapes and curves, and intact stolen furniture. Given that the source of all of Orphan's stuff was the Teutons caravans, he had developed a bit of a taste for their style. The only piece of his own Glimingish heritage that he retained was an affinity for fur lining and pelts. The finery and ill-gotten wealth of Orphan's living quarters had improved since he first woke up in them but they still paled in comparison to the home of the Winterman.

Walking to the shelves lined with potted plants and cacti, vines crawled and climbed the entire wall freely and small glowing bulbs drooped from the sides. The would-be Tyrant grabbed a watering can and began taking care of his little hobby. Aw, it would be adorable if it wasn't for the fact each and every one of these pots contained either highly poisonous or hallucinogenic plants. The time he had spent looking after his uncle's collection remained with him and the act of maintaining a garden like this was soothing. Just a very deadly version of an old lady's hobby.

Alone with his thoughts, the soul crushing reality always

returned to him even as he went through the motions of his tasks. There was not a single individual in the Hive that felt like he could talk to another person. The irony was not lost on him, before all this he was in a town that hated yet ignored him and he felt more alone now in a giant Hive filled with thousands of simple minded Imps, cruel and uncaring Demons, and a host of fanatical zealots.

Fiends were one thing, but Orphan found disappointment in his fellow mortals as well. Those that had come to serve him were either opportunistic scum or members of the Tyrannic Temple. Religion was… uncommon so to say in this world. The Church of the Orphaned World was less a religious initiation and more a bad attempt at curing a global sense at abandonment. But there was one place that still had Faith in the truest sense. Hell… or Heaven depending on who you ask. The Kingdom of Devils worshiped their Tyrant progenitors as the new pantheon of the world, and the Tyrannic Temple were their shepherds.

"Never did I think I would miss the drunk bastard and the infuriating girl." Orphan muttered to himself; he did this very often and one must think that maybe his mind was going. But unfortunately he was quite sane. Merely finding out that Fiends, hostages, and subordinates could not equal that of an equal.

He turned away from his wall of toxic beauty those deadly, poisonous plants he so meticulously tended and headed toward his dresser, readying himself for tomorrow's trials. But as he passed the full-length mirror, he stopped, frowning at his reflection. Ah, yes… still, after all this time, after all the gifts granted by the Trials and the Fiend's so-called "excellent" diet, he remained woefully underwhelming. Too thin. Too small. His bones, stunted. His muscles, underdeveloped for what they should be. And his height? A meager five-four.

He would never speak of it aloud, of course, but the disappointment gnawed at him. A Tyrant should stand tall, imposing and fearsome. And here he was, looking more like the scraps left over after a Hero's feast. Oh, the irony.

Then, something shifted. Not a sound, not a tremor in the air, but a feeling, a gut instinct, deep and primal, warning him that he was not alone. His eyes narrowed. Orphan moved as quietly as he could, slipping his hand into one of his boots, retrieving the hidden blade stashed inside. The handle felt solid, familiar, as he gripped it tight. Heal was already on the tip of his tongue, ready to counter any first strike from whatever intruder had dared to breach his sanctuary.

And then he turned.

Standing by his garden wall was a towering figure cloaked in black a mass of shadow against the pale glow of his poisonous plants.

"Belladonna, Oleander, Hemlock, Aconite... interesting," the giant murmured, his voice soft, almost contemplative. There was a light accent to his speech, one that Orphan couldn't place, but it carried a weight that demanded attention. The stranger's back was still to him, but Orphan's gut screamed that attacking would be a death sentence. "And then there's Queen's Tea, Barb Ivy, Sullen... Both magical and non-magical plants here. Fascinating."

"Who are you?" Orphan's voice was steady, but his grip tightened around the knife. "And why do you invade the realm of the Ravenous Swarm?" He tried to steady himself, recalling Abezethibou's lessons, every ounce of training in his body telling him to keep his stance strong. But the problem was glaring: this thing was nearly eight feet tall, and none of his training had covered how to fight someone like that. Especially not with such an itty-bitty blade.

The intruder turned slowly, revealing a tall, lithe figure, his skin almost as pale as Orphan's own. Long red hair, loose but interwoven with several braids, draped down his back, and heavy black robes swirled around him, punctuated only by the glint of thick metal chains hidden between the folds. His face was sharply angled, with stress lines that hinted at an impossibly long life. And there, on either side of his head, long, pointed ears. Ah, how lovely. An elf.

"Whoa, easy now," the elf said, his hands raised in a mock gesture of peace. "I thought an informal meeting would be better."

Orphan didn't relax. Pointless. There could be any number of weapons hidden in those robes, not to mention the countless ways someone his size could crush Orphan like an insect.

"And you got through the entire Hive without anyone noticing?" Orphan asked, his tone sharp, his mind already calculating the quickest route to his personal stash of weapons across the room.

The elf offered a smile awkwardly, and far from comforting. "You live as long as I have, and you pick up a few tricks along the way." The smile widened, but Orphan wasn't buying it. "Myself and those I represent, we serve Malice in all its forms, but…" The elf paused, his gaze flicking toward the garden before settling back on Orphan. "The Fiends often disagree with our vision of how a future Tyrant should be handled."

Ah, so there it was. A visitor from beyond the Swarm, bringing whispers of some other faction, some other group playing the game of power and Malice. What fun.

"Right. Still haven't told me who you are." It would be ten steps across, fewer if he tried to sprint. But then he'd have to open the cabinet before actually having a decent weapon in hand.

"I am Rhiel; my companions and I wish to dedicate ourselves to the coming Tyrant. Out of the current Masters of Sins you are the closest to gaining the Title." Oh. So that's the game here. It would not be the first time someone of not-fiendish nature came to the Hive. At the moment there was in fact a sizable minority of mortals working under a Master of Sin. But all of these so far had not proven their worth to be fit among Orphan's company as so said by the Demons.

"Is that so? Who exactly is my competition then?" If any of this was true then it did give the young man a small boost in confidence. He understood greatly that he was in a very lucky position already knowing where his Seat of Power was. But there was still always that worry that some other Devil or Cursed Born would beat him to the title of Tyrant.

"Right now there are two other Masters of Sin, of Wrath and Pride. The former however has no interest in becoming a Tyrant and is content leading the dogs of war. As for the latter… it is complicated. But suffice to say he is in no position to become Tyrant. You, despite not being Crowned, are the closest to taking the world as yours." While Orphan's trust had yet to be given, there was also no lie in the elf's words. Why would he lie about something that could be eventually verified. Not easily done but not impossible. If Rhiel was trying to gain his favor then starting on such a meaningless falsehood would be foolish. Maybe his luck was not so bad after all?

The very concept of luck hung around Orphan's mind at times. It was luck that his father was crushed to death making him an orphan in the first place. It was luck that he was blessed with the Cardinal Point of Life and so could heal from all the abuse in his childhood. It was luck that had a foreign power invade the day before his supposed last. It was luck that the Winterman took pity on him. It was luck that his malnutrition made Beelzebub pass over him instead of eating him. And it was the biggest stroke of luck of all that he just so happened to be near a Seat of Power. Now, he was being told that he was lucky enough that all his competition were effectively out of the running? If it wasn't happening all his life from the day he was born Orphan would suspect it was all someone's plan.

"And just what would you provide me as your service?" The young man shook his head, dispelling these annoying pensive thoughts. Why question fortune if it's impossible that it's anything but fortune?

"I have lived quite a long life, I have advised kings, generals, and many other leaders. Wisdom and experience are my wares." Rhiel's face grew even softer, a caring honest look of a man that knew the plight of his fellow. Sickeningly upfront and genuine bah. "Plus, I know that living among the Fiends is quite challenging for someone that does not think like them. Creatures that are born from Magic and those born of the Material simply can never fully understand each other in my experience."

"Yeah, I've been getting that lately." The Cursed Born had tried to develop satisfying bonds with the Demons, a more touchy-feely type of idiot would say he tried forming a new family with them. It just doesn't work like that for Fiends. Especially for Demons like those of the lineage of the Maggot Lord. Fiends as a whole do not have emotions in the way mortals do, they may seem to act in similar matters but the processes in their minds are completely different than how a mortal might have come to that same conclusion.

"But what do you want Orphan? Why do you work to become a Tyrant, and what's keeping you from getting it?" Cutting deep. Was the fact this was the first time he was speaking with someone that could be called an equal or even a horrible possibility that this was a safe moment to express himself? Unfortunately for all involved it was. This elf's eyes held nothing but disgustingly genuine care and reassurance. It's unnatural is what it is.

"I want… everything I never had. I want to sit among people that look to me with loyalty and not hatred, host a feast for those that I deem worthy of it, and to kill and destroy everything that threatens to take them from me. And right now, what's stopping me from getting it? It's forsaken gods' damned Fiends that keep me from seeing the sky." Death, it comes in many forms. Whether it be age, sacrifice, destruction, madness or other such scary concepts. But one that all men fear, is not only to die… but to die alone. Empty. Isolated. No one to grasp a hand as you pass on in your final moments.

"I think I can help there, as others see fit to." The elf attempted to move through the space, his size not helping him. However, while on the surface his movements looked awkward and clumsy as Rhiel attempted to avoid bumping into things Orphan had a feeling that it might be for show. He claimed to have lived for a long time, and certainly there would have been great need to learn how to move through the spaces of shorter races.

The door closed behind the elf, and after checking over the entirety of his room, Orphan finally fell back onto his bed even more exhausted. The day he could finally leave and see the outside world again was approaching, more than that he would be visiting a village that had never seen him before. What would it be like, interacting with people that didn't already hate him or were terrified out of their feeble little minds. And a Demon of Lust too. A lot would be coming for the aspiring Tyrant.

Words of the Ninth

Dogs of Loyalty, no chain
Bite and claw, no pain
Sacrifice everything, no gain

Going Off Script

For the first time in many years, snow touched his face. Orphan looked up at the sky, a sight so unfamiliar it sent an unnecessary ripple of panic through him. For so long, the only thing above him had been cold stone and rock, the oppressive ceiling of the Hive. Now, the hazy clouds of the Soarland sky greeted him, gray and white, with snow drifting lazily down in a quiet reminder of the world he had left behind.

"Is it sad that I think I prefer the cave?" Orphan muttered, though no one answered. Depending on who you ask, yes. But for Orphan, the question hung in the air, unanswered, as he stood by the rough wooden gate separating the wilderness from the makeshift fort the Imps had crafted around the cave entrance. It was designed to look like any old bandit camp, a mess of cobbled-together wood and stone. Anything to avoid drawing attention to what truly lay beneath the mountain. The guards, followers of Malice, were tied up and gagged, leaving the fort deserted. No Imps would show themselves here. The surface was no place for their kind, not near such a vital entryway.

Despite the teeming hordes that writhed below the earth, they still took care not to reveal themselves to the Glimingars or Soarlings. If attacked the Fiends had no doubt that they could survive the initial onslaught, and the second, and the third… but the Fourth? That awful fourth? No. No-no-no. Because they had guessed that would be the wave of Confederate soldiers with cannons and gun lines. Thunderous booms and cracking earth. And with the Seat of Power so close, making the possibility of crowning a Tyrant more real than ever, the Hive could not afford to draw the world's attention to itself.

Orphan let out a breath, his eyes still trained on the sky, though his thoughts were pulled back to earth as he heard the gates creak open. Slowly they swung open letting in three newcomers on horseback. Well one of them was on the back of a massive elk, but you get the idea. And the one on the not-horse was the only face that Orphan had seen before, that of Rhiel. The other two figures were strangers, their forms obscured by heavy black cloaks.

To Rhiel's right, a man with a long white beard flowed out from beneath a strange faceplate that curved back over his head, covering all but his ears and chin. On Rhiel's left was a hooded figure whose shadowy cowl obscured all but a glimpse of dark skin and a hint of a lower lip.

"Hail, Heir of Gluttony! We've come to escort you down the mountain," Rhiel called out in that annoyingly chipper tone of his, dismounting from his elk with a fluid grace. "By the weather and distance, it should be a six to eight-day ride. We best hurry if you want to beat the Swarm."

Orphan glared at the elf, feeling the sting of his forced confinement tug at his nerves. "Why am I letting strangers take me somewhere I've never been?" he deadpanned. He glanced back at the cave, then up at the sky again. Yes, strangers were better company than the Fiends for now. It was only temporary. Once he found an army, once he had taken Glimisvellir and razed it to the ground, then he would return, proud and victorious. He would not be the boy who left, but the man who came back in glory. And, if all went well, not dead by the hands of bitter Demons.

"We are members of the Cult of the Seventh Sun, an ancient organization dedicated to the Powers of Malice," Rhiel explained smoothly as he handed the reins of an extra horse to Orphan. "The Cult has advised Heirs and Masters of Sin, as well as Warlocks, Scourges, and yes Tyrants for ages. We don't trust them; we trust their vows."

Orphan frowned as he took the reins. "Great. Religious fanatics. Just like the Tyrannic Temple." It wasn't that Orphan had a problem with religion itself, but the constant subservience grated on him. Complete submission from everyone around him might sound appealing at first, but it quickly lost its charm. He longed for an equal someone he could talk to without the veil of false reverence or terror. Even the Demons, who tolerated some forms of insubordination, were far too alien to offer anything resembling true camaraderie.

"Please do not go comparing us to those fanatics. The Cult hasn't been an actual cult for a thousand years my lord, it's more out of tradition than anything." Gross, the elf is petting the horse as he so nicely explains to Orphan. Meaningless rubbing of fur aside, it is true what he says. The Cult of the Seventh Sun once started out as one of the many competitors to the Church of the Orphaned World oh so long ago. But it was completely crushed due to some events that would be called… ghastly is the right word here. Needless to say, the

Cult went into hiding and eventually evolved into what it is today.

"Aye, more like we're very bad at changing with the times," came a booming voice, thick with an accent that would sound ancient to any modern Soarling. Most would claim that he was talking like that intentionally as a joke but it came off too natural and genuine. The bearded one let out a belly laugh as he dismounted his mountain horse with a thud that shook the ground slightly. The scent of blood and iron clung to him as he approached Orphan, his bulk casting a shadow over the young Cursed Born.

"This little shrimp is what passes for an Heir of Gluttony? Where's the meat? The gut?" Serk's gruff voice was thick with skepticism, his eyes scanning Orphan as if sizing up a pig for slaughter.

Rhiel, ever the diplomat, intervened with a smile. "I think we'll find his hunger comes from other places, Serk. He won't be found lacking in that regard."

What was that? Positive reinforcement? Already this elf was spoiling the boy.

"True, eh? Well then, best see that in action," Serk replied, his hand landing heavily on Orphan's head. The pressure of his fingers ruffling the sharp quills of Orphan's hair felt more like a casual threat than a friendly gesture.

Orphan wasn't sure what to make of it. But before he could dwell on it, final preparations were made, and Orphan gave his thanks to the guards, those bound and gagged, who had been guarding the fort on behalf of the Hive before the four of them set off into the wilderness of Glimisvellir. The land outside the fort was a desolate expanse, scarred by the hasty and careless clearing of trees for construction materials.

Snow covered the stumps and gouged-out earth where the logs had been dragged away, forming a crude trail that led up from the Hive to the forest beyond.

Orphan took in the sights, a strange sense of nostalgia pulling at him, though he still felt uneasy without the familiar weight of stone around him. But the surface world, with its endless sky and open air, was a welcome change. For a fleeting moment, he allowed himself to appreciate it. Then bitterness crept back in, tainting the air, as memories of his childhood in Glimisvellir resurfaced. The cruelty, the torment. The bitter knowledge that those memories weren't muddied by time they were seared into his mind with perfect clarity. No amount of demonic whispers could convince him otherwise. He had suffered, and he would have his revenge.

Two days passed before they reached the outskirts of what was considered Glimingaric territory. Off in the distance, Orphan could see the two mountain ranges that framed the valley where Glimisvellir lay nestled. He drifted in and out of moods during the journey, brooding one moment, lost in thought the next. His companions seemed to find his mood swings amusing.

"Ha! That's the face of a man who needs to kill somethin'," Serk's voice boomed, echoing through the snow-dusted trees. His laughter seemed as hearty as the man himself. They trudged through the snow-covered trail, their horses laboring against the cold. Serk's joviality was almost contagious, though Orphan wasn't sure if it was a comfort or an irritation. This man was far too jolly, like he would be the type to entertain children with tales of blood and steel.

"We're going to be passing one of the border stones soon, from there it's five more days if we are lucky and don't hit a snowstorm." The elf tried his best to sound cheerful despite the fact he was dreading this trip. Not for its purpose or anything like that, no, but he just hated the snow. The horrible flakes of frozen water were never seen in his homeland which was mostly sandy deserts and a bit of jungle oasis.

"Five days? Nay, more like seven, for we're not takin' the main path," Serk interjected with a hearty chuckle. "Best steer clear of those southern patrols. We'll be in the wilds, and that means delays and mischief. Ha! Just adds to the thrill, doesn't it?" Serk, as a native of these lands, knew them well. The wilderness hadn't changed much since his days of raiding and pillaging, back when he was nothing more than a Soarling marauder.

"The longer we keep the contact waiting, the more likely he is to leave. We should not dawdle." The voice, if one could call it that, didn't pass through the cold air as spoken words typically would. No, it slid directly into their heads, soundless yet fully present, like a thought that wasn't theirs. Samium's method of communication was unsettling, even among seasoned followers of Malice.

"Fuck! That's how you talk?" Orphan blurted, startled by the sudden invasion of his thoughts. It was the first time the shadowed traveler had used this strange and invasive method of speaking. The young Cursed Born wasn't prepared for it, and no wonder having someone in your head without warning would rattle anyone.

"Haha! That never gets old," Serk laughed, loud and hearty as always. "Makes it easier when travelin' with a damned sober eunuch. No fun, this one." Serk's broad smile creased his weathered face, but Samium remained unphased, offering no reaction to the bearded man's ribbing. Serk's continued disappointment at Samium's lack of humor was palpable. "But now I've got better company, eh? Come now, young Heir of Gluttony, tell me it doesn't do the soul great to be out here in the chill of a Soarland winter. What could be better? Maybe if we had a real blizzard instead of this soft freeze. We of Soar's blood, we've got ice in our veins, don't we yes?"

Orphan shifted in his saddle, glancing up at the softly falling snow. The cold bit at his skin, but it wasn't unfamiliar, though Serk's words about Soar's blood weren't sitting right with him. "Despite living here all my life, I'm not actually Glimingar or Soarling. Pretty sure my mother was Neustrian. I have no idea about my father, though." He spoke bluntly, and for a moment, the weight of that admission hit him. He'd never thought much about his heritage, about where he truly came from. He didn't feel like he belonged anywhere.

He had no claim to Glimingar culture or any real connection to the Neustrian people. That hollow feeling gnawed at him, a feeling he wasn't used to confronting. Had the Glimingar shaped much of who he was? Yes… unfortunately. But could Orphan truly call himself one of them when he had been shunned from the entire culture all his life? No.

"A devil, no doubt. You're Cursed Born so it has to be. Before you took the Trials, you looked different, right? Any disgusting features you don't still have?" Rhiel's curiosity was piqued, his keen eyes studying Orphan. Devils were notoriously proud of their bloodlines, often boasting of their heritage even when they had no real connection to the victories or glories of their ancestors. But they rarely took responsibility for their half-breed spawn at least, not in a humble setting like this.

Orphan snorted. "Fish. I looked like a fucked-up fish." The memory of his former appearance was bitter, enough that he actively avoided any dishes that contained fish, a petty reminder of a past he'd rather forget.

"I'd guess of the Twelfth," Rhiel said, though his brow furrowed in thought. "But you lack the Chimera's Eye."

Orphan raised an eyebrow. "The what?"

"The Twelfth Tyrant, Captain Damophon, also known as The Chimera," Rhiel explained. "Every Devil Bloodline has one shared trait. Like those from the first all have their wings, or the sixth all have black and white hair split down the middle. For the Twelfth, it's a barnacle-like growth over one eye. But none of the other Bloodlines are known for fish-like mutations. Strange…"

"The Twelfth Tyrant, huh?" Orphan muttered. He hadn't given much thought to his paternal lineage, and honestly, it didn't matter to him. But now, the name stirred a new curiosity in him, however fleeting.

"Yes, the Tyrant of Ambition. He died seventy-six years ago, but his bloodline has spread far. You may very well be his grandson, or even great-grandson," Rhiel continued. The elf's tone was calm, but Orphan could sense the weight of the information. Devils, Tyrants, bloodlines none of it had ever meant much to him until now. Prior to this moment it had all been quite academic, like reading the script before taking the stage and living the role. The words mean nothing until they must mean something.

"Neustrian and Pelasgian," Serk mused with a mocking tone. "Well, at least one of 'em has shed its softer nature." The Soarling's eyes twinkled with amusement as Orphan fished through his coat, pulling out his mother's diary.

"All I have is this," Orphan said, holding the small, weathered book in his hands. "Arcon and Carelena refuse to translate it for me. Maybe there's something about my father in it." He handed the diary to Rhiel. For years, the book's secrets had eluded him. He'd asked Arcon to teach him the Neustrian language, but Carelena, ever cruel in her amusement, had convinced Arcon to drop the lessons, robbing Orphan of the chance to unlock whatever truths lay within its pages.

"Demons. Don't bother tryin' to understand why they do anything. Just kill 'em," Serk grumbled as Rhiel took the diary, flipping through its pages with a practiced eye. His face unreadable by Orphan except for the movements of eyes. Eventually, however, the book was handed back to Orphan with a shake of the head.

"Sorry, my lord," Rhiel began, his voice calm yet apologetic, "but it only speaks of herself. There's mention later of someone I assume to be your father, but she didn't speak of him clearly. After a certain point, the pages stop. Several are torn out. Unless those missing pages held the answers, it seems your mother was simply a disgraced Neustrian noblewoman."

That conclusion felt right to Orphan. It aligned with everything he had known about her: a woman of luxury and status, seduced or ensnared by a Devil, reduced to a hunted witch in exile by her own country. The pieces fit together, but even though the picture was clear, it left him unsatisfied. His mind churned over the details.

Why here? Glimisvellir was far from the most strategic or logical place to flee. The Soarlands were isolated, a desolate tundra nearly untouched by Devilish influence.

Only Beelzebub's wanderings had brought Fiends of his lineage here in greater numbers. If she had been running from the condemnation of her homeland, there would be better places than this icy wasteland. Glimisvellir was far enough removed that the Glimingars lacked the same deep-rooted hatred for Devils and Cursed Born that places closer to Hell's influence harbored. They might have treated Orphan more fairly if it weren't for his mother's behavior.

Memories of the desperation, the bitter isolation flashed in his mind as they descended from the mountains. He replayed those years over and over, wondering about paths not taken. What kind of life would he have led if things had been different? Only a few times had he asked the question of what if, the last answer he wished involved many taverns and Skald songs. But amid those swirling thoughts, Orphan's sharp mind observed more than just his own inner turmoil.

These thoughts of the past and possible futures he could have had plagued his mind during the trip down from the mountains. But the young Cursed Born was not without wits. He noticed things about his traveling companions.

None of his traveling companions ate in his presence. Rhiel sometimes chewed on a green paste from a pouch, while Serk would disappear for a time and return with his beard covered in blood, hinting at a fresh hunt. Samium, meanwhile, simply existed detached from the physical needs of food and drink, or so it seemed. Curiosity simmered within Orphan, but instead of asking, he chose to watch. He was learning, after all learning the ways of his companions, reading their oddities, gaining insight into these strange allies.

After several days of travel, they finally arrived at their destination.

"There it is. Not much, is it?" Serk's deep voice rumbled through his helmet as they looked over the ridgeline toward the village below. Hafnarlond, a modest hamlet on the edge of the Glacial Sea. It was surrounded by a crude wooden wall made of tree trunks, enclosing maybe a dozen log cabins of varying sizes. A place small enough to be crushed by a single Soarland captain on a whim, Serk mused.

"Yes. That is Hafnarlond," Rhiel said, his tone far more subdued than usual. His gaze lingered on the village, his lips curled into a slight frown. Something about this place agitated him. Perhaps it was the foreboding stillness, or perhaps something unseen gnawed at him.

As they trotted down the hill toward the village's open gate, Orphan allowed himself to take in the scenery. The beach was littered with countless smooth pebbles of gray and black, stretching out toward the icy blue waters that lapped at the shore. Drifting patches of ice floated aimlessly in the distance, like fragments of a forgotten world. The forest behind them had an equally grim hue, its skeletal branches covered in frost. The entire landscape seemed to repel joy and warmth, as if mirth itself were an offense to the land. There was a bleakness to it all that mirrored Orphan's own mood.

"Such a strange place to be meetin'. Not their scene, this," Serk commented as he rode beside Orphan, drawing his attention. "Tell me, boy, what did the bugs tell you about Lust Demons?"

"Not much, they've been really quiet on the other types of Fiends." He had been given rough outlines of the other Sins and their spawn. Most all of the beings of Malice despised each other to the point of active avoidance. It was a gift really to mortal kind, if the Fiends could stop being so stupid in this stubbornness then they wouldn't need a Tyrant to finally win against the inane chaos of the free peoples of the world.

"I do hope it's one of their females. Oh, I do love them plump in all the right places, and boy, do they know how to use their curves. Haha, nothing beats a woman with meat on her bones," Serk lewdly chuckled. Though Orphan couldn't see his face, he imagined there was a blush beneath that helmet. He himself retained a bit of color too, as he was still discovering just what he preferred in his women. Ah, young foolishness. So indecisive and ponderous.

"Cows. They're cows." Samium's voice cut through the conversation like a whip, his words lingering in their minds.

Yes, the Lust Demons descendants of Asmodeus, the Archfiend of Lust were known to take on the appearance of half-man, half-bovine creatures of striking beauty. They often possessed hooves, horns, tails, and the eyes of their animalistic side. These Demons, part of the Licentious Congregation, were masters of seduction and indulgence, gathering herds of mortals who sought their fiery touch. Oh yes, they are also on fire much of the time. Passionate flames indeed.

"A bull or a heifer, what shall we find?" Rhiel mused, a smirk tugging at his lips as they stopped at the open gate of Hafnarlond.

Already, something felt wrong. Where were the villagers? Not a soul was outside, neither working nor idle. As the riders entered the small hamlet, they saw signs of abandoned tasks: a pile of logs half-chopped, cloth left by a wash basin, and a deer, partially skinned, now left to the elements with its meat exposed. The entire village seemed to have frozen in time, as if its inhabitants had simply stopped and vanished.

Riding through it all until they reached the building that seemed to have any life to it. In the center of this village was the largest of the structures, the only one with two stories. There they found people, three men and two men lying on the ground and slumped along the cobblestone walls. All of them moaning and grumbling in a mix of pleasure and withdrawal. Now one might think this is expected, this seems to be signs of a being called a Lust Demon being here. But no. All three of the Cultists were confused as this was unlike a Demon of Asmodeus to leave their playthings in a state like this.

"This feels off," Rhiel muttered, his tone serious as they dismounted and tethered their mounts to posts outside the tavern. Passing the groaning villagers, they stepped inside, only to be hit by an overwhelming wave of sharp spice and potent alcohol.

The stench was almost unbearable, forcing all of them to flinch as they entered. Inside, lumps of people lay in various states of undress, sprawled across tables and the floor. Pots of burning narcotic incense were scattered throughout the room, their acrid smoke mingling with the scent of spilled liquor. The sounds of moaning and flesh slapping against flesh filled the air, creating an overwhelming sense of debauchery.

At the very center of the tavern, in a large, throne-like chair, sat a hulking figure. Several women draped themselves across his legs and feet, one tipping a horn of mead into his mouth while others caressed his body. But this was no Lust Demon as they had expected. Instead of a bullish figure with hooves and horns, they were greeted by a creature with a mane of bright red feathers, creeping scales along his upper body, a lion's tail swishing lazily behind him, and bright yellow, serpentine eyes.

"Welcome, new friendsss," the creature hissed, its voice sharp and slithery, exactly as one might expect from a snake-like mouth.

The Cultists stiffened. This wasn't the kind of Fiend they were familiar with. It wasn't part of Asmodeus's brood, nor did it resemble any known creature of Malice. A new player, then? The older men were guarded, but Orphan, in contrast, was intrigued.

"Hello," Orphan replied, stepping forward past his companions. "Looks like you've been having a swell time. I can smell the mead, but I don't recognize the incense. Something you brought?"

The two villagers at the snake-man's feet shifted lazily, their eyes glazed as they reached out to touch Orphan, running their fingers along his legs as soft, lazy pleas slipped from their lips.

"Indeed. My own blend," the creature responded with a sly grin. "Yasssmine and sssandalwood… after being soaked in a barrel of wine and opium for a month, then dried out again." The Demon laughed, sharp and cruel, as it turned to nip at one of the women's breast as she draped over him, while his hand traced the edges of another's body.

"Who are you, Demon? We were expecting a Son or Daughter of Asmodeus, but instead, we find… you." Rhiel's tone was as sharp as a blade's edge, slicing through the thick fog of lust that clung to the air. One could almost hear him cursing his contact's name under his breath, the elf inwardly kicking himself for not asking more questions when the information had been offered. Ah, the arrogance of thinking things were ever as simple as they seemed.

"Insssstead, you have found a ssson of Haborym, the current Archfiend of Lussst."

Now, that caught the group off guard, didn't it? The Cultists stiffened at the mention of any other name than what they expected. Ah, poor fools living under the illusion that their peers remain static. Asmodeus may have ruled Lust for ages, but now? Well, even the most exquisite treasures fall. The Flame of Passion, once the epitome of sinful indulgence, was no more. A tragedy, really. Oh, the performances she would put on the seduction of the dance, the fire of her embrace. Priceless, truly. A greater prize than all the gold in the world. Ah, a true loss.

"Since when?! Fuck! The most perfect set of tits gone! Ow!" Serk howled, his outburst quickly silenced by Rhiel's swift backhand to the back of his head. The man was still grumbling obscenities, but his savage tongue was far less amusing now. As for the current Lust Demon in front of them? The creature merely smirked, his hands continuing to toy with his thralls, their bodies writhing under his touch, their faces twisted in rapture. Ah, the power of lust, when wielded by a master.

"During the Lost Eleven Years of Madness," He hissed, his voice slithering through the air like smoke from a dying flame. "The Queen of Ssssteps and Sssstrides ruled Lust when it began, and by the end, the King of Eternal Celebration held the crown. My father, Lord Haborym, hasss lived in Holmgård sssince then."

A city of fire, industry, and blood. One of the few free cities of Ereth, situated at the very end of a large mountain range and a natural harbor. It climbs into the sky and digs into the earth, being built into a semi-dormant volcano. Using its mass of factories and seemingly unlimited source of iron and coal, there is no place in the world that produces more steel than Holmgård.

"But that's a hundred years," Rhiel muttered, his mind reeling. "No Archfiend outside of Dis has ever stayed in one place for that long… though, if any could, it would be an Archfiend of Lust."

Ah, Rhiel. Always so quick to catch on once the pieces are laid bare. How clever, yet how slow. The more the Cultist thought about it the more it made sense. To the point that they felt a little foolish that their order hadn't caught on. Giving a little credit, the Cult of the Seventh Sun rarely has large meetings when there isn't a Tyrant on the rise. Even that was contributing to the problem as the Tenth, Eleventh, and Twelfth Tyrant refused the Cult's services and so the members maintained their distance from each other.

The Lust Demon smile widened as he pulled away from the women fawning at his legs, his towering frame moving with a grace that belied his size. He chuckled darkly, standing before the group like a monarch before his court. "Father has kept a tight leasssh on the brood. Only two othersss of my sssiblings have left the city. Not that many want to."

With a flick of his hand, his thralls tumbled to the floor, their mewling now a background symphony to his serpentine movements. He stepped forward, the thin cloth around his waist barely containing the raw, animalistic power of his form. Bright red feathers cascaded down his mane, contrasting sharply with the creeping scales along his back. His lion's tail swished rhythmically behind him, while his snake-like eyes gleamed in the dim light.

"My name is Sagares," he hissed, his voice dripping with sin. "It is my pleasssure to meet you, Heir of Gluttony. I was told you require my influence to become a naughty-naughty boy."

"I have need of you because, so far, I've been surrounded by bugs that are incapable of understanding basic human interaction," Orphan started, stepping closer, meeting the lustful demon eye to eye. There was an intensity about him oh, this boy, this would-be Tyrant, wasn't the feeble shell of a child anymore. Orphan's voice carried a weight, laced with bitter frustration. "And an army of bootlicking suck-ups that can only be described as pure fodder."

Sagares the slithering serpent of lust, oh how he basked in his own vanity, a proud, towering form amidst his writhing thralls shifted his attention fully to Orphan now. Ah, look at him preening, the self-satisfied grin tugging at the corners of his mouth as he circled. No doubt the Demon was savoring the smell of young ambition, tempered by Orphan's devilishly handsome, albeit corrupted features. A face crafted by the gift of Guile, wrapped in layers of frustration and desperation. And lust, let's not forget the hunger in those darting eyes, glancing toward the naked forms of Sagares's toys.

"I'm going to become the next Tyrant," Orphan declared, voice steady, his conviction barely masking a simmering rage. "And in order to do that, I need more than a legion of insects at my beck and call. Tell me you can help in that."

Ah, the classic demand. What else could a young ruler-in-the-making ask for? Power. Dominion. The thrill of watching others fall in line. He's already learned enough to know that Fiends won't give him what he needs. He's tired of dancing to their whims. Now, he's calling the shots or at least, he's trying to.

"I can," Sagares hissed, the words dripping with amusement. His serpentine eyes gleamed as he circled, studying Orphan like a predator savoring its prey. "But ssshould I?"

The Demon was testing him now, circling like a viper about to strike, tasting the potential oozing from the young Cursed Born. Sagares was worried that Orphan, having been raised in the Hive, surrounded by emotionless creatures, might have been reduced to a hollow, calculating puppet. But there, beneath the surface, Sagares could sense it, ambition. If a bit aimless, it was there.

"Yeah, you should," Orphan replied, unfazed. By now, he was used to being judged, weighed by creatures who sought any excuse to dismiss him as unworthy.

"Isss that confidenssse or arrogansssse?" Sagares's voice slithered between the lines, a thin veneer of menace coating his words. "I want to believe it'sss the latter, but I need sssome proof of that. You want to become a Tyrant? Could you do it without it being handed to you?" With a sudden snap of movement, Sagares grabbed the neck of one of his thralls and chucked it at the wall, breaking it enough that the winter air blew inside. Blood sprayed, a sickening crunch echoed through the room, but no one panicked. Oh no, they were far too lost in their narcotic haze to care. The wind from outside rushed in, carrying with it the stench of blood and death. Sagares didn't so much as blink.

"And why did you do that?" Orphan asked with a raised eyebrow as the Demon slithered to stare into the Cursed Born's eyes, inches away from his face.

"I needed to sssober these thralls a little, sssso they can ansssswer some questionsss. The breeze should help with that," Sagares explained, his voice as casual as if discussing the weather. He moved through the piles of writhing bodies with a serpentine grace, stopping at two men lying back on a bed of furs. "Alssso, that woman sssmelled of fish in the wrong way, sssshe offended my tastesss."

"Right," Orphan muttered, glancing back at the three cultists, their expressions steely, their hands twitching toward their weapons. And why shouldn't they be ready? This Demon was a wild card, unpredictable in ways the typical lustful Fiend was not. Where the Demons of Lust were often affectionate patrons of their thralls, this one treated his playthings as disposable. A creature so indulgent, so drunk on vice, it seemed irrational to even the most seasoned of cultists.

Sagares continued, ignoring the discomfort of the cultists. "The two of these men came by a few days ago to collect tribute. This village is under the protection of the harbor town Narfasker. Apparently, it sssssurvived because it makesss the best mead around." As if on cue, Serk grabbed a barrel of the drink, pouring it sloppily into his mouth, half of it spilling onto his chest, though the satisfied grunt afterward suggested he didn't care. Sagares turned back to his thralls. "Hey, you two. How many ships are in Narfasker?"

"Uh…"

"I think…"

"Maybe…"

"Six?"

"No."

"Seven?"

"Yeah… that."

"Eh, best I'm going to get," Sagares muttered, stepping forward and casually crushing the two men beneath his feet. The sound of bones cracking under the weight of his body echoed through the room. Orphan frowned there went his only source of useful information. Was this Demon drunk on vice or just drunk on his own power? The boy thought to himself, the answer is yes.

Orphan's patience was thinning. "Is there a point to any of this, or are we just going to keep running through your collection of thralls?" His voice carried the edge of a blade, cutting through the absurdity of the situation. "Honestly, I'm starting to think having you around might not be the smartest idea. You're acting more like a Demon of Sloth than Lust from what I've seen."

Ah, there it is poking the beast, daring it to show its true colors. Orphan knew what he was doing, knew how to push buttons when necessary. The Demon froze, eyes burning with rage. Oh, the comparison to Sloth, how that stung. Every Demon in existence despised the Sin of Sloth. Nothing enraged them more than being compared to that miserable, parasitic brood.

"Do not compare me to thossse Failuresss!" Sagares snapped, the anger in his voice palpable. His body coiled like a serpent about to strike. "The point isss that you mussst find your own power. None will follow a Tyrant who isss given hisss power."

"He has a point, kid," Serk chimed in, ever the savage voice of brutal wisdom. "If you want to rule the Soarlands, you'll need to at least start off with your own reputation. Even if you have an army of bugs, the Sons and Daughters of

Soar will never accept a ruler who hasn't taken anything for himself."

Sagares hissed in agreement. "Narfasker isss a couple hundred people, with ssix or ssseven crews of Sssoarling maraudersss and the sssupporting villagesss. Conquer it, and you have the makingsss of your own Jarldom. A bare minimum if you want anyone to take you ssseriously, brat."

Orphan's lips twisted into a smirk. "Again? Is another Demon telling me to conquer something before it'll help me?" Ha! Well you do wish to be a Tyrant, that's what they do.

Words of the Tenth

Sheep lost, shepherd astray
Screams of humility find their way
Lullaby hums, pride at bay

Esamoair zd hahittgn

A door swung open to a cacophony of clinking mugs, raucous laughter, and the tangy smell of ale. Orphan and Rhiel slipped into the rowdy tavern unnoticed, cloaked in the shadows and noise. Coins flew across the bar in reckless arcs, landing in waiting hands or scattering onto the sticky floor. The tavern's owner, sprawled on the ground with one hand clutching an axe and the other greedily snatching the offerings from the Soarlings, looked to be somewhere between gratitude and terror. Clearly, something had stirred up a rare bout of festivity in this dark corner of the world.

"It's refreshing to see this place so lively," Rhiel remarked, eyeing the revelry as they claimed a corner for themselves more accurately, as they tossed out the drunkards who had already claimed it.

"No," Orphan murmured, scanning the room with a knowing squint. "It's fake. I know when someone's smiling to hide how they really feel." But even as he spoke, a real grin toyed at his lips, fleeting and faint. A silly thought, a glimpse of a future that could never be. The boy watched, entranced, as a pair of Skalds took turns on their instruments, sparring with sharp words and slick insults in a flyting duel that brought the room to a crescendo.

So there they sat, the Elf and the Cursed Born, cloaked in shadow at the back of the tavern nestled in the heart of the sleepy harbor town. One of many scattered along the Soarland coast, these quiet ports, called Havnskar by the locals, had become sanctuaries from the endless cycle of Soarling raids. Tradition and practicality had kept these towns standing, and few reached populations into the high thousands, too many young lives lost to the allure of raiding, the call of adventure on the seas, or just the plain old death, disease, and murder that swept through life here.

This particular Havnskar, Narfasker, was oddly bustling. Its cobbled streets swarmed with a motley mix of sailors, traders, fishermen, and marauders alike. Orphan and his company had arrived at just the right time, it seemed. Ship holds brimmed with the spoils of recent raids, gleaming loot, and southerners chained in irons to be sold as thralls. There was a steady stream of ambitious travelers from the south seeking their fortunes in Glimisvellir, a shining promise on the horizon yet many of these hopefuls forgot they first had to survive the journey north. For those without the Confederate Navy's protection, the sea was treacherous, and not all would reach their promised land.

"Times have been rough for the Soarlings," Rhiel mused, his voice almost swallowed by the din. "I suspect the brief rejuvenation they had under the last Tyrant is wearing thin. The moat of floating glaciers won't protect them forever. They were already on the ropes for a couple hundred years now, I suspect this might be the last generation of true Soarling raiders." Wise words, though they might pain me to admit. The once-feared longships, the marauders brandishing axes, the proud raiders all had found their place on the edge of obsolescence. Gunlines and cannons the thunder of the south did more damage to them than any wave or storm could.

Orphan, though, barely heard him, lost in the cadence of the Skalds' voices as the next song struck up. Ah, let the Elf worry about fading glory. The Heir of Gluttony had his eyes on the new performance.

In the land where the fjords touch the sky,
Where the mountains are mighty, and the seas never dry,
There came a swarm, darkening the day,
Locusts of gluttony, in the fields they lay.

Sing of the locusts, the feast that they bring,
A tale of the gluttons, the songs that we sing.
In joy or in sorrow, let the voices ring,
For the feast of the locusts, let the taverns swing.

They devoured the harvest, their mercies unkind,
In the halls of the craven, their feast they did find.
From the richest of kings to the humblest of men,
No table was spared from the swarm's gluttonous den.

Sing of the locusts, the feast that they bring,
A tale of the gluttons, the songs that we sing.
In joy or in sorrow, let the voices ring,
For the feast of the locusts, let the taverns swing.

The mead hall was filled with their buzzing and hum,
As the gluttons feasted, the skalds would strum.
A lesson in life, to find what one can take,

In the swarm's shadow, any man can break.

Sing of the locusts, the feast that they bring,
A tale of the gluttons, the songs that we sing.
In joy or in sorrow, let the voices ring,
For the feast of the locusts, let the taverns swing.

So raise up your horns and remember the tale,
Of the locusts and gluttons, and how they prevail.
They move through the world, devouring their morsels
And we take the scraps and scavenge the corpses.

Sing of the locusts, the feast that they bring,
A tale of the gluttons, the songs that we sing.
In joy or in sorrow, let the voices ring,
For the feast of the locusts, let the taverns swing.

May our holds be full, our tables be barren,
In the echo of locusts, let us return to our cabins.
With gold and iron we take what we please,
A song of gluttony, we thank those pesky fleas.

"It sounds like news of the Ravenous Swarm's presence in the Soarlands has spread," Rhiel muttered, his eyes scanning the lively tavern as he and his new charge lingered in a shadowed corner. Around them, Soarling raiders lifted their voices in raucous, cheer-filled songs, seemingly thrilled at the prospect of Beelzebub's brood scouring the land. Only vultures like these would sing praises for a force as callous and all-devouring as the Swarm. It takes a special kind of stupidity or bravery, I suppose to find glory and riches in the wake of Fiendish devastation. Though, more often than not, it's the former.

"Do people really have songs about Fiends like that?" Orphan asked, glancing around with mild curiosity, his voice carrying just the slightest tinge of amusement. Ah, but of course they do, dear boy. Many a soul has found profit in the powers of Malice and learned to respect, if not cherish, the ruin it leaves behind in this twisted world.

"Different peoples have different opinions on Fiends," Rhiel explained, nodding toward the revelers. "Some Sins are more hated than others, but Soarlings well, they have a particular fondness for the kin of Beelzebub." He'd seen it plenty before: Soarling raiders following a Swarm downriver, drawn like wolves to carrion. Beelzebub's kin have no interest in gold or treasure; they consume only flesh. So, when a Swarm has devoured every edible morsel in a village, they leave behind a wealth of untouched valuables. And even when armies are sent to exterminate the Swarm, that too provides opportunity whether it's the remnants of the Fiends or the weakened soldiers who survive, the Soarlings relish easy prey.

"Well, hopefully, this will make everything all the easier for me." Cocky, the young man leaned back in his chair, taking a horn of mead from a nervous serving girl who seemed unsure whether to look him in the eye. Rhiel managed a thin, uneasy smile, still cautious about the workings of Orphan's mind. After several days in Hafnarlond, the boy had gathered the Cultists of the Seventh Sun and declared he had crafted a way forward, a plan to begin the march toward his own ascendancy.

Of course, to move forward, Orphan had to take Narfasker.

Not only would claiming the town bring another Demon to his banner, it would establish him as a genuine threat, a leader worthy of commanding the powers of Malice. And let's be honest: the boy was tired of waiting. All those endless days spent training, studying, stewing in the depths of the Hive, being told he'd one day conquer the world. What fun is a destiny of domination when you're kept in a cave? He'd prove it to the Demons, regardless of their Sin, and to himself, that he could rise beyond the weak, powerless urchin he'd been in Glimisvellir. This? This would be his next grand step forward.

The two waited patiently until the last few patrons stumbled out, leaving the tavern finally empty. With some… encouragement…the few stragglers were swiftly dealt with. The owner? He was taking a little nap, tied up down in the cellar. Now, the tavern stood quiet, chairs and tables pushed aside, the floor left bare and ready for the night's final guests.

"Who the fuck got White Blood Serk to call us?" The doors were kicked open, and nine figures filed in, tough and hard-eyed, each one dressed in furs and chainmail, trophies of raids gleaming from their belts and shoulders. Axes, hammers, knives, more axes. A collection of Soarling captains, the kind who've lived long enough to carve out bloody names and who fear nothing, least of all the skinny, pale Cursed Born standing calmly in the middle of the tavern floor.

"Devil spawn," one muttered, scratching his greasy, booze-stained beard. "He'd fetch a high price down in Marrakesh." The others chuckled.

"But he's cute," another, a woman with a voice like a blade across stone, sneered. "Might just keep him as a bed warmer."

"Enough, all of you!" The largest of the group, a towering man with a thick battleaxe resting against the floor, glared at them into silence before turning his scarred gaze onto Orphan. "Whelp, just how do you know White Blood Serk?"

Orphan kept his gaze steady, a smirk on his lips that looked confident. Internally, however, he was coiled tight, fully aware he had no chance in a one-against-nine brawl. The reason he couldn't just fight his way to their loyalty was obvious: he'd never be able to kill them all before they banded together, fled, or worse. But dirty fighting? Now, that was a language he spoke fluently.

"Glad Serk managed to gather you all here tonight." His voice was calm, cool, with that same sardonic edge, belying his racing heartbeat. He was betting it all on this, knowing there'd be little chance to escape if things went sideways.

"When White Blood Serk demands something, we listen or do we want our throats torn out?" the largest captain growled, the others bristling like coiled wolves.

"Serk's no longer part of this," Orphan replied, his tone unwavering, "but he did me a favor to bring you here."

The captain grunted, hefting his axe with a dangerous glint in his eye. "I don't care how a whelp like you gets a favor from White Blood Serk. All I'm hearing is that we can kill you or waste our time without worry." His grip tightened on the axe, and the rest of the captains readied their weapons, each one taking a step forward. Now, only ten paces separated Orphan from nine seasoned killers.

"Wait!" Orphan raised a hand, and they paused, amused at the defiance of this lone devil spawn.

"Why?" one of them scoffed.

"Wait!" For a laugh they all did. "I have asked you all here for one simple request, that you all submit to me." Two seconds. That's what it took for them to begin laughing at Orphan. Deep hearty laughs, the kind you rarely have and just have to savor when you get the chance. Just as planned. "Li-Me-Me-Li Bel-Me-Me-Da Er-Li-Er-Fir Bel-Bel-Me-Me Da-Me-Da-Li."

"Shit! He's casting!" It was too late, the first thing everyone knew when fighting a Mage was to stop them before they finished their Sets. But their little laugh had given Orphan plenty of time to start his chants of the Words of Invocation. The nine paces that they needed to take to get to him was only four by the time the Cursed Born reached out and from his five glowing fingers extended out fleshy tendrils from his fingertips.

They whipped and lashed out, splitting into nine deadly ropes of sinew that all found their place in some patch of flesh in their targets. The captains froze as they felt something needle their skin and then recoiled as they realized just what kind of magic Orphan had used. Fleshcrafting. The Compound Magic of Life and Dark, one of the most feared magics in all the world for very-very reasonable reason. How could you not fear the concept of being changed from the inside out, your very meat rebelling against you and morphing to the whims of some deranged mage. The Soarlings stood frozen, even the largest and bravest of them had grown still as he felt the tendril pierce his neck.

"Excellent, now we understand each other," Orphan declared, a grin spreading from ear to ear as he looked over his captive audience. His voice held a dark amusement, his eyes gleaming with malicious satisfaction. "Now, the spell I just cast? It isn't finished yet. In a few days, you could find yourselves sprouting lovely growths, sacks of pus bubbling up in your guts, turning you into something even a leper would pity."

Ah, that look in their eyes a mix of terror, disbelief, and dawning horror as they realized this bratty mage held their lives on a string. Orphan could almost taste their panic. These seasoned captains, each one convinced this scrawny Cursed Born was just a lucky whelp, now stood shackled to his whim.

"You have our interest, boy," one of them growled, though his voice wavered. "Spit it out."

Orphan's smirk only widened. "You're all going to die. That part's set. But whether it's in a few days or a few months? That's up to how you behave." He flicked his wrist, the tendrils retracting and snapping free, leaving each captain clutching their chest, foolishly relieved. Did they think the danger had passed? As if he hadn't just warned them? Their fates now hung over their heads like a noose, tightening with each breath.

"You'll be coming to me every couple of weeks, if you want to stave off the inevitable. I think you get the idea."

"Yeah, we get it." The bravado had thinned, replaced by resentful murmurs and fearful glances as they shuffled out of the tavern, clutching their chests and muttering curses. Each one had come expecting a legend, a tale of White Blood Serk. Instead, they found themselves tethered to the will of a pale Cursed Born barely out of boyhood, afflicted with a sickness only he could control. How delightful.

Orphan waited until the door shut behind them before he let out a long, shuddering sigh of relief, the tension draining from his body as he fell back onto his rear. He laughed, faintly at first, then louder as he realized he'd just pulled it off. The whole thing was a bluff! A risky, beautifully orchestrated bluff. Every ounce of bravado he'd shown? All pure nerve. Orphan knew exactly three spells. Three. In all his years of painstaking study and frustrating effort, he'd managed only three spells.

There was Heal, of course a spell that had saved his life countless times as a child. Then there was Bear Fruit, a bit of Life magic that enlarged fruit-bearing plants to, well, the size of small bears. The Imps had cheered at the increase in rations when he'd discovered that one. Two spells of the Cardinal Point of Life, handy but far from impressive. And then there was String of Sinew, the Compound Magic of Life and Dark. A fearsome name for something that amounted to creating a few tendrils of muscle from his fingers. Nothing more, nothing less.

Unashamed, Orphan crawled over to a nearby table, grabbed an abandoned mug, and took a long, indulgent gulp, sighing as the ale's warmth spread through him. The nights he'd spent muttering incantations, hoping for some spark of magic to finally take shape it had all seemed so futile at times. None of the Demons cared much about his magic beyond Heal, but Orphan knew he needed more. Any magic, no matter how small, could become a weapon in the right hands. And finally, his diligence had paid off.

This… this was his victory. A sense of pride, foreign and almost overwhelming, swelled within him. Looking down at his hand, the skin still bearing the faint, leathery marks of his Fleshcrafting, Orphan felt a fierce satisfaction. Unlike his escape from Glimisvellir, his encounter with Beelzebub, or the skills drilled into him by the Demons, this achievement was purely his. His plan, his magic, his victory.

"By the fact you aren't a bloody mess on the floor, guess they bought it, lad?" Serk's booming voice cut through the empty tavern as he and the other cultists entered from the back. Orphan, by this point, was three horns deep in his drink, still sprawled on the floor, his back propped against an overturned table.

"Aye! They're at the table now. Just need to get them to eat the meal," he replied, his words slightly slurred but his grin unwavering. Indeed, the real work had just begun. His first foothold in the Soarlands was secure, but becoming a Jarl in his own right, that was a far trickier feat.

The Soarlings' hierarchy was simple yet brutal. At the bottom were Chiefs, who ruled the smallest villages or wandering bands, and Captains, who commanded ships and held absolute power while at sea. Whenever they docked at a Havnskar, they shared power, but the authority here was fluid and cutthroat. Above them were the Jarls, the rulers of a Havnskar and the final authority within its walls though, by tradition, a Havnskar rarely went without at least two Captains to keep the Jarl in check. Jarls and chiefs, in truth, were essentially the same rank, just expressed in different dialects of the Soarlings' native tongue. Then there were the Havi, three kings of sorts, each reigning over one of the Soarlands' so-called "cities."

The term "city" was generous; only one of these places even vaguely resembled one, and that was because it had been founded by a Naga prince who'd failed to foresee the perils of building a colony in a frozen wasteland. The other two cities clustered around ancient castles from the Age of Gods, far larger than Glimisvellir but unimpressive by any other standard.

But for Orphan, a would-be Tyrant, this step on his Path to Conquest was vital. Controlling a Havnskar wasn't just about having captains under his thumb; he'd have to earn the allegiance of the town's people. They wouldn't submit to a Cursed Born simply because he had a few captains cowering before him. No, they were Soarlings proud, blood-hardened folk who respected strength and despised anything weak or unproven. As he'd said, he had them at the table, but now he had to make them swallow every bitter mouthful.

"Your plan is working, young lord," Rhiel remarked with a smirk as he settled down across from Orphan, taking his own mug of ale. "I must say, I am impressed."

Serk jumped onto the table beside them, grinning as he slapped Orphan's shoulder in approval. "It's only working because I indulged him! Ha! Worth every second to see those milksops crawl out of here so destroyed! To die in a bedroll, not on the field having your own flesh betray you? Nothing's more shameful for a true son of Soar!"

Serk's laughter echoed through the empty tavern, his boisterous voice filling every corner. The others chuckled politely, though Serk's raucous glee was a thunder unto itself, a storm of old glory and rough pride that shook the walls.

"Serk!" Orphan yelled up, ooh… the drink getting to him a bit isn't now. "Why did they call you White Blood, there must be a story behind that."

"Ah little lad, there isn't. It is but a name given to me by those that recall me and the blood stained on my beard. So often it's covered in the crimson nectar. It is an old name; I do not recall to whom gave it to me."

Those listening, save for Orphan, had heard the tale many

times. An ancient warrior, clad in blood and renown, whose brutality had soaked into the soil of countless battlegrounds. There was always blood in his wake, an endless river that flowed through his life.

Orphan took another swig. "Just… how old are you?"

"Hmm… Rhiel, do you remember?" With a chuckle, Serk pulled off his helmet, as if he'd only just realized he'd been wearing it. He scratched his head and stroked his long white beard, the crimson gleam of his eyes now fully visible, lined with blackened stains that dripped down from the edges like molten pitch. But it was his mouth that held the others' gaze two rows of jaws, each filled with jagged, gnarled teeth that had likely torn through bone and sinew more times than any cared to know. His only softening feature was the mass of thick white hair that framed his grotesque face.

"You're the third oldest among us, Serk," Rhiel said, though even he couldn't hide his distaste at the sight of the vampire's monstrous visage. "Only milady and the High Priest are older."

"Fourteen and thirty-six hundred years," Samium intoned, his voice cold and dispassionate.

Orphan's eyes widened, the concept almost impossible for him to grasp. He'd grown up thinking his life would end at thirteen. "Four… what?"

"Yes," Rhiel went on, indulging Orphan's shock. "You see, the Cult of the Seventh Sun has two requirements to enter." No, far more, but go on. "You must pledge yourself to the powers of Malice… and you must not be capable of dying."

The Cult existed purely for the service of the Powers of Malice, and of course Tyrant as the most manifested form of that power. Service is for eternity. Membership in the

Court of a Tyrant also grants immortality of sort, allowing the courtiers to live so long as their lord does. But die once the Tyrant does. All that experience and wisdom gone. And then there's the Cult, made up of those who have slipped free from death's hold through their own means. The Cult has served since the Third Tyrant, holding memories, knowledge, and secrets through countless ages.

"Aye," Serk said with a grin, blood seeping between his fangs with every syllable. "I've been this bloodsucking creature since I was turned all those years ago. But who cares? Monster or not, I was always a beast at heart."

Serk laughed, blood spitting out from between his teeth with every word. A literal ocean of blood has passed through that deep gullet, untold numbers of bodies eaten and drained of their crimson life. In the Soarlands, the name Jarl Serk was spoken with a mixture of fear and twisted reverence, a tale of horror told to frighten children in the southern lands, who believed all Soarlings were cannibals because of him.

"Among my people, magic is a rare gift," Rhiel added, his voice softer, yet not without a note of pride. "I gained the Majorus of Death, and found a spell to extend my life beyond my kin's who already live quite long, mind you."

But what a cost, elf. Banished, shunned, and left wandering. This longevity had earned him nothing but disdain and exile from those he once called his own. He, too, had walked the path alone for centuries. But the elf-thing wasn't concerned with that now he'd reconciled those questions long ago.

All eyes now turned to the final figure. Samium, the silent shadow, sighed and answered in his usual blunt fashion. "I'm already dead. I'm a specter."

It was true; the empty robes held no body, no substance.

Samium was merely an echo, a memory of flesh and blood long since claimed by the soil. He was a relic of a past life, a rare specter who had endured the Shattering of Death and remained whole, with mind and will still intact.

Once, the gods had jealously guarded the souls of their followers, permitting no spirit to linger in the mortal realm. But the gods were gone, and cairns and graveyards now echoed with wailing ghosts. Even so, a specter with a conscious mind was a rarity, a ghost that had retained its sense of self despite the horrors of death.

"We have served all the Tyrants that have passed since the third... except the past three. Both the Tenth and Twelfth didn't seem to appreciate the Cult's value and actively shunned us. For different reasons though." The former was a Devil of Hell that had hated the elites of the world and saw the Cult of the Seventh Sun as just that... and he wasn't wrong. Meanwhile the Pirate King of Terror and Cruelty did not see the value in what could not die, where was the challenge and risk in the unliving?

"And the Eleventh was fuckin' crazy!" Serk bellowed, his laughter so hearty it spilled him onto his side, along with the contents of his mug. "But hey, there's a reason those three had the shortest reigns of all the Tyrants!" His booming voice filled the room, though the waste of perfectly fine ale dampened the cheer ever so slightly.

Indeed, history had shown that a Tyrant's success often aligned with their willingness to listen to the Cult. But then again, success is a subjective thing, defined differently by the prideful, the mad, and the ambitious. Who could say for sure, ey?

"And so, what? I should always listen to my great and

very handsome new friends?" Orphan drawled, the snark unmistakable in his tone. It earned him a few chuckles and nods from his companions. Precocious little scamp, who's a budding dastardly mastermind? Yes you are.

"I merely suggested a less deceitful approach," Rhiel countered, his voice clipped with faint disapproval. "Lying only begets misery."

Oh, the irony. Words spoken by an elf who had spent centuries weaving lies so artful even he likely believed some of them.

"You've never had the stomach for shadows, Rhiel. That's my domain." Serk leaned back against the table, his monstrous grin flashing through the dim light. The vampire, for all his brutish veneer, was far more cunning than most gave him credit for. He was a hedonist, a vain creature who had survived his long existence by mastering fear, terror, and deceit. While others might seek glory in battle, Serk was far more likely to bloody his rival's bedchamber or leave a trail of whispers in his wake. He was a beast of the shadows, and he wore the role with pride.

"Fleshcraft," Samium said with a faint shudder. "No one ever wants to meet a mage capable of it. Even hearing the First Set spoken is enough to turn most men's blood cold. But our future lord here? He used his tools to their best effect. Would you serve a lord who misused his tools… again?"

The shadows in the room seemed to shift, as if leaning into the specter's words. And all those of vaunted age noticed.

The weight of Samium's pointed remark wasn't lost on anyone, least of all Rhiel. The elf's jaw tightened, but he said nothing. For all their bravado, the Cult had yet to fully commit to Orphan's cause. To them, this was still a performance, a passing entertainment until the boy claimed his throne and earned the Title of Tyrant. They had seen the script but not yet taken to the stage, waiting on the lead's performance to see it worthy of their presence next to the spotlight.

"And that's exactly what I was counting on," Orphan cut in, his voice laced with youthful confidence. "Fear makes people do stupid things. It makes them easy to trick, especially when they've already convinced themselves the threat is real."

Ah, such a splendid student. The boy had been under the tutelage of Igurim for only a short time, but he'd taken to the Demon's lessons on fear with a natural talent. The art of wielding terror, of planting dread so deeply it became self-sustaining. Yes, the brat had learned well. But the conversation was to be cut short as an unwanted spectator had his fill of waiting and the three cultists knew it.

"Enough of our sob stories. You did it kid, I might have tossed you the axe but you're the one that split the log." Serk grinned as he and the other two immortals subtlety began inching away. Orphan was too busy basking in the glow of this acknowledgement of the moment that he didn't notice.

"I did it," he whispered, his voice tinged with awe. "Me." He clenched his fists, the sense of accomplishment washing over him like a long-awaited sunrise. But looking back up... they were gone.

The sound of boots against the hardwood floor cut through his reverie like a knife. All eyes turned toward the shadowed doorway as one of the captains stepped forward. The same captain who had led the group earlier, his stoic demeanor now laced with a cautious edge. Yet, despite the tension, there was a smugness about him, a confidence that danced dangerously close to arrogance.

Orphan's smirk didn't waver. "Need something? We'd be happy to help."

"I think only you can." The captain's response was casual, almost lazy, as he scratched his stubble and let the moment stretch, drawing Orphan's focus. "That was a fast cast, kid. Impressive. But you only cast one spell: String of Sinew. You didn't also cast Molded Maleficence."

The words hit Orphan like a blade hidden in silk. He kept his expression neutral, maintaining the lighthearted veneer with a click of his toes and a practiced smirk. "Maybe I don't need that spell. Could have something all my own. That's the fun thing about us spellcasters, bit of randomness with what you get."

How does this man know of Fleshcrafting spells? Any Cardinal Point or Compound Magic spells are tightly guarded by their practitioners, common names for the same effect or ability form and are spoken of but rarely known to a wider public. Orphan only knew the name String of Sinew as it was found mentioned in a tome that had been stolen in of the Feind's caravan raids. No Sets were given but the effect matched what Orphan had discovered. He never heard of the spell Molded Malfeasance however, and it irked him that this Soarling captain knew it.

"Could be," the captain replied, his tone still infuriatingly calm. "But I also know what it's like to feel a twisted mass of hate and bile swelling in your body. To feel your own flesh fail so miserably it starts eating itself alive."

With a practiced motion, the man pulled back his hide shirt to reveal a grotesque scar, a mangled patch of tumors and growths twisted together dangerously close to his liver.

Burn marks and lumpy nubs dotted the surrounding skin, the telltale signs of failed attempts to remove the affliction by fire and blade.

"I've been looking for a Fleshcrafter to barter with. To fix this mess," he continued. "I've been sailing for ten years. I want to die by a worthy foe's lucky axe swing, not my own body giving out."

Orphan tilted his head, feigning a smirk to mask the knot of dread forming in his gut. "Ah, yes. The great dream of every Soarling to die gloriously, remembered by… what? A couple dozen people for a little while? Come on. Few get songs or sagas told about them."

He waved his hand dismissively, every movement calculated to distract. His eyes flitted subtly over the room, searching for an acceptable weapon. Coming here unarmed had been part of his ploy, a calculated gamble to put the captains at ease. But now he was alone, unarmed, and staring down an axe-wielding man with more experience and malice than he'd anticipated. The sweat beading on his brow betrayed the cracks in his composure.

"Tsk, you're a brat," the captain growled, his eyes narrowing. Yes. Yes he was. "And tell me, brat, why shouldn't I end you right now? You've got those milk-drinkers out there fooled, but I felt nothing when you cast that spell. If you can't cure me, what use are you?"

The thud of the captain's axe hitting the floor sent a shiver through the room. It was a big, ugly weapon, the kind designed for pure brutality. Its weight alone could turn Orphan's skull into a messy pulp, and the captain knew it.

"I know Heal," Orphan said with a shrug, letting the words hang in the air like a taunt.

"Really? A Life Majorus, truth be told I've met more Dark Majorus than Life. But none that had both. So brat, we can make a deal. And seeing how White Blood Serk and the other two have abandoned you I supposed whatever deal you had with them is at an end now?" Possibly, just as the Demons suffered no unworthy master neither did the Cult. Any sign of weakness or failed opportunity to prove oneself resulted in both parties devouring the unworthy candidate. In Serk's case quite literally.

"Seems so," Orphan replied, his voice steady despite the roiling thoughts in his mind. His eyes darted again, taking stock of the room. Three knives within reach, five with a sprint. Bone, not iron, but sharp enough. Options. Ideas. Dangerous ones, but familiar.

This was an old feeling being threatened, being cornered. It felt natural, even comforting in a twisted way. His body tensed, adrenaline coursing through his veins, not unlike those days in Glimisvellir when survival meant sharp instincts and even sharper teeth.

Threats of violence were nothing new to Orphan. The Glimingar had issued them constantly, and all he could do was grit his teeth and endure. He had no power to retaliate then, no way to fight back beyond hoping they'd dismiss him as beneath their time. The Demons had been no different, their taunts and tests battering him daily. Killing them had been unthinkable not until recently, when his power began to shift. Even now, they were too useful to discard.

But this man? This captain? He was disposable. And Orphan was confident.

The captain's threats were laced with years of experience, with the weight of violence as natural as breath. But they clashed against the overconfidence of a pale, lanky youth determined to prove himself. Orphan moved first, tossing his drink directly at the captain's face. The liquid splashed against his clothes, the stench of ale clinging to the man's chest as he let out an annoyed roar. He raised his axe high, aiming to cleave the boy in two, but Orphan had already rolled under the table, emerging on the other side like a shadow slipping through cracks.

Grabbing another horn of ale and a bronze knife, Orphan threw them both in quick succession. The horn crashed harmlessly against the wall. The knife missed by a puzzling margin, its arc far too wide for what should have been a perfect throw.

His aim was never this poor. Something was wrong.

The captain snarled, unfazed by the failed attack. "You little whelp!" With a roar, he grabbed the edge of the table and flipped it forward, sending it crashing toward Orphan. The boy's eyes widened, but his instincts kicked in. Agile as ever, he darted aside, his movements quick and slippery. The space between them felt tight, the air alive with tension. He scanned the room desperately, seeking another weapon, but taverns like this rarely housed true arms. Soarlings preferred fists to settle disputes, their weapons reserved for war and raids. A hammer or blade might ruin the fun, and these people were nothing if not devoted to their chaos.

"Why can't I hit you?" Orphan growled under his breath, dodging another wild swing. This time, instead of hurling another object, he lunged forward, closing the distance. He slipped beneath the wide arc of the captain's axe, weaving through his reach to go straight for his head. The bone knife in Orphan's hand gleamed briefly as he thrust it forward but it passed harmlessly aside the man's head, as if guided off course by some invisible force.

The captain's head snapped forward, delivering a crushing blow to Orphan's skull. Pain exploded in his vision as he crumpled to the ground, coughing up a blot of blood. The sound of the captain tossing his axe aside barely registered before a fist slammed into his face, and then another, each blow heavier than the last.

"Lucky little shit!" the captain snarled, his words fueled by frustration and jealousy. "I get Dark Majorus and Fire Minorus. The shadows blur my outline so no one ever lands a hit. But you?" Another punch cracked against Orphan's cheek, splitting the skin. "You have Heal? Heal?! Do you even know what I'd give for that?"

Crack. Smash. Each punch brought new sounds: bone breaking, skin splitting, flesh squishing under the force of his fists. This wasn't just violence; it was pettiness incarnate, a jealous rage made manifest. Orphan felt his skull crack. The room spun as blood dripped from his split lips, pooling on the tavern floor.

He wasn't going to survive this.

The captain yanked Orphan up by the collar, slamming his back into a support pillar. The wood groaned under the force. "You... your..." Orphan tried to speak, to deflect with a quip, but only blood and broken words spilled out.

"Thanks, brat." The captain grinned darkly. "I needed this. A beatdown always clears the head. I'll even let you live if you fix my body."

The words hung like a noose around Orphan's neck. The captain's fingers tightened, one hand wrapping around the boy's throat while the other grabbed Orphan's trembling hand, forcing it under his armor to press against the mass of tumors. "Do it. Heal. Now."

"I'm cold," Orphan murmured, his voice distant, faint. "Aren't you?"

"What?" The captain paused, confused. "Get on with it, brat wait… yeah. What the fuck?"

A cruel, bloodied grin spread across Orphan's face as the captain's body began to freeze. The booze Orphan had splashed on him earlier was still wet, and with a snap of his focus, the liquid hardened into ice, spreading rapidly across the man's armor and skin. His movements slowed, his muscles locked in place as frost spread up his arms and down his chest.

"Li-Me-Me-Li Bel-Me-Me-Da Er-Li-Er-Fir Bel-Bel-Me-Me Da-Me-Da-Li." The Words of Invocation spilled from Orphan's lips, and once again, tendrils of flesh erupted from his fingertips. This time, they were no mere pricks. His hand, still pressed against the captain's tumors, sent the tendrils burrowing into his body. They tore through the flesh like hungry worms, rupturing sacs of pus and aggravating the already inflamed mass.

He screamed as the pain fueled a panicked breaking of the ice, throwing Orphan aside in an attempt to get him away from his body. But the damage was done, pieces and scraps of innards mangled and torn spilled out of a fresh hole. The strong and grizzled ship captain stumbled and tried to maintain his balance but the pain and blood loss won in the end, tumbling face first into the stained tavern floor. Silence then. Broken by some heavy breathing and hasty speaking of Words of Invocation. Orphan healed his face and body as quickly as he could before standing up and approaching the still body on the ground.

"Don't worry, I'll heal you just enough for us to discuss things like rational people. Can't have me losing someone… oh… wait. Are you dead?" Slowly, the young man stepped forward and then again and again until he was standing over the motionless form of the Soarling Captain whose name he never got.

Softly glowing green eyes moved ever so slightly as they took in the sight. His breath was still but the fingers that had been used to create the tendrils of flesh that did the deed twitched slightly. Ears listened, and heard nothing. No groans of pain, no gasps of breath, nothing at all. And that's what Orphan felt. Nothing. No guilt nor any pleasure. There wasn't this regret at taking another's life, snuffing out what they had been and what they could be. Bloodlust wasn't there either, neither satisfaction nor ecstasy came with the kill.

The young man leaned down, touched two fingers to the Soarling's neck and confirmed what he already knew. Nothing more, he walked away. Closed the door behind him and silently began to walk down the path toward the inn he and the Cultists had been staying at. Vaguely he began listing off in his head some combinations of Sets and Words of Invocation he had yet to try and musing what might the inn serve for breakfast the next day.

As Orphan disappeared into the night, leaving his first kill behind, Rhiel emerged from the shadows. The elf's sharp gaze fell on the fallen captain, his lips curling into a thoughtful smile. "Wasted potential…" he murmured. With whispered Sets of Invocation, a faint light flickered in the corpse's eyes.

Yes, potential like this should not go to waste.

And people thought Serk was the worst of them.

255

Words of the Eleventh

Truth in the minds of the Lame
Lies in the hearts of the Vain
Madness is only for the Sane

The Triumphant Return of the Leading Man

"Do you have any idea how important this is?"

"We don't think you grasp the situation, much less possess the right to accuse us of inaction."

"Two years! Two years our Heir has been missing gallivanting with the Suns and a Whore of Lust! And every attempt to track him down has resulted in the same dead ends and dead Imp parties!"

Ah, my dear Listener, behold a charming scene of camaraderie and professional discourse. Pause for effect. No? Too transparent? Fine, let's drop the pretense. What we truly have here is a delightful shouting match between two Demons, neither of whom has ever been accused of rational thinking.

Igurim and Arcon stood maw to maw in the Spawning Chamber, the air between them crackling with tension. Around them, other Demons of Gluttony lounged in the shadows, each watching the squabble unfold with amused detachment. The Chamber itself, a masterpiece of fiendish stonework, served as the Hive's primary meeting space, a grand arena where schemes were plotted, grievances aired, and fresh Imps were kicked about for sport. A most versatile venue.

"This argument happens every time we get a hint of the young lord's whereabouts. What's it about this time?"

The speaker, a recent permanent resident of the Hive, Lirochi, stood apart with Carelena and Ormenu, observing the scene with faint disinterest. For two years, this same tired quarrel had erupted whenever the smallest whisper of Orphan's movements reached the Hive. Igurim always insisted on hunting him down and drugging him into submission, while Arcon's preference for dragging him back kicking and screaming had become almost endearing in its simplicity. Talking, of course, was far too mundane and not nearly bruising enough.

"I was out raiding the countryside a bit," Ormenu began, his deep voice as smooth and oily as a well-polished gem. "Got a little peckish you two understand and one of the Soarlings started crying out to White-Blood Serk. Naturally, I got curious. Played with my food a bit and found out that Serk's been seen in the area. Apparently, the old man's been recruiting young, stupid men for the brat's army. But the juicy bit?" He grinned, sharp teeth glinting as he idly turned a ring on his clawed finger. "He let slip their next target: Kalfskinn."

Three ticks of a claw against his ring one, two, three and the room grew quieter, the other Demons leaning in just slightly. Ormenu's words hung in the air, their implications dripping like honeyed poison. He knew what they were thinking. Every previous sighting of Orphan had been happenstance, a stroke of luck by an Imp patrol or the whispers of mortals who feared his growing shadow. But Serk's involvement? That was deliberate.

When one of the most slippery spymasters in existence so casually spilled such crucial information, it wasn't mere coincidence. And Serk, for all his theatrics, was no fool.

Ormenu chuckled inwardly, savoring his own cleverness. Of course, he had lied. The location he'd given the Hive was close enough to seem plausible but distant enough to keep the Demons chasing shadows. Kalfskinn was a harmless bait a Havnskar near the two already under Orphan's control. The real target, however, was far more ambitious: a village under the thumb of a Jarl sworn directly to one of the three Havi.

But Arcon and its ilk couldn't see it. The blind spots of Fiends are as vast as their appetites. They still saw Orphan as a child, untested and unproven. They couldn't fathom the audacity required to challenge a Havi's dominion with only three Havnskar and a handful of ships. They underestimated him as mortals often underestimate Fiends. And yet, just as mortals can never truly comprehend the malice of Fiends, Fiends themselves can never grasp the mortal drive for ambition and change.

Ormenu, however, could see it plainly. He saw the boy they once knew, yes but also the budding monster, the hungry predator desperate to carve out his own throne. And oh, what a bloody throne it would be.

Amusement flickered in Ormenu's predatory eyes as he watched the Hive's Demons dissolve into disarray. Igurim's shrieking tantrum echoed through the Spawning Chamber, matched in pitch and volume by Arcon's snarling retorts. The other Demons and Imps kept to the shadows, observing with that peculiar mix of detached interest and veiled derision that Fiends so excel at. The scene was chaotic, a delightful mess of shouting and misplaced fury, and Ormenu found himself thoroughly entertained.

This was their weakness, after all. A Hive without its Heir was directionless, functional, yes, but lacking cohesion. When no leader emerged, the Hive could act as solitary hunters, each pursuing their own ravenous hunger. But the moment even the shadow of a ruler appeared, their nature compelled them to fall in line. The Hive needed a monarch. Without one, it was little more than a squabbling nest of beasts. Abezethibou, the only Demon that could possibly put an end to this mess, had not been seen for several weeks. And even then... the lazy bastard mostly ignored the affairs of the Hive in favor of its own lounging.

Ormenu's lips curled into a smug grin as he turned his attention from the gleaming gemstones on his rings to the disordered display before him. His Sin wasn't so different from theirs, truth be told. Greed, like Gluttony, required an Alpha. There must always be someone at the top of the heap, hoarding the greatest treasures, commanding the others to serve their ambition. It was simply the way of things.

"They might actually do something this time," Carelena teased, its voice carrying an edge of amusement as it sauntered up beside him. Its serpentine gaze flicked toward the escalating chaos with clear disdain.

Ormenu followed its gaze. The shouting match between Igurim and Arcon had devolved into barked orders, the Spawning Chamber alive with the scurrying of Imps being herded into formations. The plan was obvious: a small swarm would be sent to raid villages, culminating in a strike at Kalfskinn. It would be a lesson, no doubt a show of dominance meant to remind the wayward Heir of his place.

Fools. None of them seemed to grasp the bigger picture.

"I'm going to find a breeder and have some fun. Enjoy your elders' tantrum," Ormenu drawled, rising sluggishly to his full height. His powerful frame stretched, muscles rippling beneath his furred form, before he turned and lumbered away.

Carelena gave a languid wave as he departed, its eyes narrowing as it watched him leave. But Ormenu's path was not toward the mortal settlements within the Hive where women unlucky enough to catch his eye awaited. No, his destination lay above.

The fortified encampment above the Hive was a far cry from the grandiosity of the Spawning Chamber. It looked, to the untrained eye, like a well-established bandit camp wooden palisades, makeshift towers, and the scent of un-washed men and cheap ale hanging heavy in the cold moun-tain air. The illusion was deliberate. It kept the Glimingar and their ilk at bay, with only the occasional foolhardy raiding party daring to test the defenses. Those that did found themselves shredded by the Hive's ravenous spawn.

Only once had a true threat emerged: a detachment of Teuton soldiers hauling cannons up the treacherous mountain path. Ormenu fondly remembered that day not for the bloodshed, but for its lack. While the Demons and their spawn had prepared for battle, the wolf-thing had simply strolled into the enemy camp and handled matters the smart way. One of his lesser rings had purchased the soldiers' silence, sparing the Hive the spectacle of cannon fire. The few who refused the bribe? Disposed of by their comrades, of course. Mortals were such predictable creatures when properly incentivized.

"Byrnwold!" Ormenu's roar echoed through the fort as he approached, sending the stationed men scurrying like frightened rats. Though each had come to the Hive as a follower or servant of Demons, their fear of Fiends was ever-present. And rightly so.

The summoned man emerged, better armored than the others and bearing a scarred visage that spoke of hard-earned experience. Byrnwold approached Ormenu without hesitation, a glint of confidence or stupidity in his gaze. Even sheep know to fear the wolf, yet this one walked straight into its jaws.

"Yes Lord Ormenu, going out for a hunt? My scouts reported an elk this morning and I have yet to tell the bugs about it." Hearing that caused the Demon to lick his lips and feel a bit of a rush to claim such a meal before the bottomless pit that was the Ravenous Swarm could get to it. But he had to contain his urges but for a moment.

"Not today," he replied, his tone low and dangerous. "I'm going to retrieve our wayward Heir. The boy has been shirking his responsibilities, and I think old Arcon misses its favorite student." A dark chuckle followed, carrying with it implications Byrnwold dared not question.

"Only that I wish you luck being the vanguard of the Swarm, my lord." Already the Demon of Greed was reaching to one of small pouches that lined his rear armor to pull out the sufficient bribery that would need to take place here.

"Ahh, that's what I like about tyou. You don't seek to plunge every morsel down your gullet, that's not your sin of choice is it? Let's see… about fifty Teutonreach Vints should do it unless you wish to test your greed against mine?" And what a foolish endeavor that would be. Fiends of Greed do not become Demons by selfishly hoarding every last piece of gold or silver they grasp, or those that do are seen quite low, but knowing how best to use one piece of their horde to gather another greater piece. Coin is everywhere. It's painfully common to a Demon that lives so long as don't get sloppy. But worthy men? Loyalty to a preferred patron? That was worth any pile of measly gold.

"Forty should do it, me and the lads can survive off jerky and piss ale for a while longer." Just as equally a man might know when to pick such moments to be greedy and to be reserved. Demons must abide by their nature; mortals have the luxury of complexity.

"You'll take the fifty, eat too little and your strong bodies wither." Investment, not sentimentality.

"Very well my lord, happy hunting that elk." The mortal man took the bribe with a smile and several of his men made happy glances at each other knowing that they would be getting their small cut.

The gates of the Hive parted, and with a blur of motion, Ormenu surged into the snow-covered wilderness. The wolf-thing moved with a ferocity and speed that seemed to mock the natural world, his powerful legs propelling him through the trees, over rivers, and across the craggy ridges that defined the Glimingaric lands. What might take a mortal rider days, Ormenu accomplished in hours.

A Neustrian saying flickered through his mind: The greediest hand is the quickest to the rich man's pocket. It was often spoken as a warning against shortcuts to ill-gotten gains, but its origin lay in the Fiends of Greed, whose unnatural speed often left mortal eyes wide with disbelief. Ormenu was no stranger to embodying this particular maxim.

Two sets of powerful legs rushed out of the lands of the Glimingar, he had to be quick even by his own nature. The Swarm would move not nearly as fast but faster than the mortal man could. They would be going in the opposite direction towards a town that might have started preparing itself for a fight… not with a horde of hungry Imps and very annoyed Demons but still. Ormenu hoped that this would allow some aggression to be worked out and a fourth town under Orphan's banner. Meanwhile he was heading south where Kalfskinn was north of the swath of land the Hive knew Orphan had taken for himself.

Far in the distance, the gray expanse of the ocean appeared, shimmering like dull steel beneath the overcast sky. The wolf-thing's sensitive nose caught the acrid scent of smoke and blood, and his ears twitched at the faint echoes of screams. His pace slowed as he neared a ridgeline overlooking the forested coastline. Below, the Havnskar of Dritsker was aflame.

The town's palisades had been scaled, its defenses shattered. Fires raged at its center, their flickering light casting eerie shadows across the snow. The chaotic clamor of combat filled the air Soarling raiders clashing with the town's defenders, their battle cries mingling with the wails of the terrified. Ormenu cocked his head, observing the scene with a detached interest.

"Rough work," he muttered, his voice a low rumble. "Not much of value here, I suppose." The town wasn't worth much effort, but the disorganized brutality of the assault was of mild interest. Ormenu suspected Orphan's forces were testing themselves a skirmish to blood the inexperienced, not a calculated raid.

Then a particular scream pierced the din, a woman's voice, shrill with terror and hoarse from overuse. It was close.

Ormenu's ears perked as he scanned the tree line below, catching sight of a woman in a tattered gown. Her torn clothing hinted at finery, as fine as the Soarlings ever managed. She fled through the snow, stumbling and flailing in her desperation, pursued by a massive warrior clad in iron.

The wolf-thing's eyes narrowed as he studied the scene. The woman's cries marked her as someone of importance. Nobility, perhaps, or at least a favored concubine. She had the tenor of someone accustomed to being valued. But his interest lay in her pursuer.

The warrior was a towering figure, perhaps seven feet tall, his form encased in Soarling iron. The helm he wore bore no trophy horns; instead, a crown band and a shawl of chainmail adorned it, a striking combination reminiscent of Neustrian aristocracy. Ormenu's sharp mind connected the dots. This was no ordinary raider, this was one of Orphan's chosen.

"Ah, Orphan always did have excellent taste," Ormenu mused, lowering himself onto the snow-dusted ridge to rest after his journey. His amber eyes followed the unfolding drama below. "Big, strong, and useful. Yes, you'll need more like him, boy, if you're to rule with your frail little body."

The wolf-thing chuckled darkly. It was no secret among the Hive's Demons that Orphan would not be a Warrior-King. His malnourished childhood had stunted his physical growth, and though his mastery of Heal had kept him alive, it had come at a cost. The energy spent fueling his magic had drained what little reserves his body could muster. He would never be a brute force on the battlefield, but a Sorcerer-King?

A King of Shadows? That, Ormenu could see.

Below, the woman stumbled, her desperate pleas scraping against Ormenu's ears. "Please stop! I've done everything I was told! Have I not been useful " Her words were cut short as she tripped, sprawling into the snow at the edge of the tree line. The warrior loomed over her, his silence more damning than any words.

"Whimpering. Disgusting," Ormenu muttered, watching her futile attempts to crawl away. "Every creature must prove its worth, or it becomes a burden. The weak have no place in the world the Powers of Malice demand."

The warrior's spear descended in a sharp arc, and her screams were silenced. Blood pooled in the snow as her body stilled. Ormenu's tail flicked lazily, his interest waning.

But then the warrior looked up, his iron-shod visage turning toward the ridgeline. Ormenu smirked, unbothered by the cold, emotionless gaze that met his own.

"Is that so? And just whose lord do we share, mutt?" The warrior's voice sliced through the cold air, dripping with disdain. Ah, the cheek on this one. Feels familiar.

"Mutt?" Ormenu snarled, his hackles rising as his fiery eyes narrowed to slits. "I am as pure-blooded as they come, a Demon of the line of Mammon, Progenitor Archfiend of Greed. You will watch your tone, mortal, or I shall teach you the reverence a mere follower of Malice should show one of its incarnations."

Growl and bark all you wish, wolf-thing. A touchy subject indeed among the Voracious Pack, whether one was spawned pure from the pools of Malice or birthed from the wombs of breeder-slaves. Ormenu was of the former, and like his spawned kin, he wore his origins with pride.

"Teach me, then," the warrior replied, resting his spear casually across his broad shoulders. His stance was deceptively relaxed, but there was a tautness beneath a coiled spring ready to unleash. His voice held a mirthful whimsy, yet beneath it lay steel a confidence born of conviction that few ever attain. "I have so much to learn from you, apparently."

"And you will regret it."

In a blur of motion, Ormenu launched himself from the cliff's edge. The sheer rock face was nothing to him; he bounded down with lethal grace, his massive form hurtling toward the warrior below. Claws outstretched, fangs bared a whirlwind of fur and fury intending to end this farce with a single, decisive blow.

But as the Demon descended, the warrior moved with uncanny speed. In an instant, he planted his feet firmly, pivoted, and brought his spear up in a fluid arc. The shaft met Ormenu's bulk with a resounding crack, the force redirected expertly. Using the Demon's own momentum against him, the warrior leveraged the spear to vault Ormenu over himself, sending the wolf-thing crashing into the snow beyond.

"You!" Ormenu spat, scrambling to his feet amidst the shattered remains of a tree he'd obliterated upon landing. Splinters clung to his fur as he shook himself, eyes blazing with disbelief. "You reacted to me? And countered!?"

"No, I didn't," the warrior retorted, his tone mockingly innocent. "Clearly, since I'm lying in pieces after your devastating attack."

He settled into a stance then, spear held with practiced ease. It was a warrior's stance, disciplined and precise not the wild posturing of a Soarling raider. Ormenu might have found it odd, had his pride not been stinging.

No more teasing. With a guttural roar, the Demon charged again, snow exploding beneath his paws. This time, he unleashed a flurry of slashes, his claws cutting through the air with lethal intent. He closed the distance swiftly, aiming to nullify the spear's reach by getting in close.

Yet the warrior was undeterred. His size, impressive for a human, allowed him to wield the spear with surprising agility. He spun it in tight arcs, the blade and butt both in play. Metal met claw in a rapid sequence counter, block, block, counter, block, block, counter. The rhythm was almost musical, a deadly dance where one misstep meant death.

Ormenu snarled in frustration. He attacked from every angle, feinting left and striking right, but the warrior anticipated each move with uncanny precision. It was as if he could read the Demon's intentions before he made them.

"Stand still, you wretch!" Ormenu barked, lunging forward with a feint to the left before twisting right, his jaws snapping inches from the warrior's neck. But the warrior dipped beneath the lunge, bringing the haft of his spear up to crack against the Demon's ribcage.

"Is that the best a Demon of Greed can muster?" the warrior taunted, a sly grin hidden beneath his helm. "I've met beggars with more bite, their hunger sharper than your spite. Your eyes are gems, your teeth are stone. You howl loud but all I hear are cracks in bone."

"Such pretty words, what are you some pathetic poet or is this the famous flyting of the Soarlings? Fine then, I'll play with my food a bit." With a snarl that echoed through the trees, Ormenu tapped into his innate magic. The air around him seemed to ripple as his form blurred, moving faster than before. He became a whirlwind of claws and fangs, his strikes a frenzy designed to overwhelm.

"You dare yap with blood still fresh? Your blade still dull, your tongue still mesh. I've skinned men sharper than your, and used their pride to line my vest." Is was the best he could come up with at the time given that as the warrior held firm they both gained no ground. He moved with a grace that belied his size, each step deliberate, each parry precise. Snow kicked up around them, a swirling tempest as the two clashed. The ground trembled beneath their feet, the very air charged with the intensity of their battle.

Then, seizing an opening, the warrior spun his spear in a full arc, the blade slicing across Ormenu's cheek. A sharp sting followed by the warm trickle of blood.

Before the Demon could react, the warrior reversed his grip and slammed the butt of the spear into the side of Ormenu's head.

"A vest of pride? How fine, how grand. Do you sew with hooves or one hand? Your trophies rot, your stories crawl. The wolf who howls but can not maul." Stars exploded in the Demon's vision as he staggered, the world tilting precariously. He hadn't been struck like that in centuries. Rage boiled within him, a seething cauldron of wounded pride and simmering fury. Ormenu's eyes cleared a bit and opened in bloodshot rage as he felt his body get a little lighter.

"Big mouth for a whelp with no name, I'll... fuck... where is it..." The little game of words was not even close to the forefront of his mind as he checked over his body. A Demon of Greed knew the weight of each and every piece on their bodies. So they knew when one was missing. Wildly spinning and standing back up, all he could see was red as in the warrior's hand was one of the many pieces of jewelry that adored the wolf-thing's frame.

"A rhyme lost? How tragic, beast of the den, your wit runs dry like the scraps in your pen. This trinket? It slipped... no, I plucked it with flair. You guard your gold, not the fool's vacant stare." The string of gems and pearls was a gaudy thing of no real artistry even as it playfully circled around the warrior's finger. But it mattered not, it belonged to the demon and thus it was enough of an injustice that it was not in his possession.

"Stealing from a Demon of Greed, I don't care if you're Orphan's favorite tool or even if you're his favorite set of holes... your skull will be skinned, boiled, and studded with fine jewels as I make it My least favorite goblet." Snapping and sharp, every word from his jaws bit and promised he would keep his word on the threat and more Only to be confused as the warrior tossed back the necklaces that had been previously stung along Ormenu's lower flank. "Oh... that worked? That's disappointing. By the fourth's rusted hooves, you ruined the grandness of it all."

"Just wanted to prove something, Ormenu." At last the warrior reached up and removed his helmet, and surprise-surprise he had lightly glowing green eyes and pale skin spiderwebbed with black veins. A literal jaw dropping moment for Ormenu, though obviously not so for the astute Listener to this tale.

"Fuck, strap a saddle to me and get to bucking! How in the... you did it... you found the Sets to Divine Body, didn't you?" Ormenu's voice crackled with disbelief, his wolfish features betraying a mixture of awe and begrudging respect. The spell, after all, was the stuff of whispered legends, a Life spell that granted its user the body of a divine being, perfected in every conceivable way.

Orphan smirked, the edges of his mouth tilting upward as he shifted his weight with newfound ease. "I mean, I didn't know its name, but yeah, it's the spell I've been trying to crack since I learned I had the Life Majorus. It feels great being tall, though doors have become… annoying."

Ormenu let out a booming laugh, his deep voice carrying across the frosted landscape. "Doors! Don't ever go to the Syndicates, kid. Damn dwarves don't build their homes human-size friendly, let alone for someone like us."

Their laughter filled the air, a rare camaraderie between Demon and Heir. Yet as Ormenu's gaze drifted to the motionless body sprawled on the ground the woman's fine gown torn and bloodied it darkened. "Who was that?"

"Wife of the Jarl," Orphan answered bluntly. "He raped and beat her. It wasn't hard to get her to switch sides; she forged an order from her husband to the guards at the gate, welcoming reinforcements from the Havi. But once a betrayer, always a betrayer. She was just a loose end to take care of."

Logical. Responsible. Not a shred of guilt or cruel satisfaction laced his tone. The words were clinical, detached. Ormenu tilted his head, studying Orphan with renewed curiosity. The boy's voice, now deeper and more authoritative, hinted at maturity, but also a lack of sentimentality. There was no enjoyment in the act, just a sense of duty, as if taking a life was as routine as sharpening a blade. Perhaps resentment lingered beneath the surface, but nothing more.

"You're a killer now. What was the first? Did the Suns grab some poor criminal and hold his neck out for you?" Ha! If that had been the case there was no doubt that Ormenu would have a mind to continue the fight and end it for such an act of cowardice. But the shake of Orphan's head saved them the trouble.

Orphan shook his head, his expression unchanged. "No, it was by accident. I wanted to take him as a subordinate, but he fought back. I was unarmed and desperate. Still… he had Seidr, and he was skilled. I wanted that power for myself. Tore into his guts didn't mean for it to be lethal, but I hit a diseased spot. Caused more damage than I expected. And that was it."

A shrug, recounting as if recalling a particularly memorable and lucky catch while out fishing but nothing more than that. The Demon studied the man, no longer a boy. Impressed and excited for the future, it would be long and thrilling serving under this man as Tyrant.

"You speak plainly. Banal. Bored." The Demon paused, letting his words hang in the air. "You don't enjoy killing, do you?"

"No, not really," Orphan replied, his honesty surprising. "Serk says I'll come to crave it, and Samium expects me to break down from guilt. I've felt worse hunting a fox than I have killing a person. It's just a chore and a waste of a resource, but it has to be done."

Ormenu's lips curled into a toothy grin. "The Eighth Tyrant, the Sin of Envy, did you know he hated killing? Tried to avoid it whenever possible. Sure did a lot of it, though. But none of the Powers of Malice respect him, nor his legacy. Even his Fiend line distances themselves from his memory."

"They're the tree ones right? Don't they all live still in his Seat of Power?" Quite yes they do, much to the chagrin of their neighbors and the people that once inhabited the island that Seat rests on. Now it is entirely covered in a dense... dark... damp forest where anything with a thinking brain and opposable thumbs gets torn to pieces.

The wolf-thing's tone shifted as he continued. "The last Tyrant, the Twelfth your ancestor, the Pirate Tyrant, Sin of Ambition. He craved blood, pillaging and sacking towns in the cruelest ways imaginable just to attract stronger foes. Lived for the kill and the pleasure of it. Dumb bastard never felt satisfied. Eventually gave up and committed suicide by charging a Teuton gunline. Sure, it was a lot of fucking guns, but still."

"I get it," Orphan muttered, his tone laced with exasperation. "Both extremes are bad. Ow!" He flinched as Ormenu's massive paw cuffed him lightly across the back of his head.

"What I'm saying," Ormenu growled, his voice low and deliberate, "is you've got the right mindset. Killing itself doesn't have to excite you. But take satisfaction in the skills you use to deal death and in what that death achieves for you. Regret the loss of potential or usefulness but never for their sake."

A twisted lesson passed from elder to younger psychopath. Beautiful, in its way a scene that might stir a dark heart with pride.

The Demon and Cursed Born trudged through the snow and came to the town of Dritsker, the battle was over and the remains were being picked at. The defenders that still lived were being tied to stakes lining the main road into the town itself. Meanwhile the dead of both sides were being tossed into carts to be piled up far away and then burned. For many centuries corpses have been seen as well... a bad omen. Seeing how a Demon of Sloth could turn a graveyard into an army, it posed genuine reason. Nearly the entire world now cremated their dead.

Contrasting the carnage was the jubilant reception awaiting Orphan. The Soarling raiders, wearing sigils of the Havnskar now claimed under his banner, greeted him with shouts of triumph. They hailed their leader with unrestrained camaraderie, eager to recount personal victories from the battle. Orphan met their cheers with familiarity, calling out names, exchanging jokes, and sharing in the moment. It was all a lie. Wolfish eyes could see it plainly, these víkingr were indulging Orphan out of their own greed and fear of him. The Soarlings for years now had felt the gnarled fingers of desperation at their heels and this silly Cursed Born was a possible escape to them.

As they entered the town, the heavy stench of ash and blood saturated the air. Rubble from torched buildings had been hastily repurposed into makeshift pens, corralling the defeated civilians like livestock. Fear and anger lingered in their eyes, but Orphan's forces were efficient, sorting through the remnants of the population with methodical precision. It was clearly Arcon's teachings here at work Ormenu suspected.

Their climb to the longhouse was marked by another macabre display. Above the gates hung the mutilated remains of the town's Jarl, splayed open in the bloody shape of a Soarling "bloody eagle," his insides spilling down in a grotesque pool below.

"Serk's idea, but it gets the message across." Over the puddle of blood below the mutilated man the two walked into the longhouse. The shadows covered most of the hall, a scant few torches were lit and the cooking pit was cold.

Where this was once a place of revelry and pathetic bonds of community now it was silent and empty. Saved for four figures. "Rhiel! Ormenu found us, the Hive shouldn't be long behind."

"The fact you underestimate both my intelligence and ability is maddening." Both Orphan and Ormenu froze as they looked to the west end of the longhouse where Abezethibou was waiting for them. Sitting on the throne of the Jarl and the three Cultists of the Seventh Sun lightly beaten and tied up at its clawed feet. Around the edges of the room, dozens of Imps squabbled and stared, their glowing eyes reflecting the dim firelight.

Ormenu froze, his darting eyes narrowing as he scanned the longhouse. His gaze flicked toward the Imps and back to the elder Demon, suspicion brimming in his tone. "How the fuck did you beat me here, you ancient locust?"

"I went on a light jog." Glowing yellow eyes of an insect met the amber eyes of a wolf. At first neither backed away from this standoff, pride met self-control and in the end the beast was the first flinch. With an irritated growl Ormenu turned away and continued to knock aside obstacles as he found a place to lay down on the other end of the longhouse. "As for you…"

"What? Going to drag me back up the mountains and stick me in a cave for a few more years?" Oh, there comes a point in every man's life when they step up to their elders thinking they can win that fight. Tis funny, they all think they can actually win. Time makes fools of all of us, muscles grow limp and bones become brittle. There does come a day when a son defeats his father and assumes the mantle of patriarchy. This is not one of those moments and this not that kind of relationship.

"Pathetic, you mammals disgust me. You think just because you get a bit of meat on you suddenly you're stronger? And in my opinion you could use a bit more, Divine Body or no you're still a bit on the lanky side brat." The Cursed Born's blood boiled at the ridicule that they both knew to be only that. Divine Body was perfection, that was the entire point of the damn Blessing magic. Didn't mean that such comments didn't have their effects on him.

"I'll remember this when I'm Master of Gluttony," Orphan growled, his voice tinged with both venom and juvenile defiance. Despite the growth in his stature, his words betrayed the lingering traces of a child lashing out at a world he couldn't yet dominate, a young man weighed down by grudges and an overinflated sense of self-importance.

"They all say that," Abezethibou replied coldly, its faceted eye unblinking. "Rarely have they had the opportunity to carry it out."

The insectoid Demon turned its attention away from Orphan, its gaze now fixed on the three Cultists at its feet. "As for you three," it began, voice dripping with disdain, "you've done an acceptable job pushing this brat down the Path of Tyranny. But let's not celebrate mediocrity, fulfilling your purpose to Malice is the bare minimum."

Serk, ever the provocateur, barked out a laugh, struggling theatrically against the flimsy ropes that bound him. "Ha! Yo' wouldn't be talkin' so high and mighty if you fought us properly instead of sneakin' behind our backs!"

"The irony of you saying that, Serk, is so thick it's not even funny," Abezethibou snapped, its tone sharper than the Imps' chittering laughter.

Rhiel, sensing the futility of Serk's bluster, stepped in with calm reasoning. "You've made your point, Viceroy of the Maggot Lord. But we have important matters to discuss. The Havi of Horga will soon learn of Orphan's attack on one of his vassals. Retaliation is inevitable."

The elf's appeal to logic pierced through Abezethibou's towering pride. With a single, dismissive motion, the Demon cut the Cultists' bindings, the ropes falling away like strands of cobweb. "Ambition has always infected the young," it mused, leaning back into the Jarl's throne, the wood creaking under its weight. "It was only right to make it a Sin."

The Cultists rose, their gazes locking onto the Heir of Gluttony, who now stood once more before the insect Demon. Abezethibou's chitinous head swiveled back to him, its single eye gleaming with a mix of judgment and scorn. "Arcon is leading a Swarm on Kalfskinn, with orders to preserve it. Four Soarling towns do not an army make, brat. And to take Horga, one of the three Soarling cities, you'll need an actual army."

"I have an army," Orphan shot back, his voice brimming with unearned confidence. He stepped closer, his shadow crossing into Abezethibou's domain as if challenging its authority.

"No, I have an army," the Demon corrected, its voice low and menacing. "And I wield it by the viceroyship of Lord Beelzebub. What you have is a tattered warband. Do not mistake 'Heir' for 'Master.' You've yet to take Glimisvellir my stipulation for recognizing you as worthy of our Lord's faith."

The air in the longhouse grew heavy with tension as the two forces of Malice stared each other down. Abezethibou's mind raced through its plans. It wanted to deny Orphan's growing influence, to keep the Hive's forces under its control. But the situation was precarious. Orphan's actions had set a chain reaction into motion.

By attacking Dritsker, the young Tyrant hopeful had forced a response from the Havi of Horga. Abezethibou knew what was coming. Havi Värmod Balkisson wasn't just a figurehead; he was a living legend. A master of the Water Majorus and Death Minorus, he had risen to power in the aftermath of the Twelfth Tyrant's fall. His cunning and combat prowess were bolstered by Magic that kept his aging body unnaturally capable. The Hive had always planned to court him as an ally. Orphan's audacious assault had threatened that strategy.

"You say I can't lead the Hive until I take Glimisvellir, but you also say I can't leave the mountain to find my own army." Orphan's voice cut through the silence like a blade. "Can you see how those things don't make sense? Madness isn't supposed to be your Sin."

Abezethibou's eye focused sharply on the Cursed Born, its alien mind calculating a dozen responses at once. Then, unexpectedly, it spoke. "Hit me."

Orphan blinked, caught off guard. "Gladly!" he snarled, surging forward without hesitation.

The hall erupted into chaos as Orphan charged the throne, fists clenched and glowing faintly with the faint shimmer of Life Magic. His steps thundered against the blood-stained floor, every movement crackling with tension. This wasn't just defiance; it was a declaration of war against the very forces that had raised him.

A simple broom was Abezethibou's chosen weapon of all things as it smoothly dodged Orphan's initial strikes, seizing the tool from beneath an overturned table. Wood met metal and flesh as the broom parried Orphan's spear with unerring precision. Every thrust, every swing of the spear was either blocked or deflected, and yet Abezethibou never struck back. That wasn't the purpose of this match. It was a test, not a fight, and the elder Demon had no qualms about delivering a humiliating beatdown if Orphan failed to demonstrate his growth.

The clash was chaotic. Tables splintered under the force of their movements, benches skidded across the blood-slick floor, and bits of half-eaten food sailed through the air. The longhouse, once a place of Soarling revelry, was now a battleground of cacophony and carnage. A basket of apples, seemingly untouched in the earlier carnage, was sent flying into the rafters.

Cheers and jeers filled the air as the Imps looked on in gleeful delight, their cacophonous voices forming a discordant chorus of amusement. To them, the spectacle mattered more than the victor. On the other hand, Ormenu watched with a more discerning eye. The wolf-thing's gaze followed every movement, every blow, silently judging Orphan's performance.

Orphan's technique was raw, but far from sloppy. In Ormenu's estimation, the boy's skills were on par with the finest knights, champions, and lone warriors who had made a reputation cutting through armies. Yet, for one walking the Path of Tyranny, that was merely a starting point. The true foes of a Tyrant were rarely human; they were monsters shaped like men.

To the fight happening in front of him, it was the same even after roughly five minutes of lamentably one sided flailing about in a semi-coordinated manner. Orphan for his part had a plan. A scheme. A stratagem if you will. For you see, the messy thrashing about that has happened so far was all in purpose of a tried and true plan of the Cursed Born. Get things wet. Ale and mead froze just as well as plain water. While not a drop had gotten on Abezethibou due to the bug's skill and grace naturally having it slide between the splashes. But with a glance Orphan did it, froze a puddle of booze just under where Abezethibou's foot was about to step. Such dastardly cunning.

The result was… underwhelming.

Instead of slipping as intended, Abezethibou's clawed foot shattered the ice, digging firmly into the stone beneath. No stumble, no falter. Only a sharp, unamused glance at the frozen puddle betrayed the Demon's acknowledgment of Orphan's effort.

"Predictable," Abezethibou scoffed, locking its gaze onto Orphan, who had thrown his spear into the air. "Only a child would abandon a weapon of reach and utility for a desperate-"

Plop.

Ormenu's roaring laughter echoed through the longhouse, overpowering the Imps' shrieks of delight. "HAHA! Don't look up, bug!"

Abezethibou froze mid-sentence, its faceted eye narrowing as it stared at the offending apple now rolling on the floor. Slowly, its gaze lifted to the ceiling, where Orphan's spear had lodged itself into the rafter, piercing the bottom of the dislodged basket. A cascade of apples had followed, and this one had landed squarely on the Demon's head.

From the wreckage of a long table, Orphan rose, brushing

splinters off his shoulders with exaggerated nonchalance. His cheeky smirk widened as he spread his arms in mock triumph. "I hit you. I win."

Abezethibou's single eye burned with unamused fury. "You played games, boy. And I am not amused by games." Its voice dripped venom as it glared down at the bruised apple under its clawed foot. With a deliberate motion, it stomped the fruit into a pulp, its chitinous leg grinding the remains into the floor. "I will not-"

"Break thy word, Abezethibou."

The declaration came from everywhere at once. Every Imp in the longhouse, their multitude of voices blending into a singular, resonant tone, turned their gazes to the elder Demon of Beelzebub. Their shared gaze bore the weight of a collective will far beyond their individual forms.

"Oh-ho-ho! Now you're in it," Ormenu howled, his laughter echoing off the longhouse walls as he set himself upright. He lumbered toward Orphan, a grin stretched across his lupine maw. ""Ooh… you in the shit now. Big bad bug coming in to spank his child"

Orphan, for his part, was just as stunned as Abezethibou. This was far beyond the scoldings and harsh lessons he had come to expect from his supposed guardians. This was something else entirely.

"Lord Beelzebub," Abezethibou said, its voice trembling with reverence and urgency as it dropped to a knee. "I only wish to fulfill thy mandate as thy viceroy. Say the word, and I shall take the Swarm to devour the whole of the Soarlands."

"We have chosen Orphan as our Heir; dost thou think we have erred?" The Imps spoke in eerie unison, their bodies moving with unsettling synchronicity. "Dost thou deem him unworthy of our Crown? He is not at least, not yet. Five Heirs have we had since the Tyrant of Wrath, and five times have they failed us. Dost thou not think it is time for us to have a master?"

The voice of the Archfiend of Gluttony carried the weight of centuries of frustration and unmet hunger. Though boundless in its power, even Beelzebub knew that it could never sate its eternal appetite alone. A swarm needed guidance as much as it needed sustenance.

"You are our master!" Abezethibou cried, its voice cracking with desperation. The demon's steel was unyielding in its loyalty, but the undertone of longing betrayed a fear of failing its progenitor. "I need no other!"

"I need? Nay, I need others, for a swarm is naught without the crop to consume. A farmer is as much the swarm's master as he is its victim." The imps that carried the voice of the Archfiend moved with synoicous grace, eerie in how still these normally fidgety and flighty beings could be. It could be that their forms did not accurately enforce the fear or loyalty of Abezethibou as the Demon felt able to protest further.

"Lord Beelzebub," the viceroy began again, its voice now pleading. It was the last of the first clutch, those that lived and served during Beelzebub's first days as an Archfiend. It had been so different then, not even the stage let alone the plays of those times remained. Only aging actors that could vaguely reminisce.

"Enough! Thou hast already been chastised with the Helm of Denial wilt thou go without feeding for another hundred years?" The Imps' collective voice thundered, silencing Abezethibou. The threat carried the weight of millennia, a reminder of the Hive's merciless discipline. Abezethibou flinched, its resolve momentarily shaken.

Orphan, emboldened by the Archfiend's intervention, attempted to speak. "Does this mean that "

"Two favours hast thou! For thy Greed and Gluttony that bestowed upon me remembrance of the Master and Mistress. The first was to take thee as Heir. The second is to meddle in my viceroy's affairs, ill-conceived though they were." Hehe, oh the sassiness of a bug. Rare as it is, enjoy it while it lasts. But humor notwithstanding the eyes of the Imps now were focused in two directions before a third joined in.

"Where does that leave them then, or are you going to interrupt me as well?" Demons hold no inherent deference for the Archfiends of other Sins, respect or fear perhaps but never submission.

"No, hunter of Mammon. Thou hast earned our respect for steering through these times with a clear mind."

The Imps' focus shifted again, dividing between Orphan, Abezethibou, and now Serk, who visibly tensed under their attention. For all his bravado, the Soarling hated the scrutiny of such a powerful force.

"White Blood Serk," the Imps intoned, their collective gaze locking onto him.

"Yes… my fellow hungry maw?" Serk's tone betrayed his unease, though he masked it with a crooked grin.

"You three, make haste to the Husk of the World Tree. We know that thou know'st the way."

"Aye, I do," Serk replied, his voice a mix of deference and annoyance.

"Escort the Heir and my Viceroy; there shall we await."

Words of the Twelfth

Dismiss the call to stay and try
Freedom's song is born to die
Chains are broken, one must comply

Changing of the Age

A crackling fire fought valiantly in a small pit, its embers struggling against the relentless bite of the northern winds. Here, on the edge of the tundra forest, far enough north that even the memory of Glimisvellir seemed distant, a camp had been set. Tents groaned under the weight of the tempestuous gusts, though none of their occupants Orphan, Abezethibou, and Serk truly needed the shelter. The cold, the wind, the bitter bite of the high north all such discomforts were meaningless to a Demon, a Vampire, and a brat blessed with the body of a demi-god.

The camp itself was less a necessity and more an excuse for pause, a placeholder against the blizzard roaring through the valleys ahead. That vicious storm was a wall no mortal or immortal could cross, not even the audacious trio.

For now, only two figures occupied the space. Orphan stepped from his tent, his eyes scanning the emptiness for Abezethibou, who was conspicuously absent. That left only Serk, crouched by the firepit, poking at the dying embers with a stick.

"The bug left an hour ago. Said somethin' about finding bears to play with. My words, not its." Serk grumbled, his sharp-edged voice laced with derision as he worked to revive the fire. The smoldering logs resisted, their last embers sputtering out as the vampire's fetid blood stirred sluggishly in his veins.

"Which would you rather fight, boy? A bear or a pack of Greed Imps?" Serk's lips curled into a crooked grin, his tone teasing. "I'll never forget the sight of you scuttlin' about when those mutts tried to sack Narfasker. That was somethin'."

"The bear. Any day of the week." Orphan plopped himself down by the extinguished fire, indifferent to the lack of warmth. "At least a bear from this land would stay in the fight. Those little bastards never shut up. They'd rather steal everything in sight and run off than finish what they start." His tone was light, but his smirk hinted at genuine annoyance.

Orphan leaned forward, squinting into the void of the stormy night. "But why would Abezethibou even want to fight a bear? It's not the sort to enjoy a fight, and it doesn't even have a mouth so eating it is out of the question."

"Oh, it's got a mouth, boy. Just can't use it." Serk chuckled, a dark, rumbling sound, as his deformed grin stretched wider.

"What? Where?" Orphan tilted his head, curiosity lighting up his features. He leaned in, like a mouse sniffing at the promise of cheese.

"That thing on its head it's not just some fancy helmet. It's another Fiend, made by the Maggot King himself. Punishment for Demons that step out of line." Serk's voice carried the satisfaction of one who relished the suffering of others. "It clamps down and keeps their mouths covered, even when they're starving, desperate to eat. Fitting, ain't it?"

"That's…" Orphan hesitated, the mental image tugging at his sense of morbid fascination. "…horrifying."

"Fitting," Serk corrected, shrugging. "A demon's gotta eat, same as me, same as you. It's a cruel trick of Malice, making us crave what we can't have." The Soarling downed a swig from his waterskin, his sharp teeth briefly catching the firelight. "Poor bastard's punishment wasn't just the muzzle, though. That's only part of why it's different."

"Different how?" Orphan asked, his intrigue deepening.

"It's from the first clutch," Serk said, wiping his mouth with the back of his gauntlet. "The first seven Imps, they're not like the others. They actually have a spark of their own. A mind, like yours or mine."

Orphan blinked, caught off guard. "Wait, what? You're saying the others don't?"

"It's like… fuck me how did that twig put it. There was this doctor down south I was workin' on, he was spoutin' off things, trying to claim he knew why I was the way I was and he could help. Yes! The inner and outer minds he called it. One is just you, thinking about and the other is your instinct, the stuff you do without thinking about it. All of the Fiends of Glutton, their inner mind is just Beelzebub, it's the Archfiend. And the line between the two is smudged a lot. Abezethibou and the other seven in its clutch weren't like that." To be born with a pack, to run free through plains and hunt as part of a greater whole. Serve faithfully and be given the greatest honor of apotheosis into something more. But there's no more pack. No more running. Now there's hunger. But the memories of the pack remain, so it's not all that surprising that one might try and make a new pack.

"I think I follow," Orphan said, though his brow furrowed with the effort.

"Enough to know this: Abezethibou's different, and in a

Hive, different is a death sentence. It's only at the top because it's stronger than the rest or maybe smarter. But don't let that fool you. In a swarm, the nail that sticks up gets hammered down."

The fire had burned low by the time Abezethibou returned, dragging the mangled corpse of a massive frost covered bear behind it. Serk, ever the opportunist, feasted well that night, his grotesque maw splitting wide to drain the creature of its still-warm ichor. Orphan, by contrast, refrained from partaking. He sat by the fire, idly watching the embers struggle against the encroaching chill. No words passed about the earlier conversation between Orphan and Serk; neither hinted at their musings to the Demon, who regarded them both with an inscrutable intensity.

Paranoia and distrust, such companions Abezethibou carried like a second skin. To it, mortals, no matter how steeped in Malice, were inherently unpredictable. Fickle. For all its movements and actions, the ancient Demon acted with one purpose: to serve its Lord. It was not out of a sense of integrity, or righteousness, or even something as disgusting as justice. But debt. A Demon's mind does not have such complicated issues as mortals do; when a matter is settled it is settled and only then. Many regard this differently, but Abezethibou considered its very life and independence as a grave debt to its sire. A debt that had yet to be paid.

But enough of such introspections; they sap the blood of the tale. The three travelers had a purpose, a destination, and no amount of awkward silences or brooding musings could deter them. Once the blizzard had thinned to a tolerable roar, they pressed on through the frozen mountains. Not that the storm abated it merely lessened, its howl still tearing through the peaks and valleys like an unseen predator.

The journey turned brutal as metal clung to flesh and frost nipped at anything exposed. And then, at last, they crested a ridge, and the horizon opened to reveal the object of their quest.

The Husk of the World Tree.

The sky above was an unnatural shade of yellow, threaded with dark brown veins the enormous, petrified branches of the Tree, piercing the heavens like ancient scars. Atop the highest peak, it loomed, casting a shadow that could smother cities. Its blackened bark was ridged, frost-covered, and dead. Cracked roots coiled and broke across the mountain's base, remnants of a once-great anchor to the earth. No leaves stirred. No life lingered. It was a monument to ruin, a skeletal relic of a world that had long since crumbled into ash.

But the power... it was in the air. Orphan could feel it, something deep inside of him felt whole. Reassured. An ominous feeling that if he just believed enough, all would finally make sense. That the very nature of the world had answers and this presence had them. But that presence was long gone. Abandoned this world long ago. This was the Divine and its folly. The people of this world know that gods are real, and they know they are no longer among them.

Thankfully, the bright and sensible Cursed Born banished these feelings as the weakness that the Gods attempted to instill in mortal kind. The three marched on forward into the valley at the base of the mountain, their last leg of the journey illuminated by the eternal rise and fall of the sun ever behind a pane of clouds. It wasn't hard to find their quarry, they just had to follow their noses.

The three descended into the valley at the Tree's base,

guided by the rancid stench of decay. The source became evident quickly: a towering pile of corpses, stacked like refuse in front of an ancient temple. The structure was hewn from solid stone, its architecture brutal yet alien. Massive curved pillars jutted from the ground like ribs, each etched with runes long eroded by time. The faint outlines of figures adorned the stone, their faces and forms blasted away, as though obliterated in deliberate censor.

The air was heavy with death, the stench mixing with the mournful whistle of the wind. Every step brought the crunch of bones, the squelch of rotting flesh, and the subtle hum of something… alive.

"Lord Beelzebub, we have arrived." Abezethibou dropped to its knees without hesitation, prostrating itself before the colossal, writhing form of its Lord.

The Archfiend of Gluttony, the Maggot King, loomed over the pile of corpses, gorging itself with grotesque efficiency. Talons, writhing limbs, and mandibles tore chunks of flesh from the mound, feeding an insatiable hunger. For a long moment, it gave no response, save for the wet, sickening sound of consumption.

"It's really here," Serk muttered, his voice a mixture of reverence and disbelief. "She wasn't lying." The legendary Temple of the Bifrost one of the rare relics to survive the Era of Chaos. The ruins of the Divine's hubris, and now the seat of a force far darker.

"So this is the Seat of Power." Orphan's voice was quiet, measured. "I can see why it's needed to become a Tyrant."

The word Tyrant hung in the air, and Beelzebub stilled. The sickening sounds ceased as the Archfiend rose to its full, terrifying height. Its many glowing yellow eyes fixed on them, devoid of emotion but full of weight, a gaze that seemed to pierce through the flesh and into the marrow.

"What is a Sovereign without their Throne?" Beelzebub's voice was a low, rasping rumble, its chitinous plates creaking as it moved. "But a despot, held aloft by the whims of fate."

"My lord, we have arrived as you commanded." Abezethibou remained kneeling like the dutiful servant it was. But its lord did not reciprocate, in fact it would seem oh so terribly that Beelzebub could care less. Its winding body writhed around the group, taloned spears that acted as legs pierced the ground creating a chilling rhythm that shook the soul. Overly dramatic without even trying.

"Heir of Gluttony, you have grown, and you have suffered," Beelzebub intoned, its voice resonating like the grinding of distant glaciers. "Do you still hold that hunger for more for everything this world has to offer? By what right do you stand before me, the Archfiend of Gluttony, and claim to be worthy of my crown?"

The Archfiend's serpentine neck coiled around Orphan, its countless appendages rising and falling in an unsettling sequence, brushing against his skin with an almost delicate touch. The sensation was not comforting; it was invasive, as if measuring him from the inside out.

"The same right that any Devil or Cursed Born has," Orphan answered, his tone bold, his words cutting. "The Divine Right of Sovereign is in my blood. The only difference between me and them is that I'm here and they aren't."

Bold... to admit that you aren't any different from any other decedent of the First Tyrant. But it was humorously true. Orphan's tale is not too dissimilar to many of his ilk that live outside the Kingdom of Hell. Spat upon, reviled, and more often than not killed in quite gruesome fashions.

Beelzebub pulled back, its expression unreadable. Satisfaction? Disappointment? Perhaps neither. Without a word, it turned and began its slow, deliberate advance toward the looming temple.

The structure was monolithic, hewn from ancient stone and weathered by countless centuries. Twin slabs of rock stood as pillars to a gateway flanked by walls that descended deep into the mountainside. Fallen spires and scattered rubble gave the impression of something long dead, its bones exposed to the sky. Above, the shadow of the Husk of the World Tree stretched across the landscape, its skeletal branches threading the heavens with brown veins against the sickly yellow and white sky.

"I'll take that as the best answer I'll get," Orphan muttered, his frustration thinly veiled. "But what about my men and territory? It's been weeks. The Havi of Horga will have heard of us by now. You said you'd handle it."

Beelzebub offered no response, its attention fixed solely on the temple. As usual, Abezethibou stepped in, its tone dripping with annoyance.

"Do you think Lord Beelzebub acts the mindless beast needlessly? It only does so when guiding the Greater Hive. The longer we distract it, the longer the Hive goes without its direction."

That's only half of the story, as it also reverts to a hungry monster with no wit or sense when it's without food. Only once it's filling its bottomless stomach can it talk all poetically and fancy.

Serk, lounging nearby, gave a resigned shrug. "Don't worry, lad. The Demons and Rhiel will see to it that your Swarm and warband are still in one piece when you get back. Maybe. Soarlings aren't exactly great at sittin' still or getting' along."

His humor was dampened, though, by the sight of the World Tree. The Husk loomed above them, a monument to a bygone era. To Serk, it embodied the fate of the Soarlands: once mighty raiders who terrorized the world, now a shadow of their former selves. The glory days of plunder and power were gone, replaced by infighting and decay.

And here, beneath that symbol of faded grandeur, stood four figures agents of Malice at the threshold of its temple.

"Inside lies your fate, Heir of Gluttony," Abezethibou declared. Its voice carried a solemn weight. "This is your greatest test. Complete it, and you shall be our master in all but name. Though the crowning shall wait until you have fulfilled our misguided viceroy's challenge."

Ah, the sting of shame laced its words as it glanced at the Maggot King, now reduced to primal feeding once more. But Orphan barely hid his frustration. He was growing tired of these tests, these trials imposed upon him by others. He felt he had proven himself long ago. I disagree. A few villages and some Soarling captains do not a Tyrant make.

"What am I looking for?" Orphan asked, his tone sharp.

"We do not know," Abezethibou replied with infuriating simplicity.

Serk snorted, shaking his head. "Here's a better bit of advice, kid: look for somethin' shiny and surrounded by things that want to kill'ya."

The vampire's irreverence earned an indignant glare from the Archfiend, but Orphan nodded at the practicality of the suggestion. Without another word, he stepped forward, his figure swallowed by the shadow of the stone pillars.

The darkness of the temple yawned before him, vast and unknowable.

Behind him, Serk spoke again, his voice quieter now, as if the place itself demanded reverence. "You know… my sire used to tell me stories about this place."

"All of them true, I'm sure," Abezethibou replied, its tone mocking but hollow.

"Hush," Serk shot back, his gaze lingering on the temple. "How did the saga go again?"

In the shadowed halls where the winds do howl,
The nameless king returned, his heart grown foul.
From blood-soaked fields where his glory lay,
He sought his kin, in the cold light of day.
But silence greeted his weary stride,
No laughter, no warmth, no place to bide.
Empty hearth, and a throne of dust,
All he loved, turned to rust.
To the sacred grove, his feet then led,
Where gods once walked, where oaths were said.
But the stones were cold, the altars bare,
No whispers of fate, no godly glare.
In anguish, he cried to the empty sky,
"Why have you left me, gods on high?"
But the void replied with naught but air,
Their realm, too, was desolate, stripped bare.
Alone he wandered, a king of none,
In a world where both man and god were gone.
All that remained a spear of gold,
How could his soul feel ever so cold

"There are a lot of bones here," Orphan muttered, his voice breaking the oppressive silence. His footsteps sent echoes ricocheting down the unseen halls, each one accompanied by the dry, brittle crack of ancient remains snapping underfoot. Every step churned up more fragments of long-forgotten skeletons, the fragments clattering against the cold stone.

He paused, looking around in the blackness that even his sharp senses struggled to pierce. Something about this darkness was… wrong. It wasn't simply the absence of light; it felt alive, as though the shadows themselves drank in every glimmer, every glow of his faintly green eyes.

"This could make me a lot of money," he mused, breaking his own tension. "Pitch it to farmers. Bone meal by the pound…" His smirk faded as he crunched forward, pushing the thought aside. "Ah, thoughts for later."

The sea of bones extended endlessly, his boots leaving faint impressions in the debris as he pressed deeper into the temple. Every so often, he heard the faint scrape of metal on stone or the brittle rattle of bones that weren't his doing. He was not alone. But fear? That was for lesser creatures. Orphan had endured far worse than the unsettled dead.

A prospective Tyrant does not fear the waking dead. For what are they but failures of life?

Paths split and branched in nonsensical patterns. He navigated without hesitation, letting his instinct guide him, a skill honed in the dark alleys of Glimisvellir and sharpened by his time among Demons. Yet something in the oppressive silence gnawed at his mind. Fleeting impressions, green eyes meeting his in the dark, echoes of memories that weren't his own. They were not hostile, but they were not benign either.

What lingered here? The dreams of Gods, perhaps, even

after their waking abandonment of the mortal world? Were these faint, fleeting remnants their severed fates, seeking new hosts? The thought irritated him. Mysteries for their own sake were little more than distractions.

Time slipped through his fingers, unnoticed in the eternal black. The stagnant air offered no clue to the passage of days or hours. Orphan's Divine Body required neither rest nor sustenance, but his mind wasn't immune to the tricks of timelessness. Had it been days? Weeks? Months? For all he knew, he could have wandered here for a year and not noticed until he emerged bearded and worn.

Still, he pushed onward, the endless halls filled with a monotony of ancient carvings and half-erased sagas etched into stone. His fingers brushed against the walls, tracing the worn grooves. The runes and scripts were meaningless burned away or defaced long ago in the Gods' final, vindictive act of erasing themselves from mortal memory. Their pettiness clung to this place like a stain, and Orphan couldn't help but sneer at the thought.

But the images… those remained. He stopped at one, drawn by something he couldn't quite name.

The carving depicted chaos and glory: men and beasts locked in battle, a figure wielding a hammer casting bolts of lightning, winged women descending to carry the dead. There was joy in it, as strange as that seemed. A celebration of something lost to time. Then, another image caught his attention: a man with a spear and two circling ravens, facing a snarling wolf that loomed over him.

This one was untouched, unburned. Deliberate? Or had the Gods missed it in their tantrum? He stared at it for a long moment, feeling the weight of meaning beyond his grasp.

Whatever story it told, it wasn't meant for him. He moved on, shaking off the nagging sense of familiarity that brushed against his thoughts.

Eventually, his path led to something new. A staircase, lined with frosted marble that glinted faintly in the shadows, descended into the cold depths. He could feel the chill emanating from below, a faint breeze cutting through the stagnant air.

"A draft," he muttered, hope stirring in his chest. A way out, perhaps. He moved faster now, his feet careful to avoid the growing patches of ice that slicked the ground. The temperature dropped sharply with every step, his breath turning to faint mist despite his resilience to the cold.

Then, at last, he reached the end. Before him lay something vast and terrible, something he had been searching for, though he hadn't known it until this moment.

The cavern sprawled before Orphan like a glimpse into a forgotten age, vast and breathtaking in its grandeur. The ceiling stretched impossibly high, fissures breaking through the stone to let in a pale golden light. This glow cascaded over the scene, lending the chamber an ethereal, almost holy aura that clashed with its sinister reality. The roots of the World Tree snaked and twisted down from above, their gnarled forms coiling through the hall as if to choke the life or death out of everything below.

Orphan emerged onto a winding plateau of roughly hewn stone. The path circled the edges of the cavern, descending to a jagged ravine that separated him from the chamber's focal point: a flat central plateau where a throne stood starkly against the backdrop of eternity.

The sounds reached him first. Soft and rhythmic, echoing

like a somber melody. He stepped cautiously to the edge, peering down into the depths. There, hundreds of skeletal remains shuffled and clashed, locked in a mockery of battle. Their motions were mechanical, almost lazy, as though the fight was little more than an instinctual routine. Broken weapons scraped across the stone; shields splintered without force. It was as if the dead themselves had forgotten why they fought, but fought nonetheless.

Orphan's eyes were drawn upward, past the chaotic rabble, to the throne itself. It was disturbingly pristine, save for the frost creeping up its base and the frozen figure slumped upon it. The body was ancient yet remarkably intact, encased in layers of ice that preserved its decayed dignity. Sunken features stared out, hollow and cracked, framed by tattered robes and rusted armor. Two items stood out in pristine defiance of time: a golden crown band on the corpse's brow and a gleaming spear clutched in its skeletal hand.

Orphan's blood roared in his ears. The sight twisted something deep within him, a primal yearning that clawed at his mind and body. It was his. The throne, the spear, everything in this place belonged to him. The voice of his ancestry thundered through his veins, urging him forward. He took a step, reaching instinctively.

Then the corpse moved.

"Havi? Have you finally returned?" The voice echoed like the crunch of ice beneath a boot, jagged and fractured, yet heavy with misplaced joy. It filled the cavern, reaching every shadowed corner. The figure stirred, its joints cracking like dry timber as it rose from its icy seat. "I have stayed, Havi. I have stayed here and awaited your return. Please... let us share one more drink... one more story of battles long fought."

The sight froze Orphan in place. His pulse raced, but his curiosity outweighed his fear. "How can I understand you?" he called out, cautiously pacing along the edge of the plateau. "Anguish wasn't even compiled by the Church yet when you were around."

The answer was plain: this was a Seat of Power. Understanding was a mere trifle in a place that bent the rules of reality itself.

"You... you are not my Havi," the corpse croaked, its frozen features sagging into something far more pitiful. The glow in its eyes dimmed as its shoulders slumped. "I see. So the Dread Wolf was victorious in the end. Ragnarok has come at last."

"No, I'm not your Havi," Orphan replied, stopping in his tracks. "I have yet to take that title." He almost smirked at his own words, already envisioning the title of High King to follow. But the words stirred something in the corpse, its sunken sockets lighting once more.

"Title? No... no... no... it is no title. It is my lord." The figure shattered the ice that encased it with a sharp, resounding crack. Rising to its feet, it slammed the pommel of its spear into the ground, sending vibrations through the stone. "I see you. I see you, Dread Wolf. You have taken my Havi from me. Now you wish to consume not only his flesh but his very name."

"Wait, I think you're mistaken," Needlessly the Heir of Glutton raised his hands in a foolish gesture before remembering he's not some weak mortal man afraid of a fight. This was always going to happen. This ingrate was sitting on His throne... and holding a very fine spear that Orphan now considered his too. The dead don't have property rights, that's just ridiculous.

"There is no mistake! You come here! You come to die by a poor man's last act of faith!" The spear glowed… and oh my… now the frozen zombie is in front of Orphan. Weapon raised, mid launch, only perceivable to this unlucky Cursed Born because of his Divine Body and Gift of Sensation. And only thanks to his other gifts did he not turn into a skewered lump of meat spattered across the cavern's walls.

Blood sprayed from Orphan's mouth, his abdomen torn open by a savage blow. His ribs ached, possibly shattered, as he slammed into the unyielding stone wall, the impact shaking the cavern. Pain seared through his body, but pain was an old friend, one he'd learned to work alongside rather than fight against. He gasped, blood trickling down his chin, but he was alive. And if he was alive, he could still fight.

The Nameless King lunged again, golden spear a streak of death in the dim light. The second, third, fourth, and fifth strikes came in rapid succession, each one carving new craters into the rock as Orphan rolled and dodged, narrowly avoiding annihilation. Between each desperate move, he muttered the Sets of Heal under his breath, the magic knitting together the torn flesh and broken bones with brutal efficiency. Yet every use of magic drained his reserves.

Divine Body also had another benefit for Orphan, since it was so efficient at using the energy he received from basic nourishment, to the point he would only need to eat a single meal a month to live. It also meant that that same energy could be stored and used for other matters than just living. Say… spamming magic spells that would normally kill the user through starvation just by casting it. That did not mean he had an infinite amount of uses. Four or five more hits like that and Heal would likely kill him faster than that dastardly lethal spear.

The golden spear smashed into the stone floor, sending jagged shards flying. Orphan darted to his feet, ignoring the pain that would have felled lesser mortals. His ribs screamed with every breath, but he did not stop. His own spear lashed out, a desperate thrust meant to force the Nameless King back. The ancient corpse barely moved, pivoting as if bored with the attempt. It roared, a sound that carried the weight of centuries of anguish and rage.

"Is this what you offer, monster?!" the King howled, its voice echoing with unearthly force. "How could something so weak have slain the High One?"

The King's movements were deceptively fluid, each step cracking away more ice that had encased him for eons. Orphan's spear lunged again, only to be deflected with an almost lazy flick. The Nameless King retaliated with a brutal blow from the pommel of his weapon, striking Orphan across the face and sending him hurtling into the wall once more. Stone cracked under the impact as Orphan tumbled to the ground in a heap.

"Damn it!" Orphan hissed, spitting blood as he staggered upright. "I'm not this Dread Wolf thing! But you're not listening to me, are you?" His voice dripped with frustration, but his mind raced. He couldn't beat this ancient warrior in a fair fight. That much was clear. But he smiled, as winning by playing fair was no way to win at all by a devoted follower of Malice.

The Nameless King advanced, each step deliberate, his

golden spear glowing with an otherworldly light. Orphan stayed where he was, leaning against the cracked stone as if defeated, though his mind was anything but idle. His sharp eyes studied the King's movements, the nuances of his attacks, and the cracks in his ancient form.

With a roar, he leapt from his position, the Nameless King already reacting with a sweeping strike meant to end the fight. Orphan ducked low, rolling beneath the blow, and came up with his spear aimed for the King's midsection. Divine Power hummed in the air as the two combatants clashed again. Sparks flew as their weapons met, each strike sending shockwaves through the cavern.

Below, the undead army stirred. Their guttural chants echoed in time with the battle, a rhythmic cacophony of swords striking shields and boots stomping on stone. They were no longer the entertainment, they were the audience, captivated by the spectacle unfolding above them.

The Nameless King moved like a predator, his spear a golden blur. Orphan could barely keep pace, his own weapon striking only air as the King's movements defied human limitations. Each failed strike widened the gap between them, forcing Orphan closer to the edge of the plateau. A misstep would send him plummeting into the undead horde below.

A thrust made too wide and Orphan with a simple move of his shoulder was able to dodge. Fast enough that he was able to react with a gambit of his own. He grabbed ahold of the shaft of the golden spear and everything made sense. Just about this fight and how he could win. But this land. This temple. The World Tree and the Gods themselves. He could not name their names but he knew them in that very instant like they were family. Devoid of any true feelings of family, this did not stop Orphan. A yank to disarm, but failed as the Nameless King shouted in manic rage at the attempt and flailed about like a panicked dog whose bone was almost taken away.

But a mad dog is easily put down by a steady hand. Orphan shifted the tempo of the fight, launching his own series of strikes. None landed at first, but tides change and all that. For a moment, it seemed as though he had gained the upper hand. He drove the Nameless King back across the cavern floor, each of his attacks coming closer to finding their mark. Just as he thought he had broken through the King's defenses, the ancient warrior shifted his stance, pivoting with a sudden burst of speed that caught Orphan by surprise. The Nameless King's spear lashed out like a viper, and with a sickening crack, Orphan's spear shattered in two.

"I remember your name, Dread Wolf," the Nameless King intoned. "All other names have fallen from my ears, lost to the threads of fate. But my despair and anger are stronger than any curse beset by your betrayer father. You may have killed my Havi, but I shall end you, Fenrir." Nearly half of the ancient Soarling's body was now exposed, the ice chipped away by his movements and Orphan's strikes. His skin was blackened and stretched taut over bones, muscle a forgotten concept.

"Happen to know the names of any other gods? The Church gives out rewards that rival kingdoms' treasuries for one," Orphan quipped, spinning one of the broken hafts in his hand. Truth be told, he was scared. He now knew how to win, but executing it wasn't so easy. This man might have once been a great warrior, likely one of the best of his time. But his body was so far removed from those days it was pathetically laughable. Only one thing was keeping him together: that spear.

The broken weapon clattered to the ground, leaving Orphan with nothing but the jagged remnants of the shaft. He barely had time to react as the Nameless King pressed the attack, forcing him to parry with splintered wood. Each impact sent jolts of pain up his arms, the rough edges digging into his palms as he struggled to maintain his balance. The King's strikes were relentless, pushing Orphan further back until he found himself pinned against the cavern wall.

But Orphan was far from defeated. Gritting his teeth against the pain, he tossed aside the remnants of his spear and lunged forward, closing the distance between them. His hands, now free, became weapons in their own right. With speed and ferocity born from years of surviving harsh conditions, his fists connected with the Nameless King's chest and face, each blow delivered with the precision of a seasoned fighter. More ice cracked and broke, falling to the ground in pieces.

Undeterred, the Nameless King swung his spear with enough force to send Orphan sprawling across the cavern floor. He rolled with the momentum, coming up in a crouch just in time to dodge another bone-shattering strike. The spear gouged deep into the stone where he'd been moments before, sending debris flying. Orphan surged forward, his bare hands a blur as he struck at the King's joints, seeking to cripple the undead warrior.

The battle grew more brutal, more bloody. Cuts and cracks were inflicted upon each other countless times. Orphan's mouth never stopped chanting Heal, trying to fix the damage where he could between blows and dodges. This wasn't training with Demons or fighting forgettable raiders; this was a moment that would never leave him. The wailing, the air nearly aflame with cold as Divine Right fought Divine Remnant. The pain would certainly be delightfully traumatic. But the brat was ruthlessly stubborn.

His strikes were precise, aimed at weak points where the King's decrepit body might give way. He targeted the ancient sinew that held the bones together, using his superior agility to outmaneuver the spear's deadly reach. Despite the King's immense strength, Orphan's speed allowed him to stay just ahead of the killing blows, his hands a blur as he danced around his opponent. But the corpse refused to break! This stubborn walker defied the natural order.

Regrettably, the Nameless King was no mere opponent. With a bellow that echoed through the chamber, he shifted his stance, spear sweeping low in a wide arc. Orphan leaped over the attack, but as he landed, the King was already upon him, spear swinging in a devastating overhead strike. Orphan barely managed to sidestep only enough not to die.

"Fucking bastard…" Orphan panted heavily, reaching up to touch his head. A large gash across his cheek now split his mouth wider than he'd like. This had to end, now, before his luck ran out.

Gathering his strength, Orphan launched himself at the King once more, his fists slamming into the torso with enough force to crack stone. He struck with everything he had a flurry of blows that would have felled any mortal. The Nameless King staggered under the onslaught, ancient bones cracking with each hit. Yet he did not falter. Instead, he met Orphan's assault with a brutal counter, driving the haft of his spear into Orphan's gut. The blow knocked the wind out of him, but Orphan didn't stop. He grabbed hold of the spear again, using it to pull himself closer as he delivered a devastating headbutt that sent shockwaves through the King's skull.

And then it came. In the moment of recoil from the headbutt, Orphan chanted his String of Sinew as fast as he could. Tendrils of flesh roped around the golden spear, stretching from his fingers. The Nameless King, panicking, tried with all his unnatural might to reclaim his most precious treasure, the one he'd sacrifice kingdom, men, flesh, and blood to keep. Another blow struck his strength. In an instant, all the ice on his body melted away. That tiny bit of support was the push Orphan needed to yank the Divine Spear from its caretaker.

The chants stopped. The air was still. Orphan stepped back, a little staggered but victorious. He held in his hands one of the last pieces of the Gods' presence in the world. His hands touched what something Divine had once held. He looked up to see the Nameless King stumbling forward, bits of him shedding as the only thing keeping him moving was now gone. Millennia-old frostbitten skin flaked off; finger bones clattered to the ground as he desperately reached out for his precious to be returned.

"Give it back. Give… him… back…" With one last horrendously pleading croak, the skeleton collapsed, turning to dust as he shattered upon the ground. Following their liege, the rest of the undead were finally allowed their place at the eternal feasting hall of the gods only to find it quite empty. Disappointment is not the sole property of the living.

Words of the Thirteenth

Forever made to Change
Eternally this world's Bane
At Last is Without Blame

Commence Act Three

The Sons and Daughters of Soar were once whispered across the southern lands and even farther afield, where even the east muttered their name in caution. Their longships descended like shadowed daggers from the Glacial Sea, carving a path of terror down rivers too remote to guard and too numerous to predict. The Glacial Sea itself, uncrossable by all but them, was their fortress, while the narrow strip of land connecting their home to the mainland served as both shield and gateway. Untouchable, relentless, their ways persisted unchecked. But all things end.

Time is a ravenous beast, and no wall of tradition holds it back forever. Innovation shattered their supremacy. Grand galleons of the southern navies reduced the proud longships to relics, a pitiful joke against cannon and powder. Tales began to shift; more and more did longships vanish into the horizon, never returning to port. The old graybeards, grizzled and heavy with sorrow, warned their brash young heirs to seek fortune on land, to abandon the salt and the waves. The Soarlings had not yet realized it, but their golden age was over long before the tide told them so.

Until a certain pirate king came around and filled the hearts of every rapscallion in the world with the Sin of

Ambition.

Yet even that blazing monster was extinguished, and his wake left the oceans cold once more. The age of piracy was hunted down with honor's bullets and Virtue's cannons. Shame, can't always have nice things can we?

So perhaps it is no wonder that some Soarlings looked to a bratty Cursed Born with glimmers of hope. A last hurrah, perhaps a final glorious pillage before succumbing to the slow, starving death of irrelevance.

Now, it's always a curious thing when Fiends ally with mortals. Ill omens seem to follow such unions like vultures. For what could make Fiends cooperate with anyone, let alone mortal men? Such times usually end very poorly for everyone not on the Fiends' side. And yet here we are: a young Soarling warband under the banner of a Cursed Born leader, flanked by hungry Imps of Gluttony. Always staring, always watching, those unsettling little bug-eyes glinting with something that wasn't hunger but shared its malice.

Oh, the Soarlings had enjoyed their leader's rise so far. But few of them truly expected this. Cursed Borns, Devils, these oddities cropped up now and again in the Soarlands, and most managed some success, even fame. But to claim one of these peculiarities could become an Heir of Sin, let alone a master of it? Ludicrous odds. People may know of the Path of Tyranny, but it's far different to see it forming under your feet.

To the common folk, an Archfiend is a creature of nightmares, an impossible colossus of malevolence. That Lord Beelzebub might recite a drama so profound it would move a man to tears? Madness! And the idea that such a being might go unnoticed for centuries? Preposterous! Deep down, mortals fear Archfiends with a singular wish: that they emerge far away.

But the Soarlings, ah they are cut from different cloth. Theirs is a people who favor Malice over Virtue, Chaos over Order. So, when a warband finds its leader a recently risen Cursed Born also named the Heir of Gluttony? They shrug. They build sturdier chests to store their food. They know it won't help. They do it anyway.

Of course, tension lingers. Starving dogs crammed into a cage with the promise of food later don't stay docile. The volatile blend of Soarling raiders greedy and used to taking what they want clashing with Imps of Gluttony malicious creatures devoid of mortal concerns created friction. Oh, they might align under specific conditions, but only just. And in this moment? Those conditions hung by the thinnest thread.

"It's just one thing after another." A burly Soarling, dressed in a bit of armor marking him a sailor whom has had the privilege of looting the dead of their unneeded items. This particular strapping man was doing his very best not to die in a horribly bloody and entertaining fashion. "I don't care who sang A Feast for Fles but one of you is going to the Fiend side of the camp to give them their pound of flesh. Figure it out among yourselves!"

"Yes Vifil!" Several voices rang out before a brawl among the raiders to see just who was going to meet their fate at the hands of the Demons. As it seemed the Swarm had heard the Soarlings' little song about them and were none too pleased.

It was a calculated move, and Vifil knew it. In his ten years as a raider, he had crossed paths with Demons and monsters before. He understood them as well as any mortal could.

Unlike men, Demons rarely held grudges. You kill a man's child and they never stop hunting, hurting, or thinking about you. Demons had a simpler view: debts must be paid. Once satisfaction was delivered whether that meant blood, gold, or humiliation the matter was closed. It was a cold calculus, but it worked.

As the camp slowly returned to its tense equilibrium, Vifil muttered curses under his breath. He stepped away from the murmuring clusters of raiders and toward his next destination. Passing through the Soarlings' section of the camp, he could feel the weight of the tension in the air. I wonder why, it's not like there was a volatile mix of inhuman monsters and highly aggressive barbarians… oh wait… that's exactly what was happening. Worse still, he was certain that if it came, the spark would come from the Soarling side.

He strode toward the largest and most extravagant tent in the camp. From a distance, its gilded sheen stood out like a beacon, dwarfing the other makeshift shelters. Guarding its entrance were men encased in golden plate armor, adorned with emerald studs. These were not mere raiders, they were mercenaries of the highest caliber. The ground beneath their feet glittered with coins of countless currencies and eras, discarded like gravel. Without sparing them a glance, Vifil pushed through the flaps, greeted immediately by a choking wave of narcotic smoke.

"Oh, honey, it seems we have a visitor. Do put the kettle on," came a melodious voice from the back of the tent. Sagares lounged at the head of a finely crafted table, piles of gold and jewels surrounding him. An opium pipe dangled lazily from his fingers, the smoke curling around his olive-skinned face. His appearance was strikingly human dark eyes, a strong jawline, and a body built to charm and ensnare. Unlike the Fiends of Gluttony, who reveled in monstrous forms, the Demons of Lust were masters of subtlety. Their forms could shift at will, allowing them to blend seamlessly into mortal society.

"Or you could leave, whore," snarled Ormenu from across the room, his irritation evident. The Demon of Greed was seated nearby, his massive frame hunched protectively over a chest of gleaming treasures. His sharp claws tapped restlessly against the floor, betraying his mounting frustration. "Your damn fumes are seeping into my rugs! Do you have any idea how much I paid for them?"

"It's getting worse," Vifil interrupted, wasting no time. He waved a hand in front of his face, trying to dispel the smoke as he stepped forward. "The bugs are demanding justice in the form of an execution."

Both Demons turned to him, their expressions unreadable for a beat. Then, in unison, they burst into laughter, the sound ringing out like a cruel mockery of the Soarling's urgency.

"You poor beast-pup," Sagares chuckled, leaning back in his chair. "Your people will just have to endure for a bit longer. Orphan and his entourage are surely on their way back as we speak. All we need to worry about is ensuring the warband and Swarm are ready for Havi Värmod."

The Demon of Lust took a languid drag from his pipe, exhaling a plume of smoke with a satisfied smile. But Vifil wasn't fooled. He could see the tension in both Demons' movements, the faint edge of concern hidden beneath their veneer of arrogance. They might mock the Soarlings, but they were just as aware of the Swarm's growing restlessness.

It wasn't loyalty or camaraderie that fueled their interest in Orphan's return, it was fear. Fear that the Ravenous Swarm, deprived of leadership and a proper outlet, would turn on the nearest source of sustenance: first the Soarlings, and then the Demons themselves.

"I told you to stop with that. And you, what happened that's got you all pissy?" Neurotically fidgeting over the possible damage being done to his property, the beast-thing tried to distract himself before the urge to rip out Sagares' throat grew too much.

"One of them barged into our side of the camp, killed one of my crew, and then ranted about a skald's song." Vifil's voice trembled with controlled fury as he glared at the two lounging Demons. "Petty bullshit like this is exactly why having your kind around is a nightmare."

Ormenu and Sagares exchanged knowing smirks, their disdain barely concealed. Vifil clenched his fists, his nails digging into his palms, and tilted his head until his neck cracked loudly. A low growl rumbled in his chest, slipping through his self-control like steam escaping a kettle.

"People are already on edge as it is!" he snapped, letting the edge of his Wrath bleed into his voice. "Year after year, fewer longships return. Our way of life is being snuffed out by ironclads and southern guns. We've only lasted this long because of the Tyrant of Ambition! And we all know it. Orphan is our last chance. The era changes, and we'll all be throwing away our axes to beg for scraps from the weak and soft! One last time! One last chance to die in glory!"

"Wow. Are you finished?" Ormenu gave a mocking slow clap to Vifil's outburst. Everything he said was true, the world was advancing beyond the need to fear wooden longships manned by axe wielding barbarians.

"Just tell me how to get the bugs to listen," Vifil growled through gritted teeth. "And maybe stop my men from getting any more pissed off."

"Whore, what is the height of Fiendish diplomacy amongst our kind?" Further mockery came in the form of a soft welcoming tone, the Demon of Greed even added a playful wink to the mix. How adorable if not coming from such a grizzled visage.

"Let us repeat it Mutt, Don't touch my stuff or I'll kill you." Trailing a few fingers down the side of the drooling woman that desperately clung to the chair, Sagares smiled so pleasantly that a honey bee would find it too sweet.

"Don't touch my stuff, or I'll kill you." The clinking of a many coins hitting each other as Ormenu picked up a handful and let them fall back into the pile through his fingers. They then both turned back to the Soarling with false syrupy delight to deliver the answer together.

"Someone touched your stuff, go kill them Beast."

The growl that escaped Vifil's throat was more feral this time. His body began to shift involuntarily, claws threatening to sprout from his fingers, teeth popping free as fangs forced their way forward. Bones cracked and strained against his skin, desperate to take on a more bestial form. With a monumental effort, he forced the transformation down, the pain contorting his features into a grimace. His breath came in ragged gasps as he glared at the Demons.

"Fuck both of you! She was already starting to wake and you just had to go and poke her." Unconscionable amounts of pain coursed through Vifil's body as he fought back the change being forced upon his body. He especially disliked the damage that had been done between his legs. An unfortunate side effect of the Imp nestled inside your body deciding to become female upon their accent to Demonhood.

"Aw, can you please let Shurpanakha come out? When she's not a raging bitch she's… well she's never not that but still I'd appreciate the better company." A hard annoyed glare toward the more serpentine Demon from the wolf… horse… man-thing. Ugh, Demons of Greed are always so confusing.

"I am never not grateful to every forgotten god out there that I don't remember what she does when in control of my body. I still don't believe you given how she rants about you." Finally it was too much and Vifil fell to the ground hunched over in pain. Neither of the Demons made a move to help him but instead returned to their own interests. "If you two aren't going to help then can I at least get a pass of whatever it is the whore is smoking?"

"No."

"Yes bitch, maybe I should have let you out." Vifil would not get the chance to carry out that threat as loud noise rang across the entire camp. First came a horn, singling the return of the Jarl, then the deafening sound of insect chirping excited at the coming of their line-sire. The Demons, and host of a demon, of the other Sins all regarded each other for a moment before setting aside the current motion of insults and petty drama to address the return of their lord.

The camp erupted in a celebration that felt misplaced more fitting for a victory feast than a gathering of an army teetering on the edge of collapse. Still, the air was electric with cheers, laughter, and the eager howls of warriors longing for blood and plunder. Orphan had returned, and with him, their hopes of salvation or, at least, survival.

Yet this was no triumphant return. The state of his forces painted a grim picture. The Swarm had dwindled to a fraction of its true potential, only around two thousand Imps and fewer than a dozen Demons among them. Meanwhile, Orphan's warband, once numbering twelve hundred, now struggled to maintain five hundred weary souls. Against this ragged host stood the Havi of Horga's vanguard, a well-equipped and experienced force four thousand strong, barely half of Horga's total strength. The odds were daunting, and the strain on supplies and morale had been corrosive.

The Fiends of Gluttony were little better than their mortal allies. With their voracious appetites and short-term focus, they were poor quartermasters. The Imps bickered and hoarded scraps, and tensions simmered dangerously. Hunger, fear, and the looming specter of defeat clung to the camp like a shadow, threatening to unravel it entirely.

But these silly ideas like numbers, morale, and the dirtiest word of all... logistics... ugh... were no longer on the minds of the Swarm or warband. The sight of Orphan and the cloaked figure of Beelzebub marching into the camp swept away doubts and complaints. The warriors and Fiends alike erupted into cheers, their chants of Orphan's name mixing with the eerie, synchronized chirping of the Imps.

Behind the pair trailed Serk and Abezethibou, both vanishing into the shadows as soon as they could, ever the unassuming specters of Orphan's rising dominion. Orphan on the other hand did enjoy a bit of the spotlight, the applauding crowd of his followers lit a fire of warmth in his belly like a dragon cooking a foolish adventurer party for dinner.

Yet, Vifil's eyes were drawn to the spear in Orphan's hand.

Wrapped tightly in bandages and cloth, it was indistinct, its shape teasing at something greater. Whatever it was, it never left Orphan's grasp.

"Warriors, one and all! I have returned!" Orphan's voice boomed, silencing the camp.

The crowd roared in response, their enthusiasm shaking the air.

"With me, I bring Lord Beelzebub, Archfiend of Gluttony! With its help, this war will stop being a war and become a conquest!"

More cheers erupted. Torches were raised, blades pounded against shields, and the camp seemed to come alive with fervor. The Archfiend, however, offered no acknowledgement of their adoration. It stood still, shrouded in its cloak of twitching, writhing flesh. Its silent demeanor was unnerving, but its presence alone was enough to instill awe and terror.

Without ceremony, Beelzebub lumbered to the camp's edge. There, it raised one taloned leg and stamped the ground. A rumble resonated through the earth, silencing the crowd as they stared in stunned anticipation. The ground cracked and shifted beneath Beelzebub's feet, and a smooth ramp began to descend into the earth.

The camp watched, slack-jawed, as a massive tunnel took shape, a perfectly carved pathway stretching toward Horga. It was vast, wide enough to fit dozens marching abreast, and sloped gently downward. The sheer size and precision of the work defied understanding. This was no natural cavern but a feat of Archfiend magic.

Murmurs spread through the camp like wildfire. The implications were staggering. With this tunnel, they could bypass enemy patrols and terrain, marching straight to

Horga's gates without fear of ambush or attack. The entrance could be sealed behind them, cutting off pursuit and securing their rear. It was a gift as monumental as the Archfiend itself.

Beelzebub, however, did not bask in their amazement. It simply stood there, twitching faintly beneath its skin cloak, as though the effort had barely registered.

The Soarlings gawked like children witnessing their first ship launched into the sea. Even the Fiends whispered among themselves, acknowledging the feat with grudging respect.

"By the gods," Vifil muttered, his voice low enough to be lost in the cacophony. For the first time in years, he felt a pang of hope. Yet, deep down, unease lingered. This wasn't the triumph of a people reclaiming their destiny; it was something stranger, darker, and far more dangerous.

Soon the entire camp was in a frenzy to get moving. The armies of Horga were out, no doubt the Havi of the city did not summon all his levies and men to deal with Orphan. Thus, the city was likely lightly defended. Or so they hoped. It did not matter! For how could they lose with an Archfiend on their side?

"Vifil." The Demon of Wrath host turned back as he felt his Jarl's hand on his shoulder. He looked up and could see Orphan clearly now that he was up close. Old souls know that look. That of a young man that has grown far too much in so little time. "I don't see Rhiel or Arinbjorn, show me to my tent. I'm sure you have one set up."

Vifil nodded. "Yes my Jarl, this way. But I'm sure it will be taken down soon enough now that we have a heading."

With a faint chuckle, he led Orphan through the bustling camp. The tension hung thick in the air, men and Imps avoiding each other's gaze, muttered curses mixing with the clinking of weapons and armor. Vifil knew all too well how precarious the balance was; it wouldn't take much to tip this volatile army into chaos.

Orphan's tent was modest compared to the grand extravagance of Ormenu's, but it still held an air of authority. Inside were a few spoils of war, Teutonic furniture, hunting trophies. As well as a few choice potted plants, nowhere near as impressive as his garden back in the Hive but the exact specimens here were… quite interesting indeed.

"How close were you all to killing each other without me." It was half a joke and half a bad jest. The brat knew he would be coming home to a shitshow. Soarlings at their very nature needed a strong hand to grip and direct their frenzy and thirst.

Vifil gave a mirthless laugh as he moved to light the lamps. "Closer than I'd like. Not as close as I feared." He lit the central brazier last, watching as Orphan immediately gravitated to his plants, inspecting them with the sharp eye of a master gardener. Muttered complaints about their condition escaped the Cursed Born's lips, drawing an amused smile from the veteran sailor.

"You know, three of the boys nearly died handling those," Vifil said, leaning against a table. "If not for Rhiel, they wouldn't have made it."

"They should have," Orphan muttered, snipping at a wilting leaf with his bare hand before pausing. His gaze fell to his right hand, bound tightly in bandages along with the spear it gripped. He stared for a moment, then turned to Vifil.

Without a word, Orphan walked to the central war table and began unwrapping the spear. As the cloth fell away, Vifil's eyes widened. Beneath the bandages were fleshy tendrils, pulsing with thick veins of blue and red, twisting and writhing around the spear's haft. The grotesque appendages burrowed into Orphan's hand, fusing with his flesh as though they were part of him. It was a hideous, living thing, a macabre union of man and artifact.

"What in the gods' forsaken hells…?" Vifil whispered, his voice trembling despite himself. Fleshcrafting of all the Compound Magics, it was the most reviled, feared even among those who practiced Dark Magic. This… abomination made the hair on the back of his neck stand on end.

"Please tell me White-Blood Serk or the Maggot King knows what's happening," Vifil said, his voice barely masking his unease.

"They do, they say it's an Incomplete Incarnation." Orphan replied. "This is a Divine Artifact. The personal spear of the original Havi, the god that title comes from."

New awe washed over the Soarling much like how a blizzard washed over peasant village, it left nothing else in its wake but itself. This was a weapon held by a God, one of theirs! Nearly every culture in the world wants nothing more than to have some connection back with their divine pantheons. Names. Artifacts. Seats of Power. Legends. These things hold power and sway that make kings seem insignificant by comparison. And not just small petty kings that maybe hold a dozen or so settlements but big Kings that actually matter.

"Wait," Vifil stammered. "Does this mean we know the name of a god? The real name?"

"No," Orphan said, shaking his head. "Havi is just a title, one of the names they used. Beelzebub told me if we ever found a Name-Name, we'd know. Instantly." He smirked grimly, flexing his bandaged hand as if testing the spear's grip. "But this? This is more than enough for now."

When I said power I meant Power! Anything connected to the Gods had real tangible power infused with it. Knowing the Name of a God when they had very much tried to remove them from the world before they left grants the knowledge bearer a tiny itty-bity portion of that God's power. The world is a big place… and there are a lot of people in it that run around thinking that the story is about them.

The tent's heavy canvas walls barely keep out the biting cold, but the flickering lamplight and the warmth of the brazier at the center offered some comfort. Both stone faced men sat on opposite sides of a low wooden table, a comfortable silence lingering between them. Vifil had been one of the first of the Soarling to truly come to Orphan in genuine loyalty, not for anything so banal or silly as trust or Malice forbid admiration. The old Soarling had been betrayed one too many times to fall for such useless tricks of the weak hearted. Instead Vifil saw in Orphan potential and competent instincts, far better than his own fat useless lump of a captain.

"Do you ever wonder what comes next?" Orphan, absent-mindedly rubbing the tendrils of the Divine Spear, finally broke the silence. The faint glow of his green orbs drifting along the Spear's shifting surface, as if looking for some deep meaning where there was none.

"Next?" Vifil raised a bushy brow, setting his cup down. "You mean after Glimisvellir?"

"No, I mean when we die," Orphan deadpanned before shaking his head. "Yes, after Glimisvellir. For years, all I've thought about is taking that place, making them pay. It's fueled me every battle, every trial. But now, with it so close, I can't help but wonder if that's all there is."

Vifil regarded him with a mixture of surprise and wariness. Orphan was no stranger to moments of introspection, but this felt different. "It's the Path of Tyranny, isn't it? Each step taking you closer to becoming a Master of Sin and then Tyrant."

"That's what the Demons say." Orphan's voice carried an edge of irritation. "Don't twist my words, I want it all. Power, wealth. Glimisvellir, though? Glimisvellir's different. It's personal." His jaw tightened as memories flickered in his mind. The mocking laughter of that fishmonger still echoed, not for its cruelty but for how meaningless the man's torment had been to him. "But it's just a pile of stubborn pig-headedness. Not some grand city of culture or trade, just a frozen relic with too many sagas written about it."

Vifil chuckled dryly, leaning back in his chair. "Oh, boohoo. The little Tyrant is sad his vengeance is against a bunch of backwater hicks. Maybe you're just tired. Sounds to me like you've let this grudge go cold."

Orphan glared at him but said nothing. Vifil wasn't entirely wrong. More than once, the thought of abandoning it all and raiding the southern lands had tempted him. To leave the Soarlands, to see the world outside the grim tales of his childhood was a dream that still whispered to him. To hear the songs and sagas of other lands. To hear what music and poetry could be found outside the frozen cold.

"It feels pointless," Orphan admitted after a moment. "But I can't let it go on principle. One moment, I want to burn the place to the ground. The next, I think maybe I'll just let

Beelzebub eat it and be done with it." Death and suffering would come to those that made his life horrible. The debt must be paid, with interest. But as time went on for Orphan, the urge to collect slid away like a slug down a pane of glass. Slow but inevitable.

"Um… both of those involve completely destroying Glim-isvellir." The empty eyed look that Orphan gave in response to Vifil's worried statement. The fire cracked a bit as the secret Beast poked at it, this was very unlike Orphan and possibly concerning should the wrong people hear him speak this way. If the Bugs heard him talk like that they would begin shifting from servants to devourers, rapid monsters let off their chains of duty and loyalty to Orphan's vision of rulership. The last Tyrant had been much the same way, a monster that rampaged through the world destroying everything he touched. Even a man like Vifil didn't wish to see that happen again.

"I don't see this ending any other way," Orphan said quietly. His words hung heavy in the air, their weight almost suffocating.

"So what you're saying is, you don't know what comes next after your revenge so maybe you don't actually want to have it huh? Do I perhaps find my Jarl approaching a bit of mercy in his heart?" Casually throwing mugs of ale at one's head aside, Vifil smiled at the look of disgust on Orphan's face at the concept of mercy. While the old sailor might not fully be on board with the powers of Malice, he could recognize a natural adherent to it. And so he knew where to push and prod.

Villainy comes in many forms, practiced with as much variety as the villains themselves. Orphan, for all his ambition, was no sadist. He did not seek out blood for the joy of spilling it. Our angry little ball of spite and bile did not seek out the suffering of others… but he could care less if it happened right in front of him. He felt he should. It twisted and gnawed inside him. That something should be felt in the actions and tragedies that happened around him. Bah, pointless stupid garbage I say.

"Mercy? Why would I give out something that was never given to me?" Orphan's tone was sharp, his fingers tightening around the coiled tendrils of the Divine Spear. "The Glimingar, the Fiends, even you all of you none ever showed me Mercy. Everything I've gained, I've taken, or it was given to me because the giver wanted something in return."

Vifil leaned forward, his weathered features betraying a flicker of curiosity. "Really? Not a single person ever helped you up off the ground?" His tone was half-jest, a bitter joke from a man who knew the world's harshness all too well. But he noticed something as Orphan opened his mouth to respond then hesitated. The younger man's expression shifted, his sharp gaze growing distant and contemplative. He slumped back in his seat, the firelight casting shadows across his face.

The question lingered like smoke in the air. Did Orphan feel gratitude for those who had helped him along his path? Yes, in his own twisted way. But did he believe their actions were selfless? No. Not a single one. The Fiends followed him because his steps aligned with the Path of Tyranny. The mortals followed him because of their faith in Malice, a faith either placed in blind zealotry or future payoffs. And the Soarlings? They followed because he paid them well. Every ally was transactional. Every act of loyalty conditional.

Like flipping through a book you absolutely hated to read, Orphan recalled his memories of Glimisvellir. Page upon page of hate and spite stained bloody from both sides. Until he reached… a chapter he actually enjoyed. The very why he kept the book in the first place instead of throwing it all out or more accurately and enjoyably, burning it to dust. Ah, such giddy and warm fuzzy feelings swelled in his chest… bah… disgusting. But powerful! So not all bad really. Was it enough for him? Such little bits of joy that existed within his past? Could be that the torch he lit to set ablaze Glimisvellir's very existence could be put out so easily.

"While I was away…" Orphan's voice was softer now, his eyes fixed on the Divine Spear as its fleshy tendrils pulsed faintly around his fingers. "… I met someone. They stayed faithful to someone they cared about for so long. Logically, they should've given up, moved on. But they didn't. Could I ?"

"My Jarl!" No! Interruptions are not appreciated here, damnit! But regardless of important matters, the silly whims of the cowardly masses must have their due. One of Orphan's Soarling warriors burst into his tent with a suitably desperate panicked look on his face. "The Demons! They are causing trouble, a fight has broken out!"

"Would have lost that bet, I expected this to happen sooner." Hiding behind a joke or two, Vifil remained seated as Orphan quickly rewrapped the Divine Spear and hurriedly followed the menial warrior out to confront the situation. The Beast stayed behind, not having the stomach to deal with any more Demon nonsense than he already had to. Speaking of…

"He's grown stronger hasn't he?" Pointedly Vifil did not

look toward the reflection in a nearby mirror. "Hey! Darling please look at me, the cold shoulder gets you nowhere."

"Fuck off Shurpanakha." He grunted in sheer effort to not react to the feeling of soft touches both under and above his skin. For if you had the opportunity, you could see under his armor gentle bulges underneath the skin that might reflect that of someone caressing his body like a lover would.

"That's what I love about you Vifil, your frozen heart, your ice cold veins, your anger is like a sharp piece of ice thrust into the eye socket of some poor helpless rabbit." The old sailor flinched as he felt a hand reach along the underside of his chin... while still being under his skin. The Beast known as Shurpanakha played with her host, tantalizing him with ridiculous notions of care and empathy. But he knew. She was a monster of rage and fury. So... a woman. Hehe, I'm going to be in trouble for that comment aren't I?

"Are you waking up to tell me anything of value or just to annoy me?" Light hearted jokes aside, Vifil was deeply worried by the sudden awakening of Shurpanakha. She only came to the surface when blood was being drawn or when he felt threatened. If she did start speaking during one of these calm moments, it meant she wanted something.

"I'm checking on you darling, making sure you know just who to keep your loyalty to." Before the touches were gentle and soothing... now we're getting to the fun stuff with gashes of claw marks, deep bites along the neck, and... squeezing in certain places. "There is already a Master of Wrath, first chance I get I'm taking us south to tell him about the Seat of Power up here."

"And that's why I'm not letting you out until Orphan becomes the next Tyrant."

Words of the Warlock

"All eyes are on me, every ear listens to my voice, my name is on everyone's lips. Their devotion is my bread and their undying love is my wine."
Words of Atapila, High Priest of the Third Sun Cult, speaking at his trial of heresy.

One's End is just a Stepping Stone for Another

Ships upon ships upon ships. The port of Horga, once the envy of the south, sat glistening in its fjord a shadow of its former self, yet still clinging to its pride. Long ago, this harbor brimmed with Soarling longships returning triumphant, their hulls overflowing with plunder: gold, silk, exotic foodstuffs, and tools from every corner of the known world. For generations, Horga had rivaled even the capitals of the Savior Nations in wealth, its fame whispered in foreign taverns and spoken of in trading halls. Prosperity had done the city swell... until it didn't. Now Horga sat on the brink, in truth. The population bitterly refused to leave their holey homes and gave up on the days of past. Hmm... that sounds familiar. Bah.

These ships were still traders for the most part as many a merchant dynasty had invested generations of effort and coin into building up their own presence in Horga. While much less merchandise flowed through, deals and sacks of money still passed hands. Horga was less a great bazaar of old than now a den of illegal workers and shadowy fingers sticking themselves into meaty pies. No doubt a few merchant families had become... families of a different sort in the past hundred years.

Sitting squat in the middle of the great fjord lake that centered the city, barges and roped together ships made up the actual foundation of the city. While most of the locals lived in the mountains, within short dead end tunnels that spattered the mountainside, the foreigners and visiting raiders made their lodgings in the city proper. Protruding from its very center was a great spire of stone and ancient iron pillars. The Bastard's Middle Finger as it was called by many. A castle whose proper name was long lost. Even the haughty upper class of the city, there always is such a thing in a place of wealth like this, call it by the crude name.

The day began as any other, perhaps a little quieter as many of the Havi's men at arms and several hundred able men had left the city to go quash some upstart Cursed Born playing at Tyranny. When elderly grandmothers heard of this from their morning visit to a baker they laughed at the foolishness of youth. There were no Archfiends in the Soarlands. Fiends and Demons were a Southerners' problem. Oh you might get the occasional Skinchanger here and there but that was to be expected, catching the Curse of Wrath while raiding down south.

Yes. All this talk of Bugs and a pale faced giant with black ichor for blood and emeralds for eyes was nothing but fanciful gossip.

Until it wasn't.

It began as a low rumble, like distant thunder, but quickly grew into a violent tremor that sent ripples across the fjord. Water churned unnaturally, and the first to understand what was happening were the unlucky crews of ships leaving Horga. They stared in horror as a solid dam of stone began rising at the fjord's mouth, cutting it off from the sea. Moments later, the lake itself began to drain, its waters vanishing into massive fissures that appeared beneath the city.

Panic gripped the floating metropolis. Barges tore free from their moorings, slamming into one another as the water levels dropped. Homes and markets, once resilient against storms and sieges, crumbled under the strain. The bustling port became a chaos of screams, crashing wood, and splintering stone as the lakebed emerged, leaving the proud floating city broken and stranded in the mud.

For a brief, agonizing moment, the citizens of Horga could only gape at the destruction, overwhelmed by the enormity of what had just transpired. They thought it was the final act, but no my dear Listener... it was but the setting of the stage. For the true hilarious horror would begin.

The victims of this attack were only given a brief moment to whine and complain about trivial nonsense like broken bones or dead relatives and friends. From the gaping holes that had drained the lake, they came. Giggling, chittering, and shrieking, the Imps of Beelzebub poured forth in a ravenous tide. Their insectoid forms skittered over the wreckage, pouncing on anything living and tearing it apart with gleeful malice. The Swarm was merciless, its numbers vast and unrelenting.

Since the time when Horga had been just a small little hidey hole for one very smart crew of Soarlings, its two greatest defenses had been its lake and the mountains that surrounded it. Both were now being used to devastating effect against the residence of Horga. They could not escape. They found themselves in a cauldron, very fitting imagery as now they were the Ravenous Swarm's next meal. And for those Soarlings that watched in horror from afar past the new dam in their ships, they too found themselves ambushed from the mouth of the fjord. Longships bearing the green and black of allegiance to the Heir of Gluttony flooded inward.

That very Heir of Gluttony? He was in his own tunnel along with his best and deadliest. The Demons with the highest record of stabbing things very-very well. The Soarlings raiders with years of blood and murder under their belt. They followed Lord Beelzebub under the earth until they were right under the Bastard's Middle Finger. They would breach its lowest depths and begin their slaughter all the way to the top.

"This is easier than any siege I've been a part of... kinda pisses me off, to tell the truth," Serk grumbled, casually discarding the lifeless body of a blood-drained guard. My-my, there's just no pleasing some people.

"Enough," snapped Abezethibou, its multifaceted eyes narrowing in disdain as it watched the Soarlings around them. "We need to move quickly if we're to ensure everything goes according to plan." The Viceroy of Gluttony's movements were as precise as its words, every action calculated to further their advance. In stark contrast, the Soarlings reveling in the siege treated it like a festival of violence. Shouts echoed through the stone halls, filled with excitement and indulgence.

"Time for an old-fashioned fight between Jarl and Havi!" one raider called, his voice giddy with anticipation.

"Flush out the fat bastard!" another chimed in.

"Don't let the bugs have all the fun!" came the rallying cry of yet another Soarling, his axe already dripping with blood.

The Demons of Gluttony, meanwhile, were eerily silent. Occasionally, the soft chittering of their guttural, indecipherable tongue filtered through the chaos, a sharp contrast to the boisterous noise of the Soarlings. Orphan was more like the Fiends in this moment focused, driven, and silent. He cut through the guards with an almost mechanical efficiency, his pupilless green eyes fixed on the path ahead.

As they ascended, their numbers thinned. Raiders fell to stray strikes, or they were left behind to hold the lower levels against potential reinforcements. By the time they reached the massive doors of the throne room, only the most capable remained: Abezethibou, Igurim, Serk, and Vifil. The four flanked Orphan as they stood before the towering barrier, their breaths measured, their weapons ready.

"Must he go in alone?" growled Igurim, its claws scratching deep gouges into the wood of the door. The sound was deliberate, calculated to strike fear into those waiting beyond.

"Yes, a Jarl must approach his Havi alone to challenge him for rulership. If he doesn't then it's just a normal coup, all of Värmod's men in there would attack us and we'd kill them all. We need witnesses." Vifil explained as much as it annoyed both him and Shurpanakha, truth be told he also rather just purge all of Horga of its raider ilk. The city had turned into a crime infested cesspool since its heyday. He'd rather start over, fresh and clean. Save as many civilians as they could but still start anew. But Orphan had insisted they do this the right way.

"Just get moving my lord, the outcome is already decided." Orphan regarded Abezethibou carefully, the Demon was still suspect in his mind. But with Lord Beelzebub so close, namely underneath the entire dry lake now, he doubted

Abezethibou would try anything.

The Cursed Born shrugged it off as he knew his moment had come. This would be the beginning of his saga truly. Everything before this moment wouldn't be recounted in song or tale... ahem... by lesser storytellers... but this moment was it! Yes! Here was when all the skalds and poets would speak of his great leap forward on the Path of Tyranny. Much ego stroking and self-aggrandizing played out in Orphan's mind as the Demons pulled aside the great doors and he stepped through.

A great throne room lined with marble columns and tasteful secretive alcoves. Stained glass lit up the entire hall with dazzling colors as the fires of the siege littered through. This place had been built at the height of Horga's wealth... and only its bones remained. All the finery had been striped and sold off. Bare and naked this throne room only maintained a ghost of its majesty. And one of its greatest ravagers stood at its focal point, the throne.

At the center of it all was Havi Värmod Balkisson.

"What the hell do you think you're doing, boy!" Stepping down a few of the stairs that led up to his throne dais, the great and mighty Havi Värmod Balkisson stood in fury as he glared down at Orphan, who was alone against him. A burly and stout body, bare-chested and covered in tattoos of many different cultures, Värmod commanded a great strength in his arms and belly. But the most striking of features that could be famed and awed for leagues around was his glorious mustache, bright white and long, reaching down to his groin. Oh, and there was also a peculiar collar guard built with a mangled and deformed human jawbone at its prominence. But the mustache was the important part, yes-yes.

"Taking another step." Because to Orphan, that's all that this was. Another step toward Glimisvellir, another step toward a crown and eventually a throne. The Cursed Born held up his covered spear, the tip pointed at the gutsy Havi, and continued to prove his own hubris. Indulging in the venerable Sin of pride as any excellent Tyrant should, what is life without a bit of pageantry. "I challenge you, Värmod Balkisson. I will take your title of Havi, a title none but I know its true worth."

"Ha! Listen here, lads, at the barking and yapping of a devil mongrel unfit to bear the ambition that stains his soul. Oh, to see old Captain Damophon's sin wasted on someone so unworthy." A hint of genuine emotion flashed across the burly man's eyes. Nostalgia for his youth, a poor cabin boy on the ship of the Tyrant of the Seas. Such sentimental feelings, disgusting though they were, could be useful.

"I don't know, I think I'm doing my grandfather's name proud. I'm Jarl of a warband of Soarling and have gotten the Ravenous Swarm on my side despite starting with nothing. I'd call that Ambition wouldn't you say so?" Orphan continued to grandstand and maintain his flourish of style and no substance. He had lived for so long not being able to boast, taking the opportunity to do so was a sweet treat for him.

"You? You of the captain's lineage?" Oh no. There was an edge to that question that Orphan did not pick up.

"Yes I am, my father was a Devil of his line." Hoping to get some level of respect or at worst baser feelings was all in a stupid vein. Instead Värmod spat down at the floor in front of Orphan with a smug mocking smile.

"Doubt it. You don't bear the barnacle eye of the Chimera,

the sea does not claim you. Less than a bastard, but a mongrel that does not even know his own blood. You think you can goad me into an honor duel when you have no honor to speak of?" A deep laugh echoed and was shared by his warriors. Orphan did nothing but stand proudly defiant to the mockery, though a twitch of the lip came at the mongrel accusation. This was but a man, a deadly man and one that held Magic at his fingertips, but a man nonetheless. Compared to the Nameless King, Orphan felt confident in his chances.

"No, I don't think I can goad you into an honor duel. But you're going to do one anyway." Clever little smirk there, brat.

"Aye, you're right. No one interfere! I'll butcher this mongrel myself!" Stomping his way down, the first sign of perhaps just maybe possibly a mistake being conceivably made by Orphan was that Värmod, within the span of a few seconds, cast what appeared to be three different spells simultaneously. An incomprehensible bit of gibberish spilled out of the Havi's mouth as he raised a hand, and within it formed a dark oozing liquid that shaped and froze into that of a massive battleaxe. I'm sure that Orphan had everything well in hand.

The worrying, but not at all troubling, signs continued as the floor cracked beneath Värmod's foot. He blitzed forward, mighty axe already mid-swing as he loomed over Orphan with a mad grin. Instinct and sheer panic forced Orphan to dodge, lunging forward, rolling onto his feet and knees. But he didn't have a moment of respite. Already the massive hulk of a man stomped and pivoted on his heel to use the momentum to throw the frozen weapon at where the Cursed

Born had landed.

A scream echoed through the throne room, not out of limbs being shorn from body, but from the agony of nerves feeling the flaming sting of a toxin infecting every cell. Orphan had quickly used his Minorus power to turn the axe to liquid, causing it to harmlessly spatter all over him. Or so he thought. But this was no normal ice. At this very moment, Orphan's Divine Body and Gift of Fortitude were working overtime to keep him standing. He had dealt with poisons before, his little gardening hobby ensured that, but this was a whole new level of lethal staining his skin. He felt a wave of nausea hit him suddenly, and a sharp, metallic taste filled his mouth. His vision blurred slightly, a sign that something far more sinister was already in his bloodstream.

"Impressive little devil mongrel, you survived my weakest spell. But I have found that even those that live through it have a hard time giving me trouble after." Another string of babble left Värmod's lips as he formed another battle axe out of his manifested magic. Our favored little brat, meanwhile, was glaring through his helmet and trying to figure out just what he had been poisoned with. His stomach churned, a deep, gnawing pain spreading from his gut, and his skin felt like it was crawling from the inside out. He suppressed the urge to vomit, knowing that it would only make him appear weaker. If this was something he knew, then maybe he could work with that, but if it was a wholly unique poison to Värmod's magic, then that would be even more trouble. It didn't matter; pride was on the line in more ways than one.

The two combatants resumed their fight, a growing chant of excitement coming from the surrounding crowd. Axes clashed onto shields, feet stomped to the rhythm of the fight. There was another clash going on, as Orphan avoided blocking the toxic nature of the Havi's weapon. The fleshy tendrils that enveloped the Divine Spear... well... they led back directly into his veins. Not the brightest idea to let that happen, would it? But only dodging would only get him so far, because he was so focused on the battle axe and the poison it was made out of, that he grew blind to other threats.

A kick to the gut, harder than any man should be able to do and that would smash through a body were it a lesser man. Instead, Orphan coughed up blood and felt the edges of consciousness being pulled from him. A searing pain shot through his abdomen, sharper and more intense than the blunt force of the kick alone could account for. With a strength of determination fueled by rage and spite, the Cursed Born held on. He quickly looked up to where the axe was held aloft above Värmod, and turned it fluid. It crashed on his head, staining his glorious mustache, only for the barbarian king to come out smiling and headbutting Orphan's helmet, sending him stumbling back with ringing ears.

"You are fucking half-naked! Immunity or not, that much skin contact should at least do something!" Orphan snarled, trying to ignore the way his stomach churned or the cold sweat that had broken out on his forehead. He had studied poisons, venoms, and all sorts of toxins during his years growing up among the Demons of Gluttony. One of the few ways he had been able to vent some of his anger out on them was dosing their meals with vile concoctions that even a Demon would get a tummy ache over. But this... this was different. His breath hitched as his heart began to race, an unnatural pace that set off alarm bells in his mind.

"More yapping! Do all you young bloods do nothing but howl at the moon for being too bright in the night sky? How disappointing. Seems the old bugger is going senile with age." This time, it was a pair of hand axes formed out of his frozen poison. He sharpened their edges against each other before running at Orphan in a gleeful mad dash.

There was no way to dodge this. Before, the attacks had been wide and heavy. Not easily avoided, given the superhuman speed at which Värmod seemed to be moving, but it was manageable by Orphan. Smaller and more agile weapons? Bah. He was doomed. So, what does one do when presented with no logical means to counter or dodge? You get reckless and try something stupid.

In the time since he first felt the sting of Värmod's poison, it had been on his mind just what it could be. Orphan had been well distracted since then, but he suspected it could be one of five poisons he knew of if it wasn't something unique to the Compound Magic of Poison. Two of them, he had built up some level of immunity to and knew how to cure quickly enough to survive the battle. Another two he knew couldn't have an immunity built up to. And the last one had been too rare for him to acquire enough to go through the regimen needed. His mind raced, trying to push past the growing disorientation, but it was getting harder to think straight, harder to focus on the battle at hand.

His gut was telling him to go for it. Which is why there wasn't a second of delay and Orphan rushed forward into the attack. He felt it, the blades of the axes digging into his skin. Both he and Värmod were smiling like madmen as they dove in close toward each other. There was a crunch as the Havi used his strength and momentum to break Orphan's right arm at the elbow, but the Divine Spear wasn't what Orphan was going for. One of the many knives that he kept on his person was drawn and stabbed into the graybeard's chest. The skin was like iron, and the blade sunk nowhere near close enough to his heart.

With a mighty backhand, Värmod sent Orphan flying to the other end of the throne room into the wall. The Cursed Born crashed into the stone, collapsing it partially. Everyone was silent, only the slight clattering of the dropped knife making a sound before Värmod spat out a small bit of blood onto the floor. Orphan struggled to get up, his vision swimming and his heart racing out of control. His limbs felt heavy, and his mouth was dry as if filled with cotton.

"I'll give you this, mongrel… you made me bleed, not many can make that boast." The Havi of Horga laughed as tossed aside his axes and swiped a thumb over the shallow cut that Orphan had made. The smile that had been on his face the entire time grew even wider after licking the blood off. "And you thought to poison me with your own shite brew? Ha! That's… that's…"

Aah… the choking. Just as Orphan planned. True, the poison that Orphan coated that knife with didn't exactly do its best on just a shallow cut. But ingested? That played faster with this concoction given his extensive cultivation and careful breeding to accelerate the process. Many-many a poor prisoner died for this moment. A panic began washing over the crowd that had been watching, but not from the possible death of their leader. There was a mad dash and fight over who got to leave the room first. Running away from a fate worse than a quick clean death.

"I figured it out. Your poison doesn't kill, it debilitates…

at least at first. Can't have fun killing if you kill too fast." Orphan chuckled as he continued to feel his body suffer from whatever poison was actually killing him now. It wasn't something he was too familiar with, it didn't come from a plant or animal; those he was most knowledgeable. But he knew enough to feel that he had some time. As the Cursed Born pulled himself out of the ruined wall expecting to see a dying Havi, instead he saw victory being stanched out of his hands.

Grim shadows grew from Värmod's mouth and snaked their way to every person in the room, grasping ahold of their legs. They all began to beg and panic for their Havi to spare them. A shadow attempted to reach out to Orphan only to fizzle out in a magical backlash. Orphan sensed that this was Death Magic, as his Life Majoris was its direct opposite; it gave him a small level of a shield against it. Whatever it was working fast since by the time the Heir of Gluttony had pulled himself out of the wall every single warrior that had once been so strong, so skilled, so valued by their Havi were all falling over dead. The poison that Orphan had made could kill three dozen men... so that's how many Värmod needed to drain to stave off his own death. A fair trade for the one still standing I must say.

"Y-you! You bastard mongrel! You did this! Kolfinn, Runolf, Giermund, Vandil, Thorgils, Sibbi, Tore, Elgfrothi, Vebjorn, Anakol, and every other life of my crew you took!" Rage. Anger. Fury. Many-many more words to describe the bottomless pit of anguish that was bubbling up from the Havi's stomach. Years upon years of watching these men grow and survive, he knew all of their fathers and bled alongside them. Pride could not begin to encapsulate what he felt for these hardened warriors of Soar.

"I did nothing! It was whatever Seidr you casted that did that!" The air was shifting, more and more Orphan felt his skin crackle with frost. A horrible thought passed over him, that this beast of a man had one of the most fundamental yet powerful spells unlocked, Aura.

"It is my Minorus ability. I have no control over it, it steals the life out of those around me to stave off the effects of death. I will die a terrible death no true son of Soar should, sudden and in my bed. My Minorus ability only removes the effects of death, you've shortened it no doubt but passed on the immediate symptoms onto my crew. They are dead because of you!" Mmm... blame is so difficult when it comes to these things. Was Orphan at fault? Maybe. He didn't care, the only thing on his mind was a growing fear at seeing the entire hall start to grow cold with a blanket of frost and chips of Ice. Worse still, he tried using his own Minorus ability, only for the liquid to immediately freeze back.

"I don't suppose I can threaten you to surrender by telling you I have five more knives like that on me?" That hardly mattered as a sheen of ice formed over Värmod's bare skin, every movement cracked and broke this new armor but just as quickly new ice formed to fill in the cracks. The grating sound of the ice breaking constantly did not pair well with Orphan's growing symptoms of the poison still in his system.

No further answer was given as Värmod launched himself at Orphan, smashing the two of them through the floor itself. Bare fisted the Havi of Horga began to beat on the Heir of Gluttony with wild abandon. For the poor brat's side, he could do little to change the tempo of the fight. The two broke through three more floors before finally crashing into something that didn't break. He needed to use Heal immediately, but the deluge of blows that came from this maddened berserker prevented any small hope of speaking the few sets he needed.

More and more floors were burst as the two fought, Orphan getting a small second wind as the fight became more mobile. Blows came, no longer was Värmod using poison within his icy grasp so the Cursed Born felt free to unleash the Divine Spear as it should be used. A thrust would come and slide off frozen armor, then Orphan would use the position of the spear as a way to swing into Värmod's side, sending him flying with all the strength Divine Body could grant him. Wall, floors and ceilings become tools of the fight rather than means to contain it. The entire tower shook as these two fought.

There was no absence of an audience either. Many soldiers of both of the combatants watched as one of them would commit to some sort of risky blow only to either have it pay off or be countered. They hear Orphan's never ending string of Sets to Heal himself or Värmod's furious roars of vengeance.

"Worthless mongrel! You dare kill my crew! You dare hope to usurp the captain's title?! The Chimera will be the Last Tyrant if I have anything to say about it! The final Sin will be Ambition!" Frozen tears beaded alongside Värmod's cheek as he continued to beat Orphan. A steely loyalty rang through his voice as you committed to this truth of his. Every Tyrant dreams of being the last, the one true ruler of the world. If not the last among the living, then their legacy would have to do for those that looked up to them.

Värmod grabbed ahold of Orphan and threw the poor

beaten Cursed Born across the barracks hall that they had fallen into. Crashing through several wooden beds, the Heir of Gluttony was covered in their ruble. Quickly, he sped through the Sets of Heal and fixed up his broken bones, pierced lung, and as many other injuries as he could before being yanked out once again by Värmod. Given a little bit of his health back, Orphan would not go down like a dog.

He fought back, thrusting the Divine spear toward the gut of Värmod he attempted to pierce through the icy armor that encased him. It did break through and drew blood… only for that blood to then freeze and lock in the spear. Orphan was once again pinned as Värmod took the opportunity to continue his frenzy out on the object of his rage. Blow after blow it came until at last with an uppercut Värmod sent Orphan flying out of his grasp and back down to the ground.

"What makes you think you're worthy of Tyranny mongrel? You're nothing, there's no hiding behind a fake body, merger skill, and a cur's feral guile." Was this the end? No-no-no-no. But… It felt like it. A new spear made of the darkest of ooze formed in Värmod's hand after a quick cast. No doubt this was the strongest of bile and sickness that he could summon. Or perhaps just the most painful.

"Strength, diligence, cunning. I have those things, and I do have Ambition." The Havi stopped for a moment, frozen by the Cursed Born's words.

"Ah… so that's how this is. That fucking little shit, a cowardly little mushroom feasting on the corpse of better men." A cruel smile grew on Värmod's cracked lips. Now it was Orphan's turn to freeze. "Strength, diligence, cunning? I remember a whelp that raided with my crew for some time that prattled on about those things. I hear he's chief of

Glimisvellir now. I've been toying with the idea of setting off, taking the old town, now that it has all those nice shiny guns just lying about. But the Havi of Níðavellir would make a fuss if I did. Now? Now I know you're connected to him somehow, tipping the scales. I don't care if that old hag gets uppity, I'm burning Glimisvellir to the ground with Gerfinn at its heart."

"No." New resolve built within him. Could it be that some old fondness for his dear uncle has reignited his fighting spirit?

"No? That's not the begging for your life I wanted to ignore as I killed you." Thrusting forward, the Havi of Horga aimed for the head but the spear turned to a not so harmless splash onto Orphan's face. Despite the pain, despite the horrible pain... the Cursed Born glared up at Värmod with hate in his eyes.

"I'll take what's owed to me, and burning down that pile of shit is owed to me. Not you!" There it is, the comeback moment. Oh, if only this was a story about a hero and not a half dead brat with so much lethal poison in his body that would kill a couple dozen men ten times over. Instead of victoriously standing up proud and finding some new level of power and resolve to win the day... Orphan collapsed forward, foaming at the mouth.

"That's why Ambition is a Sin boy, it makes you think you can bite off more than you can chew. But I guess Gluttony is just the same in that regard." Another spear formed in Värmod's hand as he held it behind Orphan's head. "In the end, you'll be nothing but an ugly mongrel missed by no one."

Struggling through the agony of it all, Orphan forced his emerald eyes back to watch his execution. So many years later, and not by the pyre. He wanted to fight. He wanted to claw his way back. So once again he turned the spear to a deadly shower as one last act of defiance. One last spiteful inconvenience to his killer. The Havi of Horga was not amused and continued his thrust down with only his fist. A new spatter of blood painted Orphan's body though, his eye widened as a chitin spear's blade exited out the front of Värmod's mouth. Immediately did the light from Värmod's eyes vanish... it would seem that there wasn't a lifeform nearby that could be enough for his power to save him from that.

Falling forward, Värmod collapsed on top of Orphan, a painful experience. But a deadly one. A funny thing about magically summoned matter, it disappears once the cast dies as opposed to manipulating already existing matter. The poison that had been in Orphan's body crumbled into the nothingness it once was. His body still felt weak from the symptoms, but the cause was now gone and Divine Body and the Gift of Fortitude got to work.

With no little strain, Orphan pushed off the great tub of lard that was once the Havi of Horga, only to find perhaps the person he least wanted to save him. There standing behind where Värmod had once been was Abezethibou, cleaning his spear of blood.

"Excellent work Lord Orphan, you did exactly what I had hoped you would do." It could not be more sarcastic if it tried.

"What are you talking about, I lost and was about to die. Isn't that the weakness you've always been looking for? All you had to do was let him kill me and you'd have what you wanted." Switching poison for venom, Orphan's biting words had no effect on the bug. Abezethibou finished polishing his spear and looked down upon the beaten Heir of Gluttony.

"There was no belief among us Demons that you could beat Värmod. Not only was he a far better fighter than you and more experienced with magic, he also possessed this." The Demon stepped down and grabbed ahold of Värmod's corpse by the neck. Holding him up to showcase the collar guard. "The jawbone of the Twelfth Tyrant, the remains of Divine Rights holders are powerful Artifacts in their own right. Lesser than true Godly Artifacts, but not by much. As well you should know as we taught you these things."

"You knew he had that and didn't warn me?" Accusation. Orphan stood back up while glaring at the possibly quite smug Demon. Instead of answering such an insinuation, the Demon opted to unceremoniously rip the Collar Guard through Värmod's bullish neck.

"This was always the plan, brat. Have you fight him publicly, there were many that heard and saw you two fight, they have all scattered, but they still saw. No one but us, Lord Beelzebub, and the whole of the Hive knows this secret. And once you take your crown, we will be incapable of revealing your this or any other." That was all true, but did not make Orphan feel any better. He felt cheated. Was this the glorious death that Soarlings loved to seek? That he had been deprived of. That... but also an anger still remained. A renewed anger, one that had been smothered for quite some time.

"Don't ever interfere again, all of you. I don't care if I'm going to die, I'll die by my choices and my merit. I'm not some cowardly mongrel that needs saving."

Words of the Scourge

"I can destroy a man, a beast, a demon, any single being on this earth effortlessly. But a city? That will take effort. But I'll do it my love, for you anything."
Words of Lucio Virelli, Consort to the Sixth Tyrant, two days before the destruction of the capital city of the Celestial Winds Empire.

A Short Intermission

The cold morning air hung heavy in the dense forest, the mist curling through the trees like the gnarled fingers of a dead man. Each breath was a slow, deliberate rhythm, only slightly constrained by their ill-suited attire. The elk stood just ahead, its massive form half-obscured by the underbrush, unaware of the eyes watching from the shadows but still on edge due to gaudy spectators that had no sense of stealth. Muscles tensed, ready to spring into action, the hunter's fingers tightened around the smooth shaft of the spear, its tip sharpened to a deadly point. A faint breeze rustled the leaves, but otherwise, the world was still, as if nature itself held its breath for the final moment of a worthless dumb creature.

Carefully, silently, the hunter inched forward, each footfall placed with precision to avoid the crunch of dried leaves or the snap of twigs. The elk's ears twitched, sensing something new, but it did not flee. Instead, it lowered its head to graze on the frost-kissed grass, too focused on the obvious trampling of feet just barely out of a distance that would make it feel truly threatened. The hunter paused, muscles coiled like a spring, and then, with a single smooth motion, raised the spear, aiming for the precise spot just behind the elk's shoulder. The world narrowed to a single point of focus: one strike, one chance, and the hunter knew there would be no second opportunity.

"Excellent kill my lady, well done." The trotting of horses through the snow, coming upon the downed elk already tied up for a skinning and its huntress just ready to make the first cut. To her, this hunt was a failure, the beast was puny compared to the one that had gotten away earlier in the morning. But to the sniveling followers that came with her on this hunt it was a monster of great proportions. In the many years since coming under the tutelage of the governess, she had failed in one crucial lesson… that to hide her disgust for sycophants.

"Would have been better two hours ago when I found its father." Muttered under her breath and covered by the sound of her pulling back skin and flesh from muscle. Knife work immaculate, not that it could be appreciated by her audience. A grouping of oh… seven or eight. Mostly women who wished to curry favor with the respectable Lady Delacroix but could do nothing more than suck up to the Lady's pupil. The two men that came along were the worst, however, beady eyed southerners that had many years of working their slime into the ears of empty headed heiresses. My, what challenge they must have found in Brune.

"My lady, you do not need to concern yourself with such work. That is what the menials are for." One of the two gutless rats, their hair also quite resembled that of a naughty rodent, spoke with a confidence that had continued to confound the huntress. Three years now she had to deal with these types and not once in those years did they let up on their attempts to change her and everything they touched.

Hmm… that was also around the time that her mentor had effectively given up on her grand vision of a new Glimingaric nobility… also when she started drinking more with Gerfinn. Connected? Perhaps, but which came first?

"But then I couldn't do this." A satisfied smile crossed her lips as she tossed back one of the quartered legs at the gaggle of squeamish vultures. The women cried, shameful behavior from several of them as they were of local blood. That's what Brune had come to feel the most disgust by, that where she had actually achieved some level of success of Lady Delacroix's vision of a new Glimingaric noble lady… pretty much everyone else had failed and converted to the soft and delicate ways of the foreign money that had arrived years before.

"That… that is a most funny jest my lady." Aw, he had to really push those words through his teeth like tearing a snapping turtle's clenched jaw off the neck of some dead fool.

"Shut up, go get the sled so I can take this back. If you all leave me alone for five minutes I'll tell the governess you actually helped instead of what you really did." Those horses could not have moved faster as their riders all scrambled to leave the gory scene for both their delicate sensibilities and thirst for clout. Given some peace at last, Brune knew they would be in no real hurry to return. She took her time finishing the skinning, even if it was a disappointment the kill still needed to be respected. The skin would be properly treated, and the meat all consumed. Every other part she had some idea of what to use it for.

Standing up over her work, she felt satisfied by it. Looking down, she further found glee in just how ruined this custom-made hunting habit that she was sure that her mentor had spent a decent amount of money on. It was still far too close to a dress than a practical hunting outfit for her taste… particularly the corset. Much to her disappointment, Brune did indeed end up inheriting her mother's more voluptuous shape. Though it did have its upsides she had to admit. Nevertheless here she was stained in a bit of blood, skirt torn to pieces at its edges, and overall completely unacceptable to anyone of high fashion sense.

The morning sky still drew blood, an ill omen that only sweetened her day. Anything that made her ingrate town suffer brought her no end to joy. As Brune waited for the sled to take her kill back to Glimisvellir, the quiet provided a brief moment of reflection. She was suffocating, and not just physically though at times the corset did that too, but Glimisvellir was becoming more and more insufferable. So many regrets, not taking the several chances over the years of escaping down south to the Soarlands were all her biggest. More and more Glimisvellir was being built out and up, the original settlement that had been famed for its ancient stubbornness had given way some initial comforts of modern life. A few had become quite wealthy… a few. But most now languished in possibly similar regrets as hers.

A full hour later, two Glimingar hunters showed up with a sled and a sympathetic look on their faces. It was only them that had kept to the old ways, those outriders that lived a sizable part of their lives outside the safety of the walls. There were even rumors that they had attempted a coup and failed, given mercy by Gerfinn in exchange for never speaking that such an event even happened. Brune knew it was true of course, she was there when all the hunters barred the Great Hall's doors and demanded that Gerfinn stand down and were prepared to exile the noble governess. Brune did have to admit this, the old drunk had actually improved a considerable amount when it came to his lethality.

One short trip back to the hunting camp and Brune found that the other three groups had already bagged their own prizes. The haul was smaller than she had been hoping for but at the very least it was a shorter trip than planned. It was when the huntress was standing over the pile of skins, debating on just how to use them that the very last hurdle came waddling up to her. A rather repugnant parasite of society, one whose presence was barely needed in Brune's opinion.

"A most excellent hunt Lady Svafardottir, the rumors regarding your skill among the bows and spears of the huntsmen were not exaggerated. Davvero, rare talent for a lady in waiting, but it's one of the peculiar things about Soarlings that I find so charming." A small twitch of the eye at the casual ignorance of this rotund man. Brune personally had no issue with being mistaken as a Soarling rather than a Glimingar, but it was a fact that she was very sure that he was doing it intentionally. His deep voice also carried with it a certain sense of slime that only came from years of practicing that most abhorrent of debased careers… politics!

"Thank you, Senator Vindex. But really, it's a disappointing offering this time. Especially since this hunt was hardly sanctioned by the governess." The portly man barely attempted to hide his dismissive smirk, knowing that what the governess said was hardly the law it once was. Men like him and those that came after the initial groundwork of Glimisvellir's growth knew their business very well. Great men and women begin something, then smarter and keener vultures circle and strike when the iron is hot. Or in this case, when the iron is piling up on the smelting room floor.

"Think nothing of it, it's more than enough. Our trade route down to Níðavellir has finally been secured thanks to my immaculate efforts in the senate. Many of my country men had laughed at the idea of the Soarlands providing anything of worth to the City that Never Dies Twice but do hope that you all prove them quite wrong." There were so many ways she could kill him. So many sharp or blunt objects within reach and it would be so easy. Like clubbing a fat old seal that had beached itself too far from the sea. Which reminded her, she should talk to that cheapskate that sold her diluted seal oil. It was only when the word Marriage came up that Brune returned her attention to that piggly fool.

"I'm sorry, could you repeat that?" Like a dagger hidden among a bouquet, her voice was sweet but held so much promise of so much stabbing should she hear the wrong thing.

"My cousin owns thirty ships and two ports along the Pelagia Mare. Not only that but he has several promising investments in the lumber industry. He would make a great match for a fair lady of an up and coming power, mia signora" Five times, that was the count of how many of these leeches had tried to tie her up in some sort of marriage. Despite the warnings of the locals and the southerners own bigoted views on the savage north. Each time she responded in kind.

The huntress turned to the senator with that same danger-ous smile; oh, do I love a woman that makes the meek shiver in fear. Finally, she decided on something, ripping the antler off the elk's head with her bare hand she then held its rather sharp point to the fat man's generous chin. Never once did the smile falter. Never once did her hand hesitate. Never once did she have any doubt she would, could; only if she should do this. Forget the witnesses, they wouldn't get far.

Oh, sure, the finger wagging and the dressing down would be annoying for Brune. But considering everything that she knew about this man it wouldn't be too bad. Because she knew the truth of the matter, no one in Glimisvellir that had power wanted to live in Glimisvellir. He was here to undermine her mentor for his own backers, while her mentor was here to peddle the influence of the powers that be that propped her up. Bits and bobs had been thrown about in Brune's presence, an annoyed sigh there and a shout of exasperation there... enough to give her a semi-full picture of the political situation in Glimisvellir. Senator Vindex would not be missed.

"Is this the cousin that has a disturbing amount of art in his manor all focusing on women's feet? Doesn't he also have several accusations surrounding him about stealing money from Caelora's fire brigade." I'm sure she was just getting a nasty ich, that's why she was starching the antler's tip along the folds of his chin. "Or was the cousin with the personal bodyguard of half-naked oiled men whose age just seems to be younger and younger by each new recruit. And who go missing... almost regularly. Because if you're suggesting the second one then Mr. Senator I'm shoving this antler up instead of down."

"Adesso, senta, Now see here-"

"Neither of these men would appreciate me the way I need to be appreciated. Are you advocating for infidelity, because that's the only possible way I could take this without somehow involving murder instead?" By this point more eyes had fallen on the scene, and few were willing to intercede. The few Glimingar hunters among this party already feared Brune for the 'Many' rumors surrounding her. Meanwhile those not native to the ancient town did not want to suffer either Brune's lashing, verbal or otherwise. "What do you see when you look at me Mr. Senator? Do you see a woman with dainty feet who'd cower in fear at the threat of being told their allowance will be cut in half? Or worse... a little boy covered in sleek oil?"

"No. I do not see either of those things, signora." At that answer and bit of blood dribbled off his already sweaty skin.

"Are you saying I'm not dainty? I'm offended; my honor has been besmirched." After finishing her little play of innocent sweetness, Brune laughed heartily before pulling away the sharp bone of the elk. Now with the immediate danger gone, the portly fool showed that he was no such fool for once.

"I see the rumors did you no justice Lady Svafardottir. You are indeed every bit the malicious vixen I was told you'd be. Which is why I do think that I'd be a better marriage partner than any fool in these muck filled wastes." Oh, he used an interesting word. For you see, certain words in this world were only used when absolutely necessary. Sin, Virtue, Malicious, Righteous, Good and... you get the picture. Brune stopped in her tracks as now he had her fully non-murdery attention now. Every other suitor she had gotten had been a sniveling whelp not worth the blood that coursed in their veins. To describe someone as malicious, it implied things. Things that could be far more scandalous than just a rumor that she killed her own mother or the number of infernal bedroom partners she had.

"Senator? I think I misheard you, please say that again." Looking back, she strode up to him, hands behind her and posture just so to lift up certain parts of her body. And to her surprise, he did not look down, but kept his eyes on hers.

"You do not strike me as a woman who appreciates power being held over you, no? But where does the power in Glimisvellir and the Soarlands rest, my lady?" Well… there's the actual answer, the developing answer, and the public answer.

"The Chief and Governess here, the Havi in the lowlands. Your point?" She was growing bored again, dangerous ground for many. But he had piqued her interest once so maybe he shall do it again!

"Yes, power is being held in the hands of the few. But that's not what the Third Republic wants, that's what your dear Lady Delacroix is here for. Do you wish to see it, the unwashed masses holding all that power over with the paltry idea of one vote for one man?" On the one hand this was the part of politics she detested, the reasons for politics. But on the other hand, oh did she despise the idea of some inbred Soarling peasant having a say in how things should be run. She's talked to them… she knows their ideas. But there was a nagging thought in her head.

"My dear senator? Isn't the Leagues of Víteliú a republic?" He continued to smile at her spear thrust into what he was doing. Conspiracy and plotting, devious men and women all fighting behind closed doors with words and false promises. They may preach the value of Righteousness but they do seem to be practicing something far more delicious.

"Oh is it? I must have forgotten, vecchio senatore. I must be getting on in age more than I thought." A joke, he didn't seem to be joking before. As the dear senator walked away, Brune had a solid long thought on everything that just happened. It only resolved her decision she had made several weeks ago. But this was tempting... very tempting for the chance to shove a heel into moronic fools officially rather than in bar fights. But she had made up her mind, however, this would be going on her list of regrets in the coming days.

Another long discussion with the harpies, and a few angry shouts to everyone and they were all ready to return to Glimisvellir. Two days out hunting for a prize they did not get but had to consign to a lesser. While Brune would have preferred to stay out longer in the hopes of getting a far better haul, this trip was already on dubious grounds of allowance. More and more hunts like this were being denied... all the complaining of over-hunting and delicate ecosystem grated on Brune's ears.

Returning back to the end of the Glimisvellir Valley, it felt... more crowded than in years past. Glimisvellir now extended beyond its walls, sloping up to the feet of the mountain ranges and covering what used to be large swaths of the forest. Lumber camps and half-built construction projects now littered areas where Brune used to run free in the pureness of nature. It had been a particularly bad day when she heard that the cave she and... others... used to play in had been collapsed and covered over for a factory to supply the town with iron tools. Perhaps that was the moment she decided enough was enough and that this whole Glimisvellir noble lady thing was a pile of shit.

The smell too, as she rode through the outer roads of the town... there used to be only the scent of a clean river and pine. Now it was coal, pitch, fire, and booze. More and more colonists from down south came; in the first years it was Teutons and other kinsmen of the immediate southerner lands. But then the Soarlings came. The supply of Glimingar and Teutons had been eaten up, and jobs and quotas needed to be fulfilled as the ironworks of Glimisvellir grew and grew. So Gerfinn and the governess were pressed by the powers that be in both the Confederacy and the Havi of Níðavellir to make a deal with worse than devils. Brune watched as a group of Soarlings laughed and joked as they pushed aside a Glimingar miner on his way to those same mines.

"Take my kill to the Great Hall and the rest to the usual spot, I have places to be." She stopped them at the edge of an alleyway after passing through the once great and revered Gates of Glimisvellir, now covered in dirt and soot.

"But my lady, I as a gentleman can't allow you to-" Coward. One little gesture that implied that Brune may punch him in the face and he crumpled like a discarded rag.

Hopping off her horse she trudged through the muddy street that at some point under all that dirt was cobblestone. Maybe because of what she planned on she was feeling nostalgic, though that was hard to do when so many buildings you knew growing up as a child were now torn down and replaced with ugly tenement houses. The march of progress using the masses as lubricant for its ever turning wheels, and they so often claim they are the bastions of Virtue against the tides of Sin. Maybe it was the blind eye of the church here in Glimisvellir, so focused they were on finding their long forgotten Seat of Power. Or perhaps those with the power to do something about the suffering did not care given how far Glimisvellir was from their sight. But there were those that did see and felt in their hearts the fire to do something about it.

"We will not be divided! We stand side by side as workers, not as Glimingars, Soarlings, or Teutons! These are our lands, we work them, we cherish them, we respect them! Should we not have a say in how they are used?!" A rousing speech given by a dirt covered smithy, to a crowd of factory workers, miners, and fishermen. All assembled in a crowded alleyway behind a tavern. It was here that Brune knew she would find her old friend, if they could still be called that.

The huntress sauntered up to the edge of the crowd, unnoticed by the riled up men as they were too focused on their passions of anger to give much to other passions that might be ignited by the sight of her. Standing on a soap box she saw Jorund, now a grown man with the body of one that had worked the forge for many years. Prattling on about such inconsequential things like rights, dignity, and worst of all… humane treatment. Ugh, I feel dirty just saying such words.

She waited patiently for him to finish his little speech, watched as another with him passed out crude handmade fliers, and only approached as the men began to leave. A few finally turned their heads at the presence of a female of the species among them, but upon noticing who it was they either fearfully turned away or shot a look of disgust and muttered something-something murderer something-something harlot. It mattered so little to Brune that she barely heard them beyond the sound of her own self-important thoughts.

"What happened Jorund, thought you were set on being a faithful rule follower for mommy and daddy. Now you're spouting off Dwarven propaganda, trying to turn Glimisvellir into the next commune?" It had been years since they had spoken, but they knew of each other. Both had become headaches to the growing powerbase in Glimisvellir, one the loose cannon project of the disgraced governess and the other a firebrand dissident not with the program. Jorund for his part didn't react to Brune's presence as much as she expected, instead giving a curt yet welcoming reply.

"Well when mommy and daddy get strong armed out of their family forge and are driven to drinking themselves to death, a faithful rule follower tends to question those rules." Ow, at the very least Brune had the decency to flinch at that. She heard that his parents had died, not by what or the circumstances around it. But to be fair, she believed he was already causing issues at the ironworks before they died.

"I… sorry. I didn't know." Callous, smug, arrogant, these things can describe Brune. But heartless was not one. Try as she might to kill any feeling in her soul, she couldn't. There were still those few things out in the world that caused her to think about something other than herself, a pity.

"Save it. I have a purpose, they gave it to me and that's more than any child can ask of their parents." A twinge of green envy slipped through Brune, her own parents gave no such gifts. But purpose was still there, she knew it and embraced it. "Besides, I have to thank you. Being a voice in the ear of power, turning their eyes outside of Glimisvellir more than inside."

"Yes, well, a mutual friend of ours suggested it might help. So I said a few words about other problems that need attention more than your brewing revolution." Hiding behind a scoff and a glare to a wall away from his thankful gaze, Brune knew that her influence was only partially to blame for the credit she was given. It wasn't that she was trying to cover for Jorund's efforts to unite the miners and factory workers in a combined syndicate, more or less she was just trying to keep the peace for the sake of the people she actually cared about.

"And uh… has that mutual friend said anything about me?" Now it was Jorund's turn to be on the backfoot as clearly the young man couldn't hide the blush on his face from all that dirt on it. New prey showing itself, Brune took to a teasing smile and hand to her hip as she found her new weapon in her grip.

"Verchiel hasn't said much about you, but then again you don't make for interesting pillow talk." The shy adorable blush on the firebrand's face turned sour and then schooled itself to a fake smile in a matter of a second. But Brune saw. And Brune liked it.

"Oh, that's fine. I was just hoping that he would mention me once or twice given how much we need each other. Practically allies, comrades in arms, could even say partners." Desperately trying to not give into his jealous anger, while at the same time attempting to maintain his own aloof cool as baby revolutionary. But humans are such fickle yet simple creatures. Where some predators might play with their food, Brune was ever so merciful and went right for the kill.

"Want me to tell you how big his cock is?" The words… they did not match her chipper tone and innocent giggle. Jorund for his part froze like a statue, unable to respond. "To be honest it's not all that impressive, kinda weirdly shaped too… even for a Devil."

"Stop. Just stop." Finally gaining back some of his normally quick wits, a seething glare and warning came from his eyes to Brune who with a shrug ignored it. With a confident sway, she circled the young man with a reckless thirst for picking him apart. But… there is value in knowing when to stop isn't there?

"There's power in already being hated, I can sleep around and have the fun I want without worrying about everyone whispering behind my back. Because they were already doing that. But you need to keep up this squeaky clean image to your rabblerousing friends. If the Teutons and Glimingar among them found out which bits you prefer to dine on then…" She left the threat hanging in the air to the firebrand's dead eyed thousand-yard stare. There was a reason why he hadn't reached out to Brune officially despite the possible upsides to getting her on as a comrade. Because she was like this. Instead, he took a deep breath, collected his thoughts and put back on his charming recruiting smile.

"If you don't care how people see you then why don't you just tell them that it's been you that's kept the orphanage going? I'm sure lots of people would cheer your name knowing that it was going to be shut down if not for you." Ah, the adorable crying babies of workers killed in factory accidents. The endearing whimpering of children whose parents died in a Fiend raid. In this Orphaned World, they are the most cherished… so long as the money is there.

When the Church of the Orphaned World arrived in strength they set out to build one of their famous Orphanages in Glimisvellir. But… it wasn't needed. A certain Cursed Born was the only orphan in Glimisvellir for a reason. Everyone took care of everyone else and the second a fateful death happened… woosh! Some relative would come in to take in the sniveling brat as their own. So, the Orphanage floundered and the Church refocused back onto finding their precious Seat of Power. Ironically, by the time the city held a population that did produce actual orphans the Church was stripped nearly bare from budget cuts and politicking by Gerfinn to remove an annoying rival. All hope seemed lost for those little snot nosed dears. Until a charitable and probably not homicidal benefactor came into the picture.

"I don't know what you are talking about."

"And if I were to go to the orphanage right now I wouldn't find a neatly wrapped pile of venison ready to be turned into stew for the next few weeks?"

"Truce?"

"Truce."

"Very well now that we are once again the bestest of friends, could I perchance ask for a small favor, oh most wonderful Jorund?" Batting her pretty eyelashes at someone she was just ready to continue tormenting, what a woman. But the man of the people, was not buying it and with crossed arms just stared at her petty attempt at flattery.

"What sort of favor?" He asked, not opposed to it. He had no real reason to refuse should it not be something that would inconvenience him. There was no true animosity between, only frustration and mild annoyance.

"So that smuggling thing you got going on with Verchiel, any chance you could use it to get me the fuck out of this forgotten heaven damn town." That threw him off; his first instinct was to ask just how she found out about that but then thought better. It likely involved her and the Devil alderman in positions he'd wish he could be in. It did put Jorund in a bit of a bind. If she was coming to him then...

"Why not ask Verchiel?" It seemed logical that she'd go to

him rather than Jorund, but the firebrand blacksmith wasn't ready to hear the answer.

"Because he proposed to me the other day, so I don't think he'd be very happy with my desire to leave this heap of rotting fish heads town. You, him, Gerfinn, Rinelt, and so many other people see way too much in this place… all it is and all it will ever be is a frozen turd fossilized over centuries." Poor boy, he was still frozen in his own pathetic way. Now he was very invested in getting Brune as far away from Glimisvellir as he possibly could. And she was asking for it, which meant he couldn't be blamed! Truly Fate was smiling down on him for a brief moment. "I know that it's a pain, but I have money and-"

"Deal, I can have you gone in three days." Was he going to mention that his latest shipment from Horga hadn't arrived and the last word he got was that some warlord was challenging the Havi of Horga? No… I don't believe he will. Unfortunately, for those who had the correct context for possible futures and fates… other people have plans.

"You most certainly will not." A voice carried itself down the alleyway that sent shivers down the spines of the two young adults for different but similar reasons. They turned to the source and saw the noble Lady Delacroix standing there looking most displeased. The years had been kind to her regal beauty, if a few small lines here and there, but they only refined what was already there. "Young lady, this is your fourth scheme to leave the town. Can we please dispense with these games? It's unbefitting you."

"Damn. Caught again, I'll be back Jorund… you've been the best shot so far." With a playful caress to his cheek before striding away, Jorund glared at Brune's retreating backside.

If the noble governess was spying on her student, then it was possible she heard his little rally, and his self-inflated sense of import in the goings on of Glimisvellir told him that was a very bad thing. Not understanding that the glare being shot down the alley by Lady Delacroix was entirely directed at Brune and not at all him.

The two women left the poorer quarter of Glimisvellir, escorted by armored guards and in a luxurious carriage. All throughout they said nothing, Brune stared out the window thinking of other possible means to leave the town undetected and on just how the noble governess was tailing her. Magic, no doubt. Meanwhile, Rinelt was stone cold silent. Not bored, silent like Brune but the kind that had no choice but to be silent to keep one's sanity. Perhaps the huntress would have noticed this distinction had she not been presently distracted by her own follies.

They arrived back at the Great Hall of Glimisvellir, and despite the changes that had gone about in the town this ancient building remained the same. Oh, it was renovated a bit, no longer did it host feasts for the entire town as it once did. Now it was more or less the royal palace of Glimisvellir in all but official name. To the natives, they could look and see a remnant of the old days, still the kind of grandness a slightly more advanced tribal town like Glimisvellir could appreciate. Simple yet big, rustic but historical, far from its golden days but well loved.

Entering though the great gates, they arrived into a new foyer built into the front of the original feasting hall, new stone was inlaid with the revered wood of the old structure. Everything had been carefully supervised by the noble lady Delacroix to ensure her vision of a new but recognizable

Glimingish culture. Some quite wasted effort if current rumors are to be believed. Her cousin was growing impatient and current situations back in the Confederacy were taking more precedent. Her support was waning and there were sharks circling the remains of her work.

"Go to your room and do not leave it until I say. If you are lucky it won't be before the new moon, ma fille." She warned as she strode toward her lover's study. Normally Brune would have given a token bit of back talk and pretended to do as she was told before sneaking around and listening in on Rinelt and Gerfinn's discussion until it stopped being flirting and politics and was just flirting and moaning. But this time was different. She was miffed over her latest failed attempt at getting out and now rethinking that was offered by the Senator.

Lucky or unlucky, only fate decides this, Rinelt opened and closed the doors to Gerfinn's study without a tail behind her. Normally she knew about her, sometimes, darling student snooping, allowing the young woman to learn from her meetings with Gerfinn. But this time she wasn't remotely thinking about Brune beyond doing everything in her power to keep her in Glimisvellir. As frightful as it was, the noble Lady Delacroix believed that Brune was their only backup plan to survive.

"Did she come back kicking and screaming? No? Then I win the bet." There was no time for Gerfinn's unfunny jokes. Rinelt shoved aside the work he had been doing for a change on his desk, a bit of her internal panic bleeding through her eyes. Gerfinn for his credit, blinked a few times, sighed, and looked up at his beloved lover. "Darling, dear, beautiful, what is wrong?"

"Horga has fallen, mon amour, I just got word that it has been destroyed." Pacing, she began pacing as she recovered bits and pieces of her sense of self.

"That… is admittedly not great news. But not bad, we can send word to Níðavellir and see if they-"

"Non! You're not getting it!" An outburst like that was very unlike her and now Gerfinn was starting to feel on edge if his normally calm and cool rock was acting like this. "You remember awhile back one of the hunters reported seeing a Swarm, a big one headed down south?"

"Okay, so we have a Swarm capable of taking down Horga. We know that the Demon Abezethibou was sulking about. Maybe now we can get some damn reinforcements." He tried to rationalize as best he could. A Swarm was nothing, often led by a Demon that roamed the world devouring what it could before eventually breaking apart from some sound prodding by outside forces. A Swarm led by a Demon as ancient as Abezethibou was another matter, especially if it was as large as the hunter made it out to be. It meant that there must be a Spawning Pool of a particular size, which would explain things to the ignorant fools.

"I don't know if I should be happy or wish for ignorance, because I went back and checked the written reports that we required the hunters complete. The description of the Demon that the hunter saw, does not match the Church's records of Abezethibou… and there were conflicting descriptions among the hunters." The noose was tightening, they finally started to see the knife at their throat… was in fact a very big cannon was about to lit in their dumb faces. Gerfinn's face appropriately went pale. Different Demons of Seven Times Cursed Beelzebub. That only happened under one condition. His hands began to shake as his eyes drifted to the bottle under his desk.

"That's impossible, you need an Archfiend to have a Master of Sin. Right? Right?" He begged in his eyes, that his beloved would tell him that this was all just a mistake. But she was just as distraught.

"The Archfiend Beelzebub, has not been seen since the Ninth Tyrant over three and a half hundred years ago. Soarlings claim that Fiends of both Wrath and Gluttony started appearing in the Soarlands roughly around the same time after the Ninth Tyrant's death but... Church records have the Fiends of Gluttony actually arriving thirty years earlier. The timelines match up, I've done the calculations in my head on some guesses and assumptions but... I'm confident I'm right, hélas." She was chuckling now, a pleading smile on her face as she explained the course of history. And to her credit, she was right.

Lord Beelzebub wandered for many years after the Lord of War died and bestowed the Curse of Wrath upon the world. The ancient Maggot King was drawn North for reasons only it knew. Perhaps it was simply a coincidental migration of meals, perhaps it had learned of the Seat of Power in the north. Whatever the cause may be, the Ever-Gapping Maw had found itself in the Soarlands and eventually Glimingaric lands. There it found little food and unfortunately for two hundred years the Hive had been only gently reined in by his dominant mind. Left to run rampant and easily culled by the developing powers of this modern era.

"They still need a Devil or Cursed Born, which of them are missing?" Keeping track of the descendants of the First Tyrant was a standard practice among the mortal peoples of the world. Even in those places that looked favorably on the Scions of Sovereign. In the aftermath of the Tenth Tyrant, more of the world had opened its doors to Devilkind in return for some concessions from the Kingdom of Hell, which didn't mean they weren't spied on constantly.

"That's what I had been doing all day, checking in with our watchers. All of them. Every Devil and Cursed Born that has immigrated to Glimisvellir is accounted for, tous, sans exception." Rinelt approached Gerfinn, hands clasped as if to pray to some long forgotten and lost god. Prayer that what she deduced wasn't real and that her most precious person in this world could deny what she suspected to be true. "Mon amour... you said he was dead. You saw his body right. Someone did? Please?"

"No." He both answered and denied, to her and himself. "No-no-no-no... It's not him. It can't be."

"But if it is? Could you do it? Could you kill him?" It was the only way to kill the head of the snake... or bug in this case. If an Heir or Master is killed, the Fiends that followed them often turned on themselves and the Ravenous Swarm was no exception. Lord Beelzebub was a fickle all-sire and would be more likely to turn its back and return to a new search of a worthy Heir than to babysit its frantic children.

"Maybe... we have cannons, guns, this is our land, assemble a militia alongside the soldiers. Everyone needs to fight or be eaten." Tis true, not a single soul would be left should the Swarm descend upon them with no restraint. "It's not impossible, their numbers should be less after attacking Horga."

They weren't.

"Gerfinn!" A hard slap came after, grabbing him by his

face. "There is no way around this, everything you've told me about Orphan leads me to only one conclusion, he will burn everything to the ground after letting his Swarm eat us all alive. Tell me… can you kill him?"

"That brat never stops being a pain in my ass."

Words of the Oracle

"The Mysteries of the past. The Conspiracies of the present.
And the Lies of the Future. I see them all and By every lost
god I wish I didn't."
Professor Guthmaer of the Rothland University; Magic
Division, last words spoken to his colleges before he was
found dead in his office.

Apathy, Hunger, and Change

"Another drink woman, we're thirsty!" Raucous roars of cheers and indecent hollering came from all around the feasting hall of the Bastard's Middle Finger. Though their many smiles and drunken giggles abound, every single person in this room was desperate to disregard the misery, horror, and overall awfulness that could befall them at any second. The serving girls were those that were freed from the clutches of the previous occupants of the tower. They had forced smiles on their faces in the hopes that if they appeared grateful to their liberators… those same liberators would in turn not act as their previous captors did. But it could be said those Soarlings were too busy distracting themselves with drink rather than flesh to avoid the sounds that came from below, from the remains of the city of Horga.

Meat being torn, bones crunching in the mouths of chittering monsters, no more screams… only whimpering pleading to gods so long gone it was absurd to cry out to them. The Ravenous Swarm was having a mighty feast indeed, tens of thousands of citizens of the Soarling city of Horga were now all wonderful delicacies for the ever hungry maws of Gluttony. No one was spared, age, gender, social status… it meant nothing as every mortal was little more than meat to the Imps of Beelzebub's lineage. And they were always hungry.

So, those um… allies… of the Swarm did everything in their power to not hear or see what was happening just outside the Bastard's Middle Finger. Celebration was the desperate attempt to drown out the sounds the swept up from below; barrels of booze were left open as to try and mask the wafting smell of blood and death, and every window was barred and covered so as to not catch a frightful glimpse of the bloody banquet. Hmm, they could only hope that the Swarm would not play with its food and be quick about it.

But where the mortal followers of our dear Heir of Gluttony were in the midst of revelry and debauchery, he was not so crude. Further up in the spire he sat in a big comfy chair among the room of the Havi's viceroy, and as befitting the money handler of a powerful and connected man like Värmod Balkisson… his room was nicer than his lord's. Especially now that the Havi's room was flooded due to all that ice he conjured up melting the second he died. Stupid mages are always so lazy.

He was not alone. In addition to Vifil, the Cultists all gathered about in the room. The tricky elf-thing was analyzing the viceroy's collection of books, mildly impressed by its showing. The vulgar vampire-thing was rummaging through the room as a whole, stuffing anything shiny into a sack. The ghost-thing was… haunting… doing nothing… boring. Lastly the Host of Shurpanakha was brooding as he stared out an open window to the butchery happening below.

"My-my, they could stand to be a little quieter." Rhiel

spoke knowing that it was a baiting statement. But the quiet that had settled in the room was insufferable. Or it was to someone like him, someone that liked talking about feelings and other such nonsensical rubbish.

"You mean the bugs eating a literal city's worth of people or the men trying their damnedest to drown out said bugs." The elf simply opened a new book at the old sailor's growling retort. A disappointment, it would seem that this viceroy was only a scholar and learned man when it came to money. As Riel quickly found that any tome that did not relate to gold or silver, none of their spines had been cracked even the slightest.

"It's the price to be paid. Our young lord has yet to take his Crown, the Locusts must be baited and bribed into committing to our cause until such a time. Even the great Lord Beelzebub has its limits of what it will commit before it has its master." That's the problem with immortals, they see everyone as children when it's only them that could ever live as long to see a wise old man as young. Still, the wisdom of someone that's had thousands of years to learn and grow did outweigh someone's petty life of savagery and thievery. The bugs would have eaten Horga regardless of any orders given to them by anyone, Orphan included. One, they were all hungry. And two, they thought they knew what was best for Orphan as of right now.

"Tens of thousands of people are being eaten alive and you call that a price to be paid! I shouldn't expect anything less than from someone that sees life and death like a blacksmith sees a hunk of iron and hammer!" Tempers flared but the Beast remained asleep, for she knew that all of this was bluster. They could not kill Rhiel. There was no point in wasteful slaughter if there was no death to sweeten it.

"Oy, calm down furball. The Soarlands will have new cities to clamor to. And Horga can be rebuilt, just give it time." A golden goblet studded with jewels held Serk's attention more than this conversation did. Another irritating common issue among the unliving, the valuable passage of time was meaningless to them. A day was just as important as a year, no more or no less.

"What don't you freaks get about this! I'm angry about the baker I bought bread from four years ago here, the whore that held me after having this thing crawl inside of me, the guards I played dice with every time I came to port here. Not the city, or the bugs, the fucking people that don't come back." If it wasn't for the delicious anger currently warming her belly, Shurpanakha might have taken issue with being called a thing. She did. And would carry out the punishment later. But for now she was satisfied.

"They are dead. What does it matter now? Can't change it." And with that last bit of depressing truth from the last cultist in the room, Orphan made up his mind.

"Enough, I want to be alone. Continue this fight some-where else." If Orphan was to be honest he had forgotten that there was anyone else in the entire room. He sat in the soft enveloping chair that no doubt cost a great deal to import safely from the south as nothing of this fine craftsmanship could be made by Soarling hands. Equally so was the luxurious silk robe that adored his frame, thankfully the former viceroy was a corpulent man so it was not too small on his bulk. Unfortunately, part of it had been ruined by the fact the Divine Spear still clung to Orphan's right hand. Despite the fact that wealth and more surrounded him, a frown was upon his lips. Everything he claimed to want in life, at least a small taste of it, was here… in his hands.

The others had left one by one, their presence more of an irritation than a comfort. Vifil, the old sailor, was the first to go, taking the excuse of orders to remove himself from the room before things became too heavy. The specter vanished like it was never there to begin with. Serk, the savage vampire, had slung his loot over his shoulder and happily jogged out, a sadistic grin still plastered on his face. The elf lingered a moment longer, perhaps sensing something deeper stirring in the air, but one sharp glare from Orphan sent him stalking off in silence. The door closed behind Rhiel with a soft click, and finally, the room was still.

Alone at last. Alone with his thoughts, and the remnants of a man whose shadow he had unknowingly lived in for most of his life.

Orphan sat there, motionless, his eyes fixed on the collar guard that rested on the table before him. Encased within its iron frame was the jawbone of his grandfather, Damophon, the Twelfth Tyrant. The name that had meant so little to him before, only a passing interest shoved aside once there was time to indulge in the vagaries of the small things. He wasn't even sure of their exact relation, was it his grandfather, his great-grandfather? It didn't matter. This was the man whose blood he shared, whose legacy still echoed through the world, even if only in whispers of terror.

The jawbone was a mangled ugly thing, twisted and malformed. The teeth were irregular, serrated, jagged, some curled like the fangs of a beast, others sharp like the thorns of some poisonous plant. It still maintained some resemblance to symmetry, but barely. It was as if the bone couldn't decide if it belonged to a man or a monster. Orphan had cleaned it after the battle, but the faint stain of blood still clung to it, as if the violence of Damophon's life had seeped so deeply into the bone that it could never be washed away.

"Why did they follow you, grandfather?" he asked quietly, breaking the silence. His voice was rough, almost a whisper, but in the stillness of the room, it sounded louder than it should have. "You didn't have the Gift of Guile. You didn't have beauty or splendor. They still speak of you like you were some nightmare come to life, writhing flesh, scales, fur, claws. A monster. The Chimera. An ugly beast that wanted nothing more than to kick and scream, lashing out at the world demanding it give you a reason to live. Do I have that right? And yet... they followed you. Why?"

The jawbone offered no answer. Of course, it didn't. It was nothing but bone, stripped of life and meaning. But that didn't stop the questions. Orphan leaned back in his chair, his hands gripping the armrests tightly as if he were trying to hold onto something tangible in the storm of his thoughts.

But indeed, Orphan was right. The Twelfth Tyrant, the Chimera, the Monster of the Seas, the Pirate Tyrant. Captain Damophon was a blight upon this world, savaging the coasts and inlands in a gruesome quest to finally find something that could bring him joy. Committing every vile action he could in the hopes it would inspire a Hero or even better a Savior to rise up against him. Every head on spike, every crying peasant girl, every lake of corpses he left behind was all in the hopes someone would take up that most wonderful of causes... vengeance. A man does not fight his hardest for king, country, or creed. They fight hardest for their family, their loved ones, their children. But he couldn't do it, he could kill enough of those apparently to bring him someone with vengeance strong enough in their heart to give him a challenge.

"You didn't conquer. You didn't build. You just… pillaged. Burned. Devoured. You were nothing but hunger and rage, and yet men followed you. Everything I've heard about you paints you as one of the worst Tyrants to walk this earth. What was your ambition, it had to be something great enough to stain the very idea for all mortal kind. Why did you even make ambition a Sin?"

He stood suddenly, unable to sit still any longer. He paced the room, the sound of his boots against the stone floor the only noise in the vast emptiness. His eyes fell on a gilded goblet resting on the table near the bed, filled with sweetmeats and hand-wrapped candies, luxuries beyond anything he had imagined in his childhood. The kind of indulgences he had told himself he wanted. The kind he had fought to surround himself with.

"I thought that's what I wanted, too," he muttered, picking up one of the candies and rolling it between his fingers. "Gold. Feasts. Every indulgence. I thought if I had it all, I could shove it in the faces of everyone who ever looked down on me. Who laughed at me. Starved me. Treated me like nothing. I don't need to eat now, but I will. Every day, I will eat the same amount that I watched everyone eat during a feast while I was given nothing. Every indulgence that exists in this world I want to experience. I thought that was my ambition."

He threw the candy back into the goblet, like a petulant child annoyed they now have a toothache. His fingers trailed across the silken sheets of the bed, the soft fabric foreign to him, a reminder of just how far he had come from the dirt and filth of his youth. And yet… it all felt hollow.

"Why did they follow you?" He asked again as his eyes drifted back to the jawbone, still sitting on the table, lifeless and broken. This time his voice was more forcefully spoken, as if somehow demanding an answer from the dead. "Värmod worshiped you. He was angry, angry that I was trying to take your place, angry that I claimed to be your blood. What did you give him? What made him so loyal? Why did men risk their lives for you, long after you were gone?"

His voice echoed in the empty room, the question hanging in the air like the smoke from a dying fire. He was angry now, not just at Damophon, but at himself. For not knowing. For not understanding. He had seen it in the Nameless King, too, a loyalty so deep it transcended fear, transcended logic. Men followed that kind of loyalty into the abyss, willingly, even joyfully.

But Orphan? Orphan had followers who feared him. He had an army, a Swarm, because they were bound to him by the dark threads of Gluttony and hunger. They would follow him until he died… and then they would forget him. Move on. Like nothing had ever happened.

"What is loyalty?" he whispered, almost to himself. "What do I have to do to earn that loyalty?"

The question lingered in the room, filling the air with a weight that felt brutally unbearable. Orphan's grip tightened on the armrest as if, by some miracle, the jawbone might speak. But the silence remained, unyielding, mocking. Poor brat felt the frustration build in his skull, pounding and pooling blood in places it shouldn't.

And then, a noise. A faint thud from above, breaking the

stillness. Orphan's eyes narrowed, the irritation sparking in his chest. No one should be up there, he had given explicit orders. Plus, Serk already finished looting anything of possible value though he did give Orphan a fair pick of the treasure before running off with them. Whoever was foolish enough to disobey them had chosen the wrong moment to test his patience. Naughty-naughty fools were interrupting his important time of self-reflection and... ugh... personal growth.

Slowly, deliberately, Orphan rose from the chair, the collar guard clutched tightly in one hand, the Divine Spear pulsing in the other. His irritation at the intrusion deepened with every step, the fine slippers he wore squelching as they soaked up the melted ice water. As he climbed the stairs, he could feel something... off. The air was too still, as if the very atmosphere anticipated what was to come.

The thudding continued, faint but insistent, just outside the Havi's chamber door. And in that moment, Orphan realized... whatever was happening, this would not be a simple disturbance.

What he had found standing outside the large doors of the Havi's chambers was however worth the trouble. A collection of five individuals, diverse and colorful. What adventures these five must have gone on to be so damned interesting looking would puzzle a worthy spectator. But to Orphan they were just five miscreants trespassing on his newly acquired property.

"Be quiet you idiot, or else you're going to get us all caught." Spoken as if they weren't already caught, this one was covered in green and brown, cloaks and leather, and a large bow hung on her back. If one were to get close they would only smell pine oil and squirrel innards.

"They're going to find the bodies eventually, why waste time?" Large impressive arms rested on the shaft of an equally large and impressive battleaxe. Said arms were attached to a burly man akin to the locals of the Soarlands in garb, tribal and less than one might want to have on for protection. The only bit of armor he wore was… oh… interesting… a collar guard with a jawbone attached to it. Wonder what that could be?

"Did we really need to kill those men? They were only doing as they were told." Fussy-fussy, and pointless too. Worried over the deaths of men that would without a second thought harm every hair on her head, a woman garbed in that of the priestly order of the Orphaned Church spoke in a guilty plea.

"Sister Helinda, weren't those men Soarling raiders? It's not worth it to cry over the fates of those that wouldn't do the same for you, right?" Orphan paused at this voice. It was very familiar, but distant in his memory. Not only that but it had changed, softer, older, and more… polite. But it still held a bit of accent to it, and he could never truly forget the voice of his greatest childhood tormentor.

There was also one more member of this little intruding group, but he stayed silent as the grave. Short, likely a dwarf, but covered head to toe in heavy plate armor. The helmet didn't even have any features to speak of, just a flat surface. Creepy little man.

"Thrain." Orphan said with a surprising amount of jovial mirth, he was actually happy to see the man that had chased him around so many times as a child. For… hehe… less than friendly reasons I'm sure.

The intruding agents of the Church of the Orphaned World all turned around to see Orphan standing behind them about a dozen feet away down the hallway. Thrain for his part looked puzzled as to why this, to him, unknown stranger seemed to know who he was. The others however focused in on Orphan's hands. To both the mutating Divine Spear trapped in his grip and the Twelfth's Jawbone, the object that they had come to Horga to retrieve.

They had no earthly clue that Horga was going to be consumed by the Ravenous Swarm. For the past several weeks they had been in and around the city planning and scheming to infiltrate the Bastard's Middle Finger and steal away such a potent Artifact from a man unworthy to have it. Imagine their shock and horror as they watched from their mountainside camp as the lake of which the city was so famous for drained out. And then the Swarm came. Oh the panic. Oh the hysteria. What fun.

"You, how do you know my name?" Thrain stood in front of the rest and Orphan had the urge to bury his head in his hand at the absurdity, too bad he had no free hand. But the once golden hunter of Glimisvellir had gone completely Southern. Now dressed up in garb befitting a noble from one of the Great Savior Nations and not a lick of his Glimingaric heritage left on him. Orphan found it all so amusing that it was likely between the two of them, he who hated the Glimingar probably had more in common with a man from Glimisvellir than their Hero did at this point.

"Oh my dear Havi, how does a child of your land abandon it so?" Orphan looked up to the ceiling in a mocking attempt to question the god's nonexistent sorrow. Though it would likely only confuse anyone else as that word is only known as the title of one of the three leaders of the Soarlands rather than one of the lesser names of a God as it actually was.

"It doesn't matter how he knows your name, all that matters is that The Chimera's remains are in sight and no longer attached to Värmod." The burly one smirked as he lifted his battle axe off his shoulders and got ready for a fight. But internally he hoped one would not come, as he rightly suspected the spear in Orphan's hands was the far greater threat than the bones of a Tyrant.

"This is the great Ser Thrain, I have no doubt you will easily recover the Sin of Ambition's legacy. We will return to Atlas victorious." The holy woman clasped her hands in sickening sweet hope. How naïve, like a bunny thinking it wasn't born to be the fox's dinner.

"Ser Thrain… you guys do know that this man forced his little sister to bathe with him until she was twelve, and it only ended because she kept kneeing him in the bits every time he tried after." The brat was having fun. So much fun. Seeing all, except one, of their faces at this very true comment was priceless. Orphan drank in the moment as an entire minute passed by before the others turned their head to Thrain who looked as pale as Orphan normally did.

"Now see here, there was a reason why-"

"So it's true?!" All three of the speaking companions all shouted with differing emotions. But all a mix of shock, disgust, and horror. I must feel the nauseating urge to clarify, if only not to deceive my dear and respected Listener. Thrain, is not a man that commits the most heinous of unholy desires. Much like how Brune turned to rebellion and defiance in the wake of her father's death and her mother's broken mind, Thrain also changed. Fear of further loss drove him to covet what he had left. Doesn't make how he went about this pathetic trauma any less humorously embarrassing and easily misinterpreted.

"Oh, how about her eighth birthday when you-"

"Will you not just cease speaking?!" Barely. Just barely he watched his tongue.

"Careful now Glimingar, or your dear friend and minder Iziaslav is going to have to sew your mouth shut again." The savage warned and he would do it. Orphan did take note, there were small scars along Thrain's lips. Hmm. The Cursed Born both felt satisfied and curious about this news. Nevertheless, Thrain growled a bit toward the barbarian before looking back to the source of his current contempt.

"How do you know such things? There shouldn't be a single person south of Glimisvellir that knows anything about me, so how do you?" Quickly he tacked on that last bit as to not test his luck.

"Brune told me herself, after all... I was her friend." Slowly Orphan shifted his stance ever so slightly, readying for the fight to come. There was, however, a chill running down his spine, his gut telling him that this was not going to be any ordinary fight. He simply assumed that it meant the fact he would be fighting Thrain and nothing else.

But it would come, as Thrain's face morphed from confusion, to realization, to anger and indignation. Now, do not blame him for the foolishness of it all. Orphan does not even remotely look like he once did, only a few passing features remain and even those have been refined by both the Gift of Guile and Divine Body. To anyone from his childhood he was unrecognizable. Plus, there was the fact everyone had assumed he had died out in the valley, likely eaten or frozen to death. So, that's what Thrain thought, which was why he reacted as such.

"No… that's impossible, Orphan is Dead!" The rest of Thrain's party panicked as the Hero invocated a statement. A statement that must now be true. They did not know Orphan or cared for them, it was more reflex to having a Hero speak out of turn.

The air between Orphan and Thrain was thick with tension as they stood in front of the Havi's chambers, the carnage of the Swarm's grand happy feast still echoing faintly in the below. Oh how long it has been since a Swarm had an entire city to gorge on? To long… to long. Truly it was a sign, one that could be taken differently by different people. To someone like Orphan, it was the ringing sound of his new era… to those of this Hero's party it was a sign of a new plague of locusts descending upon fields, towns, keeps, and cities. A culling of starvation might do the exploding population of the world right I must say.

As for the words that were spoken with the frantic denial of panic and dread, the weight of his Divine Right of Infallibility pressed down on the room. But something unexpected happened. A ripple in the air, a tension that made the very fabric of reality vibrate. Orphan is Dead, this statement is quite untrue. Then by the laws of the Divine Right of Infallibility that must be corrected! But. Reality itself cracked like glass under pressure, literal cracks I mean as they spiderwebbed through the very air itself between them, as the two Divine Rights fought for dominance.

For a moment, the world teetered between possibilities. If the clash tilted in Thrain's favor, Orphan would simply cease to be and this would be a very boring story indeed. The Title of Hero is a Lesser Title, and when matched against even a fragment of a Greater Title like Tyrant… like a puppy barking at an over-sized rabid dire wolf. Reality shattered much like glass in a Rights Clash, pieces of metaphysical matter broke apart into nothingness leaving Orphan standing perfectly fine. His lips twisted into a smirk as he realized Thrain's Divine Right had failed to erase him. "So, you're trying to kill me with a word, Thrain? You always were a coward, hiding behind your righteousness instead of facing me."

Thrain's eyes widened with the dawning realization that his power had failed. He hadn't intended to call upon his Right so directly. He had a great streak going too, two years since his last accidently invoked Statement. The Church had drilled restraint into him over the years, forcing him to speak carefully, always conscious of the weight of his words. Then there were the many beatings he had gotten from the Church's premier Hero Koumaïl, much-much beatings. One can only restrain themselves so much when a ghost from your past starts bringing up rather sight falsehoods regarding your actions with dear family members.

"That confirms it, there was no fuss in that Rights Clash. He's at least an Heir." From the lips of the barbarian came a resigned sigh. Oh my dear Iziaslav, you have no idea just how late all of you are to come and stop this.

"We're just going to skip over everything he said are we?" A deadpan question offered by the girl that needed to be dragged from the trees kicking and screaming. I'm not joking there, they actually had to do that.

"You're still the same twisted monster aren't you Orphan?" Thrain spat, his voice steady but laced with venom. His heart actually ached, this was perhaps the first time Thrain had seen Malice inflected on such a scale. "I should've killed you back then, maybe all of Horga would still be alive if I had?"

It had been many years since Thrain had left Glimisvellir, doing so as an arrogant manchild incapable of understanding that maybe just maybe he wasn't the center of the world. Well, when given to people that knew how to handle a petulant Hero with no understanding of their powers, one often does succumb to the truth. For Thrain it was difficult, going from golden boy hunter to unproven untested Hero. But the Church excels at not only breaking people, but building them back up as they deem they should. So now Thrain returns to the north, armed with companions, a bright shiny new moral code, and a dream. How does one fair when given such an edifice of his past self's baneful past ey?

"Do you think you're any better than the Chimera? Will you not look at the chaos you've wrought, the people you've consigned to be butchered? You couldn't be worse than the Twelfth could you? Not while you're pretending to be something better than what you are. I knew it then, and I know it now. You're nothing but a spiteful little monster."

Orphan's expression darkened at the comparison as another Rights Clash occurred between them from the Hero's reckless statement. His grip tightened on the collar guard. The twisted, monstrous jawbone of the Chimera, an Artifact of raw power, brutality, and destruction. Had he not just come from pointlessly reflecting on this very thing, the beautifully twisted legacy that man had left behind. Orphan wasn't like that. He didn't want to just destroy for destruction's sake. Life could not be enjoyed as it was meant to be for him if everything was ruins and ash. He learned well from his studies, taxes, investment, and infrastructure.

Boring things yes, but they get you shinny baubles and expensive crushed grapes that were left alone for far too long. The world was like a tree, it needed to be clipped, tended to, and then one can enjoy its fruit.

"You don't know anything asshole," Orphan sneered, what possible changes Thrain may have gone through just like Orphan were unnoticeable by the Cursed Born. All he saw was the embodiment of Glimisvellir's score for him. "I don't destroy. I conquer. I build. My grandfather… he was a monster, and I am something better."

"Will you keep telling yourself that, Orphan?" Thrain took the first step forward, the rest of his party standing back as they felt this was something their friend and… leader… needed to do. He unsheathed his sword, an elegant that continued the theme of Thrain being out of touch with his roots. "But will you not look around you, does Horga not lie in ruins, does the Swarm not feast on the flesh of hundreds of thousands of innocent lives? There isn't a single person responsible for it all other than you is there? Face it. You'll always be a monster, could you possibly be anything else? I don't think so!"

Orphan's eyes flared with fury, his vision narrowing on Thrain even as with a shout the Hero lunged forward blade ready. He was not a monster. Monsters destroy without purpose. Monsters were ugly things and he by all accounts was an Adonis. Monsters are unthinking beasts. But he was a rational and intelligent man capable of devouring libraries. The Swarm had acted on instinct, not his direct command. He hadn't told them to ravage the city, only to take it. He was above all that. He didn't do it.

That thought struck deep within Orphan, a deliciously vile

part of the mortal psyche that will do anything to survive and justify. The kind that makes a moral and just man capable of the most heinous of acts during war. Oh what a wonderful feeling it must be, to finally find yourself blameless in all things. And there it was. The thought, horrible in the way that only true realizations are, slipped into Orphan's mind like a dagger between ribs. Neatly, efficiently. All this time, he was being accused of the notion that he was somehow responsible for what the Swarm did. That their actions, their brutality, somehow reflected on him. But why should it?

This marvelously dreadful thing inside him, could have been smothered in the powers of something as bothersome as guilt, but instead it found fertile ground. Memories. Empty eyes, looking away as he lay on the cold stone road starving. His uncle was on one of his benders and passed out, he hadn't eaten in days. Everyone ignored him.

So, why should he care if a city full of those same kinds of people was now being torn apart by creatures that could probably write the word hungry as their entire autobiography? No one had cared when he was dying. They'd walked by him, eyes straight ahead, pretending he didn't exist. And now, wasn't it only fair that he do the same? The world had ignored him, and so he would ignore them.

The world had turned a blind eye to his suffering, and now he would do the same to theirs. A sense of all consuming apathy that had always lurked at the edges of his soul blossomed. Apathy for the world that had ignored him, for the people who had watched him suffer and done nothing. Why should he feel guilty for the Swarm's actions? Apparently moral and just people felt nothing when he was dying by the wayside. He wasn't responsible for their deaths.

No, the world deserved this. The Magic of Malice took note of a new form of itself, Apathic Malice… the uncaring malevolence of a spiteful soul.

"I'm only responsible for what I do," Orphan said, his voice low but filled with a newfound conviction. A bright and shiny new steel in his words, the unreasonable glory of it all. "Not for what others choose to do in my name."

Best of all came next, the very air around him shifted. There was power in convictions when held by someone with a touch of Divinity in them, resonating in those that had been marked by it. The still celebrating Soarlings below, started to truly celebrate. The sounds from below became less of a concern. They had drink, they had young bountiful women, they had song and contests to entertain them. Why should they let the bugs ruin their victory with their own spoils? Apathy to those dying below, in favor of base pleasures. Much closer to home for Orphan, the Divine Spear. The fleshy tendrils that had once wrapped around the spear, thick white liquid began to ooze out from between the fibers. It started to harden, forming bone-like plating. The spear seemed to breathe, growing stronger as it fed off Orphan's burgeoning realization.

Almost purely by a deeply in grained instinct, Orphan blocked Thrain's swing as the Cursed Born merely gave a thousand yard stare as he came to these conclusions. But it would not be the only revelation he would experience tonight. No-no-no, emotions are high, past trauma laid bare, old wounds ripped open, it is a messy breeding ground for mind shattering turmoil.

For the Hero here, it was not as such. Thrain had not the many prongs of mental attack upon his psyche that

Orphan had but instead led actual physical attacks on the Heir of Glutton. The blade danced through the air, thrusting forward and then whipping back around for a counter slash. Orphan barely registered any of this as he mindlessly blocked having been given far worse a workout by his Fiendish teachers. Thrain had continued to goad, taunt, and accuse Orphan with every strike, but it all bounced off his empty stare. It was only when Orphan heard another Statement by the Hero that there was a change.

"The floor itself comes to my aid and will break in concert with my attack." Sure enough, cracks began to form in the floor, or more accurately those that were already there by the previous battle in the tower grew even larger. Orphan, however, quickly caught Thrain's thrust, locking the Hero's arm in the crux of his own. Pulling back and using the momentum to roll forward and away from the collapsing ground. "I won't fall into this hole!"

Unlike before where the Right of Infallibility was able to easily accommodate Thrain's Statement, this was a bit more tricky. Reality itself was a lazy bum, always doing the least amount of work to make sure everything was running as it should... but it didn't get to decide what 'should' is. So, when Thrain claims the floor will break at an exact moment, that's easily made true. Thrain not falling into the very hole he created with no genuine means of doing so? Instead, Thrain just suddenly found himself back on solid ground... in front of a now awake Orphan.

Thrain raised his sword, gripping it with the kind of desperate tightness that only comes from someone realizing, too late, that they are entirely out of their depth. It was almost pitiful, really. The Hero, standing tall, blade held like some shining beacon of hope, completely unaware of just how outmatched he truly was.

But Orphan knew. Oh, he knew. And it showed in every lunge, every strike of his mutated spear. The tendrils coiled and tightened with every movement, their grotesque strength so effortless, so overwhelming, that Thrain's once-pristine training felt like a child waving a stick at a storm. The Hero's movements were clean, precise, and rehearsed everything the Church had drilled into him over the years. But what worth was precise when you were facing raw, unchecked power?

Orphan, unlike Thrain, had never been coddled. Everyone that knows the truth of the Divine Rights tiptoes around a Hero. With the slip of the tongue entire lives are upended. No kindly priest nor noble patron had guided the brat. His teachers had been brutal, unforgiving... Demons, in every sense of the word. And as Thrain struggled to counter Orphan's strikes, it became painfully clear that all the elegant swordplay in the world wouldn't save him from the inevitable truth: he was losing. Badly.

Quite ironically given their past, Orphan wasn't afraid of this old foe. Not anymore, if he ever was. Strike and assault after another, Thrain was getting cut to pieces, but Orphan was taking his time. After all this was a perfect must needed chance to work out some stress. Though with every attack he kept a sense of the rest of Thrain's party, they all seemed quite impressive and diverse. None of them really gave Orphan a sense of panic, except one. The burly one in furs and his very own jawbone collar, that one set off Orphan's well-developed instincts. Likewise, that barbarian was watching him.

"Ser Iziaslav, shouldn't we... I don't... help?" An astute

observation by the petite woman in priestly garb. Whatever was she doing here? Far too dangerous for such a delicate thing like that. But the barbarian said nothing and it was the cloaked huntress that whispered an answer to the priestess.

"Shh. Don't move your head but look up." Doing as she was told, the holy woman glanced out and nearly gasped in fear as seven creatures were clinging to the ceiling. Their skin blackened in dead cold fashion, a wafting smell of decay fluttered down, and each of them twitched in such a disturbing manner that it shook her to her soul. "I read about them in the Church's tomes, the Wraith Lord Rhiel commands the mighty and powerful after they die and come into his clutches."

"Meaning the Cult is here." A throaty chuckle came from Iziaslav as he cracked his neck. This was getting better and better by the second for him. And by the embarrassing showing of Thrain, it was only going to get even better. Getting back to that disaster of a duel, Thrain was on his knees and bleeding profusely. Dozens of shallow and not so shallow cuts littered his body. But he remained defiant, credit to him.

"You won't win, Orphan," Thrain grunted, the third Rights Clash occurring as he spat up blood upon the floor. His soon to be executioner smirking at how cute this was until Thrain continued on. "Even if you beat me, there will be others. Heroes always rise up. That's how it's always been. Saviors will come, and they will stop you, just like they've stopped every Tyrant before."

The scary part was… no Right Clash occurred. This was not a Statement that needed to be enforced as it was partly already true. Many of the Twelve Tyrants that have lived have died by the hands of a Hero or Savior. Their mighty reigns ending in blood and tragedy, their Courts dying the second they did, the Fiends set adrift again by the loss of their master, entire realms thrown into chaos now that they were free again. It was always so tragic.

Orphan paused at this, his spear raised mid-strike. Thrain's words hung in the air, sinking deep into the Cursed Born's mind. The thought gnawed at him, not nibbled, but full on ripping and tearing into the meat of his psyche. It was true, Heroes would keep coming. There would always be someone trying to take him down, to tear away everything he had worked for. Even if he succeeded today, his future would be an endless cycle of conflict. No peace. No rest. No means of truly enjoying everything he believed he deserved in life.

"No," He hissed as the realization filled him with rage. His eyes darkened, his lips curling in a sneer. He was so damn tired of all the trials and tribulations. He wanted to win, and for the win to stay a win. Thirteen years, a little over half of his life he had nothing. His Seat of Power was right there, he could become Tyrant so easily and just as easily lose everything to a Hero's blade… or gun… or fist… or many forms of blunt force trauma. The options were endless.

"Ha… even a sick and twisted monster like you has to understand the power of Righteousness in this world. You'll never-" Thrain struggled and pulled himself up, but couldn't finish his sentence as he was backhanded by Orphan and sent flying into a nearby wall. The priest girl shouted in panic and rushed over towards Thrain, setting off the next stage of the battle.

Howling in a shrill screams, the moving corpses that Rhiel

so disturbingly fancied dropped from their ceiling perches toward the Hero's party. The remaining members, the barbarian, the huntress, and the mute armored one all took their stances. Now was a true display of combat finesse. Each of them played their part, taking hits, dishing them out, or striking at the perfect moment. Like symphony well-orchestrated, they fought these ghoulish creatures as the holy woman attempted to heal Thrain. Unfortunately for them, the corpses they were fighting were of people that could easily be counted among the party's peers once upon a time. And they were not shambling zombies, but fully capable wrights just as deadly as they were in life.

A certain Cursed Born watched this and it only reaffirmed what Thrain had said. People like this would always rise up, and they would have backing. By the Church. By the Nations that opposed him. By foolish masses that didn't understand what was best for them. The entire world fought maddeningly against the forces of Tyranny for millennia... by what delusion did Orphan think they would not do the same to him? He would never know peace... until... there wasn't anyone to oppose him left.

Another puzzle piece of Orphan's emerging ethos fell into place. Peace was what he wanted. Peace to enjoy the world and everything it had to offer him. That was what he wanted all along after all, had been since he first woke up in the Winterman's home. The difference between before and after this moment is he now understood what needed to happen for him to get it. And through the connection he shared with Lord Beelzebub, the Maggot King finally felt its Heir ready for his Crown. Finally Orphan was committed to the task at hand. No more waffling about, no more indecision and certainly no more fucking excuses. It was time to Consume the World.

Swell thing too… as the Archfiend of Gluttony had already planned on killing off Orphan once the feast was done. The boy had proven himself inadequate for the ancient bug, until this moment. It had hoped that this revelation of Ambition would happen during the fight with Värmod but better late than never.

"Thank you Thrain, you've been surprisingly really helpful. Making a lot of things clearer for me." Orphan mused as he lazily walked toward Thrain, his glowing green eyes more focused on the battle between Thrain's party and the wrights. To him, whatever magic the holy woman was using wasn't Life Magic… he would recognize it. It wasn't Heal, so there was little that she could do. Though, if it was Heal then the woman would likely kill herself attempting to use it on all of Thrain's injuries.

"I don't need your mockery, you little freak." More fussing by the woman as Thrain struggled to get ahold of himself.

"Maybe you need my pity? Would you like that Thrain, pity from the Cursed Born brat that you liked to chase around because your sister liked to spend time with me more than with you." He was now having fun, this was a fun time for him. But not for Thrain, the mention of his sister was the last straw and he said something he shouldn't have.

"I've always been right about you Orphan, you deserve nothing but scorn and to be disregarded. The people of Glimisvellir thankfully came to their senses and so will the rest of the world." Oh… another Statement… but no Right Clash. This combined with Thrain's words, it made horrifying sense as Orphan thought about it. It explained why they could at the same time look upon him with such hatred whenever he looked up at them, but then in the next moment forget he even existed without his knowledge.

"You… you used your power on them, didn't you?" Orphan whispered, his voice cold and steady. How could an entire town come to hate a baby? No matter how awful his mother was he should by all rights and logic be guiltless of her sins. Especially since he was orphaned, one of the most sacred and protected people in the entire world. Unless… oh dear unless all of them had been changed.

"What? No, I was far too young. They just came to understand what a devil spawn you really were. It's as he told me." Whether by deliberate denial or a subconscious one, Thrain sputtered out his refusal to take responsibility for all of Orphan's misfortune. It made too much sense to the Cursed Born, it answered too many questions.

"That's it. That's why they hated me. It wasn't just them. It was you. You made them see me like that. You. The Hero. The town's golden boy. You did it." He changed them into something they weren't. Something he wanted them to be more convenient for him. And still the world praises him for what he is.

At last, the final click of everything is settling within Orphan's mind. He had now his Malice, his means to free himself of all wrongdoings that others may freely commit. Ambition, a Sin that had eluded him for so long, was now firmly in his grasp. These two facets of Orphan's mind alone had given him inner peace in a way. He now had the answers to questions about himself he long since been asking. But it was only now that the third and most important question for him had been answered. How can he find Loyalty?

The answer? Change.

Change people.

Change the world.

Change the very laws of reality itself.

And Orphan knew he could start to inflect this change very close to home right here and now.

"You think you can decide who I am? What I am? You call me a monster? No. I decide what I am. And now, I decide what you are." In a flash, Orphan appeared before Thrain and before the silly holy woman could do anything thrusted his spear into the Hero's heart. Two things began their final transformation.

The spear's power surged through Thrain's body, twisting and reshaping him from within. His once-handsome features began to warp, his skin stretching and contorting into something grotesque. His hair fell in patches, his jawline warped into a hideous, fish-like maw, and his eyes bulged unnaturally from their sockets. He gasped and screamed, but the sound was an ugly gargle.

Meanwhile, something far more beautiful was changing for the better. The Divine Spear. The last mental block within Orphan's soul was clear. The turmoil in his heart caused by the displays of true loyalty from the Nameless King and Värmod was dispelled. He need not be jealous of such things now that he had the answer to find such loyalty himself. So, the Spear finally attuned to his soul and magic. Becoming a living weapon. Its shaft, encased in pale, bone-like plating, pulsed with dark veins and through ornate oval holes along its sides revealed sinewy muscle and capillaries within. At its base, three sharp claws formed the pommel, able to clutch with lethal force. A slitted green eye sat where the shaft met the blade, ever-watchful. The blade itself, curved and serrated, shimmered with an eerie glow. As Orphan gripped it, tendrils of flesh reached out, merging with his arm and giving a sense of oneness with his weapon.

"Everyone thought they could shape me into something they wanted. You. The people of Glimisvellir. The Fiends. The Cult. Every damn person I've ever met has tried to change me. But now I'll change them. I remake them in my image. And now, I've remade you."

Thrain collapsed to the ground, barely recognizable. His strength was gone, his body broken, his dignity stripped away. Orphan stood over him, the Divine Spear pulsating in his hand, its new form a symbol of his complete domination over the man who had once been his rival.

Orphan's mind swirled with the clarity of a madman proven right for the first time. He could reshape the world, just as he had reshaped Thrain. Loyalty, hatred, even love... they were all malleable, just like flesh.

Words of the Hero

"To protect the weak, save the innocent, and avenge the wronged. This is my duty to the world, what I do is only right."
Vjera Kovach, Champion of the Nine Gates, the final words of her speech before doing battle with the Twelfth Tyrant.

An Exciting Climatic Return

It was not long after the destruction of Horga that the Swarm left its feasting grounds. Only a few days were spent in the former city of the Soarlands before they were back on the move, this time north. And now they moved with purpose. A distinct change had happened among the Soarlings that followed Orphan, they became colder and more detached from the woes of deemed outsiders. The fish rots from the head down, so they say, and the malicious apathy that had been birthed in Horga was certainly rotting away at their hearts.

Men and women of Orphan's warband grew selfish and callous, taking no blame for anything they had not committed themselves. They became responsible for themselves and nothing else, but in turn demanded no blame for anyone not immediately at fault. The Fiends of Gluttony took note and approved, as Fiends hold similar senses of justice. Orphan's Soarlings could easily be called cruel and uncaring, but also fair and maybe a twisted sense of justice. Such is the power of Malice and Order.

In truth, the most difficult part of this process was those that did not fall under Orphan's sway. Roughly ten percent of Horga's population survived that most bountiful of nights.

Lord Beelzebub had been directing the Hive with a heavy hand, not only to indulge in the gorging second hand but also to make sure a certain class of mortal could be salvaged. The useful and exceptional kind. Tens of thousands of impish eyes glowed with a distant intelligence, watching for those that had great beauty, stature, or those that were found in certain locations that might indicate a useful profession. Of course the great Archfiend couldn't save every one of these possible pawns of Orphan, its own passions and its progenies' alike must be sated first.

These... lucky... individuals were given chains and marching orders in exchange for their lives. Some were granted more if the Demons suspected them of being open to the ways of Malice. None of these mortals were natives but entirely Soarlings or other foreigners taking port in the city. And the survivors now suffered under the uncaring watch of kinsmen that could give not a single thought to their misery. Many died after the bloody feast of the Fiends, in captivity or marching through the snow. It's not like they were given much food for the trip.

The entire city of Horga had been ransacked of every crumble and grape. Quickly these stores were divided up among the mortal population of the army, no longer just a warband but a proper army. The fine food of Horga's elite was dug out from their storehouses and ceilers to be given to Orphan's followers. Fat and entitled little piggies they were, leaving only the bare necessities for the large number of slaves they now had accompanying them. So much grumbling and whining came from the Demons and Imps of the Ravenous Swarm, did they not have enough? No. No, they did not. Afterall, what can you expect from beings whose entire existence is hunger. Only ever briefly replaced by joy during the immediate act of shoving something down their throat. Quickly vanishing and driving them to further heights to sate this unending hunger.

For the first time in hundreds of years, a Soarling army marched up the mountains and past the border stones of Glimisvellir. The bitter wind cut through the army like a knife, the cold air biting at exposed skin and armor. Even the Swarm, for all their resilience, chittered uneasily as they moved through the endless sea of white. Pine trees loomed overhead, their branches creaking under the weight of snow, a constant whispering sound as the wind howled through the dense forest. The ground beneath thousands of boots crunched, each step muffled by the thick snow, but there was no comfort in the silence. It was the quiet before something far worse, something waiting just beyond the snow-capped horizon.

And for the first time in history an army of Fiends did so as well. Any complaints or misgivings about their duty had been dashed by their progenitor's baleful mind. Lord Beelzebub knew now it was right to give this greedy, hungry, and half mad boy a chance. Now, the ever gapping maw knew no doubt that this boy now man could do it. He might just be the... let's not get ahead of ourselves here. Nevertheless, The Fiend of Gluttony were united behind Orphan and there was a buzz in the air, hehe, among them. One final battle and a new Master of Gluttony would be Crowned.

Yes, that final battle... about that. It should have started by now. Glimisvellir had remained free and independent for thousands of years in large part due to its position at the back end of a long and narrow valley. Any army that wanted to assault it would need to travel several days through heavy snow, dense pine forests, and creeping foothills. Perfect for the Glimingar to move through their ancestral tunnel network throughout the valley, using their deep knowledge of the terrain to bite and peck at the invaders while disappearing back into the wilderness. Orphan, of course, knew all about the tunnels, though he never went into them himself. There should be no issue as the Fiends had many years to prepare their own invading tunnel network into the Glimingar's one. Nothing? Nope… the army could see Glimisvellir in the distance and not once had they been harassed.

Of course, the Glimingar knew all about the Imps and their ways. The Fiends of Gluttony were well known by the world as bugs who could tunnel as skilled as any ant could. They must have abandoned the tunnels knowing it would only be a trap. Many in the Soarling army concluded that the famed hunters of Glimisvellir would be waiting in the developing urban outskirts, as beyond the ancient stone walls of Glimisvellir had developed a thriving larger township of Glimingar and immigrants alike. The plan was obvious, fire the cannons as they approached the town and once in the streets hit them from all sides with arrows and gunfire alike. Ingenious when you think about it, tactics like this hadn't been seen yet but it was just applying what the Glimingar knew best but in a different environment.

The Swarm would go first then, Imps were as disposable as arrows themselves. The plan was made, send the Imps in to surround the town's walls while the Soarlings come through the sea of Imps with ladders. A glorious battle to end the proud legacy of Glimisvellir, ending with it being burnt to the ground and its people slaughtered! Yes! Grudges would be settled and history would be... made? Oh dear, the buildings are empty. No they're not, clearly it must be some sort of ambush. There's also a distinct lack of cannons firing grape shots into the horde of cackling and scampering imps. Hmm. Do I have the right story here? Yes? I do?

As the Imps reach the walls, they find the gates open. Mass confusion spread through the army as a whole. Even Lord Beelzebub was deeply considering plunging all of Glimisvellir into a sink hole as this was far too unusual for its taste. It had seen many things in its long life and when situations like this play out far too well it's usually a set up for an even worse boot to fall upon the squirming bug. There were calls to retreat, maybe the Church had sent more Heroes, more competent heroes, to Glimisvellir. It was known to the Cult of the Seventh Sun that the Church had some sort of magic that allowed for near instant teleportation. Others believed that all of Glimisvellir had been rigged to explode or other such grand futile gesture. Or that every person in the town had been somehow armed and were all waiting at its very center to diminish the numbers advantage of the Swarm. Not a single person thought that perhaps... Glimisvellir was surrendering without a fight?

But what about the man of the hour? What did Orphan think of this? Much of the time that had been spent bickering between his various advisors, he stayed quiet. Brooding as he looked out upon the town from the same hill that once held the campsite of the invading Teutons. He could see it all spectacularly, there was movement within the town but the snow was a bit thick today and none of the Demons or mortals could make out just what they were doing. Orphan for his part decided that if Glimisvellir was going to be difficult in not playing its part in this finale, he would at least play the part of the fearsome conqueror.

With a reassuring grip and adjusting the collar guard of the Twelfth's Jawbone, Orphan launched himself into the air much to the shock and panic of those around him. To call Orphan superhuman now was an understatement. Already his body had become the pinnacle of what a mortal could achieve, and perhaps a bit more than that. But armed with a Divine Artifact that granted the wearer the strength and durability of the Chimera, arguably the physically mightiest of all the Tyrants? Oh dear, was that a spectacle to behold when Orphan decided to unleash his full strength.

The ground shook as the Cursed Born landed at the edge of the cobblestone street that led up to the Gate of Glimisvellir. With a lazy stroll, he walked down the boulevard taking note of the new buildings and trying to remember what had been there before. Behind him was a further rumbling as the horde of Imps pushed and shoved their way among each other to catch up with their precious Heir. The rest of the army too were scrambling like rats trying to escape a flooding sewer.

Stepping past the threshold of Glimisvellir's walls, a deep sense of nostalgia washed across Orphan's mind. But that was shoved aside by a swelling ego at just how it had been prepared for him. The entire population of Glimisvellir now lined the central street as if a parade was about to take place instead of a siege. Beneath his helmet he had to smirk that difference between this and his last memories of the town. Striding forward, he drank in the forced smiles and applause that greeted him.

Orphan walked the length of the central street, his footsteps slow and deliberate, his eyes scanning every face that dared to meet his gaze. His breath hung in the air, turning to mist in the cold, a small reminder that, despite everything, he was still flesh and blood. Glimisvellir was not as he remembered it. Gone were the familiar smells of smoked fish and pine resin that had once clung to the market stalls. The lively shouts of traders and children playing in the alleys had been replaced by a disquieting silence, interrupted only by the clapping of frozen, trembling hands. He took it all in, the forced smiles, the fake cheers, this was his homecoming, but it felt wrong. There was no triumph, only the hollow echoes of a victory already won.

A flicker of something pulled at him, a distant echo of the boy he used to be, lurking in the shadows of Glimisvellir's Great Hall, watching from a corner as men feasted and drank, ignoring the hungry eyes of the orphan left to starve. So in that moment... he smiled wider. Vicious enjoyment of the reversal of fortune. An indulgent cruelty warmed his heart and made all the chill in the air meaningless. He could stand naked in the frozen wasteland that surrounded his future Seat of Power and feel like it was balmy summer's day.

They all saw it, the Swarm. How many there were. And this was not even its full breath of numbers. Certainly after that first plunge by the Swarm any and all resistance to this plan to outright surrender to the Fiends was cast aside. This was their only chance. The worst part was, none but two knew the full scope of the desperate situation here. Orphan could tell that the exact same forced grin and genuine tears were on both Glimingar and Teuton faces as he walked toward the Great Hall. The locals did not know it was him, as just like Thrain they couldn't possibly recognize either his new look or the possibility he survived at all.

The people of Glimisvellir moved with stiff but panicked movement, frozen not just by the cold but by the fear that gripped their hearts. Forced smiles stretched across their faces, but the terror was unmistakable. Orphan could see it in the nervous shifting of feet on the cobblestone streets. Eyes darted to the horde of Demons that swarmed behind him, wide and wild, as if expecting the creatures to pounce at any moment. Even in the biting cold, some were sweating, beads of moisture trickling down temples and disappearing into fur-lined collars. The Glimingars were used to hardship, but not like this... never like this. Their forced applause was a pitiful attempt to mask their despair.

Soon enough Orphan was no longer alone, Abezethibou was the first to emerge by his side. Its sudden appearance caused a momentary pause, the clapping and cheers. But the townspeople resumed, even harder both in their cheering and crying. Soon more Demons and so the Cultists all made their way to the head of the procession. Imps came next, though directed by Lord Beelzebub to remain only on the street. The Maggot King itself remained behind as it gorged itself on the last remaining stores of food they had brought for the journey. Soarling captains bullied their way to the front of the Imps, proud and smug smiles all plastered on their faces. The Glimingars and southerners alike felt safe enough giving these troublemakers scowls and heated glares.

As the procession traveled trhough the town the Fiends of Gluttony spread out like a dark tide behind him. The Imps crawled up walls and perched on rooftops, their happy little faces flickered and twitched with malicious glee. They whispered to each other in guttural tones, a constant, unsettling hum that filled the air like a swarm of locusts just out of sight. Their coal like bodies soon dusting the snow black turning the pure white that blanketed the town into something more delightfully gloomy. Meanwhile more and more Demons filtered out of the Swarm and into the road, their bodies a grotesque blend of sinew, stone, chitin, and hungry maws. Every step unsettled the already brittle nerves of Glimisvellir's inhabitants, sending tremors through the crowd.

The townspeople dared not look directly at the creatures. Mothers pulled children close, shielding their eyes from the sight of claws and teeth. Old men and women, once proud hunters of the north, could only watch in silent horror as these beings, nightmares given form, passed them by. Even the bravest among them, those who had faced wolves, wild beasts, trolls, and even these Fiends themselves in the depths of winter, found their courage faltering in the presence of these fiends. There was no fighting these monsters, no outsmarting them with traps or cunning. The cancer had grown too bloated and entrenched too deep within, to exorcise it now would only result in futile death. The Demons fed off the fear in the air, drawing closer to the trembling crowd, relishing the unease they inspired without lifting a single claw.

This sickening display of perfectly valid submission came to a close as Orphan walked the stairs to the courtyard of the Great Hall Glimisvellir. Assembled all before him were those who held any sort of power in the town or beyond. Visiting dignitaries, business magnates, military leaders, and of course the priests who were all bound and gagged. The adorable little Imps darlings they were immediately beelined for this delightful tribute and began poking and pinching at the holy men. But at the forefront of it all was the chief of Glimisvellir and its governess. Both looked up to the arriving Heir of Gluttony and did the only sensible thing one could do, they kneeled.

"Welcome my lord, I hope the trip from Horga wasn't too rough. The entire town is ready to pledge their lives to you and your cause." His head kept low, not a shred of pride in his soul kept him from speaking without guilt of what he had done.

"I was not expecting Glimisvellir's chief to make the smart call. I had come thinking that he was as all the legends say about the town, stalwart, prideful, stubbornly resistant to the outside world. But maybe what else I've heard is true… that its chief is in fact a sickly drunk with mushrooms for brains."

"Watch your cheek brat, I'm still the man that had to change your smallclothes when you were a babe." Gerfinn retorted in a brisk whisper so quiet that only he and Orphan could possibly hear. If he was wrong and this wasn't Orphan then he was surely dead… probably still as just as dead but less of a fool. He was looking straight down, the only thing of the Heir of Gluttony he could see was his boots and the tip of the horrifying spear he held.

Moments passed and nerves grew restless. The claws and blades of Demons and savages alike inched closer and closer to the necks of men who silently begged and pleaded to absent gods that Gerfinn's gambit would pay off. That submission would grant them a chance at living another day longer. They hadn't been told that the man leading the Swarm had a vendetta against Glimisvellir's very existence.

"Fuck you old man, let's talk." The gambit paid off as

Orphan strode past Gerfinn and Rinelt toward the Great Hall of Glimisvellir. A few short words to a Demon as he passed them ensured the rest of the assembled elite would remain alive for now. But for the moment, all that was left was for the new authority to speak with the old.

"Listen, Orphan about that night…" Gerfinn began where he felt most prudent as the massive doors closed behind him and his better half. But. A sudden turn and thrust of the Divine Spear into his gut stopped him in his tracks. A panicked scream came from Rinelt but no one did anything outside, they all heard… they expected it… but they did nothing… as they should.

The blade pulled out of the drunk's chest and there was not a scar or split left behind. It was as if it never happened. Of course, both the man himself and the frantic woman at his side scrambled to look over the spot, meanwhile Orphan was content to smugly stand back and watch them run around like headless chickens. Since the Divine Spear's Awakening, it had never left Orphan's side. He could now let it go but the young man refused to be anywhere without it… and I do mean anywhere.

"What… what did you do to him?" Rinelt demanded as she looked back at Orphan with a fury most men dream of seeing on their woman's face, not directed at them of course.

"One would think I'd be getting a thank you perhaps, I gave you a wonderful gift, uncle. Repayment for all those horrible days and nights taking care of me as a baby." Since the revelation of Thrain's interference in his life, Orphan had spent a great deal of time pondering the truth of the entire situation. He reasoned that initially the people of Glimisvellir treated him as one should an orphaned baby, maybe a little worse due to his Cursed Born nature and the lingering scorn against his mother. But nothing to the extent he could recall. Some point before he could remember Thrain had changed all of that, it explained how he survived his earliest childhood as there was no way Gerfinn was capable of taking care of a baby.

"I don't feel any diff… wait… I feel sober. I was not sober ten seconds ago." Unsurprisingly, several horns of ale had been consumed in preparation for this reunion or worse his first of many deaths this day. But now he felt as clean and awake as he had ever been in years. Looking up to Orphan he scowled as he realized what Orphan had done. "You not only fixed my liver but improved it didn't you?"

"You're welcome." Finishing with that smug smile of his as he removed his helmet, his face turning less jovial, sterner and a bit serious. For there were silly emotions and words that must be spoken much to their pointlessness. "That night, you tried to save me. Convince Thrain and Eberulf, to spare me. You did what you did because your hand was forced, I'm going to hold it against you."

"Oh, wasn't expecting the Master of Gluttony to be so merciful." Pushing things, careful now. Orphan only has so many limits to his ego.

"Well I'm not the Master of Gluttony yet, I'm only the Heir." As Orphan lazily walked back and through the Great Hall of Glimisvellir, taking in the changes that had become of it, he knew it was not mercy that was saving Gerfinn this day. It was that everything that happened on that night was meant to happen, if he hadn't been chased out of town, he'd never meet the Winterman again, wouldn't have learned of the Path of Tyranny, and so on and so on.

"Wait, you're not? By every lost name of the gods we had a chance!" Gerfinn shouted in rage as he kicked over a nearby table in frustration. Tis true, had Glimisvellir done their usual tactics as well as employ everything else at their disposal they could have won. Lord Beelzebub was not able to use Earth Magic on such a mass scale and control the Swarm at the same time, not without a massive quantity of food ready for it. Even the assault on Horga was timed so while the lake drained Lord Beelzebub was able to recuperate before directing the Swarm. And worse for the Fiends, they did not have the numbers purely to overwhelm Glimisvellir, not immediately. Their War-forms had yet to spawn and the bulk of their numbers were still back at the Hive some several days' travel.

"A small chance but a chance uncle, let's not go on deluding yourself." As he took an apple from one of the remaining long tables in the central hall, Orphan was in the midst of memories. Every feast he watched from a shadowed corner, all the times he wanted to join in on some game of dice being played here, or simply not cause the entire hall to grow quiet if he showed his face at all. The apple was crushed in his hands and the Cursed Born blinked at the unconscious anger that had swelled within him. It did do him well to care so much for things that once were, now that he could change what could be.

"I know, I made the right call. But I guess there's just enough Glimingaric pride in me to feel cheated of that chance because I thought it was more hopeless than it was." Following their new lord and master, the two former leaders of Glimisvellir watched as without much ceremony Orphan took to the simple throne that had remained in the Great

Hall though it had fallen out of use. Gerfinn had never liked the thing and the seat of power had effectively moved to his desk.

"That's assuming you had any Glimingaric pride left, pretty sure that all slipped out of your foaming mouth after you drank that red slop you brewed on a dare." Orphan rested upon the throne casually, giving no reverence to its history or symbolism. Correct... very correct. "How did you get all those fools out there to go along with this smart call of yours? Can't imagine it was easy."

"It was. Told them we were going to lose and then told them you had twenty thousand instead of the five you showed up with." The sight of merchants blubbering and begging Gerfinn to save them and their investments in Glimisvellir, the haughty fake bravado of the southern military commanders here to oversee their own garrisons, all melted away when faced with the grim resignation of the Glimingar hunters. They had seen the Swarm and been dealing with the Imps' raids on the routes down the mountains. Those that knew the land and their chances best had only one idea on how to survive. Perhaps long ago, before Glimisvellir's fall to the Confederacy, there were a core of hardened Glimingar warriors willing to lay down their lives for their land and people... they died... horribly to cannons and gunlines.

"Hmm, disappointing." Orphan kicked his feet playfully as he rested one of his legs on the armrest of the throne. But perhaps it was this nonchalant action that finally pushed Rinelt to strike at the heart of what needed to be discussed.

"What are you planning on for us, clearly it's not to kill Gerfinn or I as why would you change his body if not to let him live with it? From everything I have been told of you, I was expecting a burning torch and not a slave's collar." A sudden outburst and one cowed once it was done by a hardening of Orphan's gaze on her. This was no ugly malnourished boy of spite and hatred, this was adonis with obsidian veined marble for skin and emeralds for eyes. Even Gerfinn had to admit the changes that Orphan had gone through were striking to say the least. So he gave a small nudge to his woman to finish her request correctly. Years of training among the nobility of the south saved her here. "Je vous prie de m'excuser, mon seigneur, your presence inspires great emotion from your humble servants."

"Stop that." A childish groan came from the Heir of Gluttony as he rolled his eyes. "I'm not going to kill either of you. For one, I think you're the only person in all of the Soarlands I trust to speak to me plainly uncle. As for you, I know of you and you're far too useful alive both in knowledge and connections."

This seemed to relax the pair, a combination of the weariness in Orphan's voice and his initial insistence told them everything they needed to know. Here was a king whose court was filled with sycophants and bootlickers and he knew it. Rightly he now sought those that would be willing to counter him and speak the truth no one was willing to say to his face. The Fiends, of course, would immediately become unbearably loyal to Orphan upon him taking their Crown, even the most antagonistic among their number would suddenly kill themselves if Orphan wished it. Such was a Fiend's mind. As for his Soarlings and Followers of Malice, well… the latter was fanatically insane and the former too fearful of him.

Delightfully, once the panic of possible horrible death subsided... the scheming began. As both these two individuals were at their hearts, intellectuals. It was what brought them together and the very foundation of their love for each other. Thus both had consumed many tomes regarding the Tyrants and the Systems of Malice. Some of these tomes would be burned by the Church should they have learned of their existence but what danger could knowledge pose? A lot... the answer is a lot of danger. But in this insistence it provided them both with a framework regarding how to best use this sudden and unexpected situation.

"Mon cher Gerfinn, it's sounding like your darling nephew is finding himself lacking proper advisers. Perhaps you know anyone with the experience and skills of leadership, particularly over a large settlement?" Rinelt purred as she sauntered across the hall over to Orphan's side. There was no seduction here, not of the usual kind. As the woman knew better than to assume Orphan could be charmed by feminine wiles, or more accurately hers. But there are some ideas floating around in her head for later.

"Yeah me. Here's the offer brat, I keep running Glimisvellir until you become Tyrant and then you make me your Royal Viceroy." A bold demand, and it was a demand. For Royal Viceroy was the most prestigious and powerful of the Court Positions of a Tyrant. Along with being the right hand of the Tyrant in all things governance and politics it also carried with it the ability to command the Archfiends. The only person other than the Tyrant who could do so. There were other perks, most notably the innate power to appear anywhere in the Tyrant's domain in a blink of an eye and the immortality that came with all Court Positions.

"And not the Royal Fool?" A chuckle escaped the Cursed Born's lips before he retracted from a slight slap to his hand by Rinelt.

"None of that, the Royal Fool is no mere court jester as you should know. I assume that Arcon taught you better than that. If not, I will need to start giving you supplemental lessons." There was surprise on Orphan's face to learn that Rinelt knew of the sternest of bugs. The Demon had been cultivating its influence among the nobility of the entire world as a molder of minds and shaper of dynasties.

"Yes-yes, I was planning on making uncle my Viceroy ever since I learned he was actually doing a competent job here in Glimisvellir." Confusion. Conflict. Befuddlement. Orphan rubbed the hand that had been so sternly slapped and felt... odd. He did not like this feeling. She had done something to him and he was cautious to investigate it further. Don't, nothing great will come of it. Just leave it alone.

"Speaking of... what about Glimisvellir. You said you won't kill us, us... anyone else on your special list." It wasn't that Gerfinn cared particularly much for Glimisvellir even after all this time, but a grieving soul he had put in a lot of work into this frozen heap of iron and stubbornness. For his answer Orphan stood up and gave a causal stretch of his arms and neck before giving a complete and satisfactory answer.

"Seven days, then we will have my Crowning here. My people will work with you to ensure everything goes as I wish." Nothing else was said as Orphan walked past the both of them leaving them concerned about the fate of this town. Would Orphan commit to his vendetta or perhaps the worse possibility was he wouldn't.

Words of the Savior

"I am your only hope, but don't worry... I'm just as
disappointed as you."
The First Savior

The Stage is Set

"Gentlemen! We have a spectacular opportunity."

"I don't know, sounds like we're all dead men walking."

"Boss is just coping; he got turned down for the first time in his life."

"Willichar, if you say another word I'll slit your throat myself. Please don't make me, this is a new suit and I like its shade of red rather than what it would become." A rather pleased but strained voice spoke out from the front of a crowd of colorful individuals in a dimly lit warehouse on the industrial side of Glimisvellir. All of them differ from the norm of human, because all of them weren't. Devils and Cursed Born, those that lived in Glimisvellir that had made the arduous journey up north in hopes the tales of Soarling and Glimingar indifference to the Infernal were true.

And the man standing at the head of them all was likely the only one of his kind perhaps for many-many leagues about. Impeccable and stunning wings with feathers so white they almost glowed. Solid golden eyes with only the briefest hint of iris. Sharp regal features that screamed to anyone that looked upon them that this man was just inherently better than them. All clad in a finely tailored suit of the latest style complete with a gold chained pocket watch. This man was an Aurelian or if you ask him or his kin… an Angel. A direct descendant of the First Tyrant. No filthy usurper blood tainted his veins.

The crowd around him however, was of less caliber. Soot stained faces, ragged worked clothes, and a grim look of hardship in all their similarly solid-colored eyes of differing hues. Devils of many lineages were here, those that still remained in this world at least. Of them were of the Third's line, as they were the most populous of all the Devil breeds outside of Hell and the other Devil nations. Gargoyles, crackly stone skin filled the majority of the room. There were the odd Beastmen of the Ninth's blood and two twins of the Sixth whose presence everyone questioned.

And filling their numbers out were Cursed Born of the fourth's line, Satyrs. The Coven Hooved Cursed Born maintained a modicum of power by outnumbering all others. Meanwhile the rest of the Cursed Born misfits were herded away in their own corner. They had up until a few days ago lived a decent life for what someone with infernal blood could expect outside of a nation aligned with that of Malice. They were not treated as royalty like they would be in such a country, but also they were not hunted down and killed or sequestered in poverty-stricken quarters made purely for them. The Glimingars were just as the Devils and Cursed Born promised, indifferent to them.

"As I was saying, we have opportunity here. A new Master of Gluttony is about to be Crowned, how could our fortunes not be looking bright." The angelic man spoke with a light accent that bespoke to his birthplace of Dis, or as the natives of the city would insist it be called Enoch. A small flutter of his wings enhanced his every word as they moved gracefully with his performative gestures and pageantry.

"So we're still going with the uprising? I don't think the new management would be very fond of a worker's strike or even worse a communist revolution. Verchiel, it's Gluttony… they'll eat us all alive." A braying snort came from the largest of the Satyrs, thick burly arms crossed as a hoofed foot stamped on the ground in an anxious show of force. There was no docile emptiness in his eyes like other goats, despite his head being of one.

"False! If there is a Master of Gluttony then the Swarm is tamed. By the fact this soon to be Master didn't have the Swarm immediately consume the town means he wants to keep it… I hope." Those last two words were whispered under Verchiel's breath. He had risked much coming this far north, everyone in his family called him crazy for seeking to make his mark on the world instead of resting on the laurels of his ancestor. Sloth was the most hated Sin among those that celebrate the very act of Sinning. So he couldn't understand why everyone in Enoch was so willing to sit on their softening asses like they had won.

"What about your human pet, have you been able to speak with Jorund about his side of the revolution?" In truth no, much to Verchiel's frustration someone had already abducted his plaything and puppet among the human workers of Glimisvellir. Though this did fill the Angel with a bit of confidence that this new Master of Sin was intelligent. Certainly, he had been when it came to intrigue as he had not been able to find a single solid fact about him. Oh my, it's almost like fear, shadows, and death itself seem to be sowing lips shut, doesn't it?

"Yes, briefly before he was taken by our new occupiers.

There is just as much confusion and panic among the humans, if not more so than us. At least we seem to have the Master of Sin's favor for now." An educated guess that was easy to pass as genuine information. But the Angel had to admit to himself that perhaps things were getting out of hand, and he needed options.

The information of the Master of Gluttony itself was valuable. Once the Crowning took place many would learn about the event but little else. Off the top of his pretty blond head he could list off three very interested parties who'd be willing to pay the most for information. Top of the list was the Tyrannic Temple, last he heard about them was that they were very invested in getting the Master of Pride as the next Tyrant so this would be another rival for them to deal with. After them would be the House of Glut, who have been wanting to get their hands on their most famous member's Archfiend since its creation. Lastly was a certain Archfiend he happened to be acquainted with and who Verchiel knew wanted nothing to do with having a Master over him.

All but the last one were on the other side of the equator, and the latter would never show his hand to help him. The more Verchiel thought about it the more he came to the disturbing conclusion he would need to operate within the new structure of Glimisvellir. Try and salvage the powerbase he had been cultivating and get a handle on how the other players were doing. A part of him did, however, enjoy the shake up, and made things more interesting. The self-serving thoughts of ego stroking were interrupted when a shout came from the crowd in front of him. His kinsmen were fighting among themselves, with a powerful beat of his wings he sent a gust of air to regain their attention.

"Enough. All operations are to be halted until such a time I deem it necessary. Glimisvellir is hardly capital material even now. It's far more likely we are a light snack next before he heads down to one of the other cities of the Soarlands. It's very unlikely that this Master of Gluttony will be staying long. And he is not a Tyrant… yet. If he leaves we can still attempt our original plans." If being the operative word there. But Verchiel gave no room for protest as with a match struck and a cigar lit he left them all without another word. He knew better than anyone that Devils and their bastard born children were nothing if not prone to backtalk. They were all after all Scions of Sovereignty; they all wanted to have the last word.

Wrapping his wings around his body in a makeshift coat, he walked through the empty streets of Glimisvellir. Four days since the surrender of the town to the Swarm and all had been very quiet. Not the kind where nothing happened, but the kind where lots was happening but being actively suppressed. Verchiel knew personally that at least three different groups had tried to launch a counterattack against the occupiers; he could only imagine they now sat comfortably in the bellies of some Imp and if they were especially unlucky still squirming in Lord Beelzebub's bottomless stomach. A shiver ran down his spine at the sounds that often came at night as the Archfiend of Gluttony consumed piles of meat out in the middle of Glimisvellir's central marketplace. It reminded him of why he hated when his mother forced him to attend the House of Glut's many feasts… no table manners to be seen.

After taking a long breath of the fine cigar that likely cost one of his kinsmen's entire monthly pay, he stepped out on one of the major streets that led to the Great Hall. The clinking of chains filled the boulevard as throngs of slaves from both Horga and native Glimingar were marched through to where the ceremony was taking place. The angel was puzzled by one thing, and that was the soon to be Master of Gluttony's odd choice in malice. The Horga slaves made sense, but the Glimingar were odd. From what he could tell it was only natives of a certain age and up. Not a single child had been put in a stockade or slapped with shackles. No, but foolish crying happened regardless.

Next to the slaves were people in a bit better situation. Southerners, they were not in chains but also not free. They were being escorted by Soarling warriors who seemed to be completely unaffected by the suffering around them. They were called cruel, heartless, and then nothing at all after the beatings. Whiney louts need to be taught that they no longer needed a tongue if they used it inappropriately. Verchiel on the other hand, saw this as a swell sign, it likely meant that the Heir of Gluttony had some sort of Malice about him and it was affecting those under him. The Right of Sovereign at its core was about a Ruler and the Ruled after all.

His golden eyes scanned the procession of slaves being marched forward, perhaps he was looking for someone in particular. One of his biggest investments in this frozen shithole of a town. One he had felt risking his support from Enoch over but as the Succubi say, A Man will only risk his life over his money, his country, or his woman. Verchiel hated the sluts and how right they turned out to be.

"Fucking spit on a sinner Brune, why can't I find you." His teeth gnarled and bit off the cigar, ruining his day that much more. Angrily he stamped it out and pulled out a fresh one from their case. A case that had been a gift from Brune, only adding to his delightful suffering. In the past four days there had come to be thirteen people that had vanished off the face of the world. No one could find them, and Verchiel had tried… to find Brune, not the others.

New cigar lit, he continued his way toward the ceremony not wishing to be late. Imps giggled and chittered about as they passed him by. His kinsmen and he had been granted the highest status of freedom in the town. Other Devils and Cursed Born to Heir were threats, possible usurpers to the title. But for a Master they were the closest allies as inherent beings of Malice. Of such was the thought of a naïve outsider to Infernal ways. Which was another piece to the puzzle Verchiel vexed at; he had seen Arcon, and suspected the Cult was afoot. Meaning this new Master of Gluttony should know better. Devils and Cursed Born never stop being threats, even if they are less likely to steal away the title of Heir.

The entire townscape had been changed in the course of four days to accommodate the ceremony. Normally the Great Hall of Glimisvellir stood atop an elevated hill giving it a sight over the lower majority of the town. That hill had been carved and built upon over the thousands of years of the town's history and further expanded in the past years. Now there was a clear and unobstructed view for all that stood below, a great deal of land had been totally leveled so that every citizen of Glimisvellir could fit and be there for the ceremony. The remaining population of Horga were set about in the rest of the town and forced to turn to the celebrations regardless if they could see it or not. The Demons, the elite that warranted enough purpose to live, and himself among others were granted a place at the very top where the Crowning was to take place. Buzzing and the nasty smell of hive material assaulted the senses as swarms flew about and chitin spires rose from the ground. The Fiends were quickly reshaping the town to feel more homely for them.

Verchiel ignored it all as he came to the courtyard of the Great Hall, lazily his eyes scanned the assembled privileged few. Demons, check. Frightened southerner elites, yes. The heavy robes of the Cult of the Seventh Sun, confirmation. But then he spotted someone that caused the Angel to beeline straight to them.

"Jorund, where have you been?" Grabbing a hold of one of the most important assets he had in the town, the two Demons by Jorund growled but Verchiel was no scared little mortal. "Shut it bugs, I know you can't kill me."

"But we can-"

"Hurt me? Try and you will quickly find out why I'm so confident none of you can make that threat worth a damn." For a brief moment the two Demons felt ready to attempt regardless if Verchiel was bluffing or not, only for their eyes to briefly glow as Lord Beelzebub forced itself upon their minds. And Verchiel was bluffing, he was no fighter, but he knew that Lord Beelzebub would not want any incident before such a hallowed event. So he turned his attention back to his favored pet.

"I was running to our usual meeting spot hoping I'd find you, but they were waiting there for me. At first I had been blindfolded but then… I can't explain it, Verchiel. For several days I had lost all sight or hearing. It was like I didn't have eyes or ears and then this morning it all came back." Magic?

That was the only thing the Angel could think of to explain that. But what magic could do that, Shadow can rob people of their senses and Fleshcrafting could remove the organs themselves. Neither were something that Verchiel wanted to deal with.

"Well, they gave them back. Means they have a need of you and all your facilities. Take solace in that, let's get through this and then figure out where to go from there." It would be pointless to ask him about Brune given that he had effectively been in complete darkness for four days. In all honesty, Verchiel had to give it to the former blacksmith for lasting that long and not going insane. Plus, Verchiel knew that Brune was a sore spot for Jorund. A couple days before all this happened he had come to the Angel professing the mistake it would be for Verchiel to marry Brune meaning she let it slip to him about the proposal. It was just like her to do that.

Having confirmed the safety of one of his assets, Verchiel took to calming his nerves in seclusion. He knew already that he was unwelcomed by all of the other attendants of the ceremony. Those former movers and shakers that had come up from the south looked like they could crackle and fall apart at the slightest threat or insult, no fun in such easy prey. The cultists, while Verchiel was a follower of the Temple he was not a fanatic, but still he would not suffer their non-believer presence in his company. So, he suffered in solitude until it seemed to be time.

A chorus of cicada songs, a growing collective scream of excitement from all the Imps in the town. The noise was deafening and growing in rhythm until it all at once came to an end. Verchiel watched as the gates of the Great Hall opened and from it came their new lord and master, behind him the venerable Lord Beelzebub in its full glory. It towered over them all and Verchiel had to offer a brief prayer to the Seventh for thanks to be granted audience with her divine inheritor. Following the Archfiend were the previous two leaders of the town, the chief and governess. This surprised the Angel as he believed them to be dead, which seemed appropriate. But then, curiouser and curiouser there came more. Thirteen. In chains, hoods over their heads. They were forced to their knees at the very edge of the terrace that overlooked the rest of the town now bereft of the half-wall that ensured people's safety.

The silence of the moment after such an overwhelming uproar was only broken by the sound of Lord Beelzebub's talons clattering on the stone as it snaked its way behind the thirteen kneeling prisoners. Verchiel for his part was dreading the immediate thought of whom those people were as it could mean who was among them. But the Archfiend of Glutton did not seem to care about them as its large head loomed over to address all those below.

"Lo, how long have we tarried in wait for a new lord, how long have we sought one whose hunger match'd our own, how long have we lingered in shadows, bereft of purpose and starv'd of command. But no more, for the hour is nigh, and our famine shall find its end." Amusing, both the Angel and the audience did not expect such a voice from the Maggot Lord. While distinctly inhuman in its sound, the elegance of it contrasted with the alien being that it came from. "On this hallowed day, we do crown a new Lord of Gluttony. Behold, the world shall once more be our banquet. Come forth, all ye my children, and claim thy place at the table. By the ancient covenant of Order and Malice, we do pledge our fealty to our new Master. To hunger, to feast, to devour all the world in his dread name. Let us consume, let us be consumed, and let the feast never end!"

The man that would become the new Master of Gluttony approached Lord Beelzebub with an air of confident regality that Verchiel had to respect. As well as his wardrobe, a fine dark green robe with gold embroidery that contrasted well with his alabaster skin. Heavy and loose along the arms and lower half while being perfectly tailored to his body everywhere else. It cut his visage with a look of a true monarch that dignified the moment with class but kept a causal attitude that prevented the ensemble from being too serious and drab. Begrudgingly he had to admit the Cursed Born man was dashing to say the least.

All eyes were on this man as he approached the Archfiend, never kneeling but standing tall and proud before the embodiment of Hunger itself. A position that would more than likely get anyone else killed for their lack of reverence or respect. It just further proved that Lord Beelzebub thought him worthy of being its master. Verchiel could feel the blood pumping through the bodies of those around them move faster and with great stress. Perhaps they did not think this was real until this very moment like the moronic fools they truly were?

No further words were spoken between Archfiend and its new master, instead Abezethibou came in with two of the Cultists at its side. It was carrying a rather simple box. One made out of the Fiends' chitin building material that now covered parts of Glimisvellir. Lord Beelzebub nor its children gave any stock to the fine points of finery. Unseen by everyone, the ancient Demon pushed every muscle in its body to do as it was told and not ruin the ceremony with its foolish thoughts of resistance. With a hard look from its creator's glowing eyes it kneeled before the new Master of Glutton and presented the box to him.

"Behold thy crown, wrought of our very will, fashion'd by our own hands and flesh. Take it, O Master, and set it upon thy brow, that we may commence the never-ending feast of this world. Let all be devoured before thee, and let the revelry of consumption begin without end." The lid was opened and inside was the Crown of Gluttony. Made of Beelzebub's own bony hide, the band of chitin was simple and utilitarian, smooth and solid. Seven spikes formed the crown, neatly identical and sharpened well as the ringed the band. Only one spike was a bit larger than the rest to denote the crown's front.

Every soul in Glimisvellir held their breath as they watched pale hands pick up the crown, hearts beat faster as it was raised up, and in the milliseconds it was descending down upon his head… all feeling was washed away as everyone suddenly felt it. In the pit of their core, it was now empty. It wasn't like anything had been taken from them, only that they now finally realized it had been empty all along. Mouths salivated and fingers twitched, this emptiness needed to be filled. It began to grow. And grow. Moments passed by and every mortal in Glimisvellir could say they had been standing there for years feeling this bottomless pit form in them and only once the Crown was nestled so nicely on his head did it end. For just a brief moment, mortals felt what it was like to live as a Fiend of Gluttony.

As for those very Fiends of Gluttony? Well, from the

second the crown touched skin their minds adjusted to the new paradigm. What was once judgement and cruelty would turn to subservience and blind loyalty. Just like that. No more biting words, brutal beatings disguised as training, or veiled threats to murder should a certain someone fail a test of a Demon's own design. But to a wider impact, there was a more interesting story. As now there were over a billion darling little Imps sticking their heads up in understanding. The Ravenous Swarm was united at last. Lord Beelzebub can't be everywhere at once, the further a Fiend of Gluttony got from their Archfiend the less it was connected to the under-mind of Beelzebub. Never disconnected but certainly more remote. Entire Hives existed surrounding a single Demon that operated as their own master, causing their own forms of trouble. Those days were over. As finally they had a Master worthy of following. And so, the most numerous of all the Sins stopped their petty squabbles over who gets what meal, and all turned their eyes north.

Verchiel fought the urge to vomit, something not everyone was able to do. He had been told stories by family of the stories. That Crowning ceremonies can break even the best of men. They stained all who attended with Sin down to their soul. Truth be told, he didn't believe them. That was his mistake and all the funnier for it. For now, every mortal there would carry with them a hunger. It might not manifest as a hunger for food, it could be many things. But now something was missing from their lives, and now they must find and consume it.

Being one of the first to recover from the experience, Verchiel was able to watch as the new Master of Gluttony approached the first in the line of prisoners brought before the town. This was unusual as the Angel had never heard of this being part of the Crowning ceremony, meaning it was his idea. The Cursed Born tore off the hood and held out a hand where a Demon quickly brought over the most horrific looking spear Verchiel had ever seen. The Master of Gluttony gripped the thing and slammed its sharp pommel into the ground bringing all attention back on him.

"Glimingar, and others." He began with a chuckle as his voice carried over the wind and down to the audience clearly. "I thank you for your cooperation and surrender to me. Rather than a grueling battle in which many lives would be lost we instead have an opportunity. For you see, my Seat of Power lies just to the north. I have already seen it and am ready to claim it."

Dread. Absolute dread. Wonderful and ever so enchanting. A cold sweat grew on the brows of every man and woman, including Verchiel. A Seat of Power? Here? One moment he was witnessing the Crowning of a new player in the game between the Noble Houses of Enoch, the Nations of Malice, the current other Masters of Sin, and the Cult and Temple. Now that new player was at the finish line! How audacious… for everyone else. The mind is a terrible and amazing thing, able to quickly cope with the madness of reality. Verchiel for all his bravado was still a mortal man, and he chose delusion as his way to survive this revelation. Delusions of grandeur to be precise.

"I am in no rush however, there is much to do before I take the Throne and ascend to Tyrant. Work must be done here in Glimisvellir. As the closest settlement to my Seat of Power, you shall be the foundation of my… well… powerbase. So an understanding must be established." With that he spun the malevolent spear and with one slick move decapitated the prisoner kneeling in front of him. Gasps and cries from those that knew the poor man. No-no-no, the suffering shall continue poor fools.

Many watched in horror as the falling head exploded in a shower of gore. Then a scream… from the body that had been decapitated. Crunching, squelching, horrible wet noises came from it as a new face formed in the chest of the body, gasping for air as it wheezed to life. Verchiel had seen all sorts of heinous acts committed by ministers of the Tyrannic Temple and abhorrent petty violence done by vindictive Devils back home in Enoch. But this was a new level of disgust and revulsion even for him. And he despaired as there were twelve more poor souls.

"This understanding is simple, I have no mercy… only needs. I need devotion, commitment, and above all else loyalty. And what better way to ensure this from you all is to show what I am capable of." In all meanings of the phrase. He tore off the hood of the next man. This one Verchiel recognized. It was one of Jorund's. A miner that had lost an arm in an accident two months ago. He had family, children, parents and wife. People that depended on him. More importantly to Verchiel was the fact he was a damn excellent speaker at their rallies. The Angel hated to see him go, already he was planning on toting out his widow to crowds.

The spear pierced his back, and again the terrible fleshy noises came but now to the relief and shock of all witnessing it was not a fate worse than death. Budding out of the stump that had once been an arm, burst out a bone then red bloody sinew. More and more yanked itself out of his flesh and soon enough a new arm was in the place where nothing was before. Though… it was different. Not smooth clean skin but twisted and knotted hide with bony thorns peeking out.

"Punishment, reward. Carrot, stick. It is not mercy but suitable governance. I am not a monster, I cannot build a new world order without those that genuinely follow in my shadow." His speech continued, and Verchiel watched as a pattern emerged. Suffering. Relief. Suffering. Relief. A perfect reinforcement cycle to drill it into all of them his message. Serving him was not a choice, but it was as you deemed it to be. Resist and suffer the consequences. Submit and enjoy the rewards. Simple in its essence, just extreme in its application.

Verchiel watched and kept count of the order of horrific mutilation and miraculous healing. Where was she in the order of this? As best he could tell the pattern of who was getting what was hard to understand. Those that were being rewarded felt correct to him, each of them he knew to a degree and all of them would play well. Those that were known in the community, easy sob stories, the kind of person everyone would be happy to see catch a break for a change. But those getting the punishments? Random. Best commonality he could see was that they were all of a similar age. An age range that she fell under.

They all watched as he came to the last prisoner. The speech had ended with the previous one, or at least the speech that had been prepared, debated, and constructed. It had been meant to instill within those hearing it the scope of what was to come, to give a comprehensive understanding between ruler and ruled. The Cursed Born gave a deep breath as now came for his real speech. No longer coming from a place of logic or reasonableness. Spite, bitterness, and smug fulfillment now fueled these true words from his heart.

"Change. It's an odd thing, isn't it?" He began, his voice carrying an almost conversational tone that belied the weight of the moment. Taunting those listening with a shred of humanity. "It comes whether you want it or not. Whether you are prepared or not. A force that reshapes everything in its path. And yet, for some reason, so many of you resist it. You cling to the past as if it were a shield, something to protect you from the unknown. But change… change does not care about your past."

He paced slowly back down the line of prisoners, each step measured, his spear tapping softly against the stone as if keeping time with his words. Verchiel, more desperate than he cared to admit, wished that this mongrel Cursed Born would get on with it. But his trained ear picked up the shift in tone. This was personal. But why? Did this man have some sort of history with Glimisvellir? No one else that was unaware of the truth was so smart to notice yet.

"This town has stood for centuries, built on traditions, on old ways that refuse to bend or break. Glimisvellir has always prided itself on being unyielding, defiant, stubborn to the last miserable fool. A fortress of ice, set in its ways, believing it could exist frozen in time. But ice melts and nothing stays the same forever, doesn't it?" That had been proven with the Confederacy's invasion and subsequent investment in Glimisvellir. The town had been dragged kicking and screaming into the modern day. Ooh sure, they were all too happy to enjoy the money and wealth but the complaining never ceased. Even just before the Swarm had come they were ungrateful savages who were already speaking the sound of the old days.

"Change comes for us all, and those who cannot adapt are left behind. Some call it progress. Others call it ruin. But it's neither. It's simply… inevitable." A gentle hand clasped the now deformed head of the fourth man to be mutated into an ugly creature and no longer a man. Once upon a time this man was a boy, and as a boy he would run and frolic with the other kids as they mercilessly ridiculed and tormented a forgotten monster of yesterday. There was even a time this man, once a boy, led some of them in a particularly nasty rousing time. Where they dragged the little monster and locked him in a chicken coop with a fox inside. They laughed as the chaotic mixture caused much fun and amusement. Now his head resembled a chicken and his limbs were stubby and much more akin to a fox's feet than human appendages.

"I know what it's like to be discarded by a place that refuses to change. To be seen as a mistake, an anomaly, something that doesn't fit. Ignored, pushed to the side, left to fend for myself in a town that was incapable of seeing me as anything more than a thing to be reviled. But what is forgotten… can remember, can it not? Because things never stay the same, people never stay the same." He let the words hang in the air, his eyes scanning the crowd below. He could see the tension, the fear, the dawning realization that his words carried far more weight than they first appeared. For now a shadow of a memory was entering their small little minds. But denial was strong. Because if it was true? The Sin of Gluttony wouldn't be the sin they would be facing retribution for. With bated breath as he returned back to the final prisoner. They all prayed to gods that long since abandoned them, hoping a poor weak boy did in fact die out in the cold all alone.

"I offer you a choice: embrace the change, or be consumed by it. Reward or punishment. Evolution or extinction. It is not mercy, but pragmatism. It is not kindness, but necessity. I am not here to preserve your arrogantly held belief that you are safe. I am here to tear you apart and rebuild you into something I deem useful!" With that he pulled off the hood to reveal exactly who Verchiel feared it was. My, did he wish she had given him some sort of answer, because the defiant angry glare she gave the Master of Gluttony tore at his heart. This was a woman that he knew could stand with the best of the harpies and spiders of Enoch. If for no other reason than she would baffle them all to no end.

"You really like to hear yourself talk don't you? Come on! Do your worst already!" She challenged but understandably there was fear in her eyes once she had glanced over at the grotesques that had come before her. The Cursed Born raised his spear and in a moment of weakness Brune flinched and closed her eyes to what was to come. Only... no stabbing occurred, but her binds did fall apart. But she felt cold all of a sudden. And wet. Wait... did he just throw a snowball at her?

"I win. One hundred snowball fights, I win the bet."

One.

Two.

Three.

Four.

Five.

Six.

Seven.

"Orphan!" That name. It rang across Glimisvellir as Brune shouted it in joy. Leaping up onto her feat as she threw her arms around his neck and embraced him. A stream of confusion and shock left her lips as Orphan continued his parade of smugness and ate it all up.

The Glimingar, had a different frightful and panicked reaction.

The Southerners, had a more muted, confused reaction.

The Demons, found they did in fact enjoy this little ploy.

Verchiel, felt small for the first time in his life.

Orphan, finally felt the bitter taste in his mouth turn to sweetness.

Thus concludes the first part of our story. It has been a pleasure my dear Listener, for you to be here as I recite this epic tale of the Last Tyrant. I am but your humble servant Bael, eager to embark on this most delightful of tragic ends for a poor and suffering world as this.

Words of the Tyrant

"How does it feel having everything taken from you, it doesn't feel so nice now does it? Don't worry, I'll be sure to enjoy it far more than you could have."
The First Tyrant.